C000003341

To

Cancer Research

2016

LIKE FATHER, LIKE SON

Other Publications

<u>Fiction</u>

Rest in Peace

<u>Law</u>

Race Relations in Employment Law: A Brief Introduction
(booklet)

http://www.nutmeg-publications.com

LIKE FATHER, LIKE SON

RYAN CLEMENT

NUTMEG
Publications
HARROW

LIKE FATHER, LIKE SON

First Published in 2000

Published 2002 by
NUTMEG Publications

A CIP catalogue record for this
publication is available from the British Library

ISBN 0-9542528-1-0

Printed and bound in Great Britain by
St Edmundsbury Press, Suffolk

This book is dedicated to my mother,
Ann

Acknowledgements

Thanks to Caz. I give a special thanks to Susan P. James
for her invaluable comments made both during
and after the writing of this book.

I give a very special thanks to Him above for telling me the story.

LIKE FATHER, LIKE SON

About the Author

Ryan Clement was born in London. He is a lawyer
practising in England. His second book *Rest in Peace*
is due out in 2003.

Rupert

"Last day of the year and we're sitting here like two lemons!" says Dexter. "Why don't we gatecrash a party or do something – anything – just so that we can get out of this sombre mood?"

"I'm in no mood for a party," I reply. And in truth, I'm not. I have no appetite for noise and people tonight, no matter what the occasion. I still find it hard to believe that so much could have been made from so little – or what appeared to be little at the time.

"Where did it all go wrong?" asks Dexter. I resent the implication that the causes of our bout of melancholy are in any way connected, but now is not the time to be casting stones. In any case, even if the means were dissimilar, the ends were the same, so who am I to pass judgement?

"I don't know," I reply, belatedly. "But, if there is one lesson I have learnt from this year, it is that anything that is simple can soon be made unnecessarily complicated, for the tiniest of reasons. And when it's unnecessarily complicated it gets out of hand. We just can't seem to handle anything that is too simple in life. If it's basic, effortless, elementary or unsophisticated it is not worth cherishing."

"You may have a point," adds Dexter. "For a woman to be classy, she must be sophisticated. Why? Why can't she be an unsophisticated classy lady?" he asks, trying too hard to be philosophical and yet still managing to mention his favourite pastime. I refrain from attempting a genuine response, for it is clear that we are not singing from the same hymn sheet. And I am certainly not going to discuss women tonight, no matter how philosophically tempting that subject may appear. I can hear the party revellers exercising their vocal chords in preparation for their New Year's Eve celebrations. The cacophony of noise is pounding inside my head, as if a pack of hounds within scent of its prey is locked inside. Thankfully, our party of two is of a more sombre nature. There are no thrills, just us. Tonight, I need tranquillity, peace and quiet, not noise. I need to hear myself think. I need to do some serious soul-searching and that can't be done in the company of an uninhibited crowd celebrating the festive season.

"I suppose it all started to go wrong from when we were invited to Yvonne's party," I say, returning to Dexter's earlier problem. "Mind you, I say that, but the seed may even have been sowed somewhere deep inside me, from the time of my mother's death. Her death has always had a profound effect on me. And you know what?" Dexter tacitly declines to answer. "I made a vow at her funeral. If only I had kept to that vow Lord only knows how things would have turned out. But I will never know and that hurts. I search for answers but find nothing. I can't sleep, I'm tormented and I'm confused."

"The truth is," interrupts Dexter, "we both messed it up. We messed up, big time!" He was right. It was us, not them. We did it. We are solely to blame. We had it too good for too long, so we had to do something about it.

"Never a truer word was spoken," I reply. "Never a truer word."

Part One

Part One

Rupert

"Sorry, I can't come to the phone right now. However, should you wish to leave your name, message and telephone number…" I walk towards the answering machine and await the message, "…after the beep, I shall endeavour to get back to you as soon as possible." Pause. "Beep."

"Hello, Rupert it's Kelvin. How are you? Long time no speak and…"

"Hello stranger," I say, interrupting the answering machine and sounding out of breath, "I heard the phone ringing from outside and rushed in when I heard you on the answering machine. How are things?"

"Fine," says Kelvin, not sounding at all fooled by my pretence, but probably accepting that the screening of one's calls is normal business these days, "and you?"

"I'm fine, thanks."

"I was about to leave a message saying that Yvonne is going to have a party for her twenty-fifth birthday on Saturday and would like both you and Patricia to come along. I assume that you two are still together?"

"Yes, yes, we're still together," I say, hesitantly. "In fact we agreed to tie the knot only last year." I forgot to invite Kelvin and Yvonne to the wedding. No, that's not entirely true. I hadn't heard from them for some time and just assumed that our friendship had died a natural death. Kelvin was one of the few people I really liked at Bar school. He was one of the few really genuine people I met there. One knew exactly what he stood for, without having to weave through a "pile of bullshit", which was unlike many I met at that institution. We were very close in the first term but it was clear that he cared little for my sparring partner, Dexter, and later kept his distance. "It was just a small affair," I say, to ease my conscience, "close family, etcetera."

"Oh, well, congratulations," says Kelvin, not appearing to be offended. "How is the young lady?"

"She's fine, thanks," I reply, whilst shuffling through my personal organiser. "I appear to be free on Saturday but I can't speak for Pat, obviously. I'll ask her when she comes in tonight and give you a call tomorrow, if that is all right. However, if she can't make it, what say you and I meet up for a drink, in any case. It'll be nice to see you after all this time."

"Yes, why not? And how is the rest of the family?" asks Kelvin.

"What 'family'?" I reply, spontaneously and a little mortified at the clear aggression in my voice. Kelvin appears to be taken aback by my response and probably thinks better than to push this line of enquiry any further.

"Have you been in touch with any of the others?" I ask, breaking the moment's silence.

"Yes," says Kelvin, evidently relieved for the question, "I have and there should, hopefully, be a few of them at the party, if all goes well, so please do try and come along. I'm sure everyone will be pleased to see you."

"I shall, even if Pat cannot make it."

"What about you, are you in touch with anyone?"

"No, only Dexter Williams who I meet up with at least once a week for a game of squash and the occasional drink."

"How's he doing?"

"He's doing really well. He chose not to go into private practice and is now working for a small pharmaceutical company as an in-house lawyer. He and Donna are still together and they have just had a pretty little baby daughter called Dionne."

"I never thought that those two would still be together after such a rocky start." Much hasn't changed, I feel like saying but restrain myself from volunteering any further information. "Please feel free to pass on my invitation to them as well," he continues. "It'll be nice to see them, also. This could turn out to be a mini reunion if all those invited actually turn up."

"Maybe we could have a quick game of Trivial Pursuit for old times' sake," I reply. We both laugh at the suggestion, probably a little embarrassed at how childish we were during our many games while studying! Sometimes we had the most heated debates in determining whether a given answer by a player was substantially correct or substantially incorrect. How we never ever came to blows has always mystified me. "I look forward to it," I continue. "I'll speak to you tomorrow in any case, and please do give my love to Yvonne."

"And you to Pat. Bye."

"Bye."

"Hey, Pat, guess who called today? Kelvin, Kelvin Stansford. He rang to invite us to Yvonne's birthday party at their place, on Saturday. How are you fixed?"

"Oh, I'm sorry, honey, I can't make it on Saturday," replies Pat. "Jo and I are going to see The Harlem Renaissance at the Hayward Gallery. Remember, I told you some time ago? Then we'll probably go for a meal before heading to Jo's place for the night. Sorry!"

"Oh yes, I forgot," I say, whilst scanning the bookshelf trying to recall where I last saw *Native Son*. "Some of the Bar school crowd might be there and it'll be nice to see them. You know, finding out how we're all doing."

"Showing off, you mean," says Pat, which we both know is more likely the case than not.

"I'll go, if that's all right with you," I say, ignoring her correction, "and probably invite Dexter along. You know how he likes a good party."

"Don't I just!" replies Pat, choosing not to say anymore about him. Not that I would have expected anything else. Pat is not too keen on my best friend. She dislikes the way he treats Donna and is not too shy in letting my friend know, in no uncertain terms, her view on the matter. Her philosophy is, "any man who mistreats a sister, mistreats us all." With that view, I guess Dexter, on his current form, was always heading for a hard time with the Mrs. But, as she would often remind me, Dexter is my friend and not hers..

"Yes," she continues, "go and enjoy yourself. I'll give Yvonne a call in the week and make my apologies."

Pat and I were both students at Oxford University and were introduced at a party given by a mutual friend of ours, Peter "The

Swat" Stubbs. I have mixed emotions about that party. I shall always remember it for more reasons than one. In fact, I still get covered in goose pimples at its very thought. It was the end of one precious relationship and, I guess, the beginning of another. I had just returned from London where I had been visiting my mother who had injured herself in a fall. I was tired and therefore had not intended to stay at the party for very long. Pat and I were two of only three black people there. The other person being Curtis Williams. Curtis suffered from chromatophobia. He came across as being rather embarrassed both at talking to another black person and also being black. I had seen Pat once before, in the Bodleian library. On that occasion she was wearing a traditional African wrapper normally worn by the Masai women of Kenya and, in an instant, she won my admiration. She had a sense of identity that was rare at Oxford. She was in her second year, reading English Language and Literature, whilst I was a freshman. In conversation at the party, we soon discovered that our interests were not too dissimilar. She was serious about her soul and jazz music – Miles Davis and Sam Cook could do no wrong! But what really broke the ice between us that night was our love for the arts. Odd as it may appear, within only fifteen minutes of being introduced, we were comparing the works of Bernini and Michelangelo, and debating whether the Baroque period was part of the Renaissance period or a distinct period of its own. We agreed to disagree on that one. But we did agree that, architecturally, the Pompidou Centre in Paris had more going for it than the Lloyd's building in London. I remember at one time Marvin Gaye's "What's Going On?" was playing in the background and I was asking myself the same question, for I felt myself being attracted to Pat. We talked all evening and there hadn't been a single moment of boredom. Admittedly, she was no oil painting, but her faculty of reasoning, rather than her outer beauty, was what captivated me. In any case, her inner beauty gave her an ambience that no catwalk model could ever attain. She was both a good listener and a good conversationalist. She appeared to know something about everything. She came up with a theory that the reason I was so interested in Mozart and Stevie Wonder was because they were both child prodigies and I subconsciously saw myself in them. I couldn't argue with that! Later on in the evening I found myself, uncharacteristically, trying to impress her. Girls were usually impressed by the way I speak. I speak the Queen's English and I'm articulate. Some found that to be intimidating but not this lady! I told her that my favourite Shakespearean plays were *The Merchant of Venice* and *Twelfth Night*. Actually, these were the only two that I had actually read! However, in what became a typical reaction, she was not overly impressed and asked me whether I had read any Maya Angelou, Toni Morrison or James Baldwin. I told her that I hadn't quite got round to reading any of their works, as yet. I was ashamed to admit that I hadn't even heard of them!

I remember this moment as if it were only yesterday. "She's Got Papers On Me" was playing to the approval of the women at the party. The men were not so enthusiastic. Betty Wright was in the process of telling Richard "Dimples" Fields that he could take his little albums and rackety component set that never worked and he could "skat!" It was during Betty's castigation of Dimples that I received an urgent message from my room-mate, Michael, that my aunt had called to inform me that my mother had suffered a stroke whilst at work and was in Charing Cross Hospital in London. I couldn't drive at the time, so Pat kindly offered to drive me back to London that very night. When I saw my mother in the hospital I was devastated. She was totally paralysed down the left side of her body. All her outer beauty had gone. I had never cried so much before in my life. I pleaded with the Heavenly Father to spare her life and I in return would do anything He desired. Just give me the order and I would obey, no questions asked! I would go to church every Sunday. Every day if necessary. I would give up all my worldly ambitions and become a full-time missionary. It wasn't to be. From her hospital bed, my mother asked that I keep her dream alive by continuing to study hard and become a brilliant lawyer. "Look after your father in his old age and try to rid yourself of any hatred that you may have towards him. He is a good man at heart." As she said this, I could see her eyes closing as if in slow motion. That picture will remain with me for ever. Those were her final words. She passed away at 23.07 on Sunday 19 December, 1993. She had died from an acute stroke aged just fifty-four. Pat attended my mother's funeral a few days later. This, I thought, was a really kind gesture. She had only witnessed my mother alive for a few minutes.

A few days before her death, my mother had tripped on a broken pavement whilst running for the first bus. She had overslept and was late for work. That night she complained of bodily pains and a severe headache. I was in London for the weekend and she promised me that if she did not feel a lot better in the morning she would consult her doctor. In the morning, when I went into her room her bed was empty, so I guessed that everything was all right. I should have known better. I rang her at work and told her that as everything was all right I would return to Oxford that evening. To this day, I feel so guilty and only wished that I had stayed in London for at least another day but no, I had to rush back for a party!

She had an unnecessarily hard life. I say unnecessarily, because she had to work extra hard simply to see me through my schooling and my higher education. What of my father? Well, my mother was forced to leave him when I was just thirteen years old. I was of an age to know that a mother and a father were not supposed to argue as often as mine did, and that a mother was not supposed to cry from so much pain, caused by her own husband. I am not ashamed to say that I blame my father for my mother's death.

My mother would often tell me how perfectly happy she was in her mother's home before my father sent for her from St. Lucia to come to England in order to join him as man and wife. My father was a good-looking man who, to put it bluntly, liked women. I can't recall this likeness extending to my mother but I guess it must have done at one time. Many a night my mother would cry herself to sleep whilst my father was out with the boys playing dominoes, or so he tried to convince my mother to believe. Take it from me, there is nothing worse on earth than witnessing your own mother pleading with your father to stop his womanising. This claim he obviously denied and to prove his innocence he would put on his best suit and aftershave and stay out until the early hours of the morning. Some innocence! My mother obviously heard the rumours about my father being with other women. It hurt, but she kept a brave face in public. What else could she have done? The house was in his name – which I understand was a common theme in those days – even though my mother contributed both to its upkeep and to the payment of the mortgage. She had no legal right to put him out of his house and, even if she did, she could not afford the mortgage on the wages she collected from her cleaning job. He knew that.

One day, after planning it for two weeks, we left our nice house in Notting Hill Gate, London, and headed for a small, but clean, bedsit in Shepherd Bush, in West London. It was a brave move by my mother and not in any way uncharacteristic of her inherent strength. We were at peace at last. Unfortunately, she was then at an age when she was unlikely to realise her own ambitions in life. Those ended with my father. However, she made sure that I would never be without and would therefore have all the opportunities that she never had. She would achieve her new ambitions through me. She took on two more cleaning jobs. I remember calculating at the time that she survived on less than five hours' sleep a night, seven days a week. I say sleep, I guess what I really mean to say is, there were five hours between her last shift and her first.

Pat and I became very close and by the end of her second year, and my first; we were sharing a house, together with two other couples: Mark, Sabrina, Shaun and Anthea. We all got on very well and are still the best of friends today. Shaun and Anthea got married shortly after their graduation, which Pat and I attended. I knew during their wedding vows that one day I too would be saying, "I do" to the woman sitting beside me. I had fallen for Pat in a big way. True to my feelings, we were married a few years later. I make no excuses for the cliché when I say that it was the best day of my life. My mother had always said that she wanted to see me "settle down" before she visited "Our Father which art in heaven". It pains me to this day to know that her wish was never to come true.

Both Pat and I were awarded First-Class Honours degrees. I am undoubtedly indebted to her. I knew that I would at least have got a 2.1 – a Desmond Tutu was never in contemplation – but due to her casting such a critical eye over every piece of work that I had submitted, highlighting any bad grammar and ambiguities, my work was exceptionally good. As for Pat, her award was of no surprise. Not even in all her modesty could she have pretended to be caught unawares by her achievement. Her family, not to mention myself, was extremely proud of her. She stayed on at Oxford for a further two years after graduation in order to complete her Ph.D. Doctor Patricia Veronica Jackson, my wife.

Pat's parents gave us the ideal present for any newly-weds: a two-bedroomed flat in London. Not that they had much money in order to part with such a lavish gift, it's just that they had worked hard for what they had, both for themselves and for their only daughter. Their house was already built "back home". So, as they saw it, their wedding gift to their daughter and son-in-law, as they departed from the cold of England to retire in the warmth and sunshine of the Bahamas, was the very least they could do. I could see where Pat got her artistic taste from: her parents. The flat was adorned with numerous African and Caribbean artefacts, which they kindly left behind and which we were only too grateful to retain. Waking up to the likes of a beautiful twined mat made in Northern Somalia and a Basongye Stool from Zaire is a nice way to start your day.

I really do like Pat's parents, Bertran and Veronica. The "old man" and I would discuss world politics for hours on end without tire. Pat's parents are typical West Indians, in the sense that they came to England in the early 1960s, a land that was, allegedly, paved with gold. But, despite such false allegation, they did, unlike many, realise their dreams by both buying their land and building their home in the West Indies for their retirement. Mission accomplished, they duly returned.

Pat and I are undoubtedly similar in many ways. Where we differ fundamentally, however, is in our perception of race. Our equilibrium of where "tolerance" meets "not acceptable" are at different points. I'm more of a "if you're thinking about my baby, it doesn't matter if she's black or white" type of man. I have no problems with that. The world is made up of all races, colours and creeds. The way I see it, we have a short tenure on earth so let's not waste time with sub-matters that are unproductive in our enjoyment of this land. Call me too pragmatic but, to me, it makes sense. Pat, on the other hand, who is a lot more cynical than I am, is what one would perceive, I think, as being much more "pro-black" – whatever that really means – than I am or shall ever be, I'm sure. This, I guess, is something that has been inherited from her parents and, more particularly, from her mother who, at every given opportunity, would inform those around her of the many man-made injustices of the world. I recall one of my first encounters with this side of Pat that really "pissed me off" at the time. I can't quite remember how the conversation actually began, but it had something to do with my filling out a form for a grant that asked for my "ethnic background". Now, Pat had grave problems with this. Call me naïve to the ways of the world, but to this day I still have trouble seeing how such a harmless and trivial question could cause any offence to anyone – black or white. Anyway, after that first experience, I have always tried to avoid the nuclei of topics that can lead to such conversations. But, this is not always easy. Every now and again a topic with some connection to "race and the black man" would slip through the conversational net. On these occasions my advocacy skills would be called upon in earnest as I was up against a woman who was for many years a leading member of a very reputable debating society. I wouldn't have minded these conversations, as I am a great believer in "hearing the other side" – I guess this stance is due to the lawyer in me – but passions tended to run high, too high for my liking. And, what started out as a "healthy" discussion later became an "unhealthy" debate that then became an "ugly" argument. My view is that one can be too racially aware and, probably more to the point, Pat addresses this stuff to the wrong guy! I think that I have just the right attitude. I'm not a "Mister Chip-on-his-shoulder", but at the same time I'm not a "Mister Coconut", either. I'm just about in the middle. Which is where people like me ought to be. The way I see it, we live in a meritocratic society and it makes no difference what colour you are, only how good you are. You judge a man not by the colour of his skin but by the content of his character. That is my motto. Any such talk would make us vex for some time, which was never a period that I particularly liked, and would do my damnedest to bring to an end a lot sooner rather than later. Apart from these infrequent arguments, which sometimes get a little out of hand, we have a good life, a life that is often highly commended by our friends and which, I must say, in comparison to many, is very good indeed.

Patricia

Rupert and I will soon be celebrating our first wedding anniversary. To be honest, Rupert is not the sort of person that I ever envisaged that I would have married. Not that I was particularly fixed in my ways as to the sort of person I would have ended up with, mind you. Rupert is evidence of that! When I reflect on how we met, I can only think that fate brought us together. I can think of no other circumstance that could have produced such a bond between us so soon after our first encounter. We met at a party, nothing unusual about that. However, it is very rare for a person to witness the full character of another in one night, especially when they first meet! We were at this party in Oxford, where we both attended the university. I was at Jesus College studying English and he was at Magdalen College studying Law. We hit it off right from the word go. I liked Rupert but I wouldn't say that I particularly fancied him. I found him to be extremely knowledgeable and very intelligent. He came across as someone who could think quickly on his feet; the traits of a good barrister, of course! He clearly had a passion for the arts. I remember having some academic discussion, just moments after we were introduced, that made me feel like I had known him for years. We clearly felt comfortable with each other. Being together felt natural. That evening was probably the most dramatic that I am ever likely to experience. There I was enjoying what appeared to be a fairly pleasant party when Rupert received a message saying that his mother was ill in hospital in London. He didn't own a car at the time so I instinctively offered to drive the sixty miles or so back to London. The journey was, understandably, very tense. We hardly spoke a word and what had, only moments before, seemed so important to him, had disintegrated rapidly into insignificance. In the space of about half an hour I had witnessed my co-traveller metamorphose from a confident and assured young man into a very frightened, insecure and nervous individual. It was clear to me then, how close he was to his mother. I asked him about his father but he seemed not to hear, and did not reply. Obviously, I know now that he did and chose not to. We got to the hospital just before eleven o'clock that night. When we saw his mother, Rupert just lost control of himself. He couldn't stop himself crying. I tried to console him as much as I possibly could. It had not occurred to me at the time that despite having only just met I was comforting him in his hour of need. I could tell that his mother had clearly once been a very beautiful woman. She had lost the use of the left side of her body, due to a stroke she had suffered earlier on that day. The emotional intensity of that night was like nothing I had ever had the misfortune to witness. I had to fight back my own tears in order that I could be of some form of strength for the young man who was uncontrollably sobbing with indescribable pain. I heard him curse his father, I heard him curse himself, and I heard him pray. I then began to suffer from an extremely tense headache, brought on by the fighting back of my own tears. My throat was dry and my tonsils ached. Then, as if in a dream, a bright light had shone on Rupert's mother. Her time had come and she knew it. She passed on a final message to her son as the final curtain came down for the last time. Her heart was now at peace. The Holy Spirit had anointed her and her angel had come to take her home. Rupert just wept and wept as he hugged his mother bawling uncontrollably and repeating, "No! No! No!" I could not have held back any more. I had lost my fight in holding back the tears. We just sobbed in each other's arms. A few days later, I attended the funeral with Rupert. His father was conspicuous by his absence. I never asked Rupert about his father and he never volunteered any explanation. There were many of his mother's church sisters and brothers who were saying what a good woman she was. It was very emotional. I remember hearing Rupert make a vow about his father but with the singing around I didn't quite catch what he said. I guess you could say that his mother's funeral was our first date. Circumstances had brought us together. Four years later we were married.

"What time can we expect you home tonight, honey?"

"What time would you ladies wish me to stay out until?"

replies Rupert, skilfully.

"Well, the girls should be here any minute now." A quick mental calculation tells me that from seven o'clock, we would need at least an hour each to air our piece with short breaks in between.

"I would say any time after ten thirty, if that's okay." The doorbell rings. "That should be Donna," I shout, instinctively. Jo is never early.

"That's fine with me," replies Rupert, also welcoming the extra time for being with his friends.

He grabs his jacket and makes way to let in my guest. As predicted, it is Donna. Rupert and Donna exchange their greetings and then he leaves.

"Hi honey," I say to my friend. "How goes it?"

"Bearing up!" she replies, with an air of resignation.

"And trouble?" I ask, no further description necessary.

"He seemed all right this morning," she replies with an "I-couldn't-care-less attitude" that says it all. "He is more preoccupied these days with this new car he has just purchased."

I let Donna get some derogatory remark about the car and an even more derogatory remark about Dexter off her chest. It hurts to see my friend so unhappy. I sometimes feel so guilty because, apart from the odd occasion, I very rarely have anything to complain about with Rupert. Donna was such a happy-go-lucky person when we first met. We were both working as volunteers at an inner-city young women's centre. We built up this amazing rapport almost instantly. She was seeing this chap, Sydney, at the time. He was good for her, dark, handsome and very witty. But things didn't work out between them, for reasons I have never quite understood. Meeting Dexter was bad news. Dexter and I have never quite seen eye to eye. In fact, Dexter's eyes are usually roaming for women, even when he is out with Donna. He is that shallow! Dexter and Donna met at a party, given by us, at a time when Donna and Sydney were on the verge of their separation. I put Donna's lack of good taste down to her vulnerability at that time. What makes me feel so sad is that Donna was a highly confident woman when I first met her, who was full of energy and had so much to offer. Unfortunately, I would have to search long and hard to find any of that confidence in her now.

"How long are you going to continue living like this, Don?" I ask, as we make our way into the kitchen, Donna knowing exactly what I mean.

"Not long," she replies, "just give me time."

"I hate to see you like this, girl. You deserve better!"

"You know something, we had this massive row the other day about him not being there for us. He said he wasn't doing anything now that he wasn't already doing when we first met."

"That doesn't give him the right to continue living his 'Saga-Boy' lifestyle," I reply, angrily. "He has a child now. It's about time he acts like a man with responsibilities. It makes my blood boil to see what all this is doing to you, Don. Like I said, you deserve better. Don't lose sight of what you're about, girl. Don't! Don't let it happen. You're too precious to us to let some good for nothing bring you down."

"I won't, I promise," she whispers, doubtfully.

"I'm with you all the way, you know that." The doorbell interrupts as it rings again. Donna answers the door and I can hear the usual raising of voices one hears whenever Jo and Donna meet. I can hear Donna commending Jo on how well she looks. The commendation is not returned.

"Hello my darling," I say to Jo as we embrace.

"Hi sweetie," says Jo in her usual warm and flamboyant style.

"How are you, girl?" I ask.

"I'm feeling just fine and rearing to go on the gossip. What's new?"

"Plenty," I reply. "Get yourself a glass of that Chardonnay and set yourself down." Unlike Donna, Jo rides on confidence. Josephine and I go back a long way. She is probably my closest friend. We met at Crossfields All Girls School in Richmond, Surrey, when we were both just eleven years old and have supported each other through many ups and downs, since. Jo is incredibly bright and has a first-class mind for business. Her boutiques, where she sells her own designs, are always doing good business. This is of no surprise to anyone who knows her. She's good. At five feet eight inches tall and weighing around one hundred and twenty pounds she has the perfect figure to promote her own clothes. And this she does with style.

"I can't believe that six months has passed since we were all last together," says Jo with excitement.

"That was a good night," I add.

"Yes," reminisces Donna. "Alice was so enlightening."

"Your Dexter could have learnt something that night," adds Jo. Donna shuffles uncomfortably on a beanbag and passes on the invitation for comment. I chuckle to myself as I recall Jo clutching her signed copy of Alice Walker's *The Temple of My Familiar*, as if her life depended on it. "She was so calm, witty and intelligent, an inspiration to us all."

"I agree. It was nice to see such a good turn out in support of such a successful woman," I add.

"Indeed. You haven't done too badly yourself, have you, Doctor Jackson?" says Jo, proudly and sincerely. Although familiar with the title – not that I have had much cause to use it – I couldn't help but smile in acknowledgement. "I wish I had stayed on at university, like you," Jo continues, "but I really thought that Jeremy and I would have become an item."

"Same here!" I reply. "You two got on so well but that should not have prevented you from staying on at university!"

"I blame our split on his parents rather than any problems between us," says Jo, ignoring my comment on university and with a clear tone of anger in her voice. "Not so much his father," she continues, "but his bitch of a mother! She never liked me from day one."

"Why not?" I ask, rhetorically, knowing that she will tell us, in any case.

"I think she felt that her son was too good for me. Too good for me!" repeats Jo.

"What a bloody cheek," says Donna, joining in the chorus of condemnation.

"At least I got myself a good education, went to university and now run three successful boutiques. What has she done?" Donna and I remain silent, leaving Jo to continue. "All she does all day is sit on that fat backside of hers or go shopping and spend the old man's money. She is for ever arranging charity functions. Lord alone knows who half these charities are! I'm sure that Jeremy's old man is bored with it but I cannot see her father allowing the old man to keep his seat on the Board if he were to dump her."

"It must be like having a noose around your neck," I say.

"Upset the wife and you're ruined!" adds Donna.

"The sad thing about it all is that the old man is rather talented and would make it on the Board of any top company on his own merit. I'll ask him to join mine when I eventually float it on the Stock Exchange," says Jo jokingly, but confident that such a floatation will take place one day in the not too distant future. "Anyway," she continues, "I must forget that family. They were a bad dream. My business is booming and I'm happy. That's all that matters in my life at this moment in time."

"I'm glad to hear that," I say, with relief. "Your boutiques always take off when you break up with a man."

"You make it sound like it's a regular occurrence," replies Jo. Donna and I glance at each other. It is agreed that I should deliver the sermon.

"It has been," I reply. "It's the same every time, honey. You're becoming predictable and we should know, for it is Donna and I you come running to after every separation."

"Point taken!" says Jo, in resignation.

"Not that you take much note of what we say in any case," adds Donna. Jo neither confirms nor denies the accuracy of the statement. Experience has taught me that when Jo says "point taken", what she really means is stop bothering her.

"You're making me sound like I'm some sixteen-year-old who cannot function properly when she is in love." The word "love" could not have been used more inappropriately but I refrain from comment.

"Like I've said before, Jo," I respond, "if you could only give half the consideration to your choice of partners as you do to your business, I'm sure you wouldn't suffer nearly half as many disappointments as you do." Surprisingly, she refuses to comment, probably in fear of where I might tread next. "That guy from Guyana, the engineer, the one we met on our skiing holiday at Innsbruck. What was his name?" I ask, remembering but wanting her to contribute to a conversation that I know she does not welcome.

26

"Humphrey," says Jo, hesitantly, in a matter-of-fact kind of way as she opens her gold cigarette case bought for her by one of her many ex-boyfriends. Who was it that bought her that case? Jo has such a high turnover of boyfriends, I could never quite remember who was who. They never seemed to be around quite long enough for me to take too much notice of them. Here today, gone tomorrow! All I could recall of the purchaser was that he spoke as though he had a constant sinus problem.

"Yes, that's the one," says Donna, enthusiastically and enjoying the moment.

"I liked him," I continue. "Now, he was a good man. He wasn't your typical business type but he had an honest air about him. He was crazy about you. But what did you do? You played the fool with him."

"I didn't play the fool with the man!" replies Jo, defensively. "He wanted more than I could offer, that's all!" The thought of such demand is inconceivable.

"He was interested in a serious relationship and all you gave him was this holiday-romance thing. Not all men get a kick out of this loose stuff, girl. He was a gentleman. I felt sorry for him because he meant well." Donna nods her head in agreement but remains silent.

"I know, Pat. He was a nice man. A perfect gentleman if you like. And to be truthful I believed he could have made me happy for a while, but a lot of those guys I've been out with have made me happy at some time or another. However, being happy is not enough. I need excitement! Adventure! I need to feel that I have to either be with the man all the time or talk to him on the telephone when he is not around. I need to feel my body change. You know what I'm saying, girls."

"The sad thing about it, Jo, is that you didn't even give Humphrey a chance. He was always on to a loser. You mentioned that some of the guys you went out with made you happy at some time. In other words, they were no different from Humphrey. Still, you went out with them and gave them a chance until..." I stop short of saying "they dumped you" as this was not about bashing my friend per se. This is much deeper! "He was obviously too black for you," I say. Donna sips her glass of wine.

Our eyes meet and I sense her support.

"Not now Pat. I'm in no mood for a lecture," she says, pleading.

"You know I'm uncomfortable with this stuff, Jo, but you quite clearly did not even give the guy a look-in just because he was black," I say, in the tone of a headmistress reprimanding a naughty schoolgirl before her friends. "You're consciously not even giving the black man a chance." Jo suddenly feels the need to search for an irretrievable item in her clutch bag. She doesn't like where this is going but I do, so I continue. "I'm not saying that things will be any different or even better with a black man but you are discriminating against your own kind. Sorry, I should say, your own colour. That to me is immoral. It's weird! I have never known anyone like that. No, tell a lie, there was this guy at Oxford. His name escapes me. Never mind it's not important. What is it with you Jo? Is it the contrast in the skin, sex or what?"

"We've spoken about this before, Pat and you know how I feel. I just don't feel at ease. Shameful, maybe but that's the way I feel and that's the way I am. It's got nothing to do with the contrast in any skin colour and it's definitely not a sex thing! Hey, if it was all about sex, I would have no choice but to opt for my black man."

"Less of that, 'my black man', stuff. For some reason that kind of talk just doesn't ring true coming from you, Jo."

"You know what I mean, Pat."

"I know what you mean, but I'm not convinced that the choice is that obvious, Jo, if Rupert is anything to go by," I reply, allowing myself to be sidetracked. "Either Rupert is the exception to the rule or that black-man-in-bed thing and his anatomy is a vicious rumour!"

"Probably started by one of the brothers out there," says Jo, welcoming the moratorium.

"Who else?" I reply. "Rupert usually starts his performance with good intentions but that soon fades after he loses control of himself. Before you know it, the show's over and the man's fast asleep with a stupid grin on his face." Laughter ensues.

"And there's me thinking that Rupert was so innocent," says Donna. "The impression I get when I'm out with you guys, is that it is you who have to make all the moves. Rupert seems as though he'd be just as happy reading a law report."

"Don't let that fool you, Don. That innocent act is one big charade. When he's doing his business, he thinks he's doing something! That's the shameful thing about it. He's got this sort of 'I've got all the moves babe, but I'll only show you a little at a time' approach. The sad thing about it is, Rupert only has a little thing to give, all of the time!" A cacophony of laughter fills the room.

"Well I'll be damned!" says Jo, melodramatically, as the true Rupert is revealed.

"I remember when I first introduced you to Rupert," I say, getting back to the main theme, "you said that he was a nice guy but commented that he was not your type and yet you and Rupert are similar in so many ways."

"I didn't mean to offend you, Pat," responds Jo, quickly. "It's just that…"

"It was like it was taboo to even consider being with him," I interrupt. "The fact that he was a handsome and intelligent man was suddenly of little or no importance. I remember thinking at the time that you had serious problems, Jo."

"I think you're being a little unfair, Pat. Like I've said before…"

"Williams," I say, rudely interrupting her again. "Curtis Williams, that was his name, the guy at Oxford who is just like you. He had a problem with his own skin colour. It's ironic because you probably couldn't find another person darker than him!" Jo gives a nervous smile that stopped far short of a laugh.

"No. No. I haven't got a problem with the colour of my skin. I'm proud to be black and a strong-minded black woman at that, but when I first came over here from Zaire, I could hardly speak a word of English and all those black kids around gave me a harder time than the white children. The white children saw me as just another black child whereas the black children saw me as some kind of alien. It was horrible! I hated it back then. Although, in hindsight I shouldn't blame the children. At that age they probably didn't know any better but I do blame their parents for not educating them that not all black children around the world speak English and in Zaire or, more importantly, in Africa, English is not the mother tongue. I guess that that period of my life had more of a profound effect on me than I care to realise."

"But Jo," I say, sympathetically, "although I would not have experienced such a thing, I, like any member of a minority group, would know how ugly and hurtful such ignorance can be but I wouldn't adopt and implement similar bigotry as you appear to do. Prejudice is born out of ignorance but you're not ignorant, so why be prejudiced?"

"Because, Pat," she responds with a little anger, "that prejudice exists within many adult black people today. Maybe more than you care to admit. Even some Africans and West Indians cannot get on, for prejudicial reasons."

"I know exactly what you're saying, Jo. I personally find the whole concept rather sick. I am a British West Indian woman who is proud of my African roots. At the end of the day, one hundred and thirty million black people were killed during the slave trade. That should be enough to pull black people of all descendency together, not to push them apart."

"Tell it like it is, girl," supports Donna.

"I agree Pat, but look around us. It's everywhere. There will never be peace at the same time within the four corners of my mother-continent during my lifetime. So my minor indiscretion in my choice of men is not exactly going to change the world, is it?"

"It's not a case of changing the world, honey; it's a case of using that expensive education of yours to liberate your mind of any prejudgments and maybe give some of those guys the benefit of the doubt. You should know better. It is sisters like yourself who should be the role models to the rest of the family. Let's face it, you could hardly do any worse than you have already. Do you not think that an upwardly mobile brother out there would not feel just as proud having an equally upwardly mobile sister on his arm? Especially, when he goes to the restaurant, visits the museum or goes to see a show in town? Of course he would. All I am saying is that you should not date one at the expense of another just for the reasons you have given. I do not think that chastising yourself against your own colour is the solution to the problem. You've seen the movie on numerous occasions. You know how it ends. Maybe it's time to see a different movie!"

"Point taken!" says Jo, as she walks over to the hi-fi system and presses "play" on the compact-disc player, without even checking what's in the appliance and turns up the volume. Cameo's "She's Strange" blurts out from the speakers. We all look at each other, but say nothing.

Rupert

"I got a call from Kelvin Williams," I say to Dexter. "He rang to invite us to Yvonne's birthday party this Saturday night. Do you fancy going?"

"Donna will be visiting her parents this weekend. I'll be free, so why not?" replies Dexter with little persuasion. We both know that he would have agreed to go whether Donna was going out or not! He seems to do whatever he so wishes these days, with or without Donna's approval. I like Dexter. Many people, I know, find him very difficult to get on with, aloof, even. And, to a certain degree, I can understand why. He can be irritatingly argumentative. Sometimes, in my view, unnecessarily so. But I think that that kind of attitude comes from him having had to fend for himself from a very young age. In that respect, we are very similar. We were both brought up single-handedly by our respective mothers. His father died unexpectedly from cancer when Dexter was just eleven years old. Having neither sisters nor brothers to lean on, he was instantly promoted to the "Man of the House". When life imposes that kind of responsibility on you, you have no alternative other than to mature into adulthood a lot sooner than your compeers do. Such unnatural and rapid development must take effect in one way or another and can, as in the case of Dexter, lead to one being a single-minded and, sometimes, selfish person. You're warier of people and more cynical than you need otherwise be. Some interpret such behaviour as somewhat odd, which, of course, it would be, unless you had a similar upbringing. I view it differently. I see him as simply surviving the best way he knows how. He's always on his guard. Always on the look out for anyone who might wish to take advantage of him in any way whatsoever. He's built a mental barrier between himself and the outside world, so that no one, fiancée, friends or otherwise, can get too close to the real Dexter. Those not so understanding, or forgiving, as myself treat such demeanour with contempt. I agree, in some respects that such paranoia can cause him to overreact to situations where no harm was ever intended or, indeed, sustained. I can empathise with him because I too could have been like him, had I not met Pat when I did. Up until that time in my life, I had difficulties fostering any long-term relationships with girls because of the degree of my vulnerability. People don't appreciate just how emotionally vulnerable you can be when, as a young person, you are brought up solely by a parent of the opposite sex. You are always thinking that the boy with a dependable father, or the girl with a dependable mother, knows something that you could never know unless you were in their shoes. Of course, that is not necessarily the case but try convincing a young man or woman otherwise, with such ingrained beliefs, at such tender age. As a young man, growing up without my father being around, I had only ever confided in my mother, or kept matters to myself. So, whenever I had a girlfriend, despite all her good intentions, I regarded certain matters dear to my heart as those that I used to discuss with my mother or those that I reserved for myself as private. In other words, matters that were previously reserved for me, stayed with me, and, as my mother could never be substituted, there was nothing left to reveal. There lay a major obstacle that was too much for many girls to accept, no matter how much they may have claimed to have loved or cared for me. If you don't have the full trust of your partner, then you have nothing. I understand that. Pat, however, was different. She gained my trust fairly early on in our relationship. She would not have it any other way. She insisted on us being open and frank with each other from the outset, otherwise there would be no "us". I wanted there to be an "us" so I submitted. But, notwithstanding her ultimatum, she taught me to be less defensive towards people than I had ever felt the need to be, or even wanted to be in the past. And I can't say that I am any the worse for it, either. In fact, some people might say that I have probably gone too far the other way. They may have a point. Today, I could probably give Pat a lesson or two about not being too cynical. It's true that Dexter, too, has a good woman in Donna, and need not, therefore, be so shielding, but things are a little sour between those two at the moment, and I can't honestly see them surviving much longer, unless Dexter soon changes his ways. By changing his ways, what I really mean is for him to stop chasing women as a hobby. It would be sad if they were to separate after all this time together, because they do make a good couple when things are going well. The trouble is things very rarely do go well!

"Why aren't you going to the in-laws?" asks Samuel, raising his head temporarily from his Book of Psalms.

"I'm not married!" replies Dexter, sharply, irritated seemingly at the implication that there had been a change in his marital status. "And," he continues, "I have no intention of changing that for some time. In any case, without me being around, Donna will have more of an opportunity to cuss my name."

"She's probably cussing you this very minute," I say, keeping within the spirit of the whole affair. "Donna and Jo are round our place tonight," I confirm.

"Well that's that then!" mocks Dexter. "My name is already mud with Pat so I might as well pack my bags and leave now!"

"I really do think that Donna has had enough," I respond, ignoring his remark about my wife.

"You'll be crazy to let her and little Dionne go," says Sam, allowing enough time only to make his views known and then return to his Psalms.

"I'm not letting her go but if she wants to go then I can't stop her, can I?" replies Dexter. "I love Dionne, you guys know that, but since Donna gave birth to her we've barely made love and when we do it's nothing to write home about. She's lost all interest in sex. She's suffering from that post-natal depression stuff. She's gone loony, so what can I do about it?"

"She's the mother of your child," replies Sam, pausing again from reading his scriptures. "What other excuse do you need? She deserves all the support you can give her. That's what you can do about it!" he adds, angrily.

"I want to be more supportive but I can't," replies Dexter. "How can I be warm to someone who finds me cold? And my only crime? Giving her Dionne. I just don't understand the woman. She was perfectly happy when she fell pregnant with Dionne. We both wanted a baby, so what the hell is her problem?

What is there to be depressed about? I just think that she's seeking attention. Women are like that. They have all these excuses when they want more attention from their men. I should know, because I've witnessed it on numerous occasions. If they're not complaining about premenstrual depression, it's post-menstrual depression! If it's not prenatal depression, it's post-natal depression! There's no pleasing them."

"That doesn't stop you trying, though, does it?" I respond. "Also, your behaviour can't be helping matters."

"She knows nothing about my behaviour, as you put it, so that can't be depressing her. The way I see it, she's gone off sex at the moment because she blames me, if that's the right word, for making her pregnant. But she's perfectly happy with Dionne. If you can work that one out then you're a better man than I. Not every time we make love is she going to get pregnant, is she? Now she's acting like Dionne is hers alone. I have to clear everything with her before I do anything for my own child. I couldn't even buy Dionne a packet of sweets without first getting Donna's permission. You guys would act the same way if you were me, I know you would."

"You can count me out!" I reply in my defence. "I would never cheat on Pat. If I still wanted to play the field then I wouldn't have got married, period!" If I were to play Dexter's game and Pat found out, she would kick me out of our home so fast I wouldn't even have time to say "I'm sorry." Pat has fixed morals on certain issues and such misconduct is one of them, which would be totally unacceptable.

"Well, I'm not married so I'm okay!" Dexter replies, sarcastically.

"If you and Donna come to church one Sunday," says Sam, sincerely, "I can ask Pastor Benjamin to pray for you both."

"You must be joking!" replies Dexter, plainly shocked at Sam's proposal. "I'm not going to have some pastor pray for my woman to be ready for sex! That's sick! Plus, we're not even married!"

"I didn't mean that Pastor Benjamin should pray for Donna to be more sexually active, only that you both get through your current problems," responds Sam, visibly embarrassed at the misunderstanding.

"It sounds like a good idea to me," I say, supporting Sam, whose head is already buried back into his book. "In any case," I continue, "I'm sure what Donna is going through is only temporary. A lot of women go through similar phases shortly after giving birth. Just be patient with her."

"Why do I have to be patient?" asks Dexter. "She's the one suffering from this post-natal depression stuff not me! I'm twenty-four years old, virile and still in my sexual prime. I don't see why I should sit around while she clears her head. So in the meantime I shall do a bit of training until we kick off again." Ashley joins Dexter for a chorus of laughter. Up until now, Ashley seemed perfectly happy just sipping his white wine and "observing the scene" as he would often put it, in other words, looking at women with an unclean mind.

"That's ruthless!" says Ashley, unconvincingly, whilst shaking his head. "You're obviously not doing the business properly. You give the woman a child and you turn her off sex for life!" At this moment, Ashley bellows with a loud vulgar laugh that has nothing but "nasty" written all over it.

"No disrespect," replies Dexter, staring intensely at Ashley, "but you're hardly in a position to comment. Your relationship with Tessa leaves a lot to be desired."

"Hey, hey, I'm not the one with the problem. I have two lovely children and Tessa is pregnant with my third. I don't hear my woman complaining!"

"That may be true," says Dexter, "but if you were with Donna she wouldn't take that shit you dish out to Tessa, let alone give you two or three children. And if things are so good at home what the hell are you still doing with Pamela?"

"What are you still doing with Chantelle?" asks Ashley, in retaliation.

"Come on…" I say.

"Ain't nothing wrong with me and my woman," interrupts Ashley, like a child wanting the last word. "It's your woman who needs therapy, not mine!"

"This is getting a little out of hand," I say, sensing a heated argument brewing up.

"I'll tell you what," says Ashley, with a grin that Satchmo

would have been proud of, "as you and I go back a long way, I'll do you a favour. I'll volunteer to give Donna some of that post-natal servicing that she's been missing all this time. She'll be grateful for it, I'm sure! Come to think of it, so will you in the long run."

I sense that the gloves are now off and I'm in no mood to referee a fight between two grown men. Notwithstanding that, Ashley is a few pounds of muscle heavier than Dexter and I wouldn't want to see my friend's face rearranged, for better or for worse. I remind Ashley that it is his round and insist that he goes to the bar and puts this right before closing time, which I'm pleased to say, he kindly obliges.

"Don't pay him any attention," I say to Dexter, who looks as though he has just gone a few rounds with Mike Tyson and worse! He was clearly bruised by the exchange of words.

"You know what he's like when he's had a few drinks," contributes Sam.

"Just remember that you're a father with responsibilities now and therefore it would not be fair on Dionne to have to grow up hearing that her father is playing around with other women," I add. "I think you know what I'm getting at." I wouldn't wish on anyone, friend or foe, my childhood experience of growing up with my mother and witnessing what she went through with my father.

"Like I said, what Donna doesn't know won't hurt her," replies Dexter, repeating his slogan for the night.

"My relationship with Donna has deteriorated almost to the point of non-existence since you two have been having your problems," I say. "It's not fair on me because I'm caught in the middle between a rock and a hard place. You're my close friend. She's my close friend. I can't win!"

"I hear what you say, but Donna could be in her state for months, if not years. What am I supposed to do in the mean-time?" At this point, the assailant, Ashley, returns with three glasses filled with white wine and a glass filled with orange juice.

"I'll tell you what, Dexter," says Ashley, "you could always revert to the do-it-yourself method of sexual fulfilment. I think that you lawyers call it 'discharge by frustration'." Ashley gives another of his offensive laughs in self-congratulation at his own humour.

"I'm not into that nastiness," replies Dexter, defensively and loud enough for a few others outside his present company to hear, as if defending his manhood to the world. "To me that's worse than cheating on any woman!"

"Anyway," says Ashley, "if Donna's seeking advice from Agony Aunt Pat, I can't see you getting your oats for sometime, in any case!"

"Hey," I intervene, "my wife didn't create this problem."

"I'll get my oats, all right!" replies Dexter, confidently. "As long as women are attracted to this face," he says, shamelessly pointing to his face with both hands, "then my nooky is secured!"

There is unprovoked laughter between my friends and I, as we make our way out of the wine bar, all feeling a little worse for wear; except Sam, of course, who had been sipping fruit juice all night. When I arrived home, Donna and Jo were still there. Donna decided to leave as I was about to join them in the lounge for some small talk. I felt so guilty knowing what Dexter was up to and I'm sure that it showed. I'm not very good at these things but I am not my brother's keeper. Donna gave me a cold peck on the cheek as she walked towards the front door and left without even so much as a smile. The following day, Donna and Dionne left Dexter and moved in with Donna's parents.

Donna

Love is blind. My friends often told me that before I left Dexter. I wasn't blind. I could see perfectly well what was going on, but I did and still do, to a certain degree – albeit to a lesser extent than before – care for Dexter. It's not easy leaving someone whom you were once very fond of and whom you had shared four years of your life with. It's tough. The ironic thing about all this is that having sat in on numerous counselling sessions with women from the centre suffering from low esteem and depression, following the departure of their once loved ones, I never thought that one day I too would be taking fellowship. However, contrary to my friends, I don't pass all the blame onto Dexter. I too am the cause of our separation. I was a strong outgoing woman and went into the relationship with my eyes wide open. Dexter is right, he was the same person when we were together as he was when I first met him and so who was I to try and change him? If I didn't like his ways then, then I shouldn't have got involved with him. At first it was just a lust thing between us but that soon manifested itself into love. It felt nice going out with him because I could see all the ladies looking at him in admiration and at me with envy. His smooth light-brown skin with his hazel-green eyes made him an obvious eye-catcher. He loved all the attention he attracted, and so did I, for it was my bed he was coming home to! However, I should have known that if you give a young man so much attention, then it will soon go to his young head and Dexter was no exception to this. I started to get the feeling that I was no longer the only woman in his life. This didn't bother me so much at the beginning as I just put it down to bouts of insecurity. After all, I am three years older than Dexter, so moments of insecurity with such a good-looking young man was probably not so peculiar. After two years of being together we got engaged. I was surprised when he asked me to be his fiancée because he did not appear to be ready to make such a commitment. I remember Pat asking me if I was sure that he was the right one for me. She has never trusted him and those green eyes. In hindsight I guess she had just cause not to. But the way I saw it, one can never truly know when Mister or Miss Right comes along, so I gambled and took my chances. Dexter and I discussed having a child for some time and at some length. I was concerned that he might not be ready for fatherhood nor to deal with all the responsibilities that come along with such an honour. He assured me that he was, and with that undertaking we planned and had Dionne. I had a very difficult pregnancy. I was often so sick that I would just lie in bed all day. I put on more weight than I thought I would have done, but when you're bed stricken all day there is little to do but eat and not much chance of burning off those extra calories! Dexter would often comment on how my physical features had changed during my pregnancy. At first I paid no mind to such remarks but after a while they got through to me as it became clearer that what he was really saying was that I "looked" ugly! I sensed that he was becoming more and more distant during the period when I most needed him. I don't recall having a single hug from him during my nine months of pregnancy. There I was in my most vulnerable state and my partner was implying that I was ugly – an appearance that no amount of make-up could have changed! I became ill-tempered. I no longer wanted to give birth to the foetus growing inside me. It was that foetus that had made me so unattractive to a man who could easily have found himself another woman without too much trouble. Then one day, when I was visiting my gynaecologist, I met this couple who had just been told that their daughter would be born Down's syndrome. It was not the best day of their lives but all I could hear them saying was that their baby would have the best life that they could give her. I remember feeling so guilty about my vanity that I simply wept all the way home and asked that the Lord forgave me "for I know not what I do". From thereon my outlook on life had changed. My body would be the vehicle for bringing a healthy child into this world. It was no longer important how I looked. All I wanted was my child. My world consisted of me and my child. I did not want to hear a single negative word from Dexter or anyone. Dexter could not be part of our lives for that period.

We didn't need him. Mother and child were doing just fine on their own. I had gained an inner strength that told me that, for the first time in my life, I was to have something that I could truly call my own. Something I had created that was of my own flesh and blood. No rings needed to prove that bond. No wedding vows needed to prove the legality. Just my baby and me, that's all!

Dionne was born a healthy 7 pounds and 13 ounces. Dexter appeared to be visibly pleased by the arrival of his daughter into this world, but when I saw him with Dionne I couldn't help thinking there was a child holding a child. I had seen the real Dexter during my time of pregnancy and what I had seen was a boy. Someone who had made big commitments that were way above his immature head. My feelings towards Dexter didn't so much change, they evolved. They readjusted to the person they now knew. Having been re-aligned, my feelings rejected him. I no longer had the same attraction for him as I at first had. I tried to fight this but my feelings were sending messages to my brain and my brain was telling me that I was no longer in love. So, what was I to do? Here I was with the father of my child whom I no longer loved. I spent most of my days caring for my daughter. I had to. I guess it was the only way I could shut him out of our world. In any case, I had no time to be worrying about Dexter and his women. Oh yes, love hadn't made this sister blind! I knew perfectly well what Dexter was up to, but at that time he was secondary in my life. My primary love was my daughter. She's my own child of my own body. I owe her so much and would give up the world for her. A far cry from how I felt in my early days of pregnancy. Every time I see her, I feel so guilty. If only she knew how close she was to not being here today. To hear her call me "mama", sometimes bring tears to my eyes, when I think that I was once willing to sacrifice her life for some man. Some man who is probably keeping some woman's bed warm at this very moment!

When I thought of how Dexter made me feel at a time when I needed his utmost support and attention, I despised him! I didn't want him near me. I didn't want him to touch me. I didn't want him to touch my child. How could I? The first test, in which he could prove that he was a man, he failed, miserably! I often asked myself why did I stay with him for so long? Pat and Jo were mystified. Pat, especially. For she had known how frustrated I would get when the women at the centre would complain about their men but do nothing about it. Strangely, I hoped that I would change back to the way I felt for Dexter. He had been brought up in a single parent household through no choice of his mother. I didn't want Dionne growing up without her father around when her parents did have a choice to remain together. I guess that with all his womanising I was hoping he would eventually make the decision on our relationship that would save me the pains of having to make that decision myself. I knew that Dexter was seeing this woman, Chantelle, when we were together – not that I was supposed to know, of course. Rupert never once had the courage to tell me what Dexter was up to. I was just supposed to believe that Dexter was behaving himself. Brother Samuel tells me that Chantelle is very pretty, probably around Dexter's age, if not younger and that they seem very happy together. I would be lying if I said that I wasn't hurting in some way to hear that he is seeing someone else but I wish him well for I know that he would wish me the same if I too were in a new relationship.

Rupert

"I'll pick you up at about nine thirty," says Dexter, sounding happy and ready to "shake a leg", as the saying goes.

"Dexter seemed rather jolly on the telephone. Maybe he and Donna are sorting things out, at last," I say to Pat. It has now been three days since Donna and Dionne walked out on Dexter but my friend seems to be bearing up very well. Pat makes no reply to my suggestion of reconciliation and makes her way towards the front door. "Enjoy yourself," I continue, "and I'll see you sometime tomorrow."

"Yes, and you behave yourself," replies Pat, in that by-your-friends-you-shall-know-yourself manner.

"Don't I always?" I reply, defensively, why I don't know. Pat did not appear to hear my response as she closed the door behind her without reply.

The intercom buzzed just after ten o'clock. Dexter had arrived. In fact he caught me a little unawares because I usually hear his BMW approaching the forecourt. All I heard this time was a raunchier sounding engine prior to his arrival. As we leave the flat and walk out into the front, I can see this gleaming new sports car that would have set him back a few pounds, I'm sure.

"What's with the new motor?" I ask, as the lights to a brand new black Porsche 911 Carrera Sport flash at the remote command of its proud owner.

"The old car was soon up for its first 'three-year service', so I thought I'd give it change and try something different."

"You've done that all right!" I reply. "What did Donna have to say about this?"

"What could she have said?" replies Dexter with a quizzed look on his face. "I used my own hard-earned money to buy it!"

"A two-door sports car is not renowned for its convenience as a family car, is it?" I ask, sarcastically.

"Donna had her own car," he replies. "She and Dionne could

have got about in that," he adds with an air of finality as he turns up the volume to Grover Washington's "Winelight", which is playing on the compact-disc player. Maybe I was a little premature with that reconciliation talk after all. We didn't speak another word until we got to the party.

"Happy Birthday, Yvonne," I say, giving her a warm embrace and a peck on each cheek. Dexter says and does likewise.

"Where is Kelvin?" I ask.

"The last time I saw him he was in the kitchen with Wilson Pennycroft."

"Oh right!" I say, recalling the name but not quite the face. Dexter and I make our way towards the kitchen as the DJ plays Stevie Wonder's "Happy Birthday" which, judging by the reaction from the invitees, is not the first time tonight that it has been played.

"Kelvin, how are you doing?" I say, extending my hands.

"Hello Rupert, Dexter, nice to see you both," replies Kelvin. "You remember Wilson don't you?"

"Yes, I do," I say, as we shake hands. I now recall the face. Wilson was never an acquaintance of mine but we occasionally socialised in the same circles.

"Where are the ladies?" asks Kelvin.

"Unfortunately, they had prior engagements," replies Dexter, eagerly.

"I hear that you're working for a pharmaceutical company, Dexter," says Kelvin.

"Yes, I am," replies Dexter. "I guess I'm one of those people who did not quite make the grade." Kelvin looks to be a little uneasy at Dexter's sharp response as memories of an infamous heated argument between the two come inappropriately flooding back.

"We're not going to go over old ground now are we?" asks Kelvin, skilfully.

"Not at all!" replies Dexter, who seems disappointed that his subtle challenge to Kelvin is not to be taken up.

After the pleasantries, if you can call them that, I made my way out of the kitchen and circulated among the other revellers. The music wasn't too bad. They were playing quite a lot of late-seventies', early-eighties' soul and dance music that I really liked: Shalamar, Whispers, Kashif, that kind of stuff. I bumped into Dexter once or twice, who appeared to be having a good time dancing with Yvonne. I was also aware that he had had a little too much to drink. He wouldn't be driving that fancy car of his home tonight, that was for sure. I was making my way up the stairs to the "little boys'" room when I got a light tap on my left shoulder.

"Hello, how are you?" she says.

"I'm fine thanks," I reply.

"You don't recognise me, do you?" she asks. I don't. My mind is racing a hundred miles an hour in order to save my embarrassment. I concede.

"No, I must confess, I don't," I reply.

"I'm Linda," she announces, "Linda Walters. I'm a friend of Wilson Pennycroft. I used to meet him after classes sometimes."

"Oh yes, I remember." I recall that she would often accompany Wilson on our rare social encounters together but I don't think that we were ever formally introduced. After all, I'm sure that I would have remembered if we had. "Were you not into photography?" I ask, to show that I do genuinely remember her.

"Yes," she replies, to my satisfaction. "I was a photography student when you lot were at Law School."

Linda is an attractive woman and I remember thinking to myself one time what she could possibly have seen in Wilson who, by all accounts, was a bit of a "square". I seem to have forgotten that my bladder was not so long ago bursting for the lavatory. My present company is a much better proposition.

"Are you working as a photographer now?" I ask with interest.

"Yes, I work freelance."

"What sort of work do you take on?"

"At this stage in my career I take all commissions, but my main preference is fashion. I adore fashion photography," she says with detectable excitement in her tone of voice.

"I'm not averse to a bit of fashion myself. I could be your supermodel for a day," I say, rather innocently but sounding like Dexter on one of his "pulling" expeditions. "I wouldn't mind earning what they do for a day's work."

"I understand that lawyers don't do too badly themselves either," she replies staring at me straight between the eyes with an enigmatic smile. A nice smile too, I should add! "Actually," she continues, "I think you'd look really good modelling some designer wear on the pages of GQ."

"Thank you," I reply, bashfully. I think that "thank you" was in order. I'm not too sure but it sounded right.

"I see that you're wearing an Armani suit," she says, correctly. "If you are genuinely interested in fashion then maybe you might be interested in seeing some pictures that I took at the London fashion shows this year."

"Yes, I would be honoured," I reply instantly without fully considering the consequences or what I am supposed to say when I see these photographs. After all, I'm a lawyer not a fashion guru! "Where do you live?" I ask.

"We."

"We?" I reply.

"Yes, Wilson and I."

"Oh! I see." How sad but why should I care?

"We live in Kensington, on Kensington Church Street," says Linda.

"I know where that is," I reply with as much enthusiasm as I can muster. Suddenly my interest in fashion is not all that high after all. Maybe Linda thinks that Wilson and I were actually friends.

"Let me know when you can come round."

"I shall," I reply.

"Let me know before you go tonight," she persists. There's no escaping this one, I suppose.

"Definitely," I reply, as I continue to make my way to the men's while she descends down the stairs.

I noticed that Dexter was making a bit of a nuisance of himself and was still hovering around Yvonne like a bee around a honey pot. Since my friend has been having problems with Donna, he's been acting like some frustrated bachelor boy. He thinks that every woman should know that he is back in the market. His problem is that he fails to notice that many women are not necessarily that interested. I can only think that the true reason behind the recent purchase of his super-duper sports car was to increase his pulling power with the women. Fortunately for Dexter, Kelvin does not appear to be around. He is probably still in the kitchen chatting law with Wilson and the others. George Michael's "Careless Whisper" comes on. Linda is at the other side of the front room and she beckons me over.

"Would you like a dance?" asks Linda.

"Yes, why not?" I reply. We hold each other fairly close but not too tight. She must be around five six because her head is parallel to my shoulder. As we continue dancing, she rests her head on my right shoulder. I detect the strong aroma of her perfume and recognise it to be Chanel No.5. God, I love that scent on a woman! I would be lying if I were to say that this dance is unpleasant. I take the chance and close my eyes. This makes the dance a lot sweeter. Our feet don't lack the rhythm that the song's lyrics suggest they should. I have chemical reactions in my body which makes me feel guilty or blameworthy of something. I'm not too sure what that "something" is, but I can guess. I begin to break out into a cold sweat. I feel a little uncomfortable with a woman being so near and with me perspiring so much. A woman who is not Pat! After the dance we look at each other and smile. A smile that paints a thousand words.

"So, when are you going to come round?" asks Linda, putting me on the spot. Suddenly my interest in fashion has grown again and the request no longer seems like hassle. I open my mouth to reply, but say nothing, as I hear a commotion coming from the kitchen. We make our way over to see what is happening. Dexter and Kelvin are arguing about the social class structure in Britain. This is heavy stuff for a party that is playing such good music. Kelvin seems pleased with himself, as he appears to be taking full advantage of my intoxicated friend.

"Had you worked harder at law school," says Kelvin to Dexter, "you may well have been given a chance to prove your true worth where it really matters, but, if I recall correctly, you were often otherwise engaged with some woman." This remark appears to touch a raw nerve with Dexter. It's true that Dexter's style of studying was a little unorthodox, to say the least, but he got through. Kelvin and Dexter both had their different styles but I guess anyone who appeared not to be studying as hard as Kelvin did, did not, in Kelvin's opinion, work hard enough and therefore did not deserve to succeed, either as well as him or at all! I suppose, whereas Kelvin would be perfectly happy with a glass of Chardonnay or Sauvignon Blanc in one hand, and a law textbook in the other, Dexter would have been content with just the former. But, like I said, they both got through: the former with superior marks than the latter, of course! The argument was now becoming tedious and an embarrassment to Yvonne, not to mention Dexter or myself. For it was me who passed on the extended invitation to Dexter, albeit at the passing request of Kelvin. After this mess tonight, I question whether Kelvin's invitation really was supposed to be offered to my friend. It seems that old habits die hard with those two and there is no obvious indication that this habit will die tonight. That being the case, I decide that enough is enough and suggest that Dexter and I leave without further delay. Reluctantly, he agrees. As we are about to leave I apologise for the behaviour of my friend to Yvonne, and head for the door and our awaiting cab. As we make our way towards the front gate Linda runs towards me and hands me a business card. Dexter and I enter the cab and depart.

"That was a bit heavy for a birthday party, wasn't it?" I ask.

"I don't think so," replies Dexter with a staunch smell of alcohol emitting from his mouth. "The way I see it, you're all the same."

"What has this got to do with me?" I ask, in surprise. He doesn't answer and appears to have fallen asleep. I was in no mood to drag Dexter to his home at two o'clock in the morning and so decided that he could stay at our place for the night. I search for the cab fare and a business card falls out of my pocket and on to the ground. I recognise it as the one that Linda had given to me, as we were leaving the party. On the reverse side there was a handwritten message saying "Call me. Soon!" I put Dexter's right arm around my neck and help him into the flat.

By the time Dexter had awakened in the morning, he had forgotten most of the previous night's fiasco. He recalled very little when I informed him of his performance. He did, however, say that he felt like a weight had been lifted off his shoulders and that he would be perfectly happy never to see that "spoilt brat" Kelvin again. Unfortunately, this was not to be the case. In our rush to leave the party I failed to notice that Dexter had left his raincoat behind. His car keys were in his coat!

Dexter

Chantelle is now my full-time lover. She acquired that position almost the moment Donna walked out on me with my child. In fact, she spent the night at the flat the very day that Donna left. I felt a little guilty about another woman sleeping in our bed so soon after our separation, but that guilt soon wore off after the first or second hour. After all, I didn't walk out on Donna, she walked out on me, so I was entitled to seek relief in any way I saw fit. And, at least I was putting the bed to some good use! Am I sorry Donna left? Like hell I am. I needed my space. Well, my space to be with Chantelle. I miss my Dionne, of course, but I can see her anytime. I know Donna wouldn't deprive me of that. If I'm to be honest with myself, I didn't think that Donna had the courage to leave. She just seemed content with the way things were. We were effectively living separate lives for some time. And, apart from the occasional complaint, it didn't seem to bother her too much. We were sharing the same bed but not sleeping together. When I think back, it is clear to me that Donna never really got to know me that well. Sometimes, all I wanted was some space to myself but for some reason she just could not understand that. "Every man", I would tell her, "needs his space every once in a while." The way I see it, such periods could save a relationship and not necessarily destroy it. Now Chantelle, on the other hand, understands me very well. She knows what I want. She has succeeded in knowing me, where Donna had clearly failed. I really like being in her company. We have so much fun together. And there's such a big contrast between my time spent with Chantelle and my time spent with Donna. Chantelle likes her parties and clubs. We would club or party from Friday night right through to Sunday. Donna, on the other hand, was happy just staying at home looking after Dionne or visiting her friends, Josephine or Patricia. After she had Dionne, Donna was not the same woman. She had put on too much weight and had lost interest in all activities between the sheets. How can she lose interest in sex when she hadn't had any during the latter months of her pregnancy? I feel irritable without any nooky after only a few days! She kept saying that she wasn't ready yet. What is there to be ready for? I wanted sex not surgery. This is where a man is clearly different from a woman. If a woman is ready, her man is ready. He doesn't need to psyche himself up for action. It's as easy as that. What Donna failed to realise is that if a woman rejects her man often enough, then he will simply go elsewhere. It's an instinctive reaction. I think it must be in our genes or something. Animals are no different. A male chases the female until he gets her. When he does he moves on to the next. If she doesn't want to know, he moves on until he finds one that does. Simple! When Donna had Dionne, I gave her all the attention that a man could give his woman, but she was clearly unwell; post-natal depression she called it. Now, what is that all about? I'm a lawyer not a psychologist, so I left her alone to sort herself out and true to form I moved on to the next girl, Chantelle, who was not so messed up. I'm twenty-four years old and my young shoulders aren't equipped for bearing such emotional loads. That is what I like about Chantelle, she knows the score. She knows not to burden me with foolishness. She doesn't ask questions for answers that she doesn't need to know. Her and Donna are so different in many ways. She's young and vibrant. Full of energy. She makes me feel young. Donna was only making me feel old before my time. All that "settling down" talk was boring me. When you start talking like that, you start acting like you're married and I'm not ready for that kind of lifestyle just yet. So I had a homely, overweight woman on one hand and an outgoing, slim woman on the other. There was no competition. Chantelle won hands down! So, I'm happily enjoying life again, with a woman I enjoy being with. And, I haven't got that Patricia meddling in my business, either. That woman really bugs me. I sometimes wondered whether she was simply jealous of Donna. She probably wanted a piece of me for herself! It wouldn't surprise me, she's a woman isn't she? I have this effect on women. She just seemed to have the knives out for me. What was her problem? If you ask me, she is too educated for her own good.

She should try and lighten up and see life for what it really is, and not how she thinks it ought to be. Anyway, now she has the responsibility of consoling Donna who will undoubtedly be feeling the blues without me in her life. After all, she left me and I'm enjoying life better now with another woman than when I was with her. Knowing Donna as well as I do, that spells nothing but "depression". Good, that will teach her. Bitch!

Patricia

"I want a baby," I say to Rupert, who appears to be studying some brief with intense concentration.

"Whatever you say, honey," he replies, without so much as a glance in my direction.

"Rupert!" I shout, playfully. "I'm serious, look at me." After a moment's delay, as if wanting to finish the last line of a vital piece of evidence from his star witness, he rests his papers down on the kitchen table and gives me what appears to be his full attention. "Now that *Four Seasons* is more or less out of my hands and in print, I feel that I am ready to have a baby," I continue, as I put my arms around him and press my cheek against his with mild affection. He likes that kind of attention!

"If you feel that now is the right time for us to have a child then I'm all for it," replies Rupert, supportively, but with little or no conviction. He has had a lot on his mind lately. This case he is working on is taking so much out of him that there are times when I feel that he would consent to anything, just for the sake of a peaceful life. He just doesn't seem to be "all there" these days. I know that Rupert would make a wonderful father and he would give our children all the love and care that he claimed his father never gave him, but his beloved mother did.

"Don't you think that it would be nice to come home to your wife and two lovely children?" I ask, awaiting his reaction to the proposed increase in our family from one child to two children. We are both an only child and know how lonely that can be; no big sister or brother to confide in or little sister or brother to advise.

"Of course, I would," he replies, more convincingly, "but I'll leave that decision ultimately to you, for it is you who will be carrying our child for nine months, not me." I pretend to consider his comment for a moment but my mind is already made up.

"Well, I say that we go for it!" I reply, whilst pecking him on his right cheek. "Maybe Nelson could be conceived tonight," I say, in some hope that Rupert will request that we try now. He smiled in acknowledgement to the choice of name but little else. He's been having problems in that area of the bedroom lately and I know that that has been troubling him. The more he worries about it, the more of an effect it has on him. I have tried to assure him that all is fine with me, but that doesn't seem to do him any good. I think that he thinks that he is letting me down. He is not performing his husbandry duties. I can't convince him otherwise. You know how feeble some men can be. Rupert is not one who would normally require too much of an encouragement to enter into the bedroom but since this recent case, I think that I would have to dance practically naked, in the most provocative way imaginable, in order just to arouse any element of excitement within him. I do feel sorry for him – not that I let him know, of course! – because I have never known him to have this problem. Again, this whole affair is most unusual because I have only ever known Rupert to strive and keep calm under pressure. He welcomes it, otherwise he gets bored. I know that he can be a worrier sometimes. He was worse when we first met. But, such worries are very rarely, if ever, work-related. I suppose that when a man becomes impotent no matter how infrequent or temporarily that may be, it will be at the forefront of his mind until matters are satisfactorily resolved, in his mind, at least, if not in his partner's.

"What is this case all about, honey?" I ask sympathetically. It is a rule between us that I do not ask him about his work unless he chooses to volunteer that information, but I feel that now clearly warrants an exception.

"It's, it's about…" hesitates, Rupert.

"…Sorry," I interrupt. "You don't have to say anything. It's just that I thought that you might want to talk about it."

"That's all right, dear," he replies, apologetically. "It's just that I spend the whole day thinking about this case and I don't quite feel in the mood to chat about it in the night as well." With this comment Rupert holds my hand and kisses me on the cheek as if to restore any confidence that I may have lost in him which, of course, I haven't.

"I understand," I reply, as we make our way into the bedroom.

Unfortunately, despite his good intentions Rupert's effort amounted to nothing more than a gallant attempt. We spent most of the evening just lying there in bed with little being said between us. Rupert did not seem in the mood to talk and I was not going to press him any further on the matter. Like I said, to me it's no big deal but he obviously has other more important matters on his mind. I can wait.

Josephine

"Excuse me," I hear a voice say. I turn around to see what body could have discharged such a rich baritone. A tall, dark, muscular man with a Billy Dee Williams prototype smile looks down on me, awaiting my assistance. "I wonder if you can help me find a dress for my eighteen-year-old daughter?" he asks. Those brown eyes of his appear to be assessing my body with some approval. "I would say that she is around your size." Married?

"Yes, of course," I reply. "Do you know what kind of style she likes?"

"I'm afraid not," he replies. "It's the same every year but I still feel that I ought to at least make the effort rather than just give her money." He pauses, as if to consider his words carefully. "I give her money throughout the year, so her birthday should be different." Divorced! What's happened to his wife, I wonder? I bet he's a charmer outdoors but intolerable indoors? I've lost count of the number of times that I have met men like that!

"This dress, here," I say, pointing at a blue strapless dress, "is one of my latest designs which is very popular amongst the young. If she's around my size then I think that she'd look good in this." His untrained eyes scrutinise the dress. His clumsiness gives him a kind of sex appeal that I know some women will find attractive, including myself. I could see him repeatedly looking at the dress and then at me. Is he admiring the dress or me? "It looks good on a woman with a thirty-four-inch bust," I say, flirtatiously volunteering the statistics to the body he has undoubtedly been admiring. He clenches his fist to his right hand and draws it towards his lips as if holding an imaginary microphone and coughs as if appearing to clear a frog in his throat, seemingly embarrassed at my comment.

"Can I return it if it doesn't fit?"

"Yes, of course. Either you or your daughter can return the dress and I can try and find her another." I see Pat walking past and into the shop.

"Hello, girlfriend," she says.

"Hi, Pat," I reply, as we hug momentarily. I follow Pat's line of view as she looks at me and then at my customer. Her look says it all!

"I'll take it," says my customer. I can't help noticing the look on Pat's face as the bass from my customer reverberates around the shop, strong enough to shake the heart of any woman and probably break a few along the way as well. We watch my customer exit the shop with much delight. Nice butt, too!

"Hey, where did you get him from?" asks Pat, barely containing her excitement.

"I think he's divorced too," I reply, making sure that Pat takes heed of my appreciation. "For a woman to let that go, he must be trouble, surely."

"You're doing some good work here, girl" continues Pat, switching sharply from the attention of my customer to business as she walks around the shop, inspecting the merchandise with overt nods of approval. Too much thought of that man could seriously damage your heart. Mine is only just returning to a normal beat.

"I'm trying, Pat. I want to expand this year. I know my boutiques can do even better than they are doing at the moment. I want to make it big and I feel that this is my year. So, how are you doing, girl?"

"Fine, fine," says Pat with an air of reservation.

"How is Rupert?" I ask, knowing what's bothering her. What Pat and I don't know about each other, nobody does. We are very close and confide in each other about everything, literally. I think Pat has always viewed me as the sister that she never had.

"He's fine. Still working extremely hard."

"And the other matter?"

"There's no improvement on that side," she replies. Pat is such a strong, positive, confident woman that to see her going through any form of crisis, where she does not have full control over its determination, is something to which I know she is not accustomed and it must, therefore, be very difficult for her. "I have made an appointment to see my doctor about it," she continues. "In all the time that I have known Rupert, I have never known a case to have such a profound effect on him, that he feels that he cannot even discuss it with me. When I think of some of those "dry" shipping cases that we have discussed in the past, I sometimes ask myself how different can this one be. Anyway, at least I should soon know whether the problem is with him or with me."

"They do say that stress can reduce a man's sperm count," I say.

"And when he's not producing low-sperm count, he's producing nothing at all!" replies Pat. We both try to lighten what I know is being taken very seriously by my two friends. "I'll see you at the launch tonight."

"Yes, indeed," I reply, as Pat makes her way out through the glass doors. I can't help but think that Rupert's condition is affecting her more than she cares to show.

There must be over three hundred people here tonight. All here to celebrate the launch of my best friend's book, *Four Seasons*. Everybody wants to be seen with her; have their photographs taken with her; have a signed copy of her book. This is not bad for someone who has just launched her first novel. It seems like anybody who is somebody is here tonight. I can see that Rupert looks elated as he tries to escort his wife around the room.

"Hi Jo," I hear someone call. Looking over the crowd of heads, I see Donna heading towards me. This is only the second time that I have seen her since she left Dexter and I have to say that she's looking a lot better for it. There was a time, near the ending of their relationship, when she was looking so tired that she looked far below her best, but now it looks as though my friend is back with a vengeance.

"Hello my darling, you look great!" I say to Donna. It looks as though she may have lost at least a stone in weight.

"Thanks, I wasn't going to come, but Sam persuaded me to, and also I know that Pat would never have forgiven me if I had missed her big launch."

"I knew she would make it," I say, still admiring Donna's

transformation. Damn, she looks good!

"Also, Jo, I really believe that this book is going to be big. When I think of all those drafts we read and commented on, I feel honoured just to have been associated with the book in our small way."

"You're not alone, girl," I respond.

"Hi girls," says Pat, as she weaves her way through a crowd of people each wanting a piece of her attention.

"You've made it at last, girl," says Donna, who can't seem to stop smiling, not that she has cause to.

"I'm glad to see you girls," says Pat, "and Don, you know that your life wouldn't have been worth living had you not turned up tonight."

"I know, Sam escorted me here tonight," replies Donna.

"I have to tell you, Don, Dexter might be here tonight," says Pat. Surprisingly, Donna did not even flinch at the warning as if expecting that Dexter would have been here tonight, in any case. They say a new figure does wonders to a woman's confidence and Donna is certainly living proof of that! "Rupert," continues Pat, "seemed intent on inviting him along, so I gave in. Rupert is under so much stress at the moment, I didn't want to stress him out anymore over some petty invitation."

"That's okay, Pat..." replies Donna.

"...Hello," I hear someone say, interrupting Donna. That is the second time today that I have heard this voice. I turn round to see the hunk of a man who had earlier bought the dress for his daughter.

"Hi, how are you?" I say, embarrassed at my unrestrained excitement. "Did the dress fit your daughter?" I ask, just managing to compose myself.

"I believe it did," he replies. I could see that Donna was impressed by my acquaintance. "Sorry, let me introduce myself. My name is Earl." Lord, have mercy! What a firm handshake. If I don't steady myself, I know that I'm going to faint!

"These are my friends, Donna and Patricia, the author of *Four Seasons*, who was in the shop with me today."

"Yes, I recall. It's a pleasure to meet you all," replies Earl. If I have problems with dating black men, Lord make him be my cure!

At this point both Pat and Donna decide to circulate amongst the other guests. Surely, I wasn't being that obvious! I do, however, need to know about his wife, his girlfriend, even. Is either of them here tonight? Then again, if he has an eighteen-year-old daughter, how old is he? I've always told myself that beauty has no age, so I guess that we can still tango!

"So, what line of business are you in, Earl?" I ask. I hope that didn't sound as bad as it was intended. After all, a successful woman needs to know what line of business her potential lover is in.

"I'm a financier. My firm, Wright Consultants, is the major financiers to the publishers of *Four Seasons*. What happens, is that when the publishers receive a manuscript of a book that they believe is going to do big things, they send us a copy in order to seek our opinion on the level of advances to offer, should they decide to publish it. Such advance will be based on what we think that book will make by way of sales."

"Similar to what they do with film scripts."

"Yes, we back films as well. We try and promote the local film industry wherever we have an office."

"Your firm has more than one office?"

"Yes, we have three offices, London, Paris, Los Angeles, and we have plans for another two in the forthcoming year."

"What did you think of *Four Seasons*, then?"

"The book is going to be massive. I've backed many books in the past and after a while you tend to get an eye for a winner. These come around only once in a while. Patricia Jackson is a very talented woman. I have no doubt that her book is going to do very well. When you've backed as many winners and losers as I have, you know when a "firm favourite" comes along and this is one of them."

"Well, as for me, I'm the owner of three boutiques selling many of my own designs," I volunteer. So you could be the upwardly mobile brother on my arm.

"I was in one of your boutiques, today, I take it?" asks Earl, seemingly impressed.

"You were indeed," I respond, proudly. "You purchased one of my very own designs. I just hope that your daughter likes it."

"I'm sure that she will, but, if she doesn't, then there's no shortage of other good clothing in the shop, I'd noticed. I have to say, I was most impressed by the quality of the designs." I'm winning. Chisel away at men long enough and they soon become putty in your hands, no matter how masculine their voice. He clearly didn't have a clue what he was looking for when he came to the boutique, let alone appreciate the "quality" of my designs. He's shamelessly trying to impress me, but that's all right, I have no complaints about that! Maybe there is no woman in his life. Maybe he has been waiting for someone like me to walk into his life, to make him happy.

"Thank you, I hope to expand with another shop in due course."

"Very good. I had walked past your boutique on many occasions and often wondered if there were others in the chain. Where do you advertise?"

"I am my advertisement," I reply, boldly.

"No shows or anything?" he asks, clearly surprised by my reply. "And you're successful?"

"Not doing too badly," I say.

"Have you ever thought about doing some of the fashion shows? London, Paris, Milan, New York?" Maybe Prince Charming knows more about this business than I gave him credit for. I like a man with big ideas. In fact, I like him, period! But what about that wife or girlfriend of his? What's the score, Earl? Spit it out! I can't afford for that baritone of yours to break my heart, when it's only just been mended. Listen to me, I've already got this man in my bed before I can even scream "Lovelace" in a night of unadulterated passion!

"Those shows costs money and although I'm doing well, I'm no Karl Largerfield."

"Don't get me wrong, you advertise your designs very well." Oh Lord, this man is giving me the once over with those eyes. I can feel them prodding and checking for firmness. There isn't a problem there, honey. You play your cards right and it won't be just those eyes of yours that will be prodding! "Do you have any partners?"

"My father is a director, solely for the purpose of the limited company, but otherwise he plays no part in the running of the business."

"If you would like to expand and would need some extra finance, maybe you and I can put together a plan." He hands me his business card, stating, "Earl Wright" of, "Wright Consultants, London, Paris and Los Angeles".

"You're the 'Wright' in 'Wright Consultants'?" I ask, at an octave higher than normal.

"Yes, I am," he replies. "I started the business about ten years ago. After Cambridge, I worked in 'the City' for two years before going on to Harvard to study for a Masters in Business Administration. After that I set up on my own and haven't looked back since." First class résumé but what about your wife or girlfriend? I can't contain myself much longer.

"And, your daughter?"

"She has just entered university to study Chemistry," he replies. And what about your wife or girlfriend? "She lives with my ex-wife," he continues. Hallelujah! At last! Now, why did you divorce? You used to beat your wife, right? You moan too much and you're untidy. You're a womaniser. Yes, that's it, you like too many women. You've been flirting with me all night and you probably did the same with the other women as well. Our relationship is over! I'm dumping you right now before we go too far! "My ex-wife left me for my best man." Ah, I feel so sorry for him. Look at those sad eyes. The bitch left him and took away his daughter. Some women are so heartless and then they complain at the way some men treat them. I'll look after you, honey. This woman isn't running off with any man and leaving a cutey like you behind, rich at that! I know on which side my bread is buttered.

"You must have been devastated," I reply in a ridiculously sympathetic voice but I don't care, I'm on the chase. It's the next girl or me. But what about the girlfriend? "And you retaliated by going off with her best friend," I say. We both laugh out aloud but I'm not sure if he is laughing because I'm right, or because it's funny. Don't mince your words, girl, come out with it. "How does your daughter feel about you seeing another woman?" I ask.

Now that's bravery for you. Fast move, girl!

"I don't know," Earl replies. "I guess that I'll find out when I cross that bridge." That's it, your mine!

"I would like to discuss this expansion plan with you. Shall I call your office and arrange a meeting?" I ask. Blatant, I know but a man like him isn't going to remain on the market for ever!

"We can discuss it over dinner next week, if that is all right with you?" he asks.

"That will be fine," I reply, before he could finish the last word. I can see Dexter through the crowd smothering his new flame, Chantelle, excessively with kisses. I should try and find Donna and see whether she is all right.

"How does Wednesday at eight suit you?" he asks.

"That's okay with me," I say, without even checking my diary. Anything else can wait. I give Earl my address. At least this time, I shall have the best of both worlds. That is to say both a booming business and a hunk of a man. Now I know Pat would be proud of me. This girl's done good!

Rupert

I haven't contacted Linda for two weeks, following Yvonne's party. That is not to say that I haven't been thinking about her. I have been thinking about her over and over in my mind, since that night. Since I've been with Pat I have not so much as thought of another woman, in the way that I have been thinking about Linda. I believe that a married man could look at, but not touch, and definitely not lust after, another woman. I have been more than happy with who I've got and what I have. My brief encounter with Linda left me thinking about her a lot. I thought that it would be easy to forget her, forget that dance, forget that feeling, but I only ended feeling more and more excited about her. I want to see her and this makes me feel bad. The only thing necessary for the triumph of sin, is for good men to do nothing, but I need to see Linda in order to dispel any sinful feelings that I clearly have for her. I can't do this from a distance. I keep telling myself that our dance was the consequence of good wine and good music, nothing more. I'm not sure about that, but I have to tell myself that it was nothing. I have to see that it was nothing. I have to feel that it was nothing. I should have told Pat about her but I couldn't. Why couldn't I tell my wife that a pretty woman invited me to view her photographs? Why couldn't I tell her that I accepted that pretty woman's invitation? Why couldn't I tell her that I had danced with that pretty woman and how my body felt during that dance? Why, because something is not right. There is someone deep inside me that is telling me that I should not be feeling this way. I should confess. Come clean. "What she doesn't know won't hurt her". Those are Dexter's words but I'm not like Dexter, deceit does not come naturally to me; I loathe it. Maybe I'm making a mountain out of a molehill but I don't think so. The night Pat came back from Jo's we made love. I wanted to make love to Pat that night more than at any other time in my life. I wanted to prove to myself that I only had eyes for my wife. My

64

body was for my wife, only. I tried to tell myself that I was satisfied physically, mentally and spiritually, but who was I trying to fool? When we were making love one night, I momentarily thought of Linda and lost my way. I felt sick and became temporarily impotent. I could not make love to my wife. I could not even pretend. I explained away my behaviour on tiredness. Pat was understanding. Lies, when do they stop? I was lusting over a woman whom I barely knew and it was playing with my emotions. The jury sworn in, I had to see Linda.

Linda invited me round to her place tonight to finally view her photographs. I told Pat that I was going to view a private collection of photographs with a friend. I knew that Pat had little passion for prints, so I was not at all surprised when she gladly declined my invitation to accompany me for the evening. I was not disappointed. I had all but dialled the last digit of Linda's telephone number on numerous occasions before I finally braved the courage to ring her. I would be lying if I said that I wasn't nervous. What if my infatuation for her was an emotion that had not remotely been shared by Linda. I would be an embarrassment to myself. I would have acted like a young boy on his first date, not a man with a loving and caring wife.

I approach Linda's house with some trepidation. I ring the intercom and can see that I am being spied on through the camera on the closed-circuit television. Linda's soft voice, emitted from the speaker, commands me to enter at the sound of the buzzer. I have gone through many retakes of tonight's encounter in my mind, as if preparing for the closing speech to my biggest case. It is, therefore, to my surprise when Linda answers the door for I was expecting Wilson to welcome me in. After all, I know him not his partner.

"Hello Rupert," says Linda, in a wonderfully posh accent as if greeting royalty. "How lovely it is to see you again."

"Likewise," is all I can say in reply, as I hand her a 1985 bottle of Chardonnay. I hadn't realised how youthful Linda had looked, or was for that matter, and she is a lot prettier than I thought. She is wearing a purple thigh-length dress that appears to be made of pure silk. Her neck, shoulders and arms are exposed shamelessly above and around the thin shoulder strap. The dress is loosely cut but the material embraces her in a way that reveals the sensuous curvatures of her shapely body. This was not how I had rehearsed it. My script has already abandoned me. I feel unchaste as I think of Pat. A beautiful woman is one who loves me so I should be at home with my wife. I shouldn't have come; it was a bad idea. I can leave now and never see this woman or her boyfriend again. Three weeks' ago I couldn't even remember who Wilson was, not to mention Linda. But, as if by an invisible force, I remain firm-footed. My feet feel like they have been placed in quick-setting concrete and, if I don't leave now, I never will. My feet disobey my orders to about-turn and leave.

"Do come in," says Linda. Too late, the trial begins. I should be fine, I believe a man is never given more than he can handle. If I'm found guilty, then I will have no one to blame but myself. "Unfortunately," she continues, "Wilson can't join us tonight. I forgot to tell you that he is in the States preparing for his New York Bar exams. He's got this fascination about America and wants to be dual-qualified, in order to spend some more time over there."

"Oh, that's a shame. I'll catch up with him another time," I say, unconvincingly, as she leads me into the lounge. The room is artily decorated with the walls adorned with numerous photographs. On one side of the room there is a large picture of Linda, akin to one of Andy Warhol's multifaceted portraits of Marilyn Monroe. After showing me around the flat, we sit down to a main dish of monkfish with new potatoes and diced beetroot followed by a home-made apple pie with fresh cream. The dimmer on the light switch is turned down just low enough to allow the candle lights to illuminate the table. Miles Davis' "Kind of Blue" is playing in the background. Pat loves this CD. The thought of Pat makes me question my morality, as I enjoy the company of another woman for all the wrong reasons, but I'm here on a mission. I am on a mission to get this woman out of my mind and out of my system, once and for all. Linda and I chat about the times we had met in the past, when I was at Bar school and she was at Art College. After the meal we sit on the sofa. Linda shuffles through a variety of portfolios in search of her prints of the London fashion shows.

"I admire your CD collection," I say, with genuine admiration. "I never knew that Wilson was such a big jazz fan."

"He's not," she replies with disdain. "He wouldn't know Miles from Brubeck." Nervous laughter fills the air.

"These are the pictures I took last year," she says, passing me a portfolio. I look at the mixture of black and white and colour prints, whilst making the odd amateurish remark. "The pictures are very good," I say, repeatedly.

"I am hoping to cover the Paris fashion shows this year, for a few up-and-coming designers in Britain. Have you ever been to Paris?"

"Yes I have," I reply, recalling my walk down Avenue des Champs-Elysées from the Arc de Triomphe with Pat en route to the Louvre. "I know Paris very well; it is a very romantic city," I add without volunteering anymore.

"I've never been there before," says Linda, "so this assignment will be truly welcomed. If I get the job, you can show me around. Expenses on me, of course!" Her request was like a bolt from the blue. Surely a well-travelled man like Wilson must have taken her across the English Channel to the French capital on at least one previous occasion. And if not, then why not ask him? How can I explain to Pat that I am going to Paris with another woman? Another woman I hardly know! Linda was flirting with me and I knew it. This was in the other script. If I remember my lines, then all will be well and I'll be out of here before one can say "guilty". I'm supposed to tell her that I am a happily married man with a wonderful and loving wife who is waiting up for me at this very moment as we speak, get my jacket and leave. There is silence. The spotlight is on me and the audience awaits my reply with anticipation. It seems like hours have passed since her request but no one is leaving until I deliver my lines. My throat is dry as I attempt to recite what I had mastered only but a few hours ago.

"I would love to," I reply. The decibels rise as I hear the calamity of the audience, as if Romeo had just taken the poison in belief that Juliet was dead. How did those words come out of my mouth? I heard them, but I did not say them. I did not order those words. I condemn them, but don't seem able to withdraw them. The evidence is admissible. Linda looked far from displeased by my reply.

"Let's hope I get that job, then." I know exactly what she means.

I feel merry, but not drunk. I should leave, but I want to stay. I shall dispose of my script and ad lib from hereon. Linda's dress reveals more of her thighs, as she relaxes on the sofa. I can't help but admire how smooth her thighs look. I must compose myself. My mind wonders. I think of my mother. I think of my father. I think of Pat. I think of my vow. I can smell the sweet aroma of Linda's perfume. It's that perfume again, the one she had on at Yvonne's party. The aroma brings back memories of our dance and where our brief friendship began. My mind returns to the task in hand. We both stare intensely at each other. Is this the point of no return, the prelude to the original sin? Can I stop myself? Do I want to? I move closer to Linda and press my lips firmly against hers. My lips are met with no resistance. Both lips part as our tongues explore each other with eagerness, with passion, with desire. My mind is searching for approval. Searching for excuses. Anything to justify what I am doing. I find nothing but contempt: thou shalt not commit adultery; thou shalt not covet thy neighbour's wife nor anything that is thy neighbour's; the wages of sin is death. We continue to kiss wildly and passionately. Potency doesn't fail me now! I clumsily unzip the back of her dress and slip the thin shoulder straps down her arms. Her body is full and voluptuous, as my hands explore every inch of her bare flesh in more detail. Her tongue examines my body, as each piece is revealed with the removal of more clothing. We embrace tightly, not wanting to let each other go. Not wanting this moment to end. I am making love to a woman other than my wife and I am feeling good not bad. I had been dreaming of this moment for some time. It seemed harmless in a dream and it seems harmless now. I had made love to my wife thinking about this woman. Maybe now I could rest in peace. I could ask for forgiveness and all would be forgotten. An adventure I had to experience. I am now satisfied. We remained silent for what seemed like hours, without uttering a single word. I think of Pat with mixed emotions; guilty and yet content. My curiosity is no more. I can return to my wife for I have tasted the forbidden fruit and I am fulfilled. I was wrong, but I'm not solely to blame. I am a man and men are weak. That is my defence. Many have been there before me and many will again: Adam and Eve; Samson and Delilah; Rupert and Linda. The seeds were sown long before me. "All rise." The jury returns. I stand before the Pearly Gates and await the verdict. "Having considered all the evidence put before us this evening, we hereby find you, Rupert Nelson Jackson, guilty as charged. It is a man's own mind, not his enemy nor foe, that lures him to evil ways. You have therefore no one to blame but yourself. I sentence you to a life of shame and guilt. All rise!" The jury departs.

Part Two

Patricia

"Hi Jo, I'm sick," I say, bawling down the telephone.

"What's wrong, honey?" asks Jo.

"I can't have children," I reply, whilst wiping away the tears from seeping down my face and percolating into the phone.

"Oh, Pat. Where are you, girl?"

"I'm just leaving the hospital."

"Is Rupert with you?" asks Jo, anxiously.

"He's in court at the moment, so he doesn't know as yet."

"You don't sound like you're in any state to drive on your own, so I'll close the shop and be with you in a short while. Wait for me," commands Jo. I keep telling myself that I should be content with what I've got. *Four Seasons* has already surpassed all my expectations. My agent tells me that it is selling in excess of ten thousand copies a week and I'm receiving numerous requests from publishers around the world wanting the rights to publish my book in their respective countries. My parents were euphoric when they rang me last week to say that they had seen my book in a store in Nassau. There is even talk of one of the big Hollywood studios wanting to buy the film rights to the book. To see *Four Seasons* on the silver screen will be a dream come true for the many people who had encouraged me to write the book. It's all very exciting. I'm in constant demand to give lectures, write articles, appear on radio and television. I receive so much praise from so many people, my head is spinning. One could be forgiven for believing that he or she is what others say or write about them. I find such praise, however, to be unjustified. Not that I think that *Four Seasons* is a badly written book; on the contrary, if I may say so myself. But, all I did was to write a book that I felt compelled to do. I was just the messenger delivering the message. It was Einstein who said, try not to become a woman of success, but rather try to become a woman of value, and I have always tried to live my life by that rule. So, after this entire accolade, am I content? Well, how can I be when despite all this attention, such "public" success is matched by "private" failure? I feel like a circus clown who is adored and loved by all the children but deep down he is downhearted and sad. Rupert and I have been trying now for over two months for a baby and I am yet to fall pregnant. I am like a woman who has everything and yet has nothing. Of course I'm joyful for what I have achieved to date, but equally sad for what I haven't. And, if relinquishing all that I have accomplished in my career would guarantee me my first baby, then I would gladly surrender all, without so much as a moment's hesitation. I would happily trade publicity for obscurity. Anything, just so that I could feel like a complete woman, be a woman. Since the publication of *Four Seasons*, people have been telling me how brilliant I am but how can I be brilliant, exceptional even, when I am incapable of giving birth to the most natural thing that two human beings can produce between them? Even Jo and Donna, who have both been very supportive beyond all boundaries, can't fully appreciate what I am going through. I'm the tough strong-minded woman, remember, who can deal with any problem. "Problems are there to be solved," I would often tell them but that doesn't mean that I can't have feelings just like anyone else when trying to solve them. It doesn't mean that I can't have maternal feelings like the next woman does. I want a baby just as badly as the next woman does who desires to have a child. This should not be too difficult to comprehend!

"So what's the cause, honey?" asks Jo, sympathetically, who has arrived within ten minutes of hanging up the phone. I am genuinely pleased to see my friend. It occurs to me that in all the years that we have known each other, she has never witnessed me shed any tears of sorrow, only those of joy. Not that I haven't had my share of disappointments, mind you, it's just that I tend to cope without too much visible emotion, sometimes, it seems, to my detriment.

"There is a malfunction of my adrenal glands and this apparently has led to my failure to ovulate," I reply. I long ago stopped trying to stem the flow of tears that are irrepressibly flowing down my face. "I'm now on a course of fertility drugs.

Why me Jo? What have I done to deserve this? All I ever wanted in life was to work hard and do well for myself. That is all my parents had ever demanded of me. In all my life, I have always tried to help others. I have never in my life wished any harm on anyone, only good, so why should this happen to me?"

"Honey, you have much more than most women will ever have. People would give their right arm for what you have. I know everything will be fine in the end, Pat, trust me. I know how much you want a baby but worse things can happen in your life."

"I know that I should be grateful, and I am, but I can't help feeling that I'm blessed on one hand and cursed on the other. I feel so helpless."

"I wish you wouldn't keep talking as if you were in this alone, Pat. Besides your friends, Rupert is by your side too. In fact, you are both in this thing together and you'll both see this through to the end. Don't take this on by yourself, honey, it's too big."

Rupert has enough on his plate at the moment than to be bothered with his wife's infertility problems. It's at times like this when I could really do with my mother being around. I miss her advice and reassurance, as only a mother can give to her daughter. This thought only makes me feel more sorry for myself. Jo and I headed for Donna's place, where Donna had more or less reiterated what Jo had said earlier on our journey. More than ever, I realised how important those two are to my life. How important we are to each other. Jo forfeited an afternoon's takings from her shop as she refused to leave us, so the shop remained closed for the rest of the day. My girlfriends and I spent the afternoon and evening discussing whatever seemed appropriate to discuss. Their company went a long way towards relieving me of any self-pity, which is what I needed. Rupert came to collect me, after working late in Chambers. He kindly brought me a bouquet of flowers that were dominated mainly by red roses and pink carnations, a gesture that helped lighten what had been, without question, a very dark day for me. Surprisingly, he looked more guilty than sorry, but the problem, I assured him, was with me and not with him, so he need not feel so bad. Knowing Rupert as well as I do, it doesn't surprise me the way he is taking all of this. To be so tormented, he must want a child more than he leads me to believe. It will be his only opportunity to prove how good a father he could be. Possibly, even, prove how much better he could be at raising a child than his father was at raising him. Then again, it's hard to decipher what Rupert really wants these days to be honest with you. So much goes on in that head of his, I'm sure that I don't know half of what he's thinking when he's with me. What is for sure is that my infertility problem is a stress that Rupert could well do without at the moment but, like Jo says, worse things could happen in our lives, so we should be more appreciative with what we have.

Rupert

"How is Patricia?" asks Linda.

"She is as well as can be expected under the circumstances," I reply, uncomfortably. Discussing Pat's welfare with Linda whilst being completely naked in Linda's bed is not my ideal topic for pillow talk. Yes, I came back for more. My case was adjourned until next week, so I decided to pay Linda a short visit this afternoon. I had barely caught my breath from travelling across London when we were making love. Today is the fifth time that we have now made love. I tried to convince myself that the first time would have been the last time, it was out of my system, but that was clearly not going to be the case. Neither of us wanted to be a one-night stand for the other. Neither could let go. For me, the forbidden fruit was sweeter than I had anticipated and, once bitten, I wanted more. It is as simple as that. I couldn't fight it, and I couldn't honestly put my hand on my heart and say that I had tried to, either. And each time we made love, I felt less and less guilty about what we were doing. Each time it became easier than the time before. I tell myself, "what Pat doesn't know won't hurt her." It was so easy to adopt those words. I seek comfort in those words, as others just depress me.

"I hope that you weren't too late last night," says Linda.

"No, I was all right," I reply. "I told Pat that I had to work late." More lies, but what Pat doesn't know won't hurt her, remember. I put my trust in those words and pray that they fail me not.

"What are we doing Rupert?" asks Linda, a question I have asked myself many times.

"I don't know," I reply. It was clear from our first night together that our encounter was not going to be a one-off event, although I tried to persuade myself otherwise.

"Do you want us to continue?" asks Linda.

"What do you want to do?"

"I asked first," she replies, adamantly.

"You know how I feel about you, Linda," I reply without hesitation. "So, if you feel the same way about me, then why end what we both desire."

"And what about Patricia?" replies Linda. I have always tried to steer clear of thinking too much about Pat and this affair. I hate myself for what I am doing but I can't let this go. I need this. My body needs this. I need to relive this experience over and over again until my heart's content. And one day I shall view this short chapter in my life as a pleasurable and harmless experience, but now is not the time for either this chapter or this experience to end. I want more!

"I don't want to hurt Pat," I confess. "If there is any way in which Pat would get hurt from what we're doing then we will have to stop, now!"

"I don't want to hurt anyone either," replies Linda, defensively. "And I certainly don't want to be named in any divorce proceedings!" The thought of divorce hadn't even entered my mind. That, of course, is not an option to consider. Life without Pat would be too much of a high price to pay for what is at most a bit of harmless fun.

"And what about Wilson?" I ask, in reciprocation.

"I've told you before, I don't love him," says Linda. "I care for him but I don't love him." I can't help but feel a touch sorry for Wilson at Linda's confession, but any condolences from me would be a bit rich when I'm stark naked in the man's bed and having just made love to his girlfriend.

"I guess that makes it easier for you," I say.

"Why do you say that?" asks Linda, sharply.

"Well, I love my wife, so this affair is very difficult for me, even though I am fully aware of what I am doing."

"I was once in love with Wilson but I'm not now. That doesn't mean that I would want to see him get hurt, far from it. Like you, I didn't plan this affair between us, it just happened. I am just as unsure what to do next as you are."

"And does Wilson feel the same way about you?" I ask. There is a pause, as Linda appears to contemplate whether she should answer my question.

"I don't think so," replies Linda, but offers no more than this short riposte.

"Are you saying that you are with him only because he wants you to be, and not because you want to be?"

"I don't want to talk about Wilson any more, Rupert. There are only two of us in this relationship not three or four. If this relationship gets any bigger than either of us can handle, then we will simply end it without too much of a fuss. In that way no one gets hurt. Until then, let's just have fun and enjoy it."

"That's fine with me," I say. What Pat doesn't know won't hurt her!

"I could be going to Europe soon to promote *Four Seasons*, so why don't you join me?" asks Pat. "It would be nice for us to get away for a few days."

"I would love to, if I could spare the time, dear," I reply, "but you know how busy I have been lately, so I can't guarantee anything."

"I hope that you can. It would be nice to go to Rome and Paris again. I've got some fond memories of our trips there."

"Same here," I say, recollecting that Linda was also talking about me escorting her around Paris. I must ask her about that, and see whether I can kill two birds with one stone. It's risky, I know, but not overly dangerous. "Let me know when it is, honey, I shall do my best," I add.

"I hope so," says Pat. "You never know, this break to the romantic cities might be just what the doctor ordered." I look at Pat and feel bad, not as bad as when I first slept with Linda but not feeling too good, either. I can hear my mother turn in her grave at what or who I might become. That will not happen! I shall not turn out to be like him! One day I shall look back on this period as nothing more than a phase in my life. My father, too, may have once uttered these very words. But my one affair is different. Like Linda rightly said, I didn't plan for this affair to happen, it just did. My father cheated on my mother numerous times throughout their married life. I'm attracted to two women, only. I'm not a womaniser. He was. But, isn't this where it all starts? No! My case is different. I can't quite put my finger on why it is, but it clearly is. I know that, even if nobody else does.

Dexter

It was nice to see Donna at Pat's book launch the other night. She's lost a lot of weight. I'd have to say that there were some signs of improvement. Although she is still frumpy, she doesn't look as dowdy as she used to when she was with me. I know that breaking up with someone you love can sometimes make you put on weight. I'm glad to say that Donna's appetite did not get any bigger than it already was, so I guess she has a lot to thank me for. I haven't seen Dionne since her mother took her away from me but I have been so busy. Chantelle and I have done nothing but socialise. It has been one party after another. We were just about able to make Pat's party. I must say it was good to see all those eyes turn to look at us as we arrived and pulled up in my Porsche. We wouldn't have looked out of place arriving for the Oscars. I was proud to be with her and, no doubt, she was likewise with me. We couldn't keep our eyes off each other. Contrast that with when I was with Donna. Donna couldn't keep her eyes off me, but mine were always scouting for the local talent. This kept Donna on her toes, as she knew that there were plenty of other woman just waiting to step into her shoes. I have always believed that when a woman gets too secure, then she becomes complacent and complacency breeds laziness. She feels that she no longer has to look good. Well, the way I view it, a good-looking guy looks even better with a good-looking girl on his arm, so ain't no heart or mind going to rule my head, I go for beauty. Whenever Donna came into view at the party, I made sure that she saw what she was missing by cuddling and kissing Chantelle at every given opportunity. Mind you, Chantelle likes attention so she didn't mind, not that she knew what was going on, of course. "Guess who is sleeping on your side of the bed?" I kept repeating to myself whenever Donna's eye caught mine. I could see that I was having an effect on her. Remember who left whom, baby. You leave me, you pay for it. It couldn't have been easy for Donna coming face to face with the woman who replaced her in my life. Here she was having lost all this weight still looking a few sizes too big and there was my new woman who at twice her size still wouldn't be as big as Donna, even if she tried. Also, check out the clothes, Donna was looking good, I wouldn't take that away from her, but it still had a long way to go to match my woman's. Chantelle wears nothing less than designer labels, anything else can walk! So if one was to ask me if I was bitter over the whole affair with Donna, I would clearly and honestly have to say, "no". Do I sound it? Of course I don't. Seeing the two women in such close proximity only proved to me that I hadn't given up much that some man of any real substance would want for himself. Harsh but true. After all, Donna knew that I would be at the book launch, so you would have thought that she would have arrived with some dashing guy, in order to try and show me what she is capable of getting. That is what I did. I made sure that Rupert insists that Pat invited me along. Who did Donna go with? Sam, the Bible Basher. That tells me exactly what I already knew. It tells me that he was the only sad person she could get. She must now realise that being with me gave her the credibility that she would not have otherwise attained without me. She would have to do a lot better than Sam, to even remotely tempt me back. I'm not in the business of whispering sweet scriptures into women's ears. Anyway, enough of Donna, no point in thinking of someone who has probably done enough thinking for both of us and, no doubt, been cussing my name with that Patricia. Talking of Pat, I hear all is not too well. Shame! I feel absolutely nothing for her. Why should I? She wrecked my relationship with Donna. In any case, that woman has had life far too easy for my liking, going to a fancy university, gaining a doctorate degree and writing a hit novel. I hear she has been receiving offers for her book from all over the place. I read the book and thought it too disturbing for my liking. Anyway, Rupert seems to have hit the jackpot with that one. Good luck to him. The woman's going to be rich. It's just a shame that she likes meddling in people's business so much. And to make matters worse, I see her face everywhere. If it's not the papers writing about her, it's her writing some article about something or another. Suddenly, everyone wants to hear what she has to say. The opinion that wrecked my relationship is now in demand and valued by so many, well she can stick her opinion where the sun doesn't shine, for all I care. It's a pleasure to see her going through a little hardship for a change, maybe then she can appreciate how tough things can be for others less fortunate than herself. Anyway, I'm sure she'll bounce back, people like her always do. Actually, when I think about it, she probably did me a big favour in getting Donna off my back, so I should wish her well. As for my buddy, Rupert, this baby thing has really taken its toll on him. The man is all work and no play these days. We used to meet for a drink and play squash at least once a week, but that has now been put on the back-burner while he works like a madman. Working himself into an early grave isn't going to give him the child he so desires. It might do him better to take things a little easy for a while. All that work can't be helping matters. He doesn't even condemn me like he used to do. Now, that is not the Rupert I know. When Donna left me he did nothing but tell me how wrong I was to let her go, now he rarely ever mentions her name. It could be, of course, that he has seen how happy I am with my woman and that it would be pointless going back to Donna, who was less than half the fun as my girl. Oh, that reminds me, I might give Donna the shock she has been yearning for all this time by visiting my Dionne. Chantelle is going away tomorrow to the Seychelles on a modelling contract, so I shall have some time to kill. And who better for me to see in the meantime than my ex-girlfriend who I know is missing me and not getting what used to make her feel so happy.

Donna

Well, I finally got to see Miss Chantelle. Sam was right she is very pretty. And yes, they do look good together. They definitely had a lot of time for each other, that's for sure. Most couples do in the early days, even Dexter and I were once like that. But they couldn't keep their hands off each other. Every time I saw them they seemed locked in some passionate kiss. I hope it lasts. I had attempted to say hello to Dexter but he was rather hostile towards me, so I left him alone. And I didn't want him or Chantelle to get the wrong idea. I really do have trouble understanding his attitude, however. I could understand if I had walked out on him, with our child, during a happy period in our lives, but I didn't and it wasn't. I was so depressed that I had to get out. But, why should he have cause to be angry when he seems so happy with Chantelle? A lot happier than he was with me! And I wouldn't even say that he misses Dionne either. There is little to show that he has any interest in seeing her at all. For instance, he hasn't even called her to find out whether she is well, sick or otherwise. I'm not going to take her round to the flat to see him. If he wants to see his child, then he knows where she is. I would never deny Dexter his right to see her. I've told him that, and I mean it. So not seeing her is due to his volition, not mine. I think that he feels I should have continued taking his nonsense, while he continued to see Chantelle. No way! I had enough of his immature ways. Also, after a while, you start to feel tired. I could take no more without fear of having a breakdown. Anyway, that's all in the past. I'm much happier now. There was a low point in my life when I felt so worthless that I would simply stay in and look after Dionne and do little else. Now, I appreciate that I too have a life and endeavour to visit my close friends a lot more and go to the gymnasium at least three times a week. I no longer feel the need to hide. I feel rejuvenated, as if I have just awakened from a long nightmare and realised that things aren't as bad as they seem, or as they were! I can feel all my self-confidence coming back to me. And, at least, I have learnt something from my experience with Dexter. I now appreciate what some people go through when they are with someone that they love, but they themselves lead a miserable and unhappy life. They get drawn into solely pleasing their partners at the gross expense of their own happiness. Sadly, however, such efforts are not always reciprocated. They find that all their efforts are one way only and that they become content in their relationship only because their partner is happy! I think that when you are in love, you convince yourself that, despite your partner's bad habits, you are not there to change him. After all, who is to say that your ways are any better. After a while, however, he takes advantage of that tolerance and pushes for more. Before you realise it, you are so preoccupied with accommodating his mannerisms that you have no worthwhile identity of your own. You have now internalised his ways. You are no longer the person that you once were or he once liked, you are who your partner is! Now, he starts accusing you of having changed and he doesn't like you the way that you are. You're crowding him and he needs his space. There is no thought as to why you've changed or who you were trying to please, only that you have changed and that is enough. There begins his rejection of you. The irony, however, is that you have changed so much to be like him that the person he is, in fact, rejecting, is himself! Yes, he has seen what he is like and he doesn't like it. Well I say if he doesn't like a reflection of himself then why in the hell should you like him!

Josephine

Decisions! Decisions! Decisions! Life is full of them. Do I wear a thigh length, knee length or ankle length? I couldn't detect what part of my body Earl was studying most. Gentlemen like Earl are always very discreet in the way they look at their women, in order not to offend. An appreciative look from Earl would not have been offensive, but would have been warmly received. He is a gentleman, and gentlemen don't like their women revealing too much of themselves to all glaring eyes but to their own. My mind is made up. It would have to be the black satin evening dress that nearly caused that Brother Samuel to have an eye injury when I wore it to a Charity Gala for Sickle Cell earlier this year. That night I thought Sam was going to backslide there and then, his mouth was so wide open I could count the fillings in his teeth!

When Earl knocks on that door I want him to remember why he is alive. Mind you, with a body like his and with a sharp brain to match, I don't think that he would have spent too many nights alone in his life. Women would die to be with a man like him if only just for one night. Can you imagine that voice of his saying "goodnight" to you, with him wearing nothing but his birthday suit, my oh my! I can feel my body perspiring as the temperature of the room rises suddenly, higher than is either comfortable or safe. The doorbell rings. It is exactly 7.45 p.m.. The man is punctual, as well as handsome.

"You look wonderful," he says, openly inspecting my outfit, among other things. He clearly takes pride in his appearance. His well-cut suit and immaculately trimmed moustache bears testimony to that.

"Thank you," I reply. "I must say, my date for the night doesn't look too bad himself," I add. The compliment appears to have been well received, as he gives a boyish smile. A little flirting will get me somewhere, it seems.

"So what are your plans for the boutiques?" asks Earl, driving us in his green Jaguar XJ6 to what he describes as the best Italian restaurant in Central London.

"I want to build an empire that is capable of matching all the big fashion houses," I reply, with unashamed confidence.

"Have you considered how you would achieve such a goal?" he asks, unperturbed by the grand scale of my ambitions.

"No, I was hoping that you would advise me on the best approach to take."

"I was thinking that you could put on a fashion show at the same time as opening a boutique, say one in Milan and another in Paris and so on. What do you think?"

"I was thinking more of opening two more shops in England!" I reply. I can see why he didn't flinch at my earlier reply; the man has big ideas.

"Why concentrate on just England?" he asks. "If you open more shops in England then your clothes will simply be more accessible to more people, but at the same price as they are sold now or possibly lower. If on the other hand, you open a boutique in Paris and/or Milan, we're talking haute couture. When people start reading about you and see your designs on the covers of the best fashion magazines in the world, then everyone is going to want to wear your clothes. That then leads to a high demand for your garments. There's only one small problem, however, you deliberately under-supply, thus creating that element of mystique and scarcity. And, as you know from basic economics, when demand outstrips supply then prices rise to a new equilibrium." This man is a genius. I could make love to him here and now!

"I like what I hear, but how much will all this cost me?"

"Surprisingly, not as much as you might think," he replies. "I've put together some figures for you to look at. Take your time to look them over and if they interest you, then we can take matters further." There is no doubting that Earl is the kind of man who knows what he wants and would waste no time in going for it. Successful men like him never do. Whilst others are talking about it, they are doing it. That's how I want to be.

"I shall do just that, but something tells me that we will soon be partners," I respond. "After all, a man with a Master's degree in

Business is not likely to propose a plan that doesn't add up, is he?" Earl gives a smile that would melt any woman's heart.

"You're quite right," he replies, seemingly pleased by my blind confidence in his capability. "You're obviously a woman who likes to speak her mind."

"Yes I am," I reply resolutely. "I don't believe in beating about the bush. If someone has something to say, then they should say it and not wait to be asked. Because if they don't say, then they may never be asked and the other person may never know."

"I couldn't agree with you more," responds Earl. "That could be the difference between a successful meeting and a pleasurable date." Earl stares intensely at me with those dark brown eyes of his. You're doing just fine, honey. If it's afters you're seeking then you've got it. I'm sold! Remember, I don't believe in beating about the bush, nor do you by the sound of things.

"I know exactly what you're saying," are the only words I could find. I can tell that there are plenty of words swimming around in Earl's head also, but, like me, he doesn't want to reveal too much too soon. Play the game fast but not too fast. I can live with that.

"Tell me something, what are your ambitions in life?" he asks, breaking the silence. The man needs to know whether the woman he desires has room for him in her life.

"I want to be successful and happy," I reply.

"If I may say so, that is rather general and wide. Do you think that you could be happy without being successful?"

"I haven't had cause to divorce the two, but, if I was pushed to give an answer, I would say that I could, but I fear that being unsuccessful would make me unhappy."

"Isn't being unsuccessful just a lower degree of success?" asks Earl philosophically.

"Well, I guess that being unsuccessful doesn't quite have the same stigma attached to it as being a failure," I reply. This conversation reminds me of some of the discussions I used to have with Jeremy. I missed them. Some men I meet think that because I flirt a little I'm also a bimbo. It's a pleasure having good talk with a good-looking man. Earl is good for my mind and my body. And both are feeling good at this moment.

"What about you?" I ask. "What do you want out of life?"

"I would like to be happy. I have long figured out that for me to be happy then everything I require in life must be in its right place."

"Are you happy now?" I ask. Earl seems to contemplate my question for a while. His facial expression gives nothing away.

"I think that I would find it difficult to answer that question."

"I would have thought that a man like yourself, with a successful business, I presume a wonderful daughter and," I pause deliberately as if deciding whether to continue with my line of presumption, "a potential girlfriend…"

"Like I said before," he interrupts, "there is no woman in my life at the moment. In fact, there hasn't been a woman in my life since Paula left with my best man." He seems to stop himself saying more as if the memory of having been deserted for a once close friend appears to hit home again. He makes no comment on the other two components of mine, so I guess that the one out of the three is the stumbling block to his happiness. Well not to worry, the final piece of your life's jigsaw is here. I'm your woman!

"I am having some friends round for a drink on Saturday night. You're more than welcome to come round if you're free."

"I should be free on Saturday so I would be delighted to attend." He looks at me and gives a smile that is barely visible. I'm reading his mind and like what I read. "Oh no, I do have a prior engagement for Saturday." Damn! I can't hide my obvious look of disappointment. I feel like a little girl who has just had her bag of sweets snatched away from her before she could even open the packet, let alone taste any. I need to feel this man's warm body next to mine, preferably in bed.

"Unless, we could both attend," he replies hesitantly or so it appears. He's teasing me. He's probably been here before and knows exactly what he's doing. One minute we're discussing fashion shows in Europe and the next we're arranging for daughter to meet girlfriend. Anyway, I have nothing against a man who takes pride in his contact time with his child, no matter how old she is. It would be nice to meet her, so that we can get ourselves acquainted as soon as possible. You never know we might really like each other and plan to do lunch or shopping or whatever daughters and stepmothers are supposed to do.

"It would be a pleasure to meet you both," I confirm. Shortly afterwards, Earl paid the bill and we made the journey back to my flat. He walked me to my front door like a shy young man in the early days of a relationship. I can see how women could easily fall for his mixture in tempo. One time he is moving fast, all cylinders on full fire and the next we are cruising in first gear. Like a perfect gentleman he just gave me a peck on the cheek and promised to see me on Saturday. He is undoubtedly a natural charmer and this evening he had the desired effect on me; the effect he wanted to have on me. I know that he's probably broken many women's hearts by using the same strategy as he has on me, but I am truly mesmerised by his charm. I can't think of the last time that a man brought me to my door and did not make it blatantly obvious that he was contemplating what to have for breakfast the following morning, but Earl has left me wanting him more. A peck on the cheek and walk away. How does he expect me to sleep alone tonight without him? Well, if he thinks that he's leaving this flat on Saturday night, then he has another thing coming. His daughter is big enough. She can take a taxi home, alone!

Rupert

It's been a long time since the guys and I went out for a drink. Since Donna left Dexter he has been spending most of his time with Chantelle at one party or another. And since I've been seeing Linda, I have tried to spend whatever free time I've had with her. When I say free time, what I really mean, I guess, is any time that I've had when I'm not working or with Pat. Yes, I have still maintained the same quality time with my wife as I had before I met Linda. Little compensation I know, but true all the same. Dexter insisted that everyone get together this evening, only because Chantelle is away on some modelling contract. I had already planned to meet Linda tonight but, rather than having to explain my way out of the situation I agreed to meet her at the same wine bar as the gang. I arrive at the Jools' wine bar and can see Sam, Ashley and Dexter are already into a round of drinks.

"Hi guys," I say, as I notice that Ashley already had his eye on some girl on the table next but one to ours. She doesn't seem to notice that she was under his surveillance or doesn't care. Either way, she appears not to be responding to his grave efforts. "I see that while the cat is away the mice are at play," I say to Dexter.

"No way," replies Dexter defiantly. "When has any woman prevented me from seeing my pals? Anyway, I've got some big news to break to you guys. Chantelle and I are going to get married." Dexter's announcement is met with nothing but stunned silence. I could sense that the others are probably thinking what I am.

"What about Donna?" asks Sam, beating us to it.

"In case you haven't heard Sam, Donna and I have gone our separate ways," replies Dexter sharply.

"But," says Sam, "aren't you even going to try and reconcile with her, if only for Dionne's sake?"

"Why should I?" answers Dexter. "I barely feel anything for the woman. And, I certainly don't want to spend the rest of my life with her, so what's the point? In any case, I can still see my daughter when I'm married. People do manage you know, it's not beyond the realms of reasoning!" I know that I should be saying more in support of Sam but my involvement with Linda hardly qualifies me as an angel either.

"I say, let's toast to the man's happiness," says Ashley. "He said he was getting married, not that he was going to die!" Ashley was right. No one even made the effort to congratulate Dexter on what must be a bigger step for him than most people that I know, as Dexter is not your obvious marrying kind. And, if he feels that Chantelle is the woman for him, then he should do what he thinks is best. It does beg the question, however, what it was he felt for Donna.

"When did you pop the question?" I ask.

"I haven't as yet."

"Shouldn't you ask the woman first before you announce your marriage to the world?" asks Sam.

"She wouldn't mind," replies Dexter. "We've got a good thing going. She would be just as pleased as I am to commit herself to what we share together."

"Dexter, I'm happy for you and hope that it all works out well for both you and Chantelle," I say, sensing that he may be regretting having shared his good news with his supposedly close friends.

"Thanks buddy, I knew that I could count on your support."

"Hey!" shouts Ashley. "I'm on your side for a change. You go with what makes you happy. Having a child is not a licence for eternal love. If you need to breathe, then you need to breathe. It's probably better that Dionne grows up in a happy home than one where her parents are continuously at each other's throats." I rarely agree with Ashley but he does have a point. "Sam," continues Ashley, "congratulate the man!" Sam does not obey and kisses his teeth as he turns his head away from Ashley and faces what appears to be nothing or no one in particular.

"What did Donna say about this?" asks Sam. I have always thought that Sam has a soft spot for Donna and always has her best interest at heart, even if that meant her staying with Dexter. Unfortunately for Sam, I don't think that he is Donna's type. He can be too straight. He doesn't like jokes because he doesn't like laughing at carnal matters. He seems only to be truly happy when he's rejoicing in church among his church brothers and sisters. Having said all that, however, I, like a lot of people I know, can trust Sam. He is a good and trustworthy friend to have. He will never let you down and will always be there for you.

"Donna doesn't know as yet," Dexter replies. I knew that had to be the case, as I'm sure that there was no way that Donna would have known and not told Pat and, of course, Pat would have told me had she known.

"You seem to be all mixed up, if you ask me," announces Sam. "You tell the world that you're getting married without telling the prospective bride or your fiancée who is not even the person whom you intend to marry!" Sam said this shaking his head with a sarcastic smile.

"You seem to be taking this quite hard Sam," responds Dexter. "Not to worry I'm sure Sister Donna would find herself a nice brother in the church, maybe even you if you play your cards right. Escorting her to Pat's book launch wouldn't have gone unnoticed, I'm sure." They do say that the best line of defence is attack!

"Women are like meat to you, aren't they?" continues Sam. "You probably didn't even give Donna a second thought before you decided on this farce of yours." My mind began to wonder as Dexter and Sam exchanged harsh words with each other when I noticed that Linda had already arrived and was with three other girls. Our eyes met and I beckoned her towards to the bar.

"I'd better get a round in and leave you guys to fight this one out on your own," I say. "Ashley you can referee this time." Having promoted the fight, I make my way towards the bar where Linda is already waiting.

"Hi darling!" says Linda just out of the earshot of our immediate neighbours.

"Hi dear," I respond, as I give her what could only be perceived as nothing more than an innocent peck on the cheek of a friend.

"Who are your friends?" I ask, seeing one of them looking over towards us.

"They're my flatmates."

"You mean neighbours," I correct.

"No, I mean flatmates," replies Linda strongly. "I've left Wilson."

"What!" I say checking around us for any eavesdroppers who should not be listening.

"I was led to believe that, as far as you two were concerned, everything was all right. What's brought this about?"

"After much thought, I thought it better that I leave him, rather than secretly cheat on him." Hearing Linda say this makes me feel cheap and cheated.

"We agreed that this relationship was just between the two of us and that nobody would get hurt. You've gone against your word," I say angrily, and sounding rather pathetic, but this to me could have far-reaching consequences other than Wilson himself: Pat, for example!

"I haven't gone back on my word at all," replies Linda clearly hurt by the accusation, but this relationship has now moved from both of us cheating on our partners to just one, and that one is me and I'm uncomfortable with that. "If anything," Linda continues, "I have kept to my word. I didn't want to hurt Wilson any more than I had to, and figured that now was the best time to leave him."

"How did he take it?"

"As I expected, he was pretty cut up about it, we've been together for a long time."

"Don't I know it! He must have asked why you were leaving him after all this time."

"You need not worry, Rupert. I didn't mention that it had anything to do with you and it didn't. I just told him that I felt that we were staying together only for the sake of convenience, which was probably unfair for both of us. He disagreed, but I wouldn't have expected anything else."

"So where do we go from here?" I ask.

"If you're asking me if I want you to leave your wife then the simple answer is 'no'. Let me make myself clear. My leaving Wilson had nothing to do with you. Well, not directly."

"What is that supposed to mean?"

"Well, seeing you only made me realise how much of my life I was wasting by staying with someone that I no longer loved. If I loved Wilson, I wouldn't have had an affair with you now, would I?"

"I love my wife!" I say, defending my position.

"That is a matter for you and your conscience. Anyway, I don't enter into relationships lightly, unless feeling emotionally compelled to do so. When we first got together, I loved no one. Things have since changed. And I can't envisage me ever feeling compelled to love two people at the same time. In other words it must feel right for me. With both you and Wilson in my life, it felt wrong not right, so I ended it."

"I, for one, try my utmost not to feel the way you did other-wise…"

"It's different for men," interrupts Linda.

"Why should it be any different for me? I have just as much emotion invested in us as you do."

"What I meant was, that women are less likely to get involved in an affair unless they really feel something for the man. Sex is not enough. I think men on the whole are more likely than women to get involved with someone purely for convenience and nothing more."

"I'm using you for my convenience. Is that what you're getting at?"

"Why are you with me Rupert?" asks Linda out of the blue, side-stepping the question.

"If the truth be known, I don't really know, other than to say that I am really fond of you. There might lie the answer, I don't know. When we danced at Yvonne's party, I knew that we were going to meet again and maybe something would have happened between us, but I couldn't have predicted this, of course." Linda doesn't seem offended by my obvious lack of purpose for our relationship.

"There was some electricity between us that night wasn't there?"

"Not only that night!" I reply. Linda gives a girlish laugh. "I have never cheated on my wife before," I add. I needed to make this declaration, if only to give me some form of comfort.

However, I do accept that one affair is one affair too many. "So," I continue, "all this is totally new to me."

"I'm in the same boat as you, Rupert. I almost got involved with a model once who wanted more than just his picture taken, but I decided against it. Like I said earlier, I don't take these matters lightly, so count yourself lucky."

"Who was it that said that a person can't be in love with two people at the same time?"

"I don't know, but she must have been one persuasive woman."

"But some societies allow a person to have more than one partner without any problems."

"You mean a man to have more than one wife!"

"Whatever, but I guess the point that I'm making is who are these people that make these rules? Do they abide by them?"

"That is something we'll never know. These ethics and morals just evolve over time. I'm not so sure that anyone truly knows where they first originate from. Anyway, are you saying that you are in love with two women?" asks Linda adeptly. Her question catches me off guard.

"What I am saying is that I cannot see why a person can't be in love with two people at the same time. After all, the meeting of one's partner is a mixture of both timing and luck. If we had met each other before both I had met Pat and you had met Wilson, then it would not have been a problem with us being together."

"And you could have been having an affair with Patricia and me with Wilson," reply Linda mockingly.

"I may be guilty of over-simplifying something which is far more complicated, but I do think that there is some merit in what I am saying."

"I'm not knocking your theory, it's just that you explain it away as if it is a first-come-first-served type of order."

"It is in a way. I think that who one ends up with is no more than a lottery. Whom we think might be our ideal partner often ends being the complete opposite to whom we end up marrying."

"They do say opposites attract."

"They do, indeed."

"I guess we had better rejoin our groups," says Linda looking over at her friends. I have long forgotten what drinks I was supposed to order.

"Are we still on for Tuesday?" I ask, seeking reassurance that her change of heart hadn't extended to me.

"Why not? My flatmate will be away for the night so we can be alone. Also, don't forget that I invited you to a party on Saturday. Can you still make it?"

"Yes, I can," I reply, not even trying to hide the relief in my voice. Maybe I am in love with two women, for if Linda were to end our affair I would be almost as devastated as if Pat were to end our marriage. If someone whom I am not in love with can have that effect on me, then I don't know how I feel. I used to think that life is what you make it, but I didn't plan this affair with Linda, but then I used to say that I would never cheat on my wife, and didn't plan that either.

Josephine

Tonight is the night. I intend to show off my man to the world. I have been thinking about nothing but Earl all day. I'm not saying that it will be easy tonight. A handsome man like Earl obviously chooses his women carefully. I should be honoured to be next. No, we should both be honoured to be each other's partner. I can't say that I'm that familiar with having a stepdaughter around, but how difficult can that be? I'm not going to try and replace her mother, it's just her father I want. Anyway, her mother is happy with Earl's best man, so his daughter should also wish that same happiness for her father. And I can give him that happiness. I wonder if Earl uses his daughter for vetting potential girlfriends. Well, we get on so well I can't see him letting his daughter come between us, whatever she thinks of me. After all, it would be his loss as well as mine, if she were to give me the thumbs down. I'll know from how and where he looks at me whether I have his daughter's blessing. He wouldn't be able to keep his eyes off me, I made sure about that. When I think of how these past few days have been, I'm too afraid to pinch myself in case I awake from a long dream. My girlfriends are saying that Earl has brought out a glowing complexion in me, that only a woman in love can have. Having Earl in my life must be bringing me very close to the happiness we were discussing only a few days ago. Life is so strange. Pat could never understand how someone could repel against their own race. I have always tried to assure her, unsuccessfully, that that did not apply in my case but that is all water under the bridge now. Donna has tried to warn me against dating handsome men like Earl but even she wasn't too convinced by her own argument. Her only evidence that handsome men are bad news, is her constant reference to Dexter. You need more than that, dear, in order for me to wash my hands of a hunk like Earl. I think that it is better to have loved a man like Earl than to have never loved at all. Anyway, it is agreed all round that Dexter is some good-for-nothing womaniser that Donna should never have got herself involved with in the first place. Earl is a gentleman. If he has broken many women's hearts in the past then I'm sure that it has not all been his fault. Look at the way his wife treated him, and he has bided his time until the right woman has come along. Now, that doesn't seem like some womaniser to me.

Most of my guests are here, but Earl is yet to arrive. I thought that he was punctual. Maybe his daughter refused to vet another woman and didn't want to come. She will need some working on. I just hope that he doesn't listen to her too much. I'm conscious of people talking to me but my attention is fixed solely on the front door. He has to turn up, I have silk and satin sheets awaiting our midnight rendezvous. I don't think that I could sleep another night alone without him. I dream of him every night; now is the time for the real thing. The doorbell goes again and at last I can see that Earl has arrived. I dash to the door while a friend of my neighbour is in mid-sentence about some new archaeological find in Egypt. I run to the door and greet Earl with a warm embrace. I had decided that I would make it difficult for his daughter not to like me, by letting her see that we are in love. I release Earl and I notice that his daughter isn't with him, but a rather good-looking guy. That one is for Donna.

"Hi Earl," I say, barely concealing my excitement in seeing my man, not to mention what we have in store for tonight.

"Hi Josephine," he replies in that deep voice of his, "this is Rodney, my boyfriend!"

Patricia

I am still without child. Jo fell in love with a man who did not, or maybe could not, fall in love with her. Donna's fiancé of four years is going to marry another woman he has known for less than four months! Crisis? I think so. The girls and I have called for a summit. On the agenda? Life! I can't recall a time when we all went through a mini crisis all at the same time. There is usually at least one of us free from any encumbrance, in order to help pull the others through. This time there is no such pillar of strength to lean on but only our shoulders to cry on. The one I most feel sorry for is Donna. Dexter has treated her like dirt. He made no attempt to get Donna back when she left him. And she only left him because of his insincerity towards her. Donna barely turned her back before he was roaming around town with his new woman. Now he is broadcasting his marriage to Chantelle to everyone, only a few months after telling Donna that he was not yet ready for marriage. He was ready to father a child, but not ready to help mind her. He hasn't even seen Dionne since the separation. That man has no scruples whatsoever. All I'm waiting for now is the invitation to the wedding. He knows who'll be attending that! The sad thing about it all is that I wouldn't put it past him to invite both Donna and Dionne to the wedding. Talk about rubbing their noses in it. I really fail to see what Rupert sees in him. I used to say that one can judge themselves by the company they keep but outside law Rupert and Dexter have very little in common. They couldn't be more different. And if I had any inclination that Rupert was anything like Dexter, he would be going straight out of that door with his tail between his legs. I just would not put up with that kind of foolishness and he knows that.

"I feel such a fool," says Jo, opening the meeting, as our quorum of three begin to unravel the complexities of our lives. "It's not just the fact that I was flirting with Earl all the time but the fact that I told so many people about him and how I, no we, felt about each other. I can hear them all laughing at me at this very moment."

"You have no need to feel ashamed, Jo, it's just one of those things," says Donna. "It could have happened to anyone. After all, Earl is extremely handsome. You're single, he's single, why shouldn't you have made a move on a man like that? I know that I said don't trust him, but I had other things in mind!"

"I hear what you say Don but you should have seen me, I was practically all over him. And to make matters worse, the more I replay our moments together in my mind the more that I fail to see why I thought we had anything other than a potential business relationship. He made no advances towards me. None whatsoever! It never, for one moment, dawned on me that the reason he hadn't been with a woman since his wife left him was because he was with a man. I kept asking him about his girlfriend but never thought of asking him about his boyfriend. He must have been laughing at me all the time. How could I have been so stupid?"

"I think that you're being a bit too hard on yourself, Jo," I say. "None of us thought about him having a boyfriend. Why should we? And there is no obvious reason why you should have, either. Actually, because he wasn't interested, he probably didn't even notice your 'come on'."

"Oh! That makes me feel a lot better, Pat. I give a man my best shot and he doesn't even know that I'm trying to seduce him. I might as well call it a day!"

"No, that isn't what I meant, Jo, and I think you know that. All I'm saying is that he may not have been tuned into your advances because he would not have been interested from the outset. I don't honestly believe that he would have turned up at your party if he had thought that you would have been offended, he doesn't come across as the type of person who would have got a kick out of such a thing."

"You're probably right, Pat, but I don't think that I can face him again. I'll be too embarrassed. I couldn't hide the shock on my face when he turned up at the party with Rodney, and it became clear how wrong I had got things. Gosh! I even hugged and kissed him, passionately, in front of his boyfriend. I must have been the butt of their jokes all night!"

"Oh come on Jo," I say. "You said it yourself, Earl has a good business mind and he can help your business grow. Don't throw it all away just because some love dream hasn't gone to plan. If we all did that we wouldn't achieve anything in life, now would we?

"Pat's right Jo," says Donna, voicing her support. "At least you know that Earl has belief in you as a shrewd businesswoman and not because he wants your body as collateral." I felt like adding, "like Dexter would have" but now was not the time for cheap remarks, true as they are. "So you got this one wrong, that shouldn't stop you causing waves in the fashion industry," continues Don. "If you feel aggrieved at what has happened then take it out on your competitors." Now that's the Donna I used to know, the one with a fighting spirit. I could see Jo staring at the bare ceiling.

"I like what you're saying girlfriend," responds Jo. "You're right, this should only be a temporary hiccup, no, a blessing in disguise. This will give me even more determination to make my boutiques bigger and better than they are at the moment. Forget men, they're nothing but trouble! If I'm to get anything from Earl, then it would be his idea but I am going to take it to another level and make it bigger. I don't need a partner, I can do it all by myself. Earl mentioned opening boutiques in Paris and Milan. Well, I say why not open boutiques all over Europe then look to America. It can be done girls. Anyway, what have I got to lose? I design and sell my own clothes. I am my biggest asset, so if my venture goes wrong, I'll start all over again."

"That's my girl," says Don, as we raise our glasses, as if to approve the scheme put before the Board.

"I'm going to put on a fashion show in each of the capital cities of Europe and then New York. Everyone will know of my designs. Everyone will be talking about them. We're talking big time here, girls. I feel excited about this and can't wait to start the wheels in motion." You can see the determination in Jo's eyes, she means business and, like she said, this was probably just the injection she needed. Jo spent some time telling us how she was going to implement her plans. Her ideas are big but I know that she can and will succeed. One down, two to go.

"So Don, how are you taking all this marriage talk about Dexter?" I ask, knowing that this will be undoubtedly the most sensitive topic of the night, but we're on a roll, so who knows.

"To be honest with you girls, I don't know what I feel any more. When you've been through what I have, you start to build up an emotional barrier that could take almost anything. And each time something comes along it just gets higher and stronger. I don't feel any love towards Dexter, so I don't feel too bad, I guess. But I do feel sorry for Dionne. He is punishing her only because I walked out on him. Dionne has done nothing wrong in all this and he hasn't even had the courtesy to give me a call to find out how she is doing. He doesn't have to give her money. We don't need him nor his money but he should at least show to his daughter that he loves and cares for her or, maybe he doesn't." Jo and I make no comment to Don's latter remark.

"You don't seem as bitter as I thought you would have been Don," says Jo.

"I hope that you're not bottling anything inside of you, Don?" I ask.

"I'm not," replies Donna. "I don't feel bitter towards Dexter except like I said for his treatment of Dionne. Do I look like I'm scarred from leaving him? He might wish to think so, but I'm happy with my life and with myself."

"You're looking the best that I have seen you for many months," I say.

"I feel better, much better. I'm not saying that someone has to cross the bridge that I did, in order to become a stronger person, but I have come through this experience much better for it. I can now understand what some women go through when they are caught up in that maze. You just can't seem to see a way out and almost get to the point where you want to throw in the towel. But there was always a voice inside me that kept saying that I would pull through and with your continued support, I had to come through this. No, I wish Dexter and his bride all the best. In fact, I say, we raise our glasses to them." And with that request we raise our glasses again. I don't think that even Dexter, in all his egotism, could believe that we, especially Donna, would be raising our glasses in his honour. Two down, one to go.

"Well, it seems that you two are fine, now that just leaves me. And, lets face it, no amount of talking is going to give me what I want. On reflection, it's not talking I need." We all laugh.

"Pat," says Don. "Lord knows how much I pray for you to have a child but I think we have to say that, if by God's will it is not to be, then it will not be. Let's look at what you're about. We have all known each other for a long time, you two even longer than me. I think that I can safely say that you have been the strongest supportive one out of us all. You're selfless and give your all for others. You may not be blessed with a child at this moment, but you are blessed in so many other ways. You're intelligent and have a best-selling novel now selling all over the world and none of that success has gone to your head. You're gifted, Pat." Hearing Don say this makes me feel that I have truly failed to see the wood for the trees. My work is much bigger than I am. People have often come up to me after one of my lectures and have congratulated me and told me how inspired they have been by what I have had to say and write.

"I second that," says Jo. "You're special to a lot of people, Pat, not to mention your closest friends, Don and I."

"Thanks girls," I respond. Three down and nil to go.

It was resolved that our concerns were all "much ado about nothing". Resolution passed, we raise our glasses for the final time and close the meeting. Crisis? What crisis? I guess life is not so bad after all!

Dexter

"No," replies Chantelle.

"What do you mean, 'no'?" I ask in shock. I thought that there was only one option, that being 'yes'.

"I'm not ready for marriage as yet. I'm young, I want to live a little, not get tied down too early." I remember using those very same words to Donna but that was my way of saying that I didn't want to marry her then or at all!

"How can you not be ready?" I ask. "When the right person comes into your life, you should snap them up before somebody else does." I'm sure this was not received the way it was intended. "We even made love last night!" I add.

"I didn't know that sleeping with you was consenting to marriage. If that is the case then how many women have given you that consent in the past few years?" This hurts. This just can't be happening. I can hear Sam laughing and calling me "a fool!" I must rescue myself from such humiliation.

"Sorry, I didn't mean it that way, it's just that for the first time in my life I have finally met someone that I am truly in love with."

"Are you saying that you never uttered those same words to Donna?" asks Chantelle, with an "I'm-not-falling-for-your-bullshit" look.

"I probably did say that to Donna at some time or another, but I was a lot younger then and didn't really know what I wanted, but I do now and I want you. You can have me all to yourself. I would never cheat on you Chantelle, I love you too much to do that. I only cheated on Donna because I was too young and knew that I shouldn't have got engaged to her. It was a mistake. Why do you think I left her?"

"Well, it's like that with me, I don't want to make the mistake that you made, I want to be as sure as I can be when I get married, that it is the right time and to the right man. I'm not sure of either at this time. Why can't we just continue the way we were? I might feel different later on, who knows?"

What happens from now on? If we continue, then she would always have the upper hand on me. She would always have it in mind that it was me who wanted to marry. I can't live with that noose around my neck. I like to keep my women on their toes, not the other way round. I'm not giving an inch, in order to leave myself open for a mile. I can't believe that I have asked a woman to marry me who in turn gives me nothing but grief. And worse, she said "no". If she is playing with me then I shall never forgive her. But, I like this woman a lot. A moment ago, I asked her to marry me, so how can I save face and keep her? With difficulty I think. I told the guys that I was going to ask Chantelle to marry me, so everyone knows. Why didn't I just keep my big mouth shut before I asked the woman? I thought that all I had to do was ask her to marry me and the rest would be a formality. Now I have to tell everyone the shameful news of my rejection and there are many that would not show an ounce of sympathy for me. I feel like that sad guy who proposed to Melanie Griffiths in front of all those people at that party in *Working Girl*, but I feel worse, much worse. I feel sick. It's not to say that I could even hibernate either. Everyone knows me and where I am. I'm not that popular either, so my foes are going to have a field day. All at my expense! Oh God, I even started a wedding guests' list, leaving out all those who I know despise the very air that I breathe. This was supposed to be my way of snubbing them all but who is going to have the last laugh now? It won't be me, I can be certain about that!

"I think it best that we go our separate ways," I say. "I gave you a chance and I am not about to give you another. My God, I even left my fiancée for you and this is how you repay me!" This is the best that I could make up. I have to go out fighting and with some pride still left in tact. I'm telling a woman who doesn't want to marry me that I am not going to give her a chance to change her mind. It sounds foolish but what am I to do? I'm in trouble, deep trouble. My God, the shame!

"I was afraid that you would say that," says Chantelle, calmly. "You don't seem like the kind of man who can take rejections lightly."

"Well I can't see any point in us carrying on," I say, interrupting her without apology and ignoring her snide remarks about me. "If this relationship is going nowhere, then why should we waste each other's time?"

"But I thought that we were both just having some fun, having a good time and not taking ourselves too seriously, so why the sudden change of heart?"

"I don't know," I reply. And truthfully, I really don't know. What I do know is that I have made a big mistake. I dread the finger-pointing that is going to come my way, the shame. I just got carried away. I thought that as we were having so much fun together, I should secure that lifestyle for myself before some fool takes it away from me. But this is not my style. I'm not the insecure type. Perish the thought! I leave this kind of thinking to the ugly guys, the sad ones that can't pull any women. Now that can hardly be addressed to me! Maybe this was my mind's way of telling me that I had found the right girl for me to marry but now is not the right time.

"So what do you want us to do?" she asks.

"I think that you should move out tonight," I say, so as to show that although I'm a little bruised, I'm not yet down. There are many women out there who would cry out for this opportunity, like Donna, for example. All this is Chantelle's loss not mine. Next week she'll simply see me in town with another girl on my arm and looking just as good as ever. I can feel the confidence flowing back to me, even as I speak. I lost contact with a lot of my women since I've been seeing Chantelle, so many of them will be pleased that I'm back.

"If that is what you wish," she replies, sadly, looking at me intensely as if contemplating her life without me. I've seen it all before. It's the same pattern all the time. I've called her bluff. She wanted me but she thought that I would grovel. I grovel to no woman.

"That is what I wish," I reply. It surprised me how many of her belongings she had at the flat. Chantelle had practically moved in. When I think about it, we were almost living like husband and wife in any case, but I call the shots around here and as she was not prepared to abide by them, then something had to give. It might be the wrong thing that gave, but then, again, I have my pride and that is more important to me than any woman. Well, all I can say is fathers lock up your daughters because I'm back on the hunt. That reminds me: Donna. It's about time I paid her a visit.

Donna

"Hello Donna," I hear Dexter say before I could fully open the door.

"What on earth do you want?" I ask. He didn't even have the courtesy to call and check whether it was suitable to come round. No, why should he? Donna would have nothing better to do but mope around the house hoping that he will call.

"I thought that I would come round and surprise my daughter," replies Dexter. I see his shifty eyes trying to peer over my shoulder and into the house. He needn't have any concerns: my parents do not waste their valuable time thinking about him let alone be troubled by his visit.

"Well I'm afraid that she is asleep," I say bluntly.

"Can I see her, anyway?" he persists.

"I'm sorry Dexter, you can't," I reply, refusing to let him enter my parent's home. He looks visibly shocked at my stance, but this is not the Donna he left a few months ago.

"But I've come all this way, specifically to see her."

"Tough! You should have called before you came."

"I'm sorry, I couldn't find your parents' telephone number, otherwise I would have called you a long time ago."

"Really!" I reply, not remotely amused. "Everyone knows that some skirt has been occupying your time Dexter, so don't try to insult my intelligence. Lord knows that I let you get away with that for far too long."

Dexter seems uncharacteristically more shifty than usual. I would have expected him to brag about his forthcoming marriage to Chantelle and go, not hang around like he has no home to go to.

"Donna, can I come in? I would like to talk to you."

"What about?" I ask. "I would prefer it if we stayed outside. If it is your marriage you have come to tell me about then I guess you would have expected me to know by now." Dexter doesn't look too surprised by my revelation but still seems uncomfortable. "I guess we should decide what we are going to do about the flat, as well. I'm not going to have you and your bride live in the flat that my money paid for."

"Yes, we will need to discuss that, but I would like to leave that for another time, if that is all right with you."

"I think the sooner we sell it the better. I don't want things to linger on any longer than they have already. I'm sure that you and your wife wouldn't want that either."

"That is partly what I want to talk to you about," says Dexter, nervously. "There might not be a wedding."

"What!" I reply.

"I might call the whole thing off!"

"Why?" I ask, still not believing a word of what he is saying.

"After much thought, I've been thinking that maybe I'm not ready for marriage after all. Well, not to Chantelle anyway!"

"You're not making sense, Dexter. Why did you ask that woman to marry you if you weren't sure? Mind you, I was your fiancée for many years and look what happened there, so I suppose I shouldn't be too surprised."

"Since you left me and took away my child, I haven't stopped thinking about you and sought happiness in the first person that came along. It could have been anyone."

"You're trying to tell me that you asked a woman to marry you because you were thinking of me and Dionne?" I ask sarcastically. This is just too confusing. It doesn't make sense, any of it!

"That is exactly what I am saying. I now realise that I want to be back with you and my child. I made a big mistake and I want my family to come back home to where we all belong." To say that I'm in shock would be an understatement. This might explain his hostility towards me at Pat's book launch. He always said that having his space wouldn't mean that he necessarily wanted us to break up.

"You better come in for a while," I say showing him the way. I know that I shouldn't but at the end of the day my heart is not that hard so as to leave the father of my child standing outside my family home. I see the relief on his face as I guide him through to my bedroom. He knows me well enough to know that I could never be too hard on him. I have a conscience. We both sit on the bed. I haven't seen Dexter this nervous since we first started going out with each other. He is usually much more ice-cool than this. Even when he was cheating on me, butter wouldn't melt in his mouth, but I guess it's not every day that a man pleads with his fiancée to take him back.

"I'll come clean, Donna," says Dexter, in that old shy voice of his, absent of the cockiness that had became so much part of his character. He takes my hand and looks at me with those hazel-green eyes of his. Yes, it all comes flooding back, all the good times we had together. "There will be no wedding. I have called the whole thing off. Chantelle had brought most of her belongings to the flat and was hoping to move in, but I just didn't feel too comfortable with the idea. After all, the flat is yours and mine. We started a family there. There is too much history between us for me to just let it go, after a short separation: a separation that has taught me a hard lesson. Remember it was you who left me; I would never have left you. I'm not saying that you didn't have just cause to do what you did, but I am not here to cast blame, I just want my family back. I've made mistakes in my life and I'll be the first to own up to them, but nobody is perfect and even I have never claimed to be that! I want you to come home with me tonight. People will talk, I know, but I don't care about people any more. It's our life and our life alone. Everybody else can run and take a jump for all I care." The radiance of Dexter's sincerity fills the room. I know him, he really is sorry for what he has done to us.

"Dexter, I hear all that you say, but I really don't know whether I could trust you anymore," I respond. I have never been one for believing that a leopard can change its spots and, especially, Dexter so soon after I left him.

"Donna, look at you. You look good. You needed this time apart just as much as I did. I know we both feel the same way for each other. We have both had time to reflect on what we really want out of life. If I didn't want you, then I would not have called off my marriage to Chantelle for you, and if you didn't want me then you would have told me where to go the moment you answered the door, but you didn't. Why do you think that is? I'll tell you why, because we are good for each other. We need each other. We are the only two that truly understand one another. Let's not throw all that we have away for the sake of a few foolish indiscretions."

Talk about pressure. I can hear my parents, Pat, Jo, Sam, in fact I can hear everyone saying don't get involved with the man that caused me so much pain, but, like Dexter said, I understand, the others don't. It would have taken real courage to cancel his marriage to a woman that I know he was having so much fun with, just for me. It takes maturity to acknowledge that there is more to life than parties and clubs. I haven't forgotten him smothering Chantelle at every given opportunity at Pat's book launch. That was clearly his way of trying to make me jealous. It all makes sense now. He wouldn't have bothered if he didn't care. And what about Dionne? Should he be deprived from bringing up his only child? Does Dionne deserve not to have her father around? We should both face up to our responsibilities to our child.

"I'm prepared to give you one final chance Dexter," I announce to a joyous reception. The delight on Dexter's face is there for all to see. There was no hiding what he felt about my response.

"Thank you Don. Thank you. Today is the best day of my life. No, the second best day of my life. The best was when I first set eyes on you."

"Any more of your rubbish, Dexter, and it's over for good. I mean it!"

"I've changed Don, I promise you." With that he edges closer to me and we seal our reunion with a kiss that said "welcome back".

"No, not tonight," I command, as he tries to have his dessert as well. "I'm in my parents' home and I don't think it is appropriate, after all that has happened between us, to sleep under their roof tonight."

"I understand, it's just that I wanted to prove to you how much I was back for good and there is no better way of me showing my true love for you."

"Not tonight," I say, firmly.

"Will you and Dionne come home with me tonight then? I don't want to spend another night away from my family."

"Dionne is sleeping and I don't want to wake her up. Also, I have all my belongings here, so it will take time to move them out."

"Whatever happens Don, please don't keep me waiting too long. I have been away from you for too long, and I don't want that to be extended by another day longer than necessary."

"I promise," I reply. Dexter, pleading, is not a pretty sight. I let him have a sight of Dionne while she lay asleep, totally oblivious of the decisions being taken, that will affect her life. Dexter seemed genuinely pleased to see his daughter. He looked like a man whose life was finally piecing itself together. Many men don't have that chance. Let's hope he appreciates that and doesn't abuse the opportunity. My mind and body couldn't take any more of the old Dexter; it is too tired from that emotional roller coaster. After Dexter left, sometime after midnight, I went into Dionne's room and just held our baby in my arms whispering "Daddy is home, Daddy is home, everything will be all right, Daddy is home."

Rupert

Dexter and Donna are back together again, much to everyone's surprise. One minute Dexter was talking about marrying Chantelle, "the girl of his dreams" he once described her as to me, and the next minute he was back with Donna, whom he earlier professed to care little or nothing for. Everyone around here is talking about it. Much speculation has been fuelled also by Dexter's vagueness on the whole affair. Most unlike him, he has not been forthcoming with any explanation whatsoever. However there does appear to be a consensus on the "correct" version of events that night. It seems that Dexter heard of Chantelle being with another man and decided to put her out rather than face the medicine of his own treatment. This could explain Chantelle's rapid departure upon her return from the Seychelles. No one knows where she is either. Ashley says that he saw her that night and that she told him that Dexter had warned her not to show her face around these parts again. However, when you've known Ashley as long as I have, you know to take whatever he says with more than just a pinch of salt. Also, Dexter may be all things to all men but he is not the type to threaten any woman; he loves them too much for that! But, having defended him, no rumour has yet been admitted nor denied by him, which leads me to believe that there may yet be an element of truth in some, if not all, of them. In fact, no one even knows if Chantelle knew of Dexter's proposal to be. He hasn't even shed light on that! People are asking me questions, as if I know. And usually I would, but this time I'm in the dark, just as much as they are. What is also surprising is Donna's reaction to it all. All she told Pat was that Dexter had cancelled the wedding after deciding that he wanted her and Dionne back. Anyway, besides all the gossip about their love life, I'm pleased that Donna and Dexter are back together. They've been together a long time and have parental responsibilities. I don't really know Chantelle that well, but a marriage born out of nothing more than just parties doesn't seem to be a sturdy enough foundation upon which to build any form of relationship, let alone marriage itself! But what do I know? I just hope that things work out for them this time. Let's hope that Dexter doesn't put his family through a trauma like that again. However, if last week is anything to go by, it wouldn't surprise me if this whole episode rears its ugly head again. He doesn't appear to have any intention of curbing his flirtatious ways. And it is that which gets him into trouble in the first place. He tried his damnedest to get this girl from the squash club to go out with him, but I think that his reputation made that a non-starter. She was having none of it!

Since Dexter's reconciliation with Donna, I have been giving plenty of thought to me finally devoting myself solely to my wife, but have conceded that I am in love with two women. It has taken some time for me to admit this fact to myself, but the truth eventually seeped through. I know that it's wrong, only because others tell me so. I couldn't count the number of times that I too have condemned Dexter over his womanising. But, unlike Dexter, no one gets hurt with me. I tell myself that I am one lucky man to have met two women who together make me feel whole. I have the best of both their worlds. What one lacks, the other more than makes up for. How can it, therefore, be wrong for a man to receive the love of two women? Most men would be fortunate to receive the love of just one! I know Pat wouldn't quite see things that way, but then she doesn't have to know and what she doesn't know couldn't possibly hurt her, to coin a phrase from a friend. Having said all that, I do hate lying to her. I know that one day all these lies will become too big to manage. I'm not good at lying and I don't like doing it. I know that when people lie they try their hardest to maintain consistency, often at the expense of any truth whatsoever and that is where they come unstuck. And recently I have been having these weird dreams. According to Pat I mumble, toss and turn whilst having them. The dreams are the same. A duckling is hit by a barge whilst out paddling with a raft of ducks in a canal and its only saving grace is a duck who has gone paddling for the day with her mate. Friends of the young drake search and search for this one duck but she is nowhere to be found. Unfortunately, the young drake could hold on to life no longer and dies before the duck can be found. The worrying thing is that I rarely ever have dreams, so having these has left me petrified, if nothing else. Pat and I have tried on numerous occasions to decipher their meaning, if any, but as we have failed to reach any meaningful conclusion, we put them down to having no real significance. On reflection, however, my sleep is disturbed all round. I never sleep too well on the night before I am due to meet Linda, in fear that I might mumble her name whilst asleep. Be it bad dreams or mumbling Linda's name in my sleep, either would be a nightmare!

Tonight I have agreed to accompany Linda to an important party for her of agents and other influential people in the fashion industry. I told Pat that I was visiting the archives of my opponents in a big case as part of the disclosure process. I should really have stayed at home because Pat has not been feeling too well lately, but tonight will be the first time that Linda and I have had the opportunity of going to a function as a couple, so I had to make the effort. We are at that stage now where I expect to have first refusal to any invites. I've pushed Wilson off the top spot and claimed that position as mine of right. With the party being so far out of London, I could take the chance of going and not being known. Mind you, I hadn't thought of what I would do if I were to meet someone that I did know. I try to keep such thoughts at the back of my mind for as long as possible, otherwise I wouldn't go anywhere with Linda. If I'm caught with Linda and Pat finds out and she refuses to hear what I have to say, then matters would be dealt with swiftly. Pat would commence divorce proceedings before one could say "decree nisi."

Linda answers the door to her flat. She is wearing a thigh-length, emerald-green velvet strapless dress. Those thighs of hers always cause some kind of chemical reaction to my body. Her legs are so smooth. They would easily pass a silk-scarf test. My immediate thought is, let's cancel the damn party and have a quiet night in, but quiet nights are all that we've been having since we've been together, so a change should be welcomed.

"How was your day today?" I ask Linda whilst helping her into the car. I hear my mobile phone ringing; it is resting on the dashboard. That reminds me, I must change that phone. It's too bulky and I need to screen my calls. It was Dexter who was just ringing for a casual chat. When Dexter was with Chantelle he wasn't even in to make a call let alone ring for casual chats. After our brief conversation, I switch off the phone and hand it to Linda. I can't have someone ringing me tonight and hearing music blasting out in the background when I'm supposed to be researching papers.

"It's been one of those days," says Linda. "Wilson rang me today and said that he would like us to meet for a chat. When I asked him what he wanted to chat about, he replied that his work was suffering and he didn't feel that he could carry on without me."

"What does he mean by that?" I ask.

"I don't know. I couldn't talk too long on the telephone as I was in the middle of a shoot. However, I said that I would speak to him tomorrow."

An air of insecurity surrounds me, as I realise that there is always a threat that this new and exciting life of mine could suddenly come to an end against all my wishes. But I accept that my gain of recent weeks has been Wilson's loss and the pendulum could quite easily swing back from whence it came. That is the strength or weakness of my affair with Linda. I don't blame Wilson for trying to get her back. I would do the same and more, if I were in his shoes. After all, it was my curiosity which has led to him losing his woman, a woman he had been with since his student days. So any man who cares for "his" woman would do what he is doing. The truth is, you don't know how much you miss someone until they've gone. I feel bad, because if Linda were to end our affair then I would still have a caring wife to go home to, but Wilson has no one but himself.

"He might propose to you," I say. "That seems to be the flavour of the month at the moment."

"He might do, having had time to reflect on matters."

"And what would you say if he did?" I ask, not sure that I really want to know the answer.

"I can't keep repeating myself, Rupert. I've told you before how I feel about Wilson and nothing has changed since, so there is no need for you to keep enquiring about my feelings for him. I'm tired of the same questions over and over again."

"I didn't mean anything," I say apologetically.

"Sorry," interrupts Linda. "I didn't mean to snap at you, but it has been a long day and all I want to do is let my hair down and enjoy myself tonight."

"I only asked the question because we had maintained from the outset that if anyone was going to get hurt then we would end what we have. That was the only purpose."

"I would like to see you try and end this now," says Linda, confidently. I haven't the stomach to take her up on her challenge. I think my silence is the best reply that I could give in the circumstances.

The party was held in a marquee on the grounds of a large estate set in Buckinghamshire. The host, I was informed, is a big media mogul who was launching a new innovating "his and hers" fashion magazine. I had a quick scan of the guests to see if there was anyone there who would force us to make a premature departure from the party. I gave myself the all clear upon drawing a blank on the faces. This was to my relief in more ways than one, as I am sure that any such proposal to leave, would have been met with strong opposition, which is not the way to start your first date in public. And the way Linda is feeling tonight I don't think that it would take too much for her to explode.

Linda has been introducing me to many of her friends, from photographers to models and from agents to fashion magazine editors. According to Linda, anyone who is someone in the fashion world is here tonight. It had crossed my mind that Jo might be here tonight, but I think that this party has come two or three years too soon.

"Rupett?" I hear the uncertain voice call as my heart nearly leaps out of my mouth at the sound of my name coming from behind me and noticing that Linda is across the room in front of me. I turn round hesitantly to see that it is Chantelle. "What are you doing here?" she asks, clearly surprised to see me, not to mention me seeing her.

"I'm here with a friend," I reply, shocked at meeting someone that I know, albeit not that well, and, thankfully, not that closely either, but nonetheless a daunting experience all the same. In all the time Dexter and Chantelle were together I barely saw either of them. She looks as attractive as ever. There does not appear to be any signs of her fretting from being separated from Dexter.

"Right!" she replies, shaking her slender body to the rhythm of Kool and the Gang's "Celebration" blaring out of the speakers. "You're not here with Dexter are you?" she asks.

"No, I'm not. I'm hear with a client of mine."

"Oh, who is that? I might know him."

"Her," I correct, "Linda, Linda Walters." I wait with bated breath as Chantelle runs the name through her mind giving it a mental check.

"No, I don't think I do," she replies, to my relief. I could do without the added complication of Chantelle knowing Linda. "You must introduce me to her later on."

"Yes, of course," I reply. Well there is no way that is going to happen. Not tonight, anyhow. We both stand there with an air of awkwardness, while looking around and moving gently to the music as you do at a party when you have nothing more to say to the other person, but here I do have questions that need answering about Dexter. For example, what exactly happened between you two?

"How is Dexter?" she asks.

"He's all right," I reply. In fact, I don't even know if she is aware of Dexter's reunion with Donna.

"Good, I knew everything would be fine," she says, appearing to show little concern for what happened between them. After all, why shouldn't everything be fine? Dexter lost his fiancée and daughter and in the intervening period while waiting for them to return home he was seeing an attractive woman with a body to kill for. Show me any man who wouldn't be fine after that!

"I haven't seen you around since, well, you know."

"No, I moved in with a good friend of mine, Sydney. I take it that Dexter told you that he asked me to move out of his flat the day after I came back from the Seychelles."

"He did," I reply, feeling ashamed at my friend's rather cold and erratic behaviour but I'm used to it. "They say that there is a thin line between love and hate and I don't think that I had ever witnessed a better demonstration of that than what happened between you two."

"I agree. It was such a strange evening…"

"…Chantelle, darling," interrupts this tall black man as he kisses Chantelle on both cheeks.

"Hi Sydney, you made it then?" asks Chantelle.

"Yes, I wouldn't have missed this party for the world. I've got to get my picture in one of the glossies," he replies. His face looks vaguely familiar but I can't quite recall where I would have seen him before. It is not uncommon for me to have come across someone who I have met at a trial and later meet at a social gathering.

"This is Rupert Jackson, Dexter's friend."

"Yes, I remember you very well. You don't appear to have changed much," replies Sydney. We shake hands as I stare at him blankly. "You don't remember me do you?"

"I must apologise, I don't," I reply.

"There's no need to apologise, it was a long time ago. I used to go out with Donna before she met Dexter." Yes, I remember, Pat was very fond of him.

"Yes, sorry, I remember. How are you?"

"Not doing too badly. And is your beautiful wife here tonight?"

"Stop being modest," interrupts Chantelle, before I could answer. "Sydney is the hottest property in town. Every top model wants to work for him. You are in the presence of a genius." Sydney looks embarrassed by the accolade but makes no attempt to deny it. "Seeing that you two know each other, I am going to circulate a little bit and see whether I can make myself some new contacts. I shall see you two around." With that Chantelle weaves her way through the party guests.

"Is Patricia here?" repeats Sydney.

"No, I'm afraid that she couldn't make it. She is very busy these days promoting her book. So what have you been doing with yourself?" I ask, before he could even think of enquiring with whom I'm attending this function.

"Well, it's more or less what Chantelle has said. I run a large modelling agency with offices in London, Paris and New York. Most of the top models you see in any fashion magazine anywhere in the world are likely to have come through my agency at some point or another in their careers. I think that we are unique in that we only deal with the best: the best designers, the best photographers, the best magazines and, of course, the best models. We're expensive, but you pay for what you get: the best."

"And you're the top man I take it?"

"I am the sole owner of the whole empire," he says proudly.

"And how is the law?"

"My practice could always be busier to cover the lean periods but I guess, overall, I'm not doing too badly."

"What area of law do you practice in?"

"All types of commercial work. It's the area of law that pays the highest fees," I say unashamedly.

"Made your first million yet?" asks Sydney, innocently. I should say that I have no interests in money, I practise for the love of the law, but I'll have more respect for his intelligence.

"I should be so lucky. All that stuff you read about 'fat cat' millionaire lawyers is all media hype. Some lawyers do earn that kind of money but they are few and far between."

"My company commissions a lot of legal work throughout the year. I can instruct my solicitor to pass on to you as much work as you like, if you're interested."

"Definitely! I would be more than grateful to work for you."

"Then consider it done," replies Sydney in a no-nonsense businesslike manner. "I shall have work to you by Monday morning."

"Thank you," I reply. Who said life isn't wonderful?

"If I knew that I would have bumped into you tonight, I would have brought my copy of *Four Seasons* for you to get your beautiful wife to autograph for me. I don't think that I need to ask you how Patricia is doing, as it is all well documented in the media. I have always been impressed by Patricia. She is a strong woman who speaks her mind intelligently. Such attributes are rare commodities these days. You're a very lucky man to have such a talented woman as your wife. You must be very proud of her."

"I am indeed," I reply. I sure hope that he doesn't know Linda or if he does then she hasn't told him about her seeing a lawyer, otherwise it might not be too difficult for him to figure out what is going on.

"And how is Donna?" he asks.

"No doubt Chantelle has told you all that happened between her and Dexter, so there is little to add, other than to say that I understand Donna and Dionne are very happy at the way things have turned out. Actually, she seemed happy the moment she and Dexter broke up."

"I've been meaning to visit her since Chantelle and Dexter got together. I couldn't believe it when one day Chantelle told me that she was seeing this guy called Dexter whose fiancée was Donna. I just thought what a small world this is."

"It sure is," I say. And it could be even smaller if you know Linda Walters and know that she has separated from her long-term boyfriend and is now dating a lawyer and I am probably the only lawyer at this party and I am Linda's date for the night.

"I have always tried to monitor how Donna was getting on, but it has been difficult since I don't know anybody within her social circles and it didn't seem like she went out that often in any case. I thought that after Donna and Dexter got engaged so soon after meeting each other that they were a happy couple who would be together for some time, but I guess that is something that none of us can predict with any certainty. And then when Dionne was born I thought that must be it, they are settled for life." Sydney really had been doing his homework on Donna. I wonder if she had been seeing Sydney behind Dexter's back, for he seems to know so much about her time with Dexter. No, Donna is not that way inclined. In any case, Sydney is no fool and he wouldn't have volunteered such information to me so freely if they had been in touch during that time. "Is she still at her parents' house?" he asks.

"No, they have already moved back into the flat," I reply. Sydney doesn't seem surprised at this news, as if expecting that once Chantelle had moved out of the flat the family would reunite in the family home.

"I would like to pay them a visit one day," says Sydney, in a rather casual manner, as if he was referring to a friend that he had seen just the other day, not to mention that that friend has just reunited with her fiancé and her child's father. And, even though Dexter is a very open-minded guy, I don't think that even he would welcome an old flame visiting his home. "Yes, I'll pay her a surprise visit. You never know we might be able to rekindle that old magic. I don't know how she would react to seeing me again after all these years. It was both our decisions to part, due to external pressures, so it might not be too bad now that we are older and wiser. Maybe you could do us a favour and test the waters for me." I knew that it was all too good to be true. No successful businessman just hands someone work without wanting something in return. "We should never have broken up in the first place," continues Sydney before I can even consider my reply. Maybe an affirmative response was taken as granted. "But we were both too young and naïve to know better. Well, Dexter had his chance and he blew it, now it is my turn to be with a woman with whom I should never have parted. Dexter clearly didn't appreciate Donna, but I shall. It used to hurt me when I would hear how he was getting on. He was mistreating a woman that I was once very much in love with and believe me that used to hurt! I guess that one never truly falls out of love with their first true love; such love is just put on hold." I could see Linda anxiously beckoning me over towards her. I suggested that we circulate before the many people who undoubtedly wanted to meet him accuse me of having a monopoly on his precious time, and I'm not even in the fashion industry. Thankfully, he agreed and we went our separate ways before he could meet me with Linda, who was now hurrying her way through the crowd looking flustered. She seemed unable to wait for me to make my way towards her. I thought of telling Sydney that I did not think it would be very tactful for him to enter into Donna's life at a time when she had just gone back to Dexter, but I now have a vested interest and so thought better of it.

"Hi dear," I say. "Are you enjoying the party?"

"It's brilliant! I can't believe the people who are here tonight. Also, I didn't know that you knew Sydney Charles." I take out my handkerchief to mop up the perspiration which I could feel had formed rapidly on my forehead.

"You know Sydney, do you?"

"Clearly not as well as you do. I saw you talking to the great man."

"Yes, I met him a few times a long time ago. He used to go out with a close friend of Pat's."

"You must introduce me to him," insists Linda. "I have just been talking to some woman from the Arts Council. They are sponsoring a group of British designers to put on various fashion shows around Europe and I'm sure that a man of Sydney's stature would have many contacts within the various groups of organisers."

"I'll see what I can do," I say, reluctantly, to her excitement. Fortunately, such excitement did not manifest itself into any form of physical contact, as is usually the case with her.

"If I'm selected as one of the official photographers, you promised me that you would show me around Paris, remember?"

"Yes, I do."

"And that is still on I take it?"

"Of course it is," I reply. That reminds me, Pat mentioned about going to Europe to promote *Four Seasons*. "I might have to go on a business trip to France soon, so if you tell me when it is that you are likely to go, then I can make the necessary arrangements to be in Paris at the same time."

"There is Sydney coming towards us, introduce me now," demands Linda. I feel uncomfortable about this but, what the hell, let's go for it.

"Sydney," I call out, "this is a friend of mine, Linda Walters, whom I would like you to meet." Sydney greets Linda by shaking her hand in a perfect gentlemanly fashion. I could see that Linda was so excited by the coup as she began to sell herself in a more than convincing manner. I'm glad to say that Sydney didn't seem irritable at being ambushed by yet another hungry photographer craving to get on his books. I left them "talking shop" as I circulated amongst the other guests, in confidence that Linda was not going to say anything that she shouldn't do. I can see Chantelle at the far corner of the marquee chatting to a young, good-looking man. I wonder if he is the man that Dexter was supposed to have found out about who Chantelle was seeing behind his back. After a while of wondering around, I noticed that Sydney was cornered by another woman. There is no doubt that Sydney is a very popular guy. I wonder if he will visit Donna, and, if so, how Dexter will deal with it. Not very well, I should think. Dexter has always viewed Donna as a safe pair of hands. This, I think, is what has led him into believing that he could do whatever he likes and Donna would still take him back. And, I guess, to a certain degree he must be right because after the last big separation, I could only but wonder what it would take for her to rid him from her life for ever. Let's face it, crude as it may seem, but tonight, Donna will probably sleep on the same side of her bed that was, until recently, being kept warm by Chantelle.

"Hi darling!" says Linda, looking happy with herself. "You look as though you're day-dreaming. Are you ready to go?" I check my watch to see the time. Gosh! It's late and I have to change before I go home.

"Yes, it's getting late. Pat might be getting concerned that I am working too late for a Saturday night. Did you manage to sell yourself to Sydney, then?" I ask.

"Of course, you know me. We are going to meet next week to view my portfolio."

"I hope that this viewing will not end the way our first meeting went," I say, smiling at the thought.

"Watch it Jackson, you're stepping out of line. I can't believe that a man as powerful as Sydney can be so approachable. I have no doubt it is because of you. It seems like I might have to hold on to you. You're an asset!"

"I don't know him that well!"

"Well, he seemed very interested in wanting to know how we knew each other."

"And what did you say?" I ask anxiously.

"I told him the truth. I said that we were old friends and left it at that."

"That sounds harmless to me," I say, as we make our way to collect our coats.

"Rupert!" cries out Sydney's voice from behind us, as we begin to make our way out of the marquee. "I look forward to seeing you next week," he calls out to Linda. "And I shall get some of that big-money work over to you by Monday, as promised," he says to me. "And don't forget to pave the way for me with Donna. Remember, you scratch my back and I'll scratch yours."

"He's a shrewd businessman, Sydney. I like him," states Linda.

"He's that all right," I reply. "He's very shrewd indeed."

I didn't let lust get the best of me when I dropped Linda home, although temptation was there. I thought of passing round for a few minutes but I know that that few minutes would have turned into an hour or more and time, unfortunately, is not on my side. I could tell that Linda didn't want to spend the night alone, which I can understand. After all, our first real date had proven to be a major success all round and it would have been nice to end with something even more pleasurable and climatic, but I had to take a rain check on that. Anyway, I needed time to reflect on the evening's events. Check and see if I need to watertight any stories, in case Pat feels inclined to ask any questions. I'm not too happy about meeting Chantelle and Sydney. Chantelle, I think, is harmless, but Sydney worries me. Testing the waters with Donna might raise more than an eye of suspicion. Also, far more serious, if Sydney meets with the Donna then he may tell her that he saw me and where. And there is no way that Donna would withhold such information from Pat and Pat will go ballistic. Lying is not something that Pat accepts under any circumstances or for whatsoever reason. And, to be honest, I don't want to import that kind of mistrust between us. I've seen what that can do to a relationship. One only has to look at Donna and Dexter to see what I mean. I couldn't live with that. Also, I saw the mistrust my mother had for my father and it was a very unpleasant atmosphere to live in. As I drive on to the forecourt, I can see that the bedroom light is off, which, hopefully, means that Pat will have been asleep for some time and, therefore, unlikely to know what time I came home. If I had been working this late on a Saturday night, then I would have no qualms about Pat being up or not. In fact, I would probably have wished that she were. However, it is at times like this when guilt and lies make you look as though you are guilty and lying. Remain calm and play it cool. I'm going to have to get used to this until this romance thing with Linda cools off, and my body is in no mood to give that up for a long time. I'm picturing Linda and those smooth thighs of hers. Pat is asleep. Maybe I should have stayed with Linda for a short while after all. I'm turned on, my wife's asleep and my girlfriend is probably still available at this very moment. I could go back to Linda's place and call Pat later on in the morning, saying that I went back to work after coming home and finding her asleep. Sounds like a good idea to me. No, that is not such a good idea after all. That is how men get caught. They let their penis do the thinking, and become careless. No, I think that I'll play it safe. After all, it's not that I'm playing away because I'm unhappy at home, it's because I'm in love with two women. Yes, two women, not one, and that means striking a balance to keep them both satisfied, but without taking any unnecessary risks. And, at least one partner knows of the other so my job is made that little bit easier. I open the door and see that there is light coming from the kitchen.

"Rupert?" I hear Pat call.

"Hello darling," I reply hesitantly. "What are you doing up so late?" I ask. Pat catches me off guard. What did I say about guilt and lies making one act like they're guilty and lying? I hadn't checked to see whether there were any remnants of Linda on me. Lipstick! Was she wearing any lipstick? My God I could be smothered with the stuff and not even know. I rush into the bathroom before hearing Pat's reply. All is fine. I look like any faithful husband.

"I've been waiting up for you. Where have you been? I've been worried sick," she says. Lying to her generally was one thing but lying to a specific question is worse. I can't even say later on that I misunderstood the question. Let's hope that the call for such plea does not arise.

"I was at this opponent's office, dear, like I said earlier on."

"Well why didn't you have your phone on? All I could get was your voicemail." Damn! Linda has my phone.

"Sorry, I switched it off when I went to make a coffee, so as not to make too much noise." It's the best that I can do. I hadn't covered this avenue. I'm no good at lying. I can't even cover my tracks properly. How can I possibly think of everything? I hate lying.

"I was so worried, I rang Cedric."

"Cedric!" I reply. "What did you want to trouble him for?" I ask.

"Rupert, what's the matter? Why are you fretting? I said I rang Cedric not the Lord Chancellor. What was I to think? You have all these funny dreams about ducks and things and suddenly I can't find you. Tell me, what was I to do?"

"The drake is here to your rescue," I say light-heartedly.

"It's not funny, Rupert, some dreams do have a meaning."

"Sorry dear. What did Cedric have to say?"

"He didn't recall you saying that you were going to work tonight. In fact he didn't even know of the case."

"No, he wouldn't," I reply hurriedly. This is madness, I can't carry on like this. "Sometimes clients request that we don't discuss their cases with other members of Chambers. This case I'm dealing with is going to arbitration so it's going to be heard in private." I can only thank my lucky stars that Pat is not a lawyer because a lawyer would smell the bullshit a mile away. "I'm sorry, dear. I promise that I will never switch off my phone again when working away from home."

"That's all right, I forgive you this time. It's just that you will now be the sixth person to know and I wanted you to be the first," she says with the widest grin that I have ever seen on anyone!

"First to know what honey?" I ask with eager anticipation.

"Guess?"

"You've sold the film rights to *Four Seasons*."

"Better," she says, still maintaining her grin.

"It can't be…" I pause, not wanting to get this wrong.

"It is," she replies confidently reading my mind.

"You're pregnant?"

"Yes!" she shouts. "You're going to be a father." I am going to be a father. I am going to be responsible for another human being who is going to call me "Daddy". We hug each other in celebration at what is to come.

"How did you find out?" I ask.

"Well, as you know I had been feeling ill a lot recently. So this morning, or should I say yesterday morning, now, I took a pregnancy test and it came up positive, but because I, we," she corrects, "had had so many disappointments, I didn't want to say anything until I knew for sure. So, tonight, I just couldn't wait until Monday morning and so I rang Doctor Weatherspoon and told him how I was feeling and he agreed to come over right away. He came over and carried out all these tests and each one showed that I was pregnant. I think Doctor Weatherspoon was more elated than I was. He was telling me that he can think of nothing worse than having to tell a woman that her body had not responded well to her fertility treatment and that she is, therefore, unlikely to have children."

"You said that I was the sixth to know, who else have you told?"

"Well, besides me, of course, obviously Doctor Weatherspoon knows, I rang Mum and Dad, they were over the moon at the prospect of having their first grandchild and, of course, Jo and Donna." Gosh! That reminds me, I've got to speak to Donna about Sydney. I guess I should tell Pat about my meeting with Sydney, but I would have to think this one through thoroughly before I even begin to open my mouth. Mind you the state Pat is in at the moment, I think that I could tell her almost anything and it probably wouldn't even register but I don't think that it would be wise to take that risk.

"We should start looking for a new property," I command. After all, we can afford it. Pat is a best-selling novelist and I am about to become a very wealthy lawyer.

"Yes, I thought about that. I plan to go round to the Estate Agents on Monday and find out what is on the market. I want a house with a nice big garden that our child can run around and play in. This has got to be the happiest day of my life. Nothing can compare to how I feel at this moment. I have got everything I want. I have a wonderful career, I am about to have our first baby and, most important of all, I have the best husband any woman could ever wish for." If guilt isn't written all over my face then maybe I'm in the wrong profession; I should be an actor. The "best husband" that is cheating on his wife. "And you know what?" continues Pat. "You have been just wonderful throughout this period. I know that it hasn't been easy for you being around me over these past few weeks. I have been feeling low and you have been very busy, but you have always been there for me, and that has meant so much."

"I'm your husband, what did you expect?" is all I can say.

"That doesn't count for much these days as you probably know. And I hope that you're not going to chase some woman as my belly swells. God alone knows what Donna was going through when Dexter was making those horrible remarks about her."

To think that only a few minutes ago I was thinking of going back to Linda's place for a short while, and only an hour or so ago I was with the woman. I have been praised by my wife under false pretences. I did not earn them. I do not deserve them. I must end my relationship with Linda. She will understand but it won't be easy. My head is saying end it tomorrow, but my heart and my body is saying "no, wait a while." I know which makes sense but I can't just simply move in and move out of someone's life no matter what the original intention. And, although I know that Linda will understand, she will be just as hurt as I am. But, in reality where can Linda and I take our relationship? What is it built on? I'm a married man, she is a single woman. From that alone, there is that gulf between us that can't be easily bridged. Strangely enough, things might not have been too bad if Linda was still with Wilson. In that way, it wouldn't be just me who is doing the cheating. I know what I'll do. I'll give myself until Pat starts to show around the tummy before I start to wind down my affair with Linda. I would feel twice as bad if I were to sleep with Linda while Pat was showing clear signs of pregnancy. Paris now sounds like a very good idea.

"I think we should have that Paris break you mentioned some time ago," I say. "I may have a space in my diary in a few weeks' time. I should know by next week." Hopefully, Linda will know if Sydney can do anything for her.

"That would be so romantic," replies Pat. "I shall contact my agent as soon as you give me the dates." I would have a one and final romantic weekend with Linda and then we can call it a day. I am one lucky man. Not only do I have my wife and girlfriend with me in London, I get to go on holiday with both at the same time also.

"I look forward to it very much, dear. I really do," says Pat.

What a night! After so much excitement we fell asleep in the early hours of the morning. I admit that I hadn't been nearly as excited as Pat about having a child. I love children, so I think my only explanation for my relaxed mood was that I could see what it was doing to Pat and I didn't want to add to her anxiety. I shall be the best father any child can have. I shall do all the things with my child that my father didn't even think of doing with me. I feel a sadness come over me as I think of my mother, who will not be here with us in person to see her first grandchild, but I know she is with me in spirit. I slept for a while before being awakened by that dream again. Fortunately, I awoke without awakening Pat and put this recent episode down to my mind rehearsing Pat's trouble in finding me tonight. I turned to Pat and whispered "goodnight" to mother and child and could swear I heard someone say "goodnight Daddy". Maybe my mind was playing tricks on me but just in case it wasn't I replied "goodnight my child and sleep well."

Donna

"Donna, long time no see."

"My God, Sydney. What are you doing here?" I ask, stunned, shocked, everything. It must be over six years since I last saw this man. "Who gave you my address?"

"To answer both your questions, I have obviously come to see you and I have known where you lived since the time you've been living here," he replies, in that usually cool and relaxed manner.

"I was just on my way out to collect Dionne from my parents. Are you going to be in the area for very long?"

"Like I said, Don, I have come here to see you, so you take all the time you need. I will still be here when you come back." That might not be such a good idea because Dexter should be home at any minute now and although Dexter would not think twice about inviting an ex-girlfriend into our home, I have more respect for my partner, deservedly or otherwise.

"I shall call my parents instead, and tell them that I'll be late. We can go for a coffee if you like."

"I would love to but I'm in no hurry, so please don't let me disrupt your plans too much."

"It's not a problem," I reply. I hadn't appreciated how dark he was, especially when compared to Dexter. He is still as handsome as when I last saw him and he looks manlier too. He's lost some of his boyish looks; there is definitely an air of maturity about him. Actually, this could be the way he was all the time but, when you've been with a boy for the past few years, any man who remotely acts his age would seem mature to me. "This is such a coincidence," I continue. "It was just the other day that I was chatting to Rupert, Patricia Jackson's husband, do you remember them?"

"I remember them very well," he replies.

"And your name came up in the conversation," I continue. "I can't remember why, but I do recall thinking, how odd it was, because it was Rupert who mentioned your name out of the blue. I didn't think that he had known you that well, let alone bring your name into a conversation. Oh yes, that was it. He said that he had seen your picture in some magazine. I have never seen Rupert near a magazine let alone read one. Anyhow, when I begged him to show it to me so that I could see how you looked, he told me that he had misplaced it and, strangely, couldn't remember its name. I was so disappointed, because I really wanted to see your picture."

"And, here I am today, in person, as if by fate," says Sydney charmingly.

"Yes, Rupert told me that he thought you might be in the fashion industry."

"That's all he said?" asks Sydney.

"Yes," I reply. "Why, should he have said more?" Sydney seems to think about my question for a while.

"No, not necessarily. It's just that I too saw the article and I would have thought that it was obvious what line of business I was in," replies Sydney, in a manner which suggests that his mind is racing far ahead of his speech.

"So what is it that you do?"

"I run a modelling agency."

"Oh I see. You have all these beautiful women at your disposal, do you?"

"No, not quite," he replies, smiling as if there might be some truth in my statement. If there is, then this is a side of Sydney that is post me, because he was definitely no Dexter on that front. I think back to when we were a lot younger. I really loved this man. I realised that even more after our separation. This was no infatuation, this was the real thing. When we were together I could not have envisaged us ever being apart. We were that close. We relied so much on each other. We did almost everything together and experienced many things for the first time together. It was like neither of us would want to do something without the other being there. It didn't feel right explaining what you did or where you went, when the other had neither done it nor been there. You felt as though you had cheated by having an experience that should have been shared by both. Some people, I know, will find this lifestyle invading their space. I needn't mention any names. But we didn't mind because we weren't going out looking for partners, so we were content with only going out with each other. When we separated, it took months for me to get even remotely close to another man. There were a few prospective candidates, if I could put it that way, but they were around at the wrong time. A few years later and maybe they might have had a chance, but, at that time, I just didn't want to know. I guess at that time there was still a hope that Sydney and I would get back together. I was hoping that we would have bumped into each other shortly after our separation and that we would have got back together. I knew that he would also have shared my gloominess. I definitely wasn't experiencing that feeling alone. But, as time went by, reality crept in and it became clear to me that my wishes were not likely to come true. Even then, if it wasn't for Dexter's good looks I don't think that I would have got involved with a man so soon after my break from Sydney.

As we make our way to our table, I can see that Sydney has kept his body in good shape. He was a keen athlete when we were together and used to call for me early on a Sunday morning to join him for a run. I used to hate it. For months I would envy my friends for having normal boyfriends who liked to lay in bed on a Sunday morning and read the newspapers. "It's good for your lungs" he would always say. It seems silly now, but that saying became our little private joke that would be used at every given opportunity, relevant or not. Others around us could never quite get the punch line; this made our joke all the much funnier. Those days were fun.

"Don't tell me," orders Sydney. "Coffee, white with one sugar," he says confidently, as our waitress approaches our table.

"Close but without the sugar," I reply, correcting him. "How do you think I keep this figure?" We laugh, as if it were only yesterday that we were together. I always found it quite amazing how well we got on together. I'm not one for easy romance. My record with men could vouch for that! But I have always had this belief, even today, that Sydney and I were each other's ideal partner. "Every bread has its cheese" my grandmother would often say to me when I could never figure out how some people found themselves partners. I remember thinking, when Sydney and I were together, that no one could walk in and take the other away. I have always been a woman of logic, probably too logical for the complexities of today's world. But, I was of the belief that for Sydney to have ended our relationship for another person, then that other person would have had to have been better than me. And as humans are selfish beings by nature, they are unlikely to choose helpmates who are less suitable than their ideal partners whom they already have. I sought comfort in this thought, in the belief that I could never be replaced. After all, I was his ideal partner! However, life has since taught me that you can't apply logic to everything and expect a logically reasoned answer. It's all a matter of one's perception. What appears to you as better than what you already have, may be seen by others to be quite the opposite. But, like I said, it's all about our perception and sometimes we get it right but most times I think we get it wrong. I can hear Pat and Jo say, "here, here" to that. No prizes for guessing who they would have in mind!

"You're looking as well as ever," says Sydney.

"And I see that you've kept yourself in good shape. Do you still train?"

"Yes. However, I don't run as often as I would like. Do you remember those times when we used to go running together?"

"How could I forget!" I reply.

"It's good for your lungs," we both say in chorus, as if conducted by a maestro. We laugh at our childish attempts to rekindle a youth that is no longer relevant in either of our lives today.

"It's good to see you again, Donna," he adds, after what seemed like a period of reflection. "And it's nice to see that you still have that good old sense of humour that I used to love so much."

"You know, I never thought that I would ever see you again," I say. "I would sometimes think about you and wonder what you were doing with yourself. I was so curious to know how your life panned out. Were you married? How many children do you have? All these questions would often run through my mind. It was so frustrating having all these questions and not having anyone around to provide the answers."

"I always had a general idea of what you were up to. I knew, for example, when you and Dexter moved into your flat and when you moved out and went back to your parents."

"And you knew when we had Dionne?"

"Of course," he replies, confidently, as if to say "ask more challenging questions than that!"

"How did you know so much about me?" I ask, in wonderment that someone could be monitoring my every move and I am totally oblivious to it.

"Now, that would be telling," he replies with that same mischievous smile I had got to know so well.

"So you've made me wait all this time without telling me. Are you married and do you have any children?"

"I'm divorced and I have one child, Sabrina. The mother, Katherine, and I are the very best of friends and there is not an ounce of animosity between us. Sabrina lives primarily with me but her mother comes and takes her at any time and sees her whenever she likes."

Even after all this time, not to mention all that I have gone through in my own life, I felt a little jealous to know that Sydney had found someone whom he felt he could marry, have a child with and call his best friend. Hearing Sydney talk about his ex-wife and child makes me feel that, in the same period that we have been apart, I hadn't really progressed. This saddens me. There was no way, for example, that I could refer to Dexter as my best friend and be taken seriously!

"If you and your ex-wife get on so well, then why did you two divorce?"

"Good question. We were best friends long before we got married and I think that, because we were so close, we naturally became intimate over time. We were both single. By that I mean that neither of us were in a relationship and by that time, I was mature enough to make my own decisions on whom I should be with, so we decided, after a relatively short time of actually going out with each other, that we would get married. Shortly after, Sabrina was born."

"You were mature enough to make your own decisions, but

you had no further interests in me so you decided not to come looking for me," I say, as boldly as I can and mean every word.

"Are you asking me or telling me?" replies Sydney. That was a saying of his that I used to find irritating, because, most times, he was right to ask the question.

"Both!" I reply. "After all, your informant would have told you where I was, surely!"

"You're quite right, my informer, to use your terms, did tell me where you were and who you were with. Need I say more?" Dexter, the bane of my life!

"So what went wrong?" I ask, ignoring his question.

"Nothing went wrong, we just both realised that we treasured each other more as best friends rather than as lovers and so decided, quite amicably, to have a divorce and continue that good friendship. It was really as simple as that. You wouldn't believe how well we get on. She is like a sister and a friend to me. She is very special."

"You mean like how I used to be to you?"

"No, not like that at all," he replies. "No one would or could ever replace you in my life. What we had was both special and unique at an important time of our development. No one can take that away nor replace it. Those moments will remain with me for ever. If we were as strong in character as our love was for each other, then we wouldn't have parted. And I believe that we would still have been together today. I just could not see what could have been so strong outside our own families that could have pushed us apart. But, what it all boils down to is that we were young and we just did not have the might to fight for what we really wanted. I can remember the day that we broke up as if it were only yesterday."

"That was, until then, the saddest day of my life," I say, keeping to the theme.

"That is the saddest day of my life, period!" replies Sydney. We make eye contact following his remark but make no further comment. I knew that he would have made such a remark at some time or another, if only to test my reaction. Like I said, I know him well. What I don't know, however, is why has he come to see me after all this time. By his own admissions, he knows what I've been up to, so why come and see me now?

"You say that you've been aware of what I've been up to, so you obviously know that I'm back with Dexter."

"What!" replies Sydney, "Tell me that you're joking." Ah! So that is it.

"No, I'm not," I reply. "Your source of information is obviously not very reliable – slipping, by the sound of things," I say in amusement.

"After all that he has done to you and I probably don't even know the half of it, you still go back to him?" I feel embarrassed as Sydney recites what has already been said by Pat, Jo and many others. They too couldn't believe it when I told them that Dionne and I had gone back to Dexter. I felt bad then, but I know that my girlfriends will always stick by me through thick and thin, come rain or sunshine. Such support is not dependent upon their approval of any decisions I may take; decisions that I have to live with rightly or wrongly! As my grandmother used to often say, "So I make my bed, so I lie in it." Simple words of wisdom, but all so true.

"I know that it might seem like a bad decision and only time will tell if it was or wasn't, but you would have had to have been there that night when he came round to ask me back to understand why I decided the way I did." I could see that Sydney was bewildered by my compassion. But surely he couldn't have expected to come here after all these years and expect me to be awaiting him. That would be ridiculous! So I am totally bemused by his reaction.

"I'm sorry Don, I shouldn't have reacted the way that I did. I told you about Katherine and Sabrina and you barely questioned my wisdom behind the whole affair, so I shouldn't question yours with Dexter. Just answer this one question. Are you happy?" If anybody other than my girlfriends had asked me that question, I would have told them only what I wanted them to hear, true or false. But, even after all these years, I still feel obligated to Sydney to be truthful or, if not the same thing, not to lie.

"I'm probably no happier than I was before Dexter asked me back but it would have taken him some courage to do what he did just for me."

"I don't follow, Don. What did he do for you but cause you unnecessary grief?" asks Sydney who was clearly unhappy at what I was saying, and quite frankly for him to feel this way after not setting eyes on me for over six years is most peculiar. "Sorry," he says after some deliberation, "I said that I wouldn't talk like that. I apologise." After hearing him speak this way, I think that I should, at least, set the record straight, because something is clearly not adding up.

"Maybe I should go through the story and then maybe you might be a little more understanding, or, at least, know where I'm coming from. I take it that you know that Dexter was seeing some woman when I moved out of the flat?"

"He was seeing some woman, as you put it, before you left the flat."

"My oh my, you really did know what was going on. It's frightening to think that there is some Peeping Tom out there who is watching my every move and I haven't got a clue who he is. Is he watching us now?"

"No, he is not," replies Sydney. "Trust me, it is not as seedy as it may appear."

"In an odd way, it's kind of flattering that you went through all that trouble but you do hear of these stories about stalking by all kinds of strange people. Anyway, back to what I was saying. Presumably, you know that this woman's name was Chantelle."

"I do."

"Now, why doesn't that surprise me? And you know that Chantelle went away on a modelling contract."

"I do. To the Seychelles, in case you didn't know where she went." This is amazing. I'm pleased that I didn't even try to lie to Sydney, otherwise he would have seen right through me and I would have felt guilty at such an attempt.

"Well, during this time Dexter had decided that he would ask Chantelle to marry him. This I know to be true because he had broadcast it to everyone at the time, but me!" I thought that I should confirm the parts that I can in order to spare Sydney the effort of even attempting to contradict it. "Dexter later had second thoughts about marrying..."

"Second thoughts?" he interrupts.

"Hold on, let me finish," I say. "He had second thoughts when he realised that what he really wanted was Dionne and me back into his life, so he ended his relationship with Chantelle and pleaded for our return." As I went through what happened I could see Sydney metamorphose from a confused person to someone who was clearly ill-informed. He looked as though he was about to erupt! It seems like his informant failed to relay that vital piece of information to him.

"Is that what he told you?" asks Sydney with clear annoyance in his voice. I know he could be adamant sometimes, but I think that he was probably taking this a little too far.

"What do you mean is that what he told me? That is exactly what happened." I think Sydney could detect my irritation and so he should, because I wasn't trying to hide it! "There was only Dexter and myself who were party to our conversation which took place in my room. I don't think that even your spy could have eavesdropped on that one."

"I'm not talking about listening in on your conversation, I'm talking about Dexter's version of events of what took place between himself and Chantelle."

"And how would you know the correct version?" I ask in jest.

"Because Chantelle and I are the best of friends." I almost spilled my hot coffee onto Sydney's lap as these words left his mouth.

"I can't believe what you just said," I reply, completely and utterly shocked.

"I have known Chantelle for many years. She even works for my agency."

"So she was your spy," I say, still dumbstruck.

"Not entirely. I knew what was going on long before she started seeing Dexter."

"You say Chantelle and you are the best of friends. I thought Katherine and you were the best of friends. How many best friends do you have? And who's to say that Chantelle isn't the one who is lying, just to get back at me!" Sydney seemed to be offended by my attack on Chantelle, but this whole affair was becoming more and more bizarre by the minute. First I have someone watching my every move and next the news that my fiancé was dating my ex-boyfriend's best friend! What the hell is going on?

"Both Chantelle and Katherine are dear to me," confirms Sydney. "And, to answer your question, I don't know if Chantelle told me the truth, I just believe that she did." If Sydney hasn't changed, I know this to be his way of not wanting to say anymore about Chantelle but I am not letting this one lie. I may never see him again and may never get to know things that I clearly should.

"You know more about this affair than you're letting on, don't you?"

"I don't want to hurt you anymore than you've been hurt already but I must tell you what I was told and believe to be the truth. You can then make up your own mind, after you've heard what I've got to say."

"Why do I think that I'm not going to enjoy this?" I ask, but Sydney just continues.

"When Chantelle came back from her modelling contract in the Seychelles, she went to stay with Dexter for the night. In fact, I dropped her there myself, as I had gone to the Seychelles with her in order to see that everything went smoothly with my new client. Actually, the pictures Rupert saw of me were probably from the launch party of his magazine. The following day, after dropping Chantelle off by Dexter, she rang me and asked whether she could stay with me and Sabrina, which is where she is now, as Dexter had asked her to move out of the flat after she turned down his proposal of marriage."

I listened to Sydney intently without muttering a single word. I am annoyed with myself at my apparent gullibility and wish, oddly, that he could both be right whilst at the same time be wrong. At least with the latter my dignity, whatever is left of it, would still remain intact.

"How do I know whether you are telling me the truth?" I ask, as the nightmare begins to unfold.

"I thought you knew me better than to ask such a question of me," replies Sydney, seemingly hurt by my apparent disbelief in what was being revealed to me for the first time. "Like I said before, I've told you only what I know and believe to be the truth. The ball is now in your court, you can make up your own mind on the matter."

"That bastard!" I shout. I knew that there was something fishy about all this change of mind lark, but I couldn't think that even Dexter would have stooped that low. Then again, why shouldn't he have done? I fell for it just like the mug I am. I could feel the fury building up inside me. Lord knows that I've been as patient as anyone can, but now my patience has worn thin. Now is the time to put an end to this man once and for all. "I'm ready to go," I say to Sydney.

"Donna, don't do anything that you might live to regret."

"Oh, I won't regret this at all. I should have done this a long time ago." I'm furious. Well Dexter has taken this fool for one ride too many. Tonight he will see a side of me he never knew exists. Tonight, Dexter is history!

Sydney and I swapped telephone numbers before we parted, although I'm sure that he was only going through the motions, as he probably already had my number penned in his diary in any case. I went by my parents to collect Dionne but thought it better that she spend the night with her grandparents. I told them all about my time with Sydney and what he had to say about Dexter. They were shocked to know that Dexter could have done what he did. They had no doubt however that what Sydney had said was the truth of the matter. Like Pat and Jo, my parents warned me against going back to Dexter, but not even they professed to have expected this. My parents admitted to being pleased that Sydney had come round to see me. This surprised me but nowhere near as much as their confession that they had got things wrong. They apologised for how they had acted during our time together. Obviously I forgave them and couldn't help wondering what could have been, had we been left to do our own thing. That, I shall never know. Anyway, that was in the past and I have more immediate matters to deal with in the present. So much has been going through my mind, I couldn't tell you how I got home or what route I took. My mind was focused purely on my encounter to come. I could see that Dexter's car was in its parking bay where it seems to spend much of its time these days, since he has no Chantelle with whom to party with every night. I open the front door and could hear the Crusaders playing on the compact-disc player. Dexter was sitting on the sofa and was reading some papers.

"Hi Donna, you're late. Where is Dionne?" he asks, as he gives a brief glance in my direction.

"I'm giving you ten minutes to pack your bags and leave," I say. I'm in no mood to mince my words tonight. I've had enough.

"Sorry?" asks Dexter, who was clearly stunned by my opening command.

"If you don't pack your things and leave within ten minutes, then I shall pack them for you and throw them out into the street. And then, I shall throw your arse out into the street after them. The choice is yours. I don't mind either way." Dexter was clearly puzzled by my outburst and seemed not quite sure what to say. And this is the man who could usually talk the underwear off most women! Well, his charm has deserted him tonight, probably at a time when he needs it most.

"Donna, I don't understand. What has come over you? You look like a demon possessed."

"You'll probably wish that a demon possessed was all you had to concern yourself with," I reply, surprisingly calm, but my eyes do not leave his, save to blink. I see that he is rattled and can't believe what's hit him. It's nice to see him lost for words for a change.

"Donna, can you tell me what is going on?" he pleads.

"I'll tell you what is going on. I met a very close friend of Chantelle's, today, who gave me a different version of what happened that day between you two."

"What day?" asks Dexter, blatantly trying to buy time.

"Don't play the fool with me Dexter. You know damn well what day I'm talking about, but let me remind you in any case. The day when you asked her to leave the flat because you suddenly decided that you wanted me back. I can't believe that I actually believed your crap. Do you want to put your case forward, as they say in your profession, or are you going to spare me the trouble of hearing your lies."

"Donna, I don't know what you've been told but you've got to understand that Chantelle is a bitter woman. She even threatened to get her own back that very said day. She told me that she was going to get a friend of hers to contact you and ruin me. I was going to tell you, but I wanted to deal with it by myself, so as not to trouble you with this bitter and demented woman. Also, she would have heard from someone that I was going to propose to her. My only failing is that I told everyone first that I was going to ask her, so it wouldn't surprise me if someone out there told her what was to come. As it didn't happen, she is simply seeking revenge. Surely you can see that?"

"You seem hell-bent on convincing me that her version should not be believed, without even knowing what it was she said. I thought that you lawyers always believed in hearing the case against you and yet you seem not to want to know. Why is that?"

"Because I know that Chantelle would say anything in order to destroy my happy life with my fiancée and my child." Dexter was on the ropes and it was embarrassing. Here is a man who for many years, I thought could defend himself against any accusation, but tonight my shots are landing him square on the chin. I've caught him with his guard down and can see that unless he makes a miraculous comeback, he is heading for the canvas.

"You know what I think?" I ask, hounding him whilst he's on the ropes, giving him little time to collect his thoughts, "I think that you know exactly what was said to me about that day, because you know that what I was told was the truth. You've now got nine minutes, in order to sort yourself out and the clock is ticking away." I don't know where I've got this strength from but I feel solid. No bullshit from Dexter tonight could let him off the hook. And I swear by the Almighty God that if he so much as thinks that he could try and bluff his way out of this, I shall simply throw his belongings out of the window. And this time, I stay!

"You're making a big mistake, Donna. I asked for you back because I believe that a father should be with his child. I know you do too."

"Don't try and patronise me Dexter!"

"I'm not trying to patronise you. But, even if we can't work things out between us, I do think that we should at least remain together for a while for the sake of Dionne."

"When have you really cared what is right for Dionne? When you were seeing Chantelle you never so much as gave me a call to find out how Dionne was, and you expect me to believe this shit that you're coming out with. Pull the other one, Dexter, it has bells on. And, in any case, if you really think that I am going to remain with a vulture like you, who is a liar and cheat, for the sake of my daughter, whom I am perfectly capable of bringing up on my own, then you have another thing coming. You've taken me for a fool once too often and now your time is up. The clock is ticking away."

"I think if anyone should leave, then it should be you. You're the one who wants me out of the way, so why should I leave?"

"Don't try my patience, Dexter. I've told you, you're leaving tonight if I have to physically throw you out myself. You've often told me how big I am, well you will soon feel the full might of that weight tonight if you don't get out of here of your own accord. And, you're the lawyer, I thought that you'd know better. I have a young child to raise on my own. Who do you think the courts will order to leave?" This seems to have done the trick, as Dexter hurries from the sofa and checks his watch. I pour myself a sherry, relax on the sofa and reflect on a job well done. With two minutes to spare, I heard him shout out "bitch!", presumably calling one of his women, and slam the front door behind him. Moments later I heard the raucous sound of his car engine start and fade away. I made no attempt to ask him where he was going nor did I care. All I wanted was to get rid of him. Finally get him out of my life for good! I rang Pat and told her about the day's events and what I had done to Dexter. She did nothing but congratulate me on my efforts. I tried to stop her coming round tonight with Jo. But she was having none of it. To be honest, I would have been surprised if Pat had suggested otherwise. She couldn't believe how calm I was after such an eventful evening. I was feeling just fine. I can't believe what I have done and how easy it was. After all this time, I was with a wimp who had nothing but big talk. I was expecting more of a resistance than what I met, but I knew, no matter what Dexter threw at me tonight, I would have more to throw back. It just goes to show what we can achieve when we put our mind to it. Before Pat and

Jo arrive I think that I should give Sydney a call to let him know of the price of his visit. And although I am pretty certain that Dexter had lied to me, there is always that niggling doubt at the back of my mind that maybe Chantelle had not been entirely truthful either. After all, it is only natural that she would be a bitter woman for having to leave the flat when she did. And what does Chantelle owe to Sydney that she had to tell him the truth? It's pointless having all these doubtful thoughts after the event, but it is possible that Sydney may have got it wrong. I may have been too premature in throwing Dexter out. I was uncharacteristically ruthless. I didn't recognise that person in me. In fact, it wasn't me at all. I decided to call Sydney. Fortunately, he answered the telephone as I was in no mood to speak to Chantelle.

"Hello Sydney. I thought that I would tell you how tonight went before your spy reports to you. I have kicked Dexter out of the flat and I have started a new chapter in my life." I could hear a sigh of relief from Sydney as I gave him the news.

"I think that you have done the right thing, Don. You deserve a lot better," he says.

"And," I say, so as to set the record straight for whatever Sydney may have in mind, "as from tonight, any man who comes into my life will have to do so on my terms, and my terms only." Sydney remains silent and just listens to what I have to say. "I've had enough of pleasing other people at the expense of my own pleasure. Well that is no more. It's about time that I was a bit more selfish. What has been done tonight, has been done, but I hope that Chantelle wasn't stringing you along."

"No, she wasn't stringing me along, she wouldn't do that to me," he replies.

"I don't understand, Sydney. How can you be so sure that she is telling you the truth?"

"Because," says Sydney, after much hesitation, "Chantelle's real name is Katherine. Chantelle is just her modelling name."

"You mean to say…"

"…Yes," Sydney replies, reading my mind, "Chantelle is the mother of Sabrina. She used to be my wife!"

Josephine

Isn't it ironic? Dexter begged for Don to "come back home" only for Don to kick him out of the very said home that he had asked her to come back to! I didn't even know what Don had done until Pat told me whilst we were making our way over to Don's place on that night. You could have sensed the relief in Don's voice when we arrived. It was as if a great weight had been finally lifted off her shoulders. That night turned out to be quite a party, as we helped Don put the rest of Dexter's belongings into numerous plastic bin bags. She gave him seven days in his absence, to return and remove what he had left behind. If he hadn't returned by the due time, then all his remnants would be kindly denoted to charity. I'm not aware that that return had taken place, so I can only assume that some charity has had an early Christmas. And give him his dues, he had good taste in clothes. Anything else that had a shred of Dexter was disinfected, put in a bag for him to collect or simply thrown away. Not surprisingly, most were thrown away! Donna wanted neither trace nor scent of him. When she said that she wanted no more to do with him, that is exactly what she meant. Pat and I stayed the night at Don's place. We spoke about everything; Pat's baby, my business plan and about Sydney. But that night rightly belonged to Don, as one sad chapter ended and a happy one was about to begin. Welcome back girl, it's been long overdue.

I have always believed that, every once in a while, an opportunity passes one's way which must be taken there and then, or it will be lost for ever or taken by a competitor, to one's detriment. There have been numerous signs recently which tell me that my time has arrived, and if I don't grab my opportunity now, then I might never get another. For example, I have never got anything worthwhile from any man whom I had not at some time had some form of relationship. And I don't mean just as friends! Yet, this was not the case with Earl. Okay, I admit that was not my original intention but, I think, that only goes to support what I'm trying to say nonetheless. There is always some man, somewhere, who wants to give you more than just a free lunch! So, why should Earl be different? I'll tell you why, because Earl was sent to me for a purpose and that purpose was to deliver me the plan that would make my business better. Now, I could have taken his plan and thrown it away or I could have built upon it. The former had crossed my mind but I'm glad to say that my girlfriends made me see sense. One may still see my brief encounter with Earl as nothing more than just a meeting, but then the next thing happened. I went to see my bank manager and told him of my plan to hold numerous fashion shows around Europe. He was ecstatic by the idea. He kept telling me how he wanted to make that one special loan before he retires, so that he could go out with a bang. He gave me all that I wanted. Such vibes would normally be enough to tell someone that something big was about to happen, but not me. I wanted clearer signs, before my doubts could be completely eliminated. That bombshell was yet to come: Mister Sydney Charles. Everyone in the fashion industry has heard of Sydney. I have never met him but then there was no reason why I should have. So, when Don told me that "her" Sydney was "that" Sydney I nearly wet myself. Many British designers are fighting for a place on The Best of British Fashion show and my girlfriend used to go out with the man with all the right connections. In other words, Sydney can get me a slot in that show. A show that would have the eyes of the world gazing at what Britain has to offer. And, more importantly, my designs will be in a show with the appropriate superlative, the "best". Another show would not be suitable and could, in fact, give out the wrong signals. For if my designs are not of the best then what are they? Don has kindly arranged for us to meet Sydney tonight. He is undoubtedly a very busy man but still he agreed to meet Don and me at such short notice. I wonder whose using who here!

I could see why Pat liked Sydney and abhorred Dexter. To put it in a nutshell, Sydney is a gentleman and Dexter is a pig. They are that different. I'm not usually in the business of comparing one's partners but you do have to ask yourself how on earth Don got so serious with Dexter after being with someone like Sydney. Sydney is dining with us two women and he is giving us his undivided attention. Dexter would have been giving us his attention all right along with the other female diners in restaurant. With Dexter, he was never quite content with what he had. He always wanted more; that maybe suitable for some things, but not everything. And definitely not with women! You could tell that Sydney was of the Old School. You know the type that would open a door for a lady. I wouldn't mind Sydney for myself. Forget my prejudices. Forget Earl. This is a gentleman. But something tells me that I might be stepping on my girlfriend's toes and obviously that will not do. In any case, I would bet my bottom dollar that these two would be back together at some time or another. You wouldn't believe that these two hadn't seen each other in over six years, they just seem to compliment each other so well.

I told Sydney about my plans. He seemed interested but not nearly as much as he was in making up for the past few years he had been living without Donna.

"So Sydney, what can you do for Jo?" asks Don.

"Let me have a look at the designs and I shall be in touch," says Sydney facing me.

"I don't know if your spy informs you of other matters outside your immediate concern, but Jo is one of my closest girlfriends and I would be happy if you did your best for her," replies Don. Her remark about a spy went completely over my head, but meant something to my co-diners. And, as making Don "happy" is probably top priority on Sydney's list at the moment, I know that I have a better than fair chance of getting what I wanted.

"I understand what you're saying, Don, I shall do the best I can."

"No," says Don, "you will do better." This remark didn't go over my head. We both knew what she meant.

A few days after my meeting with Sydney, I got a letter from the organising body of The Best of British Fashion saying that they liked my designs and would be pleased if I would accept their invitation to join them in their expedition to Paris in order to market the best that Britain has to offer. Obviously, I wasted no time in accepting this offer. I rang my bank manager to cancel my loan. I was in no mood to place myself in unnecessary debt. He seemed disappointed. My fashion shows will be paid for by the sponsors of the shows. All I have to do is perform. I will be paid to promote my work. Like I said, these opportunities come around only once in a lifetime and you let them pass at your peril. I also rang Sydney to tell him of the good news and got the impression that he already knew, but he congratulated me all the same and said, from what he saw, I would be a success. Hearing him say this, only inspired me more. He also informed me that he had recently viewed the portfolio of a talented photographer who was looking for a designer to associate himself with, and would I mind if he gave him my details. Obviously I gave my permission. I have never had my own personal photographer before. It is beginning to dawn on me how big this event will be and I will be part of it. I am now in the big league and competition will undoubtedly be fierce. Now was the time to start my new collection for the show. I want to be the best of The Best of British Fashion. After all, this show is a means to an end, not the end itself. I want my designs to be the talk of the town. People will know who I am when the shows are over. I rang Don to tell her of my offer. She was elated and told me that she would see to it personally that Sydney be rewarded for his efforts. I didn't think it in my place to enquire as to what such reward would entail.

I couldn't have asked for more from my staff. Everyone has rolled up their sleeves and helped out, irrespective of the hours or of their respective specialities. I've got my materials' buyer, cutter and machinist working round the clock. They know that if I succeed then they do also. I know that I can't do what I am doing without them. And, furthermore, I make it my duty to remind them of that fact. I am the first among equals, only by the nature of the fact that I own the company. Besides that fact, we are all the same. The staff are my team which I am taking to Paris with me. They deserve this trip just as much as I do. Tonight, we have a private viewing of some of the designs at the local school of modelling. This will give us a chance to see what type of materials and colours suit certain designs. And, of course, it gives the models an opportunity to practise their catwalk, before they hit the big time. My photographer for Paris promised me that he would be here tonight. I haven't seen his work as yet, but I thought what better work for me to see than photographs of my designs. But, having said that, if he's all right for Sydney then he must surely be all right for me. I was talking to a model who had convinced herself that she was obese when I heard a callout for me. My photographer had arrived. I could see this clean-shaven-headed man chatting to my cutter.

"You must be Leon," I say. I suppose the cameras around his neck are a bit of a give-away. He looks no older than about nineteen, and must be well over six feet tall. He looks like he would be more at home on a basketball court than as a photographer at a fashion show.

"I am," he replies. "And you must be Josephine."

"I am," I reply, as I look to see whether Leon is the kind of man that I could work with. For some strange reason, I work better with ugly men. Don't ask me why, that's just the way things have always worked out. Starting from head to toe, Leon's face is clean-shaven but he has a moustache which is vaguely visible to the naked eye. He is lean but not skinny. He's wearing a black open-neck T-shirt, tight denim jeans – very tight denim jeans – and black boots. Is he ugly? No, but I'll give him a chance in any case. I can't deprive the man of a break because he's handsome. "I'll leave you to set up your equipment and we can discuss what you think about the show a little later on." I leave Leon to do his thing, whilst I attend to the models. Those jeans are far too tight for the young man!

The show was a success. We are not quite there yet, but we are not too far off. I think that we need another two weeks and we'll be ready. I was impressed with Leon's enthusiasm. He was every-where. He must have gone through at least four rolls of film between his two cameras and he's not even getting paid for tonight. I can't wait to see the prints, as I didn't catch as much of the show as, maybe, I should have. My attention was somewhat distracted by the hard work of the young man. I'm sorry, but those jeans are far too tight! I want the women to be concentrating on my dresses not his butt! The man has a bum like a peach! On reflection, I'm sure we can work together, for I like a young man with that kind of energy and passion for his work. I'll take him out for a meal tonight, as a "thank you" for his kind efforts and maybe we can start making plans for Paris. Like I said, when opportunities come along you should grab them with both hands!

The team and I all went for a Chinese meal, as our "after show" dinner. We decided against inviting the models on the grounds that we all fancied more than just carrots and lettuce. I thought it only proper to invite Leon, as he had worked extremely hard tonight, and it would give me a chance to find out a little more about my photographer.

"Ladies and gentlemen," I announce, "first, I would like to thank everyone for their contributions and hard work of the past few weeks while we prepared for tonight's show. I think that you will all agree with me that the show was a resounding success." Virginia, our materials' buyer, led the chorus of applause, to the annoyance of the other diners. "But," I continue, "we have the big one to prepare for, so the hard work doesn't end here. If anything, it has only just begun. Also, I would like to make just one final announcement, as I can see that many of you can't wait to start eating, but I would like to take this opportunity of welcoming a new member on board for our team for Paris, Leon, who is a photographer and comes personally recommended by Sydney Charles, so he must be good." Leon acknowledges the numerous greetings that welcome him to our party. I had insisted that Leon sit next to me, as I was the only person that he knew, albeit not for very long. I could also see that one or two of my female staff were giving him that look that I know only too well. I need to keep my team focussed on the job in hand, so any extraneous thoughts must be kept to a minimum. Also, such thoughts can hinder creative thinking, which is not what I need at this moment in time.

"I apologise if I jumped the gun tonight but I hope that you will join our team," I turn and say to Leon as it had occurred to me, when I made the announcement, that I had not formally made him an offer for him to accept.

"That's all right," he replies. "From what I've seen tonight, your collection is going to be a big hit at the shows. I don't think there can be any serious doubt about that, so it is an honour to be invited on board. And, of course, I accept. I shall let the organisers know that I am with your team." As Leon spoke, I could tell that I was becoming merrier by the minute as I consumed yet another glass of wine. I am still trying to figure out how he could have sat down in those jeans without cutting off the blood supply to his feet! I idly glance down to just below his waistline to see how a part of his anatomy was surviving such strangulation. From what I could see, it looked all right! Leon had caught me once or twice checking his physique, but I didn't care, men do it all the time with less subtlety. After all, I've been out with men who would continually stare at my boobs, as if I don't have eyes to see what they're staring at.

"I notice that you haven't been drinking tonight. Don't you drink?" I ask.

"I do but I have to ride home tonight, so I can't."

"You came here on a bicycle?"

"No!" he replies, as if to say "don't be silly", "I ride a motor-bike." I think that Leon in his "leathers" would look quite sexy. But like I said, such thoughts stifle creativity, because you start thinking about things that you shouldn't. In any case, I've been on a self-imposed celibacy course since Earl. Actually, I don't know why I use Earl as a reference point because nothing happened between us, either.

"It's a pity that you can't share in the full spirit of things by having yourself a good drink," I reply. "Do you have to travel far?"

"I have about an hour-and-a-half ride home."

"Oh no, that is a long way for you to travel at this time of the night. Most of us live locally, so some will either walk or take a taxi home. Well the choice is yours. I have two spare rooms at my place, so you are more than welcome to stay over if you wish." Leon seems to be giving my offer some serious thought.

"I would love to, if that would not be too much trouble for you," he states.

"No trouble at all. You can leave your bike at the restaurant, it will be safe round here." I hadn't finished my statement, before Leon ordered himself a pint of lager. "It's a full moon tonight, so we can have a nice walk back," I say. In all our small talk, I still hadn't got to know anything about Leon, so tonight would be a good opportunity to get to know him better.

I could see that Leon likes to have a drink. He's been "downing" his lager as if he has just returned from running the marathon in the desert. A chain drinker, if there is such a term. We made our way out of the restaurant, unsure who was supporting whom. The cool night air made my head feel even lighter than it had felt in the restaurant. Being a little unstable on my feet, I had to hold on to Leon's arm. Leon didn't seem to mind me occasionally resting my head on his shoulder. I know that I shouldn't get too comfortable with Leon, but when you've had a successful evening with good wine inside you and you're walking under the moonlight then any flirting is understandable. And, it's only a bit of harmless fun. Our walk was accompanied with little conversation, although he made an issue of telling me the names of numerous top models he had been out with. He used to be a model before discovering that he would rather be behind the camera than in front of it. I also found out that Leon was, in fact, twenty-one years old and virile by the sounds of it. When we got home, I offered to make us some fresh ground coffee to help speed up the sobering-up process and mitigate the inevitable hangover that was bound to follow. Leon, however, wanted more lager. I couldn't assist him with that, so he settled for my prized bottle of whiskey that I had bought some nine years ago during my first trip to the Edinburgh Festival. The thought of lager and whiskey mixing in Leon's palate almost made me vomit. I don't think Leon's kidneys could have been feeling much better either. I settled for the coffee.

"I'll show you to the spare room," I say to Leon. He walks towards me and away from the door. Where does he think he is sleeping? Without uttering a word, he holds me in his arms and kisses me full on the mouth. I should push him away and say that "I don't kiss strangers" but it's too late now. And, in any case, it would be rude to interrupt something that feels so good. "I'm celibate," but my body needs this and, boy, can this man kiss. I have to keep reminding myself that I am, in fact, celibate, and I can't afford to fall down at my first hurdle. My body, however, forgot what this feeling was like. If I had thought this through carefully, then I may not have been so hasty in chastising myself. Why did I impose these restrictions on my body anyway? Oh yes, I remember, such thoughts of the flesh stifles creativity. But, my body could do with a little misbehaving for tonight. It's been starved for such a long time. I'll return to celibacy tomorrow. Only I can get these things wrong. When I wanted sexual healing, I found a man who was gay. When I find a sexual healer I'm celibate. What am I doing? I can't lose my creative talent through one kiss. Next I'll be telling myself that I believe in fairy tales. Leon retreats and lets me get some air, not to mention get my breath back. I wish I wasn't breathing so heavily, but that was unexpected. Leon starts playing with my hair whilst kissing my earlobes and whispering sweet nothings. I want to say "stop" but the words won't come out of my mouth. I wish he would stop doing this because my legs feel like jelly and if he doesn't stop soon, I'll be all his for the whole night which is not what I want, obviously! I'm celibate, remember? I have to keep reminding myself of that fact, lest I forget. He is passing his hand up and down my spine. This sends chills through my body and signals to my brain. My body is telling me to cancel my subscription to the celibacy club; it's too much hard work! I'm trying to fight it, but I feel myself losing the battle. Maybe I'll win the war. That's it, I'll let him win this round but let it go no further. I feel his bare hands on my back. God, that feels good! As if by a switch of a button, I feel the loosening of my bra. Leon is no apprentice. He has clearly mastered his trade. He knows what he's doing. Well, that is it. The game is over. I conjure enough strength and push myself away from Leon. Romeo is dangerous. I've never given what he clearly wants to any man whom I barely know. I'm not that kind of girl!

"Where did you say the room was?" asks Leon. Despite Leon having moisturised my mouth with his tongue, I struggle to find the words to reply, as my throat is inexplicably dry. After a number of failed attempts, normal speech resumes.

"It's, it's upstairs," I finally reply. I can see at the corner of my eye that Leon's jeans appear to be even tighter than before! One doesn't have to be too clever to figure out that he would like to do something about it and I don't mean buy a larger pair of jeans! My heart is saying that it's all innocent fun, but my head is telling me that there is nothing innocent about what Leon has in mind at all. Not in the slightest! I walk pass Leon and make my way up the stairs and towards the spare room. Leon held on to my hand as if what we had was the prelude to foreplay. I did not pull my hand away. I open the door and switch on the light. The double bed is in full view. Usually this would be no big deal, as one would expect a bed in a room but tonight this bed is sending out signals. It's saying "I haven't seen any action, either!" What are the chances of my own bed keeping itself company tonight? As this thought passes through me, Leon continue with part two of his act. My resistance by now is far too low to do anything about it. I've been reduced to a mere spectator, albeit with a front row view. My body has been starved for far too long. Leon skilfully and unhurriedly removes my top and skirt consecutively. His warm hands patiently explore my body with a tenderness and care that makes my spine tingle to such a point that I feel like I'm going to pass out. He has now removed all my clothing except for my French knickers which I can see is a big turn on for him. He is in no hurry. He knows that I am not going anywhere tonight. He doesn't need to convince me of his suitability. I am his for tonight. He is still fully clothed. I have never been a woman who is into a man keeping on his clothes, while I lay there stark naked. I'm not there to just give pleasure to a man. I too need to be satisfied. And I sure am not going to get that from a fully clothed man. If it's me being naked that is a turn on, then I could be naked all by myself. No, I want to see what this man has to offer. Can his body match the skilful art of his wondering hands? His bare chest is smothered with a mat of black hair. I'm not too much of a hairy-man fan, but this bush of hair is confined solely to his upper torso so I shan't disqualify him at this late hour, especially with no substitute in sight, and my body having been put on alert in high expectation of what is hopefully to ensue. Leon seems to be a little bow-legged, as his lower torso appears to be struggling in those tight jeans of his. Enough is enough, I shall have to free him of those jeans. I think he has suffered enough. I undo the button flies to his denim jeans. I could just about see what he has to offer.

"Oh my Lord!"

Leon is dead to the world. My body was so relaxed that I too slept like a log. I forgot how good such a feeling could be. I don't think the same could have been said for Leon. I have no doubt that such feeling had not left his body from his previous encounter. I'm just another number on his list for him to boast about to his friends. I don't mind, I'm no spring chicken, either. I too just want to have my kicks with no strings attached. What about my celibacy? Maybe that can wait until a more suitable time. And now is not that time! The telephone rings, but has no awakening effect on Leon. And there was me hoping that we could have another session before I go in to work. It's not that I'm on heat or anything, it's just that I don't know when the next occasion will arise, so I need to be totally fulfilled to carry me through to the next time, whenever that'll be.

"Jo!" shouts Virginia. My head didn't seem to take too kindly to this woman bellowing my name down the telephone, as it gave an unexpected throb to my left temple at the sound.

"Hi Ginny," I say, in as quiet a voice as I can, hoping that she will follow suit. "Good morning to you too!" I add.

"Sorry Jo, only it is not a 'good morning'. I'm at work. We've been burgled!" I could feel another throb to the side of my head as Virginia said this, only this time it felt like someone had physically kicked me there with their steel-toecapped boots.

"Oh my God! What have they taken?" I ask, fearing the worst.

"They've taken everything. The dresses, the computers, the designs, the lot!" replies Virginia. Someone could apply the worst torture imaginable to man and it couldn't make me feel as sick as I do now.

"They couldn't have done," I reply as my voice reaches near hysteria. Even this fails to waken Leon, who is now snoring. I hate men that snore. Suddenly that session is not so appealing. I can't believe that some people could be so wicked. Who on earth would want a few designs. What use are they to them? "Has anyone contacted the police?" I ask, still hoping that this is a bad joke by Virginia, but it seems that I could be waiting for a punch line that does not exist.

"Yes, they're still here."

"Tell them not to leave. I'll be right on my way." I jump out of bed and see that Leon is still out cold. What shall I do with him? He has to go. Dirty drunkard! I can feel the tears run down my face, as I think of all the hard work that my team has put into preparing the collection. It's sickening to think that, while I was romping with some man I barely knew, thieves were stealing my dream. How can people be so cruel? How am I going to get this bloody man out of my bed? I can't leave him here. I don't even know him. I feel shame clouding over me, as my body begins to feel unclean. I can't believe that I even convinced myself that I knew him well. How many women did he tell me he knew? I know what he meant by that! I shake Leon in order to wake him up but his body is still limp. I walk to my vase with its not so fresh flowers and not so clean water. I walk to the bed and gently pour the dirty water from the vase on to Leon's face. This does the trick. Leon shakes his head, as if awakened by smelling salts. I tell him that I have to go to work and insist that he leave. He looks bemused, not to mention sozzled out of his brains, but I am in no mood for pleasantries. We exchanged those last night!

This was obviously a professional job. The thieves knew exactly what they were looking for and took them. I keep a large float of petty cash in my drawer. They left the cash, as that was not what they wanted. What they took away was far more valuable to them than that. Someone out there must have known of our every move, knew that we would've more or less finished our collection for yesterday's show and knew that our collection would have been returned in the early hours of the morning. I can see that the police are questioning Virginia and Adam for what must be the umpteenth time this morning. It was they who brought the dresses back last night and I know that, on paper, this theft appears to point to an inside job, but I know my staff. These are people who have been with me from the start. They know that we are all in this thing together and if I fall they fall also. No, I think that this is down to a gang who somehow obtained information about what was going on. The Best of British Fashion have been advertised for some time and all those taking part has been featured in various newspaper and magazine articles, so it would be almost impossible to point a finger at the culprits. It could be anyone. From the various interviews, it's clear to me that the police have very little to work on. I am absolutely devastated. All that we have worked for has just been taken away by some unscrupulous bastards! They better pray that the police get to them before I do, because otherwise it won't be just theft that the police will be investigating. When the police left, I asked Virginia to summon the other staff in to work. In the meantime, Leon had appeared, looking extremely rough. I suppose if someone had awoken me this morning with dirty water from a flower vase whilst I was fast asleep, and demanded that I leave before I could say "breakfast", I too might look a little rough. Give him his dues, he too appeared to internalise the pain we were suffering and all he had done up to now was to take some photographs. All the staff had by now arrived. I could barely believe it as I prepared to address them. They have all been told by now and look as devastated as I am.

"First, I would like to thank you all for coming in so early, especially after last night." As I said this I kept eye contact with Leon down to a minimum, in case he got the wrong impression as to what I was referring. "As you will all be aware by now, we were burgled last night. I'm no expert on these matters, but it's clear to me that the thieves were interested in one thing and one thing only; and that was our complete collection for Paris. Everything has gone." As I said this, my voice started to break and I needed a moment or two to try and console myself. "Many of you have known me for many years and have known me never to give up, but I'm afraid that we will have to pull out of The Best of British Fashion shows." Murmurs of disbelief follow. The shows were going to be an acknowledgement of their work, as much as that of mine. I could see tears forming in many of their eyes, men as well as women. This scene of emotion leaves me speechless. Virginia walks towards me and puts her arms around me.

"Gang," she says, "we all have too much invested in this project to let some bastards defeat us by their mindless theft." There is a positive response from what Virginia had said, but even I know that you can't produce a new collection in a matter of only a few weeks. "I say," continues Virginia, "that we work even harder, in order to get the show back on the road. Hands up who's with me on this." I'm not the softest of people. In this business you can't afford to be, as someone will soon tread all over you, but seeing every single hand rise, including Leon's, brings a lump to my throat.

"I thank you all for your enthusiasm and kind support," I say, "but I should remind you that we have nothing, not even our original sketches."

"Hold on," says Leon. "I have a full set of photographs of last night's show, so we can work off those." I think back to how I treated him this morning. He's not so bad, it's just that he was the nearest person that I could have taken my frustration out on, even though he relieved me of it the night before, but this is not the time to think about that!

"Thanks Leon, but there is no point now in turning up in designs that will probably be in the shops before we even board the plane for Paris. This gang was obviously a professional outfit. I don't think there can be much doubt about that. Therefore, they're probably negotiating a price for our collection as we speak."

"Well," says Virginia, "we will have to start from scratch and produce a collection which is better than the last. We designed the last collection, so we know what we have to do, in order to design a better one. Much better!" My right-hand girl seems to have caught a wave of enthusiasm from the others, I'm not so confident. "What do you say, boss?" asks Virginia, as all eyes turn to me and await the reply that would have a profound effect on their immediate futures. I know that this is not going to work, but I can tell from their eager faces what they want to hear and they have probably had more than enough setbacks to contend with for today. I suppose it would be better that they try and fail, rather than not try at all. The few seconds thinking over my answer must have seemed like minutes to them.

"If we are unanimous on this, then let's go for it," I say. This is greeted with a loud cheer and I sense the relief that fills the room. I am happy for their joy, but know that this will be short-lived. When the pandemonium calmed down, I sought a word with Leon. "I suggest that you contact the organisers to search for another designer," I say to him.

"But I would like to stay with you and see this through. I've seen your designs and I know that you can produce another collection in time. Please, I want to stay. If this is about last night, then I apologise. I shouldn't have tried it on with the boss."

"Don't be silly," I reply, embarrassed at the thought. "Nothing happened last night that I didn't want to happen. In any case, from my recollection, you did more than try it on with the boss." Leon gives a bashful look. He alone knows who he's trying to fool! No tiger in bed at night could be that shy by day. "I just don't want you to miss an opportunity of a lifetime through being loyal to me because of one night."

"This is not about one night," he replies. "This is about confidence in your ability and talent."

"I tell you what, we are going to be more than busy trying to put together a new collection. In case we fail to meet the deadline, I suggest that in the meantime, you seek a new designer. If we manage to get ourselves a good collection then you'll be more than welcomed back but if you choose not to there'll be no offence taken."

"I'll come back. You can count on that!" says Leon enthusiastically. With that he kisses me on both cheeks, and about-turns to make his way out of the office. Maybe we'll meet again, maybe we won't. Only time will tell. It was a quick, but short and spicy encounter. And one thing is for sure, our rendezvous would not have been entirely in vain. Leon was just what the doctor ordered and now it's back to work. As I watch Leon walk away from me, I still can't help thinking that those jeans are just far too tight.

Rupert

Sydney knows of my affair with Linda. Well, I don't know this to be a fact, but I think he suspects that there is something going on. He must do. I thought about informing him of my relationship with Linda long before he went to see Donna but he made his visit to her before I could contact him. Mind you, I don't think that such news would have been too well received after the high praises he gave Pat. In any case, such news could have jeopardised Linda's chances for Paris, so there was some justification for me keeping quiet about my affair. If Sydney does know, however, it mystifies me why he hasn't told Donna or at least told her that we met. I have no proof to show that he hasn't, but I don't think he has. I can't see either Donna or Jo keeping such hot information to themselves and not tell Pat. It is possible that he could have known about Linda and me from the time of the party. "You scratch my back and I'll scratch yours," seems to make more sense now. I don't think that he was just referring to the work he was planning to send me. After all, does it really matter to him who his lawyer sends his work to? Of course not! As long as the work gets done, he's happy. And how can that amount to me scratching his back? It seems to me that what he really meant was, if I were to smooth the way for him with Donna, then he would kindly reciprocate by not making the way rough for me with Linda, or more importantly, with Pat! Whatever the reasons, I'm pleased that he has kept any inferences to himself. Anyway, I'm sure that his thoughts are being put to better use than to concern himself with my personal affairs. I don't know too much about what is going on, but it is clear for all to see that Sydney and Donna are getting close, or should I say, closer. I know that they have been seeing quite a lot of each other since Dexter moved out of the flat involuntarily. Pat, I know is very pleased, as she has always liked Sydney for Donna. I still can't quite get my head around Chantelle being Sydney's ex-wife. One has to watch one's back all the time, as you never know who you might bump into. I should know! I'm pleased that Donna is happy but not at the expense of Dexter. Hell hath no fury like a woman scorned. Never has a truer word been spoken, my friend can testify to that! If you ask me, Donna was too ruthless. Her treatment of Dexter was not necessary. She overreacted. Does it really matter that Dexter asked Chantelle to marry him and she turned him down? Of course, not! There must be many people out there who have had their proposals for marriage turned down, that doesn't mean that they should be barred from ever having another partner. There is no doubt that my friend was bruised. I have neither heard from nor seen him since the incident with Donna. I have left numerous messages with his secretary for him to call me. He is yet to return any of them. Someone has rung me a few times at Chambers, when I've been at court or in a conference, but has left no name. But my clerk didn't recognise it as Dexter's voice and, in any case, there is no reason why Dexter should not leave his name. And, to make matters worse, I don't even know where he is staying. Dexter is a proud man and I'd be lying if I were to say that he was not the laughing stock around here, but I fail to see the funny side to what he went through. I guess that one has a different perspective on certain matters when what one is doing is not too dissimilar to what my friend was punished for.

Since Pat fell pregnant, I have not been to see Linda as frequently as before, so tonight is welcomed. I haven't told Linda about Pat's pregnancy. I don't know why, but I just don't think that I would be comfortable discussing this side of my marriage with my lover. And I know that Linda has been having her own personal problems with Wilson. He hasn't given her any peace since she walked out on him. Unfortunately, I think it's beginning to take its toll on her. I don't know what I'd do if one day Wilson were to see me walking into Linda's flat. I'm sure he must know where she lives. As usual, I park my car a few streets away whenever I come here to see Linda. I can't afford for my car to be seen outside where she lives. And if Wilson were to see me, he would have no hesitation in spreading the word about what he would think was going on between me and his ex-fiancée. Fortunately,

Pat is not one for listening to gossipmongers but I still don't think that she would fully dismiss a rumour without at least giving it some thought, and it is this thought that would worry me. You never know, that could lead to all kinds of unwanted revelations.

"Hi honey," I say to Linda, as we make our way into her bedroom. Being here has made me realise how much that I have, in fact, missed her. Speaking on the telephone is not the same as seeing each other in the flesh.

"Hi dear. I'm going through a bad time at the moment," replies Linda apologetically, who is not looking anywhere near her best tonight. She usually makes an effort when we meet, but tonight, she looks as though she is carrying the world on her shoulders.

"What's the matter?" I ask.

"Nothing, but nothing, seems to be going right for me just now."

"Talk to Uncle Rupert," I say playfully, whilst resting her head on my right shoulder.

"I feel so depressed; I feel flat. I might not go to Paris and I am under pressure from Wilson. Where do you want me to start?"

"As they say, start from the beginning," I reply. It hadn't occurred to me that having two women also meant having to listen to two lots of problems. This could be tough going!

"Wilson begs me to return back to him every single day. He can't understand how we could have been together for such a long time and I could end it with no quarrel, nothing. I haven't got the heart to tell him that I no longer love him. That would be honest, but I think that sometimes the truth doesn't always need to be told. The trouble is he keeps asking me whether I still love him and I keep replying, "yes". How can I say "no"? When he then asks me why don't I come back home, I'm cornered."

"What do you say, then?" I ask.

"I just tell him that at the moment I need time to myself. I need to know who I am. I have been with Wilson for so long; I don't even know myself anymore. I know what makes him happy but I don't know what makes me happy."

"I thought I made you happy."

"You know you do, but I'm not talking about you. I'm talking about my life on the whole. I think I've done Wilson wrong."

"How can you do someone wrong by looking after your best interest for a change?"

"Because relationships are far more complicated than that. Too bloody complicated if you ask me. It can't be right to be with your partner for all these years and then walk out on him because you want a change. That just cannot be right. You owe your partner more than that, surely."

"I guess I would have to agree with you, if you put it that way."

"You would be devastated if Patricia woke up one morning and told you that she wanted a divorce because she wanted to find herself, wouldn't you?" asks Linda.

"Yes, I would," I reply, not to mention that she would be taking away my child but we needn't delve into that now, if ever at all.

"So you understand how Wilson feels. I have let him down and all for my own selfish reasons. What does finding yourself mean, when it's at home, anyway? You hear people say that when they don't know what the hell's wrong with them. It's like some umbrella disease. You don't know what it is, so you put it down to wanting to find yourself."

"I can't say that I've felt the need to have to embark on such an expedition, so I don't think that I'm suitably qualified to comment," I say.

"And to add to it all, his parents are so fond of me and were just awaiting the day of the announcement of their son's wedding. I know that by hurting their son I am hurting them also, but what am I to do? Maybe one day when all this is over between us and you start being the faithful husband to your wife, I could tell Wilson that I've found myself and I'm ready to devote the rest of my life to him."

"How do you know that I will one day be the faithful husband? You read about people having affairs for many years before it comes to an end."

"Do you really believe that we can carry on like this for many years?"

"Why not?"

"Your wife is a very successful woman and you'll one day have children. Do you honestly believe that you would risk such stability just to have an extra romp in the hay whenever you felt like it?"

"It's good to know that this is all our relationship means to you," I reply. I'm a little hurt by Linda's remark because I want her to see that I am not here just for the extramarital sex, but I really do care for her. Maybe it would be easier for me to portray myself the way she thinks I ought to be. You know, the husband who has his mistress but, when things get too heavy, he runs back to the wife who he once said didn't "understand" him.

"Rupert, I am very fond of you but, at the end of the day, you have what could be, if not already, the perfect family life. You will be risking a lot, irrespective of how I might feel for you or how you might feel for me. We both have various interests outside my bedroom. I would love you to show me what your interests are. I would love to go to an exhibition where we can walk around freely and discuss the works that we have seen, go to a concert and have fun like any other normal couple. I knew that this was the way it would have to be, but I did not anticipate that we would have been together so long or got so close."

"I understand what you're saying. We should try going out a lot more. We don't always have to go out together in town. And anyway, London is a big place. Who is to say that we are together just because we are under the same roof at the same time? I've wanted to see *Carmen* at the English National Opera for some time. I shall buy us a pair of tickets for Saturday. How does that sound?"

"That sounds fine to me but don't put yourself at any unnecessary risk on my account."

"No problem," I reply. "Now that is sorted, what's the problem with Paris? I thought Sydney was going to sort you out, so to speak."

"Sydney liked my work and is trying to associate me with a designer at this late hour."

"Surely Sydney will find someone!"

"He can only find me a designer if there is one available and I think they all have their photographers already."

"I think everything will be all right but if the worst comes to the worst then we can still go to Paris for a weekend. I have to go there on business soon, so I have to go in any case."

"That would be nice. Thank you. I'm sorry that I haven't been much fun tonight, but we can't all be a bundle of laughs all of the time."

"Linda," I say, "I want to make this clear to you. For as long as you want me around, I want to share in both your good and bad times. So please don't feel guilty about sharing any problems you may have with me. In fact, I would be insulted if you chose not to."

"I know that I shouldn't be, but I think that I might be falling in love with you, even though I know that such feelings will be fruitless and can only lead to my heartache."

"I think we should just let nature take its course," I say without much thought. Her confession did not surprise me. I am not the most receptive of men when it comes to women, but the signs have been there for some time.

"And what do you mean by that, Rupert? Are you telling me that you are going to leave Patricia for me?" asks Linda with eyes piercing my soul with such intensity I turn away.

"I can't make promises about anything at this stage but if we are meant to be together at the end then I believe that it will happen," I reply. I know that I have said very little but Linda is too vulnerable at this moment in time for me to be ranting on about not wanting to hurt anybody else. Paris is still the favourite time to end this affair but I can't say that with any certainty. I'm glad that I didn't tell her that Pat was pregnant, otherwise her depression may have been too much for me to handle. Am I really fit to cope with two women's problems at the same time? I don't think so, but I am learning fast.

"I have invited Donna and Sydney round for dinner this Saturday," says Pat. "I recalled you saying that you were free this weekend, so I hope that will be all right."

"That will be fine," I reply. I shall have to cancel Linda. I shouldn't think that this would make her feel any better but there is nothing I can do. We have a problem now only because she decided to separate from Wilson, otherwise things would have been just as cool as before.

"It will be nice to see Sydney after all these years, won't it? You probably don't even remember what he looks like do you?" asks Pat.

"Vaguely," I reply hesitantly. "Has Donna heard from Dexter?" I ask changing the subject rapidly.

"Not as far as I know," replies Pat. "But, I don't think she's losing any sleep over him. She tells me that her and Sydney are getting on so well it doesn't seem like they were ever apart."

"They're probably trying to make up for lost time," I say. "I must admit that I do feel sorry for Dexter. I really do think that he loves Donna. I just think that maybe she didn't satisfy him enough, so he sought comfort in another woman that possessed qualities in areas that she lacked."

"What are you talking about Rupert?" asks Pat, clearly astonished at my theory. "I don't follow! This is not philosophy! This is real life! When you get involved with someone you take the good with the bad, the rough with the smooth, and you should be satisfied with that." There goes my defence, should Pat find out about Linda!

"Don't you believe that people can love more than one person at the same time?" I ask with interest. "We read about many people who do. They can't all be mistaken, surely," I add, testing the waters.

"I wouldn't know because I have never been in that predicament. Have you?" The question nearly made me fall off my chair.

"No I haven't," I reply. Am I glad that God doesn't really strike you down when you lie, otherwise I would have been a dead man a long time ago.

"I wouldn't say that it is impossible," Pat continues, "but I don't think it is implicit that because a person is not married then they are automatically in a position to be laissez-faire with their love life, unless, of course, they're in an open relationship: then anything goes, I suppose! Otherwise, that person should take his or her partner's concerns into consideration. It can't just be 'me, me'. One has to be less selfish. Do you understand what I am saying? There are emotions involved here and people can't be expected to switch on or off, in order to suit their partner's selfish needs, which is what Dexter was demanding from Donna. That is not fair, not that there is ever fairness in these matters."

"I wasn't really referring to Dexter alone. I was talking more on a general scale," I say.

"I was wondering why you felt so obliged to go to such lengths simply in order to justify his womanising. Then again, wonders never cease, as they say. Look at you two. You are so different and yet the closest of friends. I suppose opposites really do attract."

"I think I understand Dexter better than a lot of people that's all. I will give him the benefit of the doubt until he gives me cause to think otherwise. I think most people judge him before listening to what he has to say."

"I don't think there's much chance of that," replies Pat, "Dexter is not known for not speaking his mind!"

"True," I submit.

"Either way, I don't think that Donna should waste her valuable time on Dexter. He is a big enough man. He can look after himself, if some woman isn't looking after him already! He hasn't even tried to contact Dionne and yet he had the cheek to tell Donna that they should stay together for Dionne's sake. Well, his actions are in complete contradiction to his words. If he did more doing and less talking, then maybe one could have taken him seriously but where is he now? No one knows where the hell he is. His daughter could be sick and Donna would be unable to contact him unless through work and look at the problems you've encountered in trying to get through to him there!"

"I haven't got through at all," I confirm.

"Oh! as I mention that, someone rang for you today but didn't leave his name."

"I wonder if this is the same person who has been trying to get through to me in Chambers? Someone has been calling me, but not leaving a name. At first I thought that it might be Dexter but I can't think of any reason why he wouldn't leave his name."

"Whoever it is, it must be someone who knows you fairly well in order to have both your work and home numbers." I wonder if it is Wilson who has been calling me. Maybe he's having Linda's place watched or I may have left something behind in his flat. But, if this were true, then there is no reason why he shouldn't have left a message or come round to see me. If I found out that some man was playing around with Pat, I wouldn't wait for him to invite me round for a tea! I've heard of stiff upper lip but that's just being plainly stiff! You would have to go round and see that person right away. You would be compelled to go if only to seek confirmation of what you believed to be true. I don't think it can be Wilson. I think I'm simply being paranoid.

"If it is that important then, I'm sure, whoever it is will eventually get through to me in one way or another," I say.

Linda was okay about me having to cancel our date for tonight, or so she tried to lead me to believe. I didn't feel good about it, but there was nothing I could do. In reality we both know that Pat will always have first call on my time unless I can safely wriggle out of it. Anyway, my tickets won't entirely go to waste because Linda will be going to the show with one of her flatmates. I know where I would rather be tonight: at the show! I have a nervous feeling about meeting Sydney and Donna tonight. I wish I had spoken to Sydney beforehand but it is too late now. I can only hope that he continues to stay mum. Pat has been looking forward to meeting our guests all day. For me, it would be strange to see Donna with another man and not with my close friend, who, I should say, has finally got in touch. He didn't say very much, but confirmed that it wasn't he who has been calling me without leaving his name. He insisted that we arrange to meet but wouldn't tell me where he was staying. I couldn't bring myself to tell him about tonight, because until I talk to him I shan't know if he is licking his wounds or celebrating his freedom again. Knowing Dexter as well as I do, I would put money on it being the latter.

When Donna and Sydney arrived, Sydney and I greeted each other as if it were the first time that we had met each other for many years. That told me that he knows about Linda and me. I "tested the waters" with Donna on his behalf but that is not strong enough to buy his silence for ever. In fact, he didn't even check with me to see whether everything was all right with her, so he may not even be aware of my contribution. And our friendship, if it can be described as thus, has no real root or foundation for either to owe the other any loyalty, so I am, effectively, hanging by a thread. I don't like the idea of having my destiny in the hands of someone whom I don't know too well. Better make sure that those fees are reasonable!

"Donna tells me that you're a big-shot lawyer," says Sydney with a wry smile. He hasn't told her about us meeting at the party. And yes, there is no doubt now, he knows I'm playing around and he knows who with. This could be a long night. If only I could excuse myself and say to Linda that I can make the show after all. It might be better for me if I were to simply return Sydney's work to him and make do with the little practice I had before. Admittedly, that wouldn't erase what he already knows about me, but at least I would not be eternally indebted to him so as when he says "jump", I would have to ask, "how high?" and not say, "get stuffed!"

"I wouldn't quite put it that way," I reply. "But I'm not doing too badly." I look at Sydney, as if to acknowledge his game. At least he knows that I know he knows about Linda and me.

"Don't listen to him, Sydney," says Pat. "It's only recently that Rupert has slowed down a little bit. He was working most Saturdays up until recently. In fact I could have nearly killed him when I got the news that I was pregnant, because he had his mobile phone switched off and I couldn't find him anywhere. Not even his head of Chambers knew where he was."

"If you're not very busy, Rupert, I can arrange for my lawyer to send you some more work," says Sydney.

"What do you mean by "more" work?" asks Donna, "You don't send him any work now, do you?"

"Are you asking me or telling me?" replies Sydney, to which both he and Donna saw a funny side. I wonder whether they are laughing at me?

"Both!" replies Donna. Is she here to make me sweat tonight as well? After all, both are very fond of Pat and would probably stop at nothing in order for me to see the error of my ways. But, like I said before, had Donna known she would have gone that one step further than Sydney has and tell Pat, not play games with me.

"It was a slip of the tongue," replies Sydney, fooling the others, but not me. "I don't think my lawyer sends you any work at present, Rupert. Do you?" How long is Sydney going to keep this game going on for? If he doesn't say something soon I might do, just to put an end to it. He's almost driving me mad!

"I'm not too sure," I reply. "I would have to speak to my clerk."

"I thought you would have known from the brief. If you haven't seen my name, then you may have seen Charles' Artists Agency." It doesn't appear that Sydney is going to ease off tonight. He started this evening the way he intended to carry on. And my problem is he can go on doing this all night because Pat and Donna will be totally oblivious to what's going on.

"The name doesn't ring a bell," I reply. "Anyone for more wine?" I ask whilst picking up the near-full bottle of Chardonnay, ready to pour into glasses which are not exactly crying out for more wine, but I need to buy some time from the next inevitable bombardment.

"Well Sydney send all the work you can to Rupert," says Donna, innocently.

"Consider it done," replies Sydney. Now, where have I heard that before? "As they say, idle minds leads to idle thoughts." We all laugh, but I'm sure that the girls don't quite have in mind what Sydney has in his!

"Oh I'm not sure that Rupert has time for idle thoughts," says Pat. "There's plenty to think about around here, isn't there honey?"

"Yes dear," I reply, "plenty." It seems that I will be afforded a temporary respite as Donna steers the conversation round to some Greek restaurant she and Sydney had visited and the good quality of the food. On the last count, Sydney had won every round. And I have nothing other than my defence, which by all accounts is very weak. Am I really that blind? Here I am having what should be a pleasant evening with friends. I say friends because I don't necessarily begrudge Sydney for how he feels, I just wish that he had confronted me beforehand if he was that concerned. I couldn't have anticipated that he would feel so passionate over someone he had neither met nor spoken to in all these years. All this just goes to show me how popular and likeable Pat really is, probably not only to Sydney but to many others also. It is so easy to forget that my wife is known by so many people who dearly admire her.

"Oh," says Sydney turning to Pat, "before I forget, I have brought my copy of *Four Seasons* for you to kindly autograph for me, Pat. I hope that will be all right."

"Yes, of course it will," replies Pat.

"You must be very proud of your talented wife, Rupert," says Sydney, again!

"Yes, I am," I reply.

"You're a very lucky man. I'd hold on to her tight, if I were you," he says.

"Why, what do you have in mind, Charles? Remember she is a married woman with child!" states Donna mockingly.

"A good woman like Pat is hard to find and there are a lot of good men like *moi* who are waiting in the wings for any sign of a slip by the husband," adds Sydney jokingly, only not so jokingly!

"Is that so?" asks Donna. "Well you'll be waiting for ever because Rupert is no Dexter."

"You tell him, Sydney," says Pat enthusiastically. "He was telling me earlier on that a man can be in love with more than one woman at the same time." I look at Sydney as Pat made her remark. His look said enough.

"No I didn't," I reply firmly in my defence, "I put forward a hypothesis that a person can be in love with more than one person at the same time. It was genderless."

"And was the hypothesis proved?" asks Sydney.

"Not particularly," I reply.

"Well, I don't know the answer to that but I know that I wouldn't accept a man bringing that kind of rubbish to me as his excuse for sleeping around," contributes Donna. "I probably let that rat get away with too much when he was around." No one enquires as to whom Donna was referring.

"I think it would be a dangerous theory to accept," says

Sydney. "I can see people using it as an excuse for their reason for having all kinds of affairs. Anyway, I think it might be academic, because the question is, how many partners will accept their partner claiming to be in love with somebody else as well and stay with them? That I think is the fundamental question. Also, when one of the partners leaves then the other may not trust you because they know how prone you are to falling in love with other people."

"Well said, Sydney," shouts Pat in his support. "Because I know that no man could've fed me with that rubbish and I stay with him. I would've dumped his arse just where I found it." I notice that the temperature of the room has risen by a few degrees over the past few minutes. Sydney and Donna were in full support of what Pat had to say. I too voiced my support, albeit with less conviction than the others but with a public show as to where I stand.

"Talking of cheats, have you still not heard from Dexter?" asks Donna.

"I heard from him only yesterday, after my numerous calls to his office. He told me that he hadn't been in touch with you."

"Or Dionne!" adds Donna vexatiously. "My body cringes whenever I think about that man. And, that, I'm glad to say, is not very often. When I think of how he nearly ruined my life, I could..." I think we could all guess what Donna had in mind: it carries an automatic sentence of life imprisonment! The subject of Dexter was the first tonight that Sydney had not voiced some opinion or another on. Could this have something to do with a one time Mrs Chantelle Charles being an old flame of Dexter?

Despite my bashing I quite liked Sydney. Odd, I know, but he seems like the kind of chap that I could actually have as a close friend. And I have the feeling that we would be seeing quite a lot of him and Donna together. Donna and Sydney left just after midnight. The evening was a success and the company was good. I was boxed around the ring a bit but Sydney never produced that killer punch that could have easily knocked me out and sent me packing. However, he sent out enough warning signals for me to know that he doesn't want to see Pat hurt. And how long he will, or can, keep my affair to himself before feeling the need to tell Donna, I don't know. Hopefully for as long as it takes for the affair to come to its natural end. But, he will obviously want to look after his own interest, and there could lie trouble. If my affair is ever exposed and Donna finds out that he knew about it without telling her, I don't think that all the love in the world could keep them together. Blood is thicker than water but Pat, Jo and Donna's care and love for each other is thicker than blood. That is what Sydney would be up against!

In all the years that I have known Dexter he has never been on time. He has to be the worst timekeeper I know. Even with a thirty-minute start, he will still arrive well late. Sitting alone in the squash club, however, has given me time to reflect on how our lives have changed so much over the past few months. Dexter and I used to play squash regularly, every week without fail. No excuse to cancel was permitted, unless it was absolutely necessary. Anything short of a doctor's sick note was not acceptable! I miss those times. In the space of a few months both our lives have become so complicated that we have abandoned the very simple things that used to keep us sane and happy. What I wouldn't give to have all that back into my life again: Sam forever telling us to repent for the end is nigh, or Ashley with his nasty laugh, or my old sparring partner complaining about some injustice in the world. And, like most things, once those times have gone, you can never get them back again. Once lost they are lost for ever! It makes me question how feeble some of us men really are. I was always the main player of the gang, the bond that kept us all together. So, if you have no me then you have no gang. I knew that. And yet, despite looking forward to and enjoying my regular gathering with the boys, at the first sign of a new woman in my life, I put the whole ritual in jeopardy. Compare that to the girls and you would know what I am talking about. There is no way that they would let some man interfere with their friendship, be it boyfriend, fiancé or husband! No one, but no one could penetrate that protective sheath they surround themselves with. Women know what true friendship is all about. I'm not jealous of what they have, but I am envious of their bond. I know, however, that some partners would find such intrusions into their marriage unacceptable. Dexter, for example, abhorred the thought of Donna discussing his business with Pat and Jo, which is ironic because Dexter would normally be happy to know that a group of women were chatting about him. He would see it as inevitable. I, on the other hand, have no doubt that those girls know a lot more about me than they would ever let on, but I have nothing but the fullest respect for what they have. I only wish that I had such a bond with someone with whom I could fully and honestly confide. I would tell Dexter a lot, but not everything. For example, I haven't told him about Linda. However, this has more to do with me not wanting this affair to be anymore public than it need necessarily be, rather than any mistrust of Dexter. Maybe if I had someone with whom I could confide, I might not have gone round to Linda's place that night and had I not gone round, I wouldn't have had an affair with her. I would be lying if I said that I haven't enjoyed having Linda in my life, but I guess it's like a drug. Once hooked you want more.

I see that familiar walk hurrying towards me. No matter how late Dexter is, he will always rush at the last minute, as if saving a few seconds will make up for being an hour late.

"Hi buddy," says Dexter, panting out of control. "Sorry I'm late but the traffic was horrendous tonight. Have you been waiting long?"

"No not really," I reply, "only from the agreed time!"

"Sorry buddy, but I can assure you that that won't happen again."

"Where have I heard that before?" I ask. "Anyway, by the sounds of you, it seems as though you need a few games of squash to get you back to fitness."

"I am a little bit out of shape, I guess," replies Dexter. He does look as though he has gained a few pounds in weight, which suggests that he must be living a little too much of the high life. So much for being bruised!

"Where have you been hiding?" I ask.

"I've been staying with an old friend of mine."

"Anyone I know?" I ask, curious to know who it is that he could be shacking up with, without detection from anyone else who knows him.

"No, you don't know her. It's someone who has always been there for me. A shoulder to cry on, sort of thing." I pass on the opportunity of commenting that we were once there for each other, but it doesn't seem appropriate, especially when considering that he knows nothing of my affair with Linda.

"That's fine but I thought that you would, at least, have returned my calls."

"I should've done but I wanted to clear my head after what happened between Donna and me. I take it that you know the full story."

"I know what she told Pat," I reply. He would know that Donna would have told Pat, and that Pat would have told me.

"Good old Pat. She must be well and truly gloating over the whole affair."

"Dexter, this has nothing to do with Pat and deep down I think you know that. Your problems with Donna have nothing to do with anyone else but yourselves, not me, not Pat, not Jo, just you two and you two alone."

"I know that, but let's not pretend, we both know that I have never been Pat's favourite person and she'd rather see me away from Donna than with her, even to the detriment of Dionne." It's at times like this where I can fully appreciate why Dexter is nowhere near as popular as he is unpopular. He seems cursed with this gift of rubbing people up the wrong way. And worse, I don't even believe that he realises what he is doing or when he's doing it.

"Pat has never wished you any harm but, you know as well as I do, you can't go round upsetting Donna in the way that you have and expect any support from Pat. That just would not happen."

"You may have a point."

"You know I do," I reply robustly, knowing full well that Dexter is aware of what I am saying.

"Anyway, what has Donna been up to since I left her?" I didn't think that Dexter would dare show any outward interest in Donna let alone enquire as to what she has been up to.

"I don't know if you are aware of this, but I think that, as your close friend, I ought to at least tell you that I think Donna and

Sydney are seeing each other."

"Who is Sydney?" asks Dexter seemingly confused. I'd always thought that Dexter knew of Sydney, everyone else did! He probably never felt the need to worry about an ex-boyfriend of Donna's because his position was never under any threat, or so he thought. And what about Chantelle then? That one I can't tell him about.

"Sydney Charles is a guy who Donna used to go out with before she met you. I thought you would have known about him. Don't tell me Donna never mentioned him."

"Now I think about it, she did mention his name once or twice, I think. Where did he come from?"

"I don't know," I reply. "Pat invited them round for a meal the other night."

"That was very nice of her," says Dexter. "I think in all the years I have known Pat, she has only ever invited both Donna and me round for a meal, twice. The first time was when she first met me and the second time was when Donna and me got engaged. So, when you say that Donna and Sydney are seeing each other, what exactly do you mean? You don't mean they're going out with each other."

"I don't know for sure, but they looked pretty close to me." I might as well be honest.

"I can't believe that woman! I barely turn my back and she's off seeing some ex-boyfriend."

"Pot calling the kettle black, if you ask me," I say, as Dexter tries to come to terms with someone having replaced him in Donna's life and by the sounds of things she is doing just fine without him.

"This fling better not be too serious, otherwise I might have to take away my daughter."

"You're not serious?" I ask with more than an element of disgust in my voice. I think that he has been hard done by, but even I would stop short of using Dionne, as if she was a pawn in a game of chess.

"I don't want any man around my daughter. You hear all kinds of stories these days about boyfriends mistreating another man's child. I'm not having it!"

"Dexter, listen to yourself," I shout in astonishment. "This has nothing to do with Dionne and we both know it. This is to do with you wanting to make Donna's life as uncomfortable as you possibly can. That's not fair. If that is your way of getting her back then forget it, she'll turn off you for ever."

"I don't want that bitch back! She's lost me for good." I have never known Dexter to be so bitter, especially over Donna. The man really is a mystery.

"I really don't understand, man. You spend all this time giving the woman a hard time only to find it necessary to make things difficult for her when you are apart from her as well."

"Whose side are you on?" he asks.

"It's not a question of choosing sides. I just don't know what it is you want. When you had Donna you showed no interest in wanting her. Now she is trying to rebuild her life and find some kind of happiness again you want to wreck it. Why? If I didn't know you better I'd say you were jealous."

"Don't be so ridiculous! If some desperate man can't find himself a decent woman and finds some overweight woman with a child who wants him, then what have I to be jealous about? If I really wanted that woman, I wouldn't have slept around. Remember, you only know the half of the story that I want you to know, there have been many others." I remember Pat once saying that "by one's friends one will be judged", referring to me. It saddens me to hear Dexter speak the way he does. I could never be as nasty as he is; it's not in my nature. By one's friends one will be judged. I shudder to think that I could ever have such vile characteristics.

"What does this Sydney chap do for a living anyway?"

"If you must know, he is a top-notch in the fashion industry. He runs his own modelling agency and from what I gather he is very successful. I think by what people are saying, he is very wealthy." I could tell by Dexter's facial expression that this truth has not gone down too well. I think I would feel the same, if I were him. I don't know if it's pride or what, but if Pat had left me I don't think that I could wish for her to be as happy as Donna appears to be at this moment.

"You mean to tell me that Donna is having some man living

the fast life of sex and drugs around my daughter? What kind of responsible and caring mother would allow that?"

"Where have you got that information from?" I ask, annoyed at where this is going. Dexter can fight a dirty fight and I fear this is what is about to happen with Donna. "I don't know Sydney that well but surely you can't believe that Donna would be with a man who deals with drugs."

"She might not necessarily know. It's not like this Sydney guy needs to walk around with a sign on his forehead, promoting his habit, is it?"

"That is absurd!" I reply. "A minute ago, you couldn't even recall who Sydney was, and already you have labelled him a drug addict. I think that you're clutching at straws my friend! You, of all people, should know that you can't go round making such a ludicrous allegation without any sound evidence to back it up."

"I hear what you say, but I prefer not to take the chance. Tomorrow, I shall commence proceedings for the custody of Dionne."

"You are joking? Oh come on, Dexter. You can't really mean that you are going to try and take Dionne away from Donna on that flimsy half-concocted story of yours. It'll get thrown out before you ever get to a hearing. You don't even give Dionne any maintenance money. Why are you doing this?"

"Because I want what's best for my daughter and believe that I can provide that for her better than Donna and her lover." I can hear my mobile phone ringing. I should just let the thing ring while I try and make Dexter see sense, but it could be Pat and I remember what happened the last time. I answer the phone and hear a panic stricken Linda. I excuse myself and make my way outside. Today may have been confession day for Dexter, but I was in no mood to admit anything about my affair with Linda.

"What's the matter dear?" I ask.

"I have just received a call from Wilson's mother, saying that he suffered a relapse tonight after taking an overdose of some pills and is now in hospital fighting for his life! I've got to go to Birmingham tonight to see him."

"You don't sound like you're in any fit mood to drive any-where let alone make your way to the Midlands."

"That is why I'm calling you. I won't take offence if you say 'no' but I would really like you to go up there with me if you can. I promise that we'll be back before midnight." I gave Linda my word that I would be there for her whenever she needed me, so I must go, but what could I possibly say to Pat? I can't say that it's work, because I have already declared to her that I am not particularly busy. I could say that I was with Dexter all the time. Pat would never check with him! And anyway, nobody knows where he is and I can't see him and Donna sustaining any meaningful conversation, if he decides to carry out his threat of starting proceedings against her, for her to seek his address. I must talk him out of this craziness. The man's gone mad. I've heard of taking revenge but he's taking the piss! Also, I know that the chances of Pat finding out about me going to Birmingham with Linda is a million to one, but there is still that one in a million chance! No, I can't tell Dexter. That is a risk in itself. The man is not even thinking straight. I would have to take my chances.

"I'll come along. I take it that I shall not actually be coming into the hospital with you."

"I don't think visiting Wilson in hospital with me would be such a good idea, somehow," replies Linda. "I'm at home, so I'll wait for you."

"I'm with Dexter but I shall be with you within a few minutes." Dexter's life is important to me, but not as important as Linda's at this moment. I make my way back into the bar and notice that Dexter is reading a newspaper.

"Dexter, I'm sorry but I've got to go. An emergency has cropped up and I must attend to it. I can't say any more at the moment but please call me tomorrow, and don't do anything that you will later regret. Call me before you do anything. I think you know what I'm talking about."

"I shall," replies Dexter most unconvincingly. I could tell that his mind's made up. I guess that I could win some points with Sydney by alerting Donna of what is to come, but if Dexter fails to carry out his threat, then I might just cause unnecessary anxiety for her. And Dexter would, no doubt, find out what I did, which would be the end of us. This is not my problem. Let them sort this one out by themselves. I have enough problems of my own to contend with.

"I can't believe that Wilson would be so stupid as to try such a thing," says Linda as we make our way up to Birmingham. Memories come flooding back from all those years ago, when Pat and I first met and we were driving back to London in order to spend the last few minutes with my mother. The atmosphere in the car tonight is not too dissimilar to how it was that night. Even though Linda had told me of the pressure she was under from Wilson, I hadn't appreciated that he was in such a bad way. I feel guilty, but he doesn't know about me, so I can't take the blame. "How dare he put me through this," she adds, breaking the moment's silence. "I shall give him a piece of my mind when I see him. I shall not be held to ransom. It's not fair." The phone rings, interrupting Linda. I can tell by Linda's response that Wilson's mother is on the other end, no doubt checking to see where Linda is. Not very near by the look of things. I can see Linda place her phone down on her lap, as if in slow motion.

"How is he doing?" I ask. Linda does not reply.

"How is he dear?" I repeat.

"Wilson died of a massive heart attack a few minutes ago." I almost lost control of the car as Linda said this, and had to slam down hard on the brakes in order to regain control again. I just could not believe what Linda had said.

"Oh my God! What have we done?" was all I could whisper, hoping that Linda would say what I wanted to hear and that was that we were not to blame. Such words of comfort sought, were not given. I stop the car for a while in order for me to regain my composure, before I drive again.

"Wilson's mother said that I was neither welcome at the hospital nor at Wilson's funeral, and asked that I honour the family's wishes by keeping away." With this Linda cried in my arms for what seemed like hours. My dream of the drake in search of the duck comes to mind. Could this have been Wilson needing Linda to spare him from fatality? A tragedy borne out of curiosity. What a rotten day!

182

Part Three

Donna

I haven't been this happy in years. I feel satisfied and content. I now enjoy living not only for my daughter, but also for myself, which has not always been the case. Sydney has brought something into my life that no man has even come close to bringing. I don't know how we could have lived apart for as long as we did, but I know for sure that I would not wish to go through that again. Amongst many other qualities, what I like about Sydney is that he respects our differences. He listens to whatever I have to say. He may not necessarily agree with me, but if he doesn't, then he would let me know why, without getting personal. He is also very much a man of principle. I have been to his home, but I am yet to spend a night there. There is no particular reason for this – Chantelle, or Katherine, has moved out, and is now looking after their daughter, Sabrina – it's just that he would normally stay at my place. He did insist, however, on a complete change of bed. I would have been content with just replacing the old sheets but he was having none of it, he wanted no trace of my former fiancé, and to think of it, neither did I. I did not object.

"Good morning, my princess," says Sydney whilst balancing the reading of *The Times* and eating a large bowl of porridge with home-made wholemeal bread and two poached eggs for breakfast. How he can start his day with such a heavy breakfast is always beyond me. I can settle for nothing more than a cup of coffee and a small glass of freshly squeezed orange juice in the morning. Anything more, and my stomach show its disapproval by ejecting what has been consumed.

"Good morning, sir," I reply. "And how are you this bright and wonderful morning?" I ask.

"I'm fine, thank you," replies Sydney. "And would madam like?" he asks, pointing towards the coffee pot.

"Madam would like."

"You have some post over there."

"Only bills, no doubt. They can wait."

"Well I can't," says Sydney.

"Since when have you become so interested in bills?"

"I'm not referring to any bills, I'm referring to you."

"I don't follow, dear. What are you getting at?"

"I've been thinking about it all night. In fact, I've barely slept thinking about it. I would like you to marry me. Would you marry me, Donna?" asks Sydney looking directly at me. He's serious. I'm not surprised at the question. Actually, I was wondering what was taking him so long, but I always imagined that he would first wine and dine me and then pop the question.

"Well, I'm shocked!" I say most unconvincingly. Acting never was one of my better fortes.

"Really?" asks Sydney, unbelievingly.

"I thought that you would have, at least, proposed over an expensive meal in town somewhere."

"Oh, I see," replies Sydney with too much of a shrewd look on his face for this time of the morning. "So you were expecting me to 'pop' the question at some time, were you?"

"Sometimes Mister Charles, you're too smart for your own good."

"Oh, it's 'Mister Charles' already is it? My mother only calls my father by his surname when she isn't pleased with him, for one thing or another."

"Aren't we jumping the gun a bit?" I ask. "I can call you by any name I like, I'm not your wife!"

"So you're going to keep me waiting, knowing that I can't go anywhere."

"Why can't you go anywhere? You're a free man."

"You know damn well why, madam! You're not going to make this too easy for me, are you?" I don't think that I can keep this going on for much longer myself, but at least we both know the game.

"No man can propose to me over a breakfast table and can expect a quick and positive answer. I don't come cheap, you know."

"I would never make such a claim."

"I should hope not too," I respond and to make him wait just that little bit longer, I make my way over to the mail holder, in order to open and read my mail which, not too long ago, was of little importance. I can see Sydney watching me from the side of my eye and he knows that I'm enjoying every minute of this, and why not? If I'm going to commit myself to him for the rest of my life, I might as well take my time and consider his proposal carefully. Although there is no doubt that I will say "yes" of course, and he knows that as well, so any pretence of panicking and awaiting my reply with baited breath, doesn't wash either. As I predicted, three of the four envelopes are bills, but one of them is from Dexter. I could recognise his handwriting from a mile away. I have had no contact with him since I put him out. Or put another way, he has not dared show his face around here since. "What the hell does he think he's playing at?" I shout.

"What the hell does who think he's playing at?"

"One of these letters is from Dexter. He says that he wants custody of Dionne!"

"What do you mean, he wants custody of Dionne?"

"He has shown no interest in her until now! I doubt whether he even knows her birthday!"

"He's out of his tiny mind!" says Sydney. "Why is he doing this?"

"He says that he has reason to believe that I am not looking after Dionne properly. How dare that swine try and take away my child. What has he done for her? Nothing! Absolutely nothing!"

"You know why he's doing this don't you? He's trying to get back at us, break us up. Well, he's taken on the wrong person, I'll crush him."

"No, this is my fight," I reply to Sydney's obvious disappointment. "I'll sort him out myself. I'm not frightened of him. When I've finished with him, he will regret the day that he ever set eyes on me. Also, I don't think that he is aware of you, so there is no need for you to get involved."

"Donna, you know me better than that, a fight of yours is also a fight of mine. How can I sit by while you fight this madman alone. If you're unhappy how do you think that will make me feel? I'm not going to have that man forever ruining your life and consequently mine. He needs to be taught a lesson, once and for all!"

"He needs to be taught a lesson! I think I need to be taught a lesson. Only a few moments ago I was seriously contemplating getting married but I don't think that that would be such a good move somehow. I have seen how nasty men can be when they don't get their own way."

"Wait a minute, Donna, that's not fair…"

"Life isn't fair, Sydney," I say, interrupting him.

"There are some bad men, as there are bad women. I don't doubt that, but it would be incredibly naïve of anyone to tarnish all men and women with the same brush."

"Do you think that I could be thinking about getting married at this moment, when someone is thinking about taking away my child?"

"Donna, I know how you must feel but…"

"Do you?" I say, cutting in. "Do you really know what I am going through at this moment? You have everything that you set out to acquire. I have one thing only, and that is my daughter. Nothing else really matters to me but her." I know this would hurt Sydney but I don't care. The way I feel at this moment, he might as well be Dexter.

"I don't think that I have ever seen you so angry," says Sydney looking sorry for himself. "No, you're right," he confesses, "I can't know how you really feel, but I do know what it's like to feel and can still empathise with you. It seems to me that you have been with a man who has shown so little interest in you for such a long time, that you do not believe that someone can really care for you. I can understand that to a certain degree but you should know what I stand for. You know me better than anyone ever would or could."

"That maybe so, but I don't know how you've changed over the years, do I?"

"Donna, where is this coming from? Please don't go down that road? Don't let Dexter come between us, otherwise he will have succeeded in wrecking your life. I bet you he is nice and comfortable where he is at this moment, just gleaming to himself over what he is doing to you. It seems like he might know you better than you think."

"I saw Rupert yesterday and there was no indication whatsoever that this was to come. I can't believe that Dexter would not have discussed this with Rupert. Rupert did say that they met, but said little else. Maybe this was because he knew what was to come."

"I hope Rupert is not behind this fiasco, as I would not hesitate to make life very difficult for him," replies Sydney angrily.

"And how would you do that?" I ask. "Don't you think that Rupert was doing just nicely before you came along? So you take away your work from him, he will simply obtain work elsewhere." I know Sydney is trying to be helpful, but short of him getting Dexter off my back all suggestions seem futile.

"Oh, I have more than just work on Rupert," replies Sydney boldly.

"What are you talking about, Charles? What could you possibly have on Rupert? A few months ago you wouldn't have even remembered him and now you're saying that he owes you something!"

"I'm not saying he owes me anything, what I am saying is that I could make life difficult for him, if I wished to do so."

"And how can you do that?"

"Unfortunately, I can't say."

"Oh, I see. Not too long ago you wanted my hand in marriage, where, I thought that we were going to be open with each other and not to keep secrets, and yet I ask you a simple question and you can't answer me. And you wonder why I tarnish you all with the same brush!"

"Donna, if I could tell you, then I would, but I really can't. And, at this time, I think that we should be concentrating our efforts on Dexter."

"Like I said, this is not your fight. I don't want him or anyone else to think that I can't fight my own battles. I can stand up for myself. It's me he wants to fight with and so it shall be." Sydney doesn't reply to my gallant expression of determination, I think having thought better of it. Poor man, he has kept off the subject of marriage, also. The way I feel at this moment, I can't see myself marrying anyone for love nor money, both of which I think

Sydney has but I haven't got the strength to fight Dexter and keep Sydney sweet. Men!

"Rupert didn't mention anything about this to me," says Pat. "He would have told me if he had known. As you know, he and Dexter met the other night. Mind you, he did come in rather late for a midweek night. And, now to think about it, he did seem a little disturbed when he came in. He didn't seem quite all there."

"I can't see Rupert being too disturbed by Dexter telling him what he was about to do. But, for all I know, Dexter might have been seeking advice from Rupert on how to pursue his claim."

"I don't think that Rupert would advise him on such a thing. Anyway, Rupert would not be suitably qualified to advise him. I'm no lawyer but I can't think that there could be much correlation between commercial law and family law. In any case, why would Rupert necessarily advise Dexter to do something as horrid as this against you? And, if it's one thing I give him credit for it is that he has now stopped taking Dexter's side, just for the sake of doing so. Before, he used to back Dexter as a matter of course, rightly or wrongly."

"You're probably right," I say in resignation.

"It seems to me that Dexter is doing this to get back at you, after hearing that you're doing all right without him. He knows he hasn't got a cat in hell's chance of getting Dionne."

"I know that too, but it doesn't stop me worrying. And like Sydney said, that is what he wants: me to worry. The man has serious problems. All this rubbish about Sydney and his potential lifestyle. What the hell does potential lifestyle mean? I kept this insult from Sydney because I know that Sydney would've nigh killed the man. Sydney may be passive, and sweet with it, but he gets stink when people try to play the fool with him. And it being Dexter would have made him doubly mad, if there is such a term. Dexter would often remind me that I would never find anyone as good as him."

"Perish the thought!" says Pat. "You'd have difficulty finding someone who wasn't better! Sorry Don, this is not the time for snide remarks."

"No, you're right Pat," I reply, in no way taking offence.

"Dexter only has good looks going for him but after you've got used to that then you want some substance and there he is lacking."

"What's hurting him, girl, is not so much that you're with someone, although I'm sure he's not too pleased about that either, but that you're with someone so soon after him. He thought that you would have stayed at home brooding over him. Also, I wouldn't put it past Rupert to tell Dexter all about Sydney and about his money. I dare say that that wouldn't have gone down too well."

"No, I don't think it would've."

"A dent in the ego, I think."

"Say it, girl. You know what hurts me most of all? It is that both Dexter and I know that he doesn't want me. He showed me that he lost interest in me a long time ago. That's fair enough; he made me fall out of love with him, so I was spared any pain that I might otherwise have suffered. And you know what, Pat? Despite all that he did to me, I still wished him no harm, but what he is doing is making me dislike him more and more. And all that does is harden any defence against him. He doesn't seem to realise that. When I threw him out of the flat, it was him who gave me the strength to do it. Each time he did me wrong, I repelled against him more and more until I could have taken no more. My defence, by then, was too strong for him to break down."

"I understand what you're saying, Don."

"I think Dexter is the type of man that wants to have a woman waiting on him. You know the type of men that try to have a woman in every port they visit, in case they have to visit that port again."

"Yes, I do," replies Pat passively listening to me getting everything off my chest. "They give women some money now and again and then they think that that is enough to keep them. They own them!"

"Exactly! Only, Dexter never tried that with me because he never gave me any money unless it was strictly for food or directly for the home."

"I suppose if there is anything good to come out of your relationship with Dexter, it was little Dionne," says Pat.

"Yes, I wouldn't change her for the world."

"The more I think about it, Don, the more I'm convinced that Dexter is just doing this to cause you anxiety. I don't think that he would have the audacity to carry out his threat," says Pat confidently. I wish that I could feel the same way, but it's not easy: my child is at stake!

"I wouldn't put anything past him, Pat. Nothing surprises me with that man anymore."

"What has Sydney had to say about all this?"

"He's been very supportive of me, but I've been giving him a bit of a hard time since all this surfaced."

"Take it easy, girl. You don't want him to slip away again," says Pat showing genuine concern. "You might lose him for good this time. And you know who would come out the winner don't you?"

"Dexter!" we both say in chorus.

"Well, don't let him get his way," demands Pat. "He's done that for far too long; it's about time he was stopped!"

"That reminds me!" I interrupt. "I almost forgot. Sydney has asked me to marry him!"

"What! Congratulations, girl," says Pat excitedly. "That's what I call playing it cool. When did he pop the question?"

"Two days ago."

"And you're just telling me now?" asks Pat sounding a little offended.

"Yes, well with all this business with Dexter going on, I've had little time to think of anything else. Sorry."

"That's all right. So, when is the big day?"

"Well, at this moment in time, there is no big day."

"What are you talking about, girl? Tell me you didn't turn the man down!"

"No, I didn't turn him down," I reply, trying to dispel Pat's apprehensions; she seems genuinely concerned that I may have said something that I might live to regret. "But I didn't accept either."

"You're not having doubts about him are you, Don?" asks Pat, still not entirely satisfied that all will be okay. "Sydney is good for you, girl. You must know that. Since he's been back into your life you have been a new woman. Have you forgotten how depressed-looking you were with Dexter?"

"I wasn't 'depressed-looking', Pat," I correct, "I was depressed, period! It was just bad timing for Sydney that's all. I was actually on the brink of accepting his proposal when I read Dexter's letter, telling me what he was planning. At that moment I just lost all interest in wanting to tie myself down to a man, knowing full well that one was already giving me grief. I took it out on Sydney when, God bless him, it was Dexter I was mad at. He took it well, though. He knows me well enough to know that I'm not truly mad at him but at Dexter."

"So when are you going to put the man out of his misery?" asks Pat seeking further reassurance that I will not pass on the opportunity. "You can't keep him hanging on for too long, you know."

"I know but let's face it, Pat, we've been apart for one hell of a long time and if he really wants me, then I'm sure that another few more days or so isn't going to make too much difference."

"You're probably right," concedes Pat, "I think!"

"Why couldn't I have found love and married that person first time, like you?" I ask.

"I wouldn't quite put it that way. I didn't particularly fancy Rupert when I first met him, he just grew on me."

"That may be so, but at least you went for the brains where there was a good chance that a decent relationship would evolve from it. I had to go for looks!"

"Rupert is not that ugly!" says Pat defensively.

"You know what I mean, Pat. Rupert is nothing like Dexter in so many ways."

"I have often asked myself how it is that neither has influenced the other when it comes to women."

"Dexter is not likely to persuade Rupert to be like him," I say. "Rupert is far too mature and sensible to get himself mixed up in any affair. In fact I couldn't think of anything more inconceivable. Rupert appreciates and is satisfied with what he's got, Dexter didn't and wasn't. And the joke of all this is that Dexter's only serious contribution towards Dionne, if you can call it that, was a sixty-second romp in the bed. Actually, it wasn't even in the bed, I think it was on our living-room floor! And, he mentions Sydney's potential lifestyle; what about his? How does he think he would cope with constantly having to look after Dionne instead of arranging a date with some floozy? He must think that looking after a child is a part-time job. Does he really think that he is prepared to act the mature father and pay due attention to his daughter's every need? If he had to choose between getting his leg over or spending a quiet night in with his daughter, I know which he would prefer. And before you know it, Dionne's had more babysitters than hot dinners."

"Ooh!" says Pat, whilst clutching her stomach."

"I'm sorry, Pat. Here I am going on about my problems and I haven't even asked you how you're feeling."

"Well, I still feel rough in the mornings. I heard about women suffering from morning sickness but I never thought of it as a real sickness. I feel so ill first thing in the morning, I dread going to sleep in fear of having to wake up and face that feeling again. It's horrible!"

"You remind me of when I was pregnant with Dionne. As you know I too had a difficult pregnancy but when you see the reward it makes it all worthwhile. And you know what?" I add. "I would go through it all over again knowing what is at the end of it all. Only this time, preferably with a man, not a boy, who would be a true father to my child."

"Who is going to be a true father to your child?" says Rupert's voice emitting from the passageway.

"It's never good to interrupt big people's conversation," says Pat to her husband. I was going to add, "didn't you're mother ever tell you that?" but even today, and I never knew her, I am always on my guard so as not to trigger off any painful memories that could arise in Rupert with regards to his late mother.

"Hi honey," says Pat. "We didn't hear you come in."

"Just as well, it seems. Am I not the true father?"

"I hope you're not having second thoughts of becoming one," says Pat playfully.

"I didn't say that. I was just making further enquiries, in case there is something I need to know."

"It seems like you've been around Dexter too much," I add.

"Not everyone is as slack as he is, you know!" Rupert gives a nervous smile to my comment but then he always was a staunch defender of his friend, despite what Pat says.

"You tell him, girl," says Pat in support. "Well, you're not in court now so you need not enquire much further. I think that on the balance of probabilities, to put it into your legal jargon, the evidence suggests that I am pregnant."

"I don't think I like the sound of that," says Rupert. "There should be no doubt at all who the father is. It should be way beyond reasonable doubt. A lesser standard of proof will not suffice!" he adds, seemingly content with his closing remarks.

"Okay, to put your mind at ease, provided that I have not immaculately conceived then you can be rest assured that you are the lucky father."

"Or should that be that you are the lucky mother of my child."

"Don't push it, Jackson!" commands Pat.

"I think that I can safely referee this one and say that you are both lucky to be having each other's child," I intervene diplomatically. "I only wish that Dexter was as grateful for having a child as you two are for yours to be.

"Talking of Dexter," says Pat. "Can you believe how low he has sunk to this time?" she asks Rupert. I watch to see his reaction to what Pat was about to say. I never did manage to extract from Sydney what he could possibly have over Rupert but whatever it was he seemed sure that it could be damning. "He is threatening to take Dionne away from Donna." Rupert seems to give nothing away by way of emotion.

"Did you know about this, Rupert?" I ask calmly. Rupert says nothing as if waiting for the question to register at his central processing unit. The expression on his face now changed from giving nothing away to saying plenty.

"Rupert!" says Pat with a look of astonishment, as if in disbelief at what his silence proclaimed.

"No, I didn't," replies Rupert very unconvincingly.

"Rupert, I don't believe you. How could you keep this to yourself?" Like me, Pat had totally ignored what Rupert had said and read his body language that had conveyed a different answer. Rupert says nothing. He looks like a schoolboy who has just been caught stealing from the school kiosk.

"Rupert," I say, not so calmly this time, "I know Dexter is a closer friend to you than me. I take no offence at that; somebody has to like him. But I thought that you would have, at least, made him see sense, not encouraged him! I thought you would know better." I look at Pat and I can tell that she was embarrassed to know that her own husband could be embroiled in what Dexter was doing to me.

"Wait there, Donna. It's not the way it seems," says Rupert in his defence. "I would never encourage Dexter to do such craziness. You know me better than that!"

"I have my doubts if I do, Rupert," I say without an ounce of venom in my voice. I think that I should be angry with Rupert, but I'm not. I simply pity him for how Pat will deal with him later.

"He told me about his intentions and I spent most of the night trying to talk him out of it. Pat will tell you, I came in late that night, or should I say the following morning. I could see that I wasn't getting through to him, so made him promise me that he would not do anything until we spoke again."

"It's unlike Dexter to break a promise," I interrupt.

"Why didn't you tell me this, Rupert?" asks Pat. I could tell that Pat was angry at what she had to witness, at the same time as me. I got the impression that had I not been here now, Rupert would not be having as easy a time from Pat as he is now. I can't guarantee it will remain this way when I leave.

"When you didn't hear from Dexter," says Rupert to me, "I just thought that it was a threat that he wouldn't really carry out. He was just overreacting."

"Overreacting to what?" I ask.

"I told him about you and Sydney."

"So that's where he got all this rubbish about Sydney and his potential lifestyle. You must have carried out a character assassination on Sydney for Dexter to feel so strongly about someone he has never met?" I state.

"I said nothing bad," replies Rupert. "There is nothing bad to say."

"You must have said more than just complimentary things,

otherwise why would Dexter feel the need to take such drastic action, when we all know that he probably cares little more for Dionne than he does for me?" Pat adds nothing to what I'm saying and simply leaves me to deal with her husband.

"Donna, I don't think that I need to tell you anything about Dexter that you probably don't already suspect," he says. "Dexter would have acted this way no matter who you were with. I could not have sung Sydney's praises any higher. We all know this has nothing to do with Sydney. Dexter's pride has been dented and he's a wounded man."

"Did he tell you he was wounded?" I ask.

"Not in so many words but I know him, and he is hurting, believe me. I don't know what comes over him sometimes but I don't think that he would have wished for things to turn out the way they did between you."

"Really?" I ask. "Well he went about it in a strange way. Having all those women was a way of showing me how much he loved me, was it? I don't see you having plenty of women to show your love for Pat." Rupert coughs, clearly appreciating my point.

"He knows where his backside would end up, that's why," says Pat, still angry.

"Hey, girls don't turn on me," pleads Rupert. "We're talking about Dexter here, remember?"

"Rupert, make him come to his senses," commands Pat.

"Like I said, Pat. I told him not to do anything before speaking to me. I'll try and see whether I can contact him at work and speak to him again. What has Sydney made of all this?" asks Rupert.

"He is furious. I believe in fighting my own battles but I cannot guarantee that I can keep Sydney out of this for ever. After all, this is bound to affect him in one way or another. And he has already told me that if he gets involved, people will suffer." As I say this I look at Rupert, in search of clues. He doesn't look very comfortable. Maybe Sydney's work is worth more to Rupert than I had realised. "He must know something that I don't," I add.

"Beats me!" replies Rupert with an 'I understand' look, only I don't, but wish I did.

"Honey," adds Pat in a rather peaceful manner and barely

audible, but telling voice, "I don't want Donna and Sydney to go through any more of this and I definitely don't want us falling out with them because of your association with that toe-rag." There is no way that my relationship with Pat could possibly come under strain over this business, but the words are very effective. It has never ever occurred to me that Pat and I could fall out over anything. Not that we don't have our disagreements, everyone does. It's healthy. But to fall out so that we don't ever speak again, we become foes, is inconceivable!

"I would like you to do the best you can to bring this to an end," she continues. "I'm sure that if anyone can persuade him to drop this action then it is you. Promise me that you will."

"I'll do my best, I promise," says Rupert. He was clearly feeling uncomfortable over the whole affair. A lot seemed to be resting on his shoulders. Maybe unfairly, I don't know. Only time will tell. He made his way out of the room rather lethargically and staggered upstairs.

"Don't you think that we were a little bit too heavy on him?" I ask Pat, who was obviously not at all pleased about Rupert's involvement with Dexter over this affair.

"Not at all!" replies Pat. "I know my husband; he works well under pressure. I know his pressure points well and exerting a little pressure in the right places will make sure that he will do all that he can in order to get Dexter to change his mind."

"What's this about us falling out over this? That couldn't possibly happen, you know that?"

"Of course I do, but I still don't want you going through this with or without Sydney, and if Rupert or I can help bring this about then so we shall. Ooh!"

"Are you all right, Pat?" I ask, as she holds her stomach again.

"Yes, I'm fine. It's just that I sometimes get these very bad tummy aches that makes me want to lie down."

"I'd better leave you to lie down. I'm sorry that I have come here and all I have done is blabber about my problems."

"Don't be silly," says Pat. On that note I make my way out of the door feeling rueful. I know that she hasn't been feeling too well and yet I burdened her with my troubles. True to her character, she listened and tried to find a solution. A friend in need...

Josephine

"Oh! Baby, that was good," says Leon, looking pleased with himself. Leon has, surprisingly, been very supportive. He has been faithful to us despite me advising him otherwise. He's had offers from other designers for The Best of British Fashion shows but has kept them on hold, until we make our final decision whether to participate or not. I don't know how long such loyalty can be sustained under the pressure of Sydney who understandably wants everything and everyone in place well before the tour. Sydney is a staunch perfectionist, so any last minute arrangements are definitely out of the question. And I'm well aware that had it not been for Donna then he would have pulled the plug on us by now. He is giving us all the breaks we need, but even we know that can't last for ever.

Leon calls about once a week, and we have met a few times with the inevitable consequence. I don't mind the consequence, with all my problems at the moment my body needs pleasure not commitments. I have never asked him about other women and he has never asked me about other men. I get what I want when I want it. In that respect, I'm in control. We meet, we talk and we make love. It's as simple as that. That's all I want in my life at the moment. I know that there are plenty of men who would be only too kind to perform such a role, but then they would be only interested in satisfying their own needs. Leon knows how to make my body feel good. He knows the pleasure points and uses them to both our advantage. He is what I call a Class-A lover. Men think it's only them that score a performance. I've been scoring men since I was experienced enough to know what's what. I have three classes of men. There is the Class-C lover. That is the man who has lost the plot. He knows that he should be making love but is not sure why, to whom or to what! I sympathise with him but I have done my apprenticeship, I don't need to be used as a training ground for anyone! I want pleasure just as much as the next person. My discovery days are long gone. So he is of no use whatsoever. Then there is the Class-B lover. This is the most popular category. He is what I call the selfish lover. I'm sure that women have come across many like him. This is the guy that just wants to get his end away. And, the sooner he achieves that goal the better. He has no interest in satisfying you whatsoever. Before you can ask, "are you satisfied?" he is fast asleep. You are there solely to give him pleasure and nothing more. In many respects this guy is worse than the Class-C lover. At least there is hope that one day the Class-C lover will get round to reading the script. The Class-B lover knows the plot, but still screws it up, if you excuse the expression. Then there is my man, the Class-A lover. He is rare. I call him the selfless lover. He's read the script, learnt his lines and mastered the plot. He gives pleasure to the woman, as well as to himself. And when it is over, it's not over. He will caress me and continue to give me the attention he gave me only but a few moments before, whilst we were making love. That is Leon.

"Your body feels tense, baby. What's the matter?" asks Leon.

"Nothing, I feel this way whenever I put together a collection, and after the theft of the last one, I feel a little nervous, that's all."

"Baby, you're going to be fine. Why don't you take the day off. We could drink champagne and fine wine all day and not put a foot out of the bed."

"I don't think I can stomach alcohol so early in the morning. Don't you think that you should be cutting back on all this drinking anyway?" I ask. I normally take people as I find them but Leon drinks far too much. He is abusing his body. His body is lean and firm but I wouldn't like to say what his hard drinking is doing to his inside.

"Did Samson need a haircut?" asks Leon. "Baby, I need my drink in order to get me through the day. Some people take drugs, I take alcohol. At least alcohol is legal!"

"That's no excuse to abuse yourself," I reply.

"It's not called abuse, it's called survival. It's called remaining sane when all around you appears to have gone mad. You see what I do. Where do you think I get the nerve to do all that stuff. People all around me keep telling me how good I am. They tell me that I can make the camera see things that are invisible to the naked eye. One reporter, after viewing a collection of my photographs at an exhibition, when I was just seventeen, wrote that I would be the best: 'you could set music to his pictures.' That's pressure, baby! I'm twenty-one years old and people pay me a fortune simply to take a picture. I am already branded the best that Britain has to offer. And you think that I could get by in an ordinary day without some help? I need to be high to cope with people's expectations of me and I need to be high to cope with the pressure."

"But like you said, you are one talented guy," I reply, sympathising with him. But I can't condone his alcohol abuse. "It is you that has the talent to produce all those wonderful photographs, not the drink that makes you do it."

"To tell you the truth, baby, I don't think I can do this whilst being sober. It would frighten me shitless. Think about it, in my profession, it could take years to discover what it is that makes people move close to tears when they see your pictures. You need to be able to take that picture that is unique, a scene that will never be seen anywhere in the world. The capturing of a single moment in time that will soon pass and be gone for ever, never to return. If you fail to take your chance at the first time of calling then you have failed outright. There might be a second picture, it might even be similar to the one that you missed, but in my eyes it is still not the same picture. It is a different photograph. That in itself is not a problem. I could live with that if it were up to me alone but it invariably isn't. The clients call the shots. They pay the money and they call the tune. And that can be where the pressure lies."

"It's only money," I say. "If people don't like what you have done then return their money. It's not worth ruining your health for it. Your work should be a slave to you not you to it."

"I'll remember you said that, if your pictures of Paris don't come out and every fashion magazine in the world is begging for pictures of your collection for their front cover." I could see where he was coming from. No money in the world could compensate me in such predicament.

"I understand," I reply. I couldn't lie. "Unfortunately, I can't stay in bed all day. I have work to do and so have you, for that matter." Leon helped himself to a can of beer that he kept in the bedside refrigerator. I left him in the flat and made my way to the office.

I can't say that I particularly look forward to these meetings. I tend to find them frustrating to the point of almost wanting to pack up and give in. And, if it wasn't for the others, I probably would've done that a long time ago, but this project is not just about me it's about them also. We have had numerous brainstorming meetings and cut just as many samples, but have yet to get that design that has made me feel that "this is the one". You can't explain that empty feeling you have when someone takes away your work without either permission or merit. You feel like your privacy has been invaded, without your consent. I cannot walk past a boutique without scrutinising the designs for any hint of my creative work. As anyone from this profession knows, such mission is bound to result in a fruitless exercise.

"Good morning team," I say, opening the meeting. Despite the negative vibes I may have within me, I always try to give out as much of a positive vibe as I can muster. I always feel that they have a longer way to go in their part of the industry, to establish themselves, than I do. Next year I shall have a new collection come what may, with or without them, preferably with them of course. But, at the end of the day it is my name that will stand or fall by the quality of the collection. They get no public acknowledgement but from me. Paris would go some way towards bridging that gulf of recognition that they duly deserve.

"As usual, I have made a few sketches that I would like us to consider," I continue. "They don't have any particular theme to them but I thought that a mixture of black and grey would be reflective of our mood." As would normally be the case in our meetings, I pass copies of the sketches round, commencing with Virginia to my right and absorb the expressions on the faces of the team as they try to interpret what I am trying to achieve. I feel that I can get more from watching them than from anything they may have to say, despite their honesty. Silence befalls us, as each critical eye is poured over the sketches. It's always interesting to hear the diversity of views that reflect the various skills and ambitions of each member. Virginia sees no boundaries to what can be done. "If it can be thought then it can be done," was her motto for a while. You would be amazed at the impact those few words had on us. We would think deep for any ounce of ingenuity. We kept telling ourselves that the designs only reflected the limits of our imaginations and not the limits of our talents. I take back what I said earlier on, I would have to have Virginia by my side, I think. She is a great motivator. She and Adam are constantly arguing as to what can and cannot be done. Adam is more cautious than the rest of us, often reminding us that he has to cut the cloth. Such debates are fascinating to listen to and are the healthiest you can witness, because what is often extrapolated is an idea worth pursuing. I guess I couldn't do without Adam, either. Without giving it too much thought, I probably attach more weight to what he has to say than the others. Most of our conceptual input is obviously at the outset of the design process, whereas what the public sees are the finished products that were cut by Adam. Like Virginia, he is one of the original members of the team and knows how I think. I trust them both. Both couldn't be more different in backgrounds and influences. Virginia is a dark-skinned Grenadian woman, who gives us all the influences that the Caribbean has to offer. I met her when she was on a visit to England having just finished a Master of Business Administration at the University of the West Indies. She reminded me of Scarecrow in the Wizard of Oz. She has an incredible bank of quotations that she would effortlessly use in support of her views. We hit it off right away. She was, and probably still is, one of the few people I have met who is not afraid of a challenge. During a heated debate one time, between her and Adam, she quoted Edward Kennedy as once saying "some men see things as they are, and say 'why?' I dream things that never were and say 'why not?'" and informed Adam that that was what he would always be up against. I met Adam on a train. I jumped on a train just as the doors were about to close and he kindly kept them open for me. We got chatting and I invited him down to see what I was about. At that time, I was cutting my own cloths and had not considered trusting someone with my materials, let alone my ideas. Adam comes from fashionable Chelsea in the heart of South-West London. Adam, I must admit, is the scruffiest person I have ever met. He is so untidy I sometimes wonder how someone like him could ever have any interest in fashion! There are no obvious signs that he does. His hair and clothes are always in such a mess. I often compare him to the Adam in the print we have on our wall of a painting called *Paradise* by Lukas Cranach. Like couples who sometimes tend to look like each other when they have been together for many years, so like Adam who seems to look like his namesake in the picture after many years of sitting just below the print. I guess that Virginia and Adam are akin to the recording artist who needs to know that her engineer will give her exactly what she requires, which is not always easy to put into words. They know what I mean, even though I may not have said it. I think that is the best way of describing our chemistry.

"I can see something there, but we are going to have to work on it," says Adam.

"What do the rest of you think?" I ask. Similar murmurs are made in reply. It is difficult to produce inspired work without the inspiration. I sometimes feel like saying, "maybe these are signs that we should pull out of the shows", but such words can't seem to find their way out of my mouth. The print on the wall to the right of *Paradise* is a lovely picture that was given to me by Jeremy, Paul Gauguin's *Woman Holding a Fruit*. Seeing this picture reminds me of Jeremy who was not a great lover of meetings. He often saw them as an expensive way of doing very little. I could see what he means. I wonder what he is doing now? I am sometimes curious to know how he is progressing, now that he is on the board of his grandfather's company.

"It seems to me that this meeting has come to its natural end," I say, breaking the silence that filled the meeting. I couldn't help saying this in a tone of "resignation".

"I think that we should have at least one more meeting before we throw in the towel," says Virginia. "If we cannot then produce something that we feel is worthy of our talents, then I'm afraid that time may have defeated us." I could sense the tension in the room and the air of anxiety, but everyone knew that Virginia was absolutely right. We all thought it, but were afraid to say it. The door is not yet shut and definitely not yet locked, it is ajar, but only just. Adam did not reply to what Virginia had to say. He looked no happier than his namesake in the picture above him. At least the Adam in the picture is consuming an apple that gave him knowledge, albeit to the detriment of "man". What I would give for a fraction of that inspiration now.

"Remember team," continues Virginia. "We are all in this thing together, so let's say we give it our best shot next time. Ask, and it shall be given you; seek, and ye shall find; knock, and it shall be opened unto you. I think you all know what I am saying." Hearing Virginia say this reminds me of my mother, who would use every given opportunity to quote something from the Bible and, if you were lucky or unlucky depending on your point of view, she would start to "preach the word" there and then.

We've had so many of these brainstorming meetings over the past few days I've started counting the number of apples in Cranach's *Paradise*. I've counted "thirty-eight" more times than any other number so I guess, on the law of averages, that must be the correct number of apples. I don't think, in all the years that we've had this painting, that I have so much as given it more than a second glance, let alone a second thought. It is rather symbolic that the simple act of biting an apple could have led to the growth of such a multi-billion-dollar industry. For, if my memory serves me correctly, it was only after Adam bit the apple did he know that he was naked. Once man had this knowledge then it was up to my predecessors to clothe him. Mind you, we haven't always rushed to fully clothe ourselves, have we? I do sometimes wonder why people from different societies feel more or less shy about revealing their bodies. We all originate from Adam, so why do we all feel ashamed of our nakedness? I guess the woman holding the fruit in Gauguin's painting is half-way between those who are shy of their God-given bodies and those who are not, covering only what some deem to be offensive. Only, what's deemed to be offensive is most coveted. We all yearn for it at some time or another in our lives. Many even pay good money for it, so it can't be that offensive. It's a matter of covering the bare essentials when what is not on view is not on offer. I like that. It has an advertising ring to it. 'Ladies, this collection is only a matter of covering the bare essentials when what is not on view is not on offer." "The bare essentials", that's not a bad name for a collection. But you can't have a name of a collection without the collection. Maybe there is more to those pictures than what meets the uninspired mind.

"I've got it!" I shout out shamelessly. They know me. I have these flashes of what I call inspiration every now and again. Some are brilliant and some not so worthy of the acclaim, but this could be of the former.

"Bare Essentials!" I continue as I am met with puzzled expressions. I look at the pictures for more food, as my mouth had prematurely revealed a concept in its infancy not yet ready for its premiere. I am creating a design that is a few instructions ahead of my brain. Sometimes these are the best, as such thoughts are pure and unrefined.

"How many of us here today have ever spent time studying the pictures we have on our walls?" No hands are raised. They all face and look at the pictures on the walls as if for the first time in their lives. I can now feel my thoughts cementing. The idea is making sense. My imagination is maturing into reality. This can work.

"Look at the pictures behind Adam, *Paradise* and *Woman Holding a Fruit*. When I look at these pictures I see a naked Adam and Eve to a semi-naked woman."

"I'm with you there!" says Diane, our seamstress, with more than a hint of sarcasm. I ignore this remark as she probably only beat somebody else to it.

"Well you keep with me, Diane, because you're going to have to sew this stuff. I want our design to reflect both innocence and sensuality. Each dress outfit will display at least one erotic fruit." I could see that there was now an air of intrigue and possible support for what I was proposing.

"I like it, boss," says, Adam.

"We'll transform a completely naked body," I say, acknowledging Adam's endorsement, "leaving nothing to the imagination, to a minimally clothed body, leaving very little to the imagination but still leaving something to the mind."

"Yes!" says Virginia shaking her head in approval as my plan begins to sink in.

"The latter," I continue, "being more sensuous as onlookers lust to see what is not on view. But what's not on view is not on offer." Short of making love, I have always thought this to be far more erotic than the full exposure of a naked body. It's like yearning for something that you know you can't have, wanting the forbidden fruit only because it is forbidden. "The Bare Essentials will be our most provocative and exciting collection to date," I say, finally.

"You know what we got to do team, so let's get to work," says Virginia. I can tell that my plan was well received. I feel that what is being proposed could be our most ambitious collection to date, which, if it is to work, will give us the recognition that we all desire, bigger than the one it replaced. Paris, here we come!

Rupert

"I didn't think that I would have missed him as much as I do, but then again I didn't count on him taking his own life," says Linda.

"That is understandable," I respond. Linda has taken the death of Wilson very hard. Her work has suffered badly. She seems to have very little enthusiasm to do anything, as if that is her way of punishing herself. A self-imposed punishment that she is telling herself she deserves.

"I too am a victim of all this. I had a great relationship with Wilson's parents. They loved me. I could do no wrong in their eyes. When people who loved you turn so much against you, in the way they have, it's hard to take. Especially when you know that the premise they are working from is a false one."

"You can't make people like you," I say, trying to comfort her as much as I can. "You have a life to live as well. If you were unhappy then you were right to do something about it."

"But they were such lovely people, Rupert. I feel like I have helped take away the only thing that was worth living for in their lives."

"You can't shoulder this blame, Linda. You did not take Wilson's life away from them; he took his own life."

"And you're saying that had absolutely nothing to do with me."

"That is not what I am saying, but, before you go running around accusing yourself with aiding and abetting, you should look at the wider picture."

"I think the wider picture includes me, doesn't it?" interjects Linda.

"Of course it does, but what I am trying to get at is that you two were together knowing that it could not have continued indefinitely. You know that."

"Yes, I do. You know that and I know that, but his parents don't!"

"What can you possibly do about that?"

"Speak to them. Explain to them how things really were behind closed doors. Make them see that all was not as it may have seemed."

"Linda," I state rather impatiently, "they don't even want to see you. That is not your fault. They have chosen to cut you off without telling you why."

"That, I think, is what's hurting most. I don't know what Wilson told them and I have no way of putting my side of the story. He must have told them something that displeased them otherwise they would not have ostracised me."

"It sounds like you are seeking their blessing in order to allow you to continue with a normal life without their son."

"It's not their blessing I require, it's their forgiveness."

"I only wish I knew what it is that you are seeking forgiveness for. I hope whatever it is, however, you get it soon because you need to get back on your feet. You seem to be letting yourself slip."

"Thank you very much. Let's hope that you never have to experience what I have."

"I'm only trying to be helpful, Linda."

"Sorry, I didn't mean it the way it appeared. But this is not easy for me. I think I need to get away and think a lot of things through. I have a friend who lives in Barcelona. I haven't seen her for a while, maybe I should visit her for a few days."

"That might do you some good," I add in support. "Talking of abroad, what is going to happen with Paris? Are you still interested in going?"

"Of course I am, but I am not in the mood for working at the moment. I think that I would be a nervous wreck if it were left to me to capture a show on camera. I am going through a bad run at the moment. They say it never rains but it pours. Well I'm in the middle of a monsoon with not a glimpse of sky in sight. Even your friend Sydney has given up on me. At one time he was very helpful, now I can't even get through to him at his office and he never returns my calls. He used to before. And when I have managed to catch him on his mobile, he has always been busy saying that he will call me back which, of course, he never does!"

"I haven't spoken to Sydney for a while so I don't know what is going on. His company doesn't seem as busy as it was before. He's probably just busy trying to sort out business matters. I wouldn't take it personally if I were you."

"How do you know that his company isn't so busy? What do you know that the rest us don't?"

"I have no inside information. It's just that I am one of his lawyers and I have not been sent any new briefs recently, so I presume that that is a sign of the times at Charles' Artists Agency."

"It could be that he is just not sending you any work."

"That had crossed my mind but he would have no cause to do so. He hasn't complained as far as I know about the quality of my work, so I presume that my work has been all right."

"He likes your wife doesn't he?"

"Sydney is very fond of Pat, yes. Why do you ask?"

"Maybe he has found out about us."

"I don't think so," I reply. I had explored the possibility that my lack of instructions from Sydney might be due to matters other than the quality of my work but he would have known about Linda, I'm sure from the outset, so I can't believe that it has anything to do with her. But, in the state that Linda is in at the moment I'm definitely not going to reveal to her that such thought had even remotely entered my mind. She is too weak for such frank admissions. "I can't see what could lead him to have any such suspicions. I don't think he suspects anything, but I wouldn't ask him, just to be on the safe side."

"I may be depressed but I'm not mad with it!"

"I don't think anyone can accuse you of that, dear!"

"Could you not ask that designer friend of yours whether she would need someone?"

"I don't know whether she is still going. Her collection for the show was stolen a few weeks ago, and as far as I am aware, she hasn't managed to locate them. In any case, I vaguely remember that she already had a photographer, some ex-boyfriend or someone."

"Well, if she doesn't need a photographer, then she might know someone who does."

"I don't think that that would be a good idea," I state firmly.

"Thanks! You sure know how to give a girl confidence when she's down."

"Oh come on Linda, Josephine is one of Pat's inner circle of friends. We don't know where such introduction might lead. It would be too risky."

"You really do think I'm stupid, don't you?"

"Of course not. And, if this is your way of starting a fight then let me know beforehand so that I can leave you to it on your own. I'm in no mood for a fight!"

"How convenient. Has it ever entered your mind to leave me?"

"I'm still here aren't I?" I reply.

"That's not answering the question," Linda responds adamantly. Such thoughts enter my mind as regular as clockwork. I have a special love for Linda. I can't deny that. She has been good for me too. I can't explain quite what it is. I think it runs deeper than just satisfying my ego, although I don't think that it has done it any harm, either. Linda came into my life when I was happy with my life but it lacked any real excitement. This is no reflection on Pat, I would never wish to hurt her. This is not a "my wife don't understand me" thing. And, this has nothing directly to do with Linda, it is to do with me. This is simply about two women making me very happy. My affair with Linda has gone far beyond anything I could ever have imagined was possible between another woman and me outside my marriage. I never for one moment thought that I could deceive Pat for such a long time without her suspecting that I was misbehaving. My guilt for that conduct peaked a long time ago. I can only think that it is a pattern that we all go through. Such guilt never lasts for ever. That's not to say that it disappears for good. It's cyclical. It's always there, but it's more a question of degree. Some days you feel that you should be at home with your wife and the next you feel that you should be with your lover. I think I came closest to ending my relationship with Linda when Pat became pregnant. I remember making plans for ending it in Paris. I felt an extra sense of responsibility towards Pat, especially when considering how hard we tried to have our baby. At that point I told myself that enough was enough. I had had the fling. No one, luckily, got hurt. Let's end it while that was still the case. In that way we would both have had fond memories of what we alone shared: an experience that neither would forget, our "Casablanca". However, all was not to be. I wasn't, of course, banking on the tragedy that followed. Wilson's death was the worst thing that could have happened to us at that time. I hate the thought of what he did. It gives me nightmares. And I have nightmares about not having "that" nightmare, as if to confirm that it died with the reality. A reality I could have prophesied if only I could have interpreted that dream. I couldn't leave Linda when Wilson died; she was far too vulnerable to face such a rejection. And I was not prepared to take advantage of her vulnerability, catch her with her guard down. I loved her too much for that. I love her now but maturity, late as it is, has taught me that you cannot always have everything that you want. Pat was right. You must think about your partner. I must end it at some time but how and when, I don't know. I see my wife's belly growing bigger by the day. I hear my wife complain how ill she's feeling. She is not having an easy pregnancy. She needs me. She needs to know that I am there for her. And I am. But, I am also there for somebody else, as well. My wife has sacrificed a painless and comfortable life in order to carry our child. I share her burden as much as a man can in mind, if not in body, but I replace some of that burden with my own pleasures with another woman.

"No, it has never crossed my mind to leave you," I reply.

"You don't know how that makes me feel," says Linda, clearly happy by my answer to her question. "I was really scared of being alone when Wilson died. I'm still scared now, but knowing that you're here for me makes me feel wanted and a lot more secure than before. I know you said you would have been there for me, but I've learnt to rely on deeds from people not words."

"You can always count on me, Linda," I say, reassuring her. I uttered these words because they seemed appropriate to say. There were no alternatives and it was my cue.

"Like you said, Rupert, I need to sort myself out and get back into work. Will you speak to your friend Josephine for me?" I hesitate, as I really don't want Linda getting mixed up with Jo. It's too close to home for comfort.

"Rupert!" Insists Linda, just short of a shout, "are you going to help me out or not? I'm not going to try and get invited for tea round at your place, if that's what's worrying you. Give me more credit than that!"

"You're right, I'm sorry. I'm just being paranoid. I just don't want to take any chances. Josephine is very close to Pat. If she gets so much as a whiff of what we're up to, she'll tell Pat faster than you can take a picture. Trust me, I know what I'm talking about."

"I'll be careful. Just ask her whether she knows of anyone who is looking for a good photographer. I'm not asking for any more than that. She doesn't even have to meet me, so she need not know who I am except by name.

"I'll speak to her."

Dexter

"I don't want to get even, John, I want revenge!" I tell John Pot, our Family Law specialist.

"You can't sue her because she hurt your feelings, Dexter," confirms John. "Thankfully, we haven't reached such a stage of desperation in our legal system." John sees a hole where others see only a gap, if they're lucky. He is among one of the brightest lawyers I know and will, undoubtedly, be made a partner within a year or so. He seems to leave no stone unturned within the twinkling of an eye. If I can get something from Donna, then he can get it.

"I was set up, John. That ex-boyfriend of hers got his girlfriend to befriend me so that he could get back with Donna."

"Hold on a second! This all sounds rather fishy to me. Are you sure about this?" asks John with his mind working overtime.

"I am damn sure! I was going out with Chantelle, who was also the ex-boyfriend's girlfriend at the time."

"Has this ex-boyfriend got a name? It's a bit tiring referring to him as the ex-boyfriend."

"Sydney, is all I know and, apparently, he is a very successful businessman."

"And you're saying that this Sydney was using his girlfriend like some kind of pimp?"

"Hey, John, I like the way you think."

"Thank you for the compliment but I am merely thinking aloud to which no reliance should be sought."

"It's me you're talking to, John, not one of your dumb clients."

"You say that he is a very successful businessman, doing what exactly?"

"He has a modelling agency. I am told that he is one of the market leaders. Apparently, every cute little thing is on his books."

"Really?" John replies with more than an eye of suspicion. I can see his sharp mind at work. Donna, you have chosen the wrong person to tread on.

"If Sydney is a pimp then he is clearly living off immoral earnings which will not be very well received, even if your allegations are false. And people always think that there is no smoke without a fire."

"Brilliant! So even if I am wrong, his business may still take a bruising."

"After all," continues John, "would you leave your angel in the care of Sydney after such allegations? Obviously not!" says John answering his own question.

"You're a genius," I say, "but where does this leave Dionne?"

"Well, there are two possible outcomes. First, is that you win the case, thus damaging both Sydney and Donna. Or second, like we said, what mother would allow her baby daughter around someone with such a reputation. Remember it is not about truth, it is about public perception. You're a lawyer, you know the score."

"Fast life, fast women. We could raise enough doubts in people's minds to question his relationship with Donna. I know what Donna is like: she will not be able to handle the pressure. She would leave him. Then she will be right back where she started from. People will ask the question, what is a top business-man like Sydney doing with a 'nothing-to-offer' pauper like Donna."

"Precisely! Is she his next target to work the streets? And with any luck, you might get the pauper back."

"She's not worthy of my attention," I say, confirming how I genuinely feel. "No, she can stay there and rot for all I care."

"Aren't we forgetting someone? Dionne. What happens to her if you win the case?"

"Well, you tell me; this is your field."

"Obviously, you get custody. But, have you seriously thought about how you would bring her up on your own?"

"Come on, John. I can't be the first single father who will be raising his child. I shall raise my child to the best of my abilities. I shall hire the best nanny available. Also, I have plenty of girl-friends who will be only too glad to help me out when I am in a jam."

"You best keep that girlfriend stuff to yourself at any hearing. I don't think that we are yet ready to accept such unorthodox method of raising a child. If anything, that will work against you, I have no doubt about that."

"Actually, the more I think about it is the more I like it. Women love a man with a baby. Especially, when I say that the mother was no good and I had to battle for the custody of my child in order to rescue her from an environment that was unfit for her."

"You're sick, Dexter, you know that. You're sick. Anything for a woman."

"Damn right you are," I reply. "This way I get to have my cake and eat it. Ruin Donna and get more women for my troubles. When do we start?"

Am I angry? Of course I am. I know that I have never been that popular with many people, but you know what? I couldn't give a shit! What are these people to me? I see things very much in black and white. And the way I see it, if you're not for me then you're against me. What else is there? Donna and I didn't have what one would call a rosy relationship, but I gave her a break. I could have been a bigger womaniser than I was. There were many women queuing up for me, but I contained myself to only a handful. And what do I get in return? The bitch hooking up with some sad ex-boyfriend. Why is he back? Probably, because no one wanted him. How can you run a modelling agency, a successful one at that, and not sleep with some of those babes. Donna must be incredibly naïve, or this boyfriend of hers is so ugly as to make her feel secure. He could give her the security that I couldn't or, should I say, wouldn't. Why should I have given her any false sense of security? A woman should know when she is with a good-looking man that is in demand. So, if she wants to keep her man then she has to keep him happy. I see nothing wrong with that! If you don't keep them on their toes then you will feel insecure. I have been there and I don't like it, so I don't put myself in that position.

All these people walking around talking about being in love, they don't know Jack Shit! Love is just an excuse to act like a fool. They say, "love is blind"; I say, "love is foolishness". When a rich man says he's in love with some poor woman, that makes big news. Why? Because people know the man is being a fool. It's a game. That's all it is. I sussed that out a long time ago. We play games until one can take no more. Each relationship is a new game; you win some, you lose some. Some lasts longer than others. No different to a game of chess, if you ask me, except in a game of chess once the game is over it's over. Relationships are rarely that simple. You see, I don't believe that Donna truly likes this ex-boyfriend of hers. She knew that I would find out what was going on. I used to tell her that she would not find someone as good as me, so this is her way of trying to prove me wrong: another game. Well, I thought she knew me better than that because from now on I will make it my lifetime's occupation to make her unhappy.

I have no answer for why I feel the way I do. Every once in a while, someone does something to you which you can neither forgive nor forget, and I think that Donna must be one of those people to me. She should have shown more remorse when I left the flat. It hurts me to know what she is telling other people, people who will always volunteer a listening ear to hear anything said against me. Donna didn't throw me out of the flat; I left of my own accord. Do you really think that she could have thrown me out, if I didn't want to leave, of course not! I wouldn't have raised my hand to her, I would not stoop so low but there would have been a fight of some kind and the loser was not going to be me! When I'm ready both her and her man will be kicked out of my home. That is to come. I'm in no hurry. I'm with Sonia at the moment and things are cool between us. Sonia is similar to Chantelle in many respects, not as good-looking but has a fitter body. She doesn't ask too many questions. She has me to herself only sometimes and that's all she needs to keep her content. She's a busy and successful woman in marketing and has no time for men that hang around for too long when they're not required. When I think about it, I could have gone round and showed off Sonia to Donna. Let Donna see the sacrifices I made when I was with her. By that I mean the quality of women that I was capable of getting, but chose to give her some street credibility instead. I gave her some respect and this is how she repays me. Well, nobody's going to publicly humiliate me like that and get away with it. Bitch!

Patricia

"It's official!" I proclaim. "As from today we are officially millionaires. That letter you gave me was from my European publishers enclosing a cheque in the sum of just over one and a half million pounds. We're rich!"

"The girl's done good!" says Rupert.

"No," I correct, as Rupert begins to scrutinise the numbers on the cheque in order to confirm whether my interpretation is in fact true, "the girl's done brilliantly!"

"I've never seen so many numbers on a cheque before," he admits. "It is traditional for authors to frame their first royalty cheque."

"That may well be so, but not when it has so many noughts on the end! I'd be more than willing to frame it if you will compensate me for my loss."

"I thought that I had already compensated you," he replies with his boyish smile, whilst passing his hand back and forth over my swollen and impregnated tummy.

"Is that so? If you could get a million and a half for every child you fathered, I would advise you to have more, because it would be quite a lucrative business. Especially when bearing in mind that you are usually conked out after only two minutes!"

"I don't recall you complaining!" replies Rupert, as if he has something to boast about! "In any case, what you have inside you is priceless, and no money in the world could buy what our baby is worth to us."

"Here! Here!" I respond and raise my imaginary glass of champagne as a gesture of my agreement to what was said.

"I can't wait for our little prince or princess to be born," says Rupert. We decided that we would not seek the sex of our baby, as it matters not to us what sex it is. We will love it either way. "I don't think Bertran and Veronica will be able to contain themselves when they see their grandchild for the first time."

"I agree," I reply. "You should have heard how excited they were when I told them that I was pregnant. I thought that Mother was going to wet herself whilst we were talking on the telephone."

"How do you know that she didn't?" he says, laughing.

"It wouldn't surprise me if she had, to be honest," I reply. Mother is a very emotional person and would never dream of holding back how she really felt in any given situation, be it in private or public.

"I just hope that they will be over here in good time," says Rupert. I can see Father and him discussing world politics and deciding on the best way forward for the world in which a child and grandchild can be safely brought up. "Personally," he continues, "I think that a week before their grandchild is due is cutting things a little bit fine."

"Mother wanted to come round the moment we told her, but she would have been unbearable if she was over here all this time, especially during my recent sickness."

"She might as well have been over here because you two talk every night. It has cost us more in the telephone bill than it would have for the flight!"

"Well, we can afford it now can't we? A woman needs her mother's support during her pregnancy. She needs to talk to someone she can trust, someone who has been there before. It was only after when Mother told me what it was like for her when she was pregnant with me did I begin to relax a little. There are so many things that I didn't even know about. And I'm sure that my mother would not have told me unless I was going through what I am today. She never told me how difficult it was for her to get pregnant or the pains she suffered when she was. I didn't even know that I was born by way of a Caesarean. I appear to be going through the same things as my mother did when she was pregnant with me.

"It could be hereditary," says Rupert. "How would you feel if you had to have a Caesarean?"

"I would do anything to have our baby. Like my mother told me when I asked her why she hadn't told me before, she said that she never saw it as a problem, as nothing could have been a problem for her to give birth to me. And I feel exactly the same way."

"I just wish that my mother was here to see her first grandchild," says Rupert with sadness in his voice. It never ceases to amaze me how the death of someone close to you can change your personality when least expected. There is no warning. It just happens. And you only realise the seriousness of the statement or comment after it has been said. By then, of course, it's too late.

"Your mother is with us," I say. "She is looking down on us and I know that she is proud of her son, very proud."

"I want our child to be proud of us too. You hear so many horror stories about parents failing their children."

"I hope we don't become one of them, I really do."

"If our child is not proud of us as parents, then we will have failed, miserably! We will have no one to blame but ourselves. But I think that we will do well. We have waited for this moment for a long time. We have spoken about everything and we're prepared. We couldn't have prepared ourselves any better."

"You seem very confident," I say.

"I am," he replies very confidently. "I have seen how to do it right and how to do it wrong. Or, nearer the truth, how not to do it at all. Pat, I want our baby, badly. I feel that this is an opportunity for me to make amends for what my father did not do for me. I have to prove to myself that my father's neglect of me was not my fault. I have to prove to myself that whatever led him to neglect me as a child had nothing to do with me."

"How could any dereliction of duty by your father have been your fault? You were only a child!" I say. It's a subject that is as sore today as it was when I first met him. I sometimes feel that he believes that he must have done something wrong, in order to warrant such disregard as a young boy. "Why else would a man father a child then care less about the innocent one's upbringing?" is his dilemma. "No amount of soul-searching will amount to you being at fault," I reassure.

"I just want to be a good father. I made a vow at my mother's funeral that I would never be like my father."

"I remember you saying something to yourself at the time but I didn't quite catch the words." Rupert seems to be reflecting on the standard that he had set himself. A standard which by his own account was not too difficult to surpass. How difficult can it be to be a better man than a cheating and neglectful father?

"If only Dexter was as caring for Dionne as you will be for our baby, things could have been so different between him and Donna. One thing is for sure, he wouldn't have embarked on this crazy campaign of his."

"What's the latest on that?" asks Rupert.

"When I last spoke to Donna things were getting a little out of hand. He is now accusing Sydney of living off immoral earnings and being, therefore, a danger to his daughter."

"He's gone mad, I swear," says Rupert shaking his head in disbelieve at his friend's tact. "I can't even talk to him. He never returns my calls and is forever in meetings. Our relationship may have soured over this whole affair. I don't even know what all this has to do with me!"

"He's afraid that you'll talk some sense into him. He is obsessed with making Donna unhappy. I really can't understand why. It's an odd jealousy: 'if I can't have you then nobody can.' Let's hope for his sake that Sydney doesn't get involved. So far Donna has managed to keep him out of the quarrel, but for how long she can continue doing that I don't know."

"Talking of Sydney," says Rupert, "has Donna mentioned anything about Sydney's business being in any financial trouble?"

"No, on the contrary, she is forever saying how well he is doing and how she does not want him to think that she only took him back because of his money. Apparently, his involvement in The Best of British Fashion will net him a fortune. All his models are fetching top prices for the catwalk, as his "supermodels" are barely enough to go round. Why, do you know something that I don't?"

"No, it's just that he has stopped sending me work, so I thought that that might have something to do with his agency being in some sort of trouble."

"Well, we are hardly strapped for cash, so I wouldn't worry about it. Maybe he is just keeping you on your toes in case you become too complacent. He is a friend but he is also a hard-nosed businessman who is probably not in the business of letting go of his money very easily."

"You're probably right, although if there was a problem I would prefer it if he told me rather than keep it to himself."

"Well, Donna hasn't mentioned anything to me so we can assume that my version of events is nearer the truth for now. I hope that a rift doesn't develop between you two, because we are all going to spend some time together in Paris."

"Are we?" asks Rupert, surprised. "I thought that you were going to take things easy from hereon."

"I am but we must give Jo our full support. Also, my agent is going to arrange some book-signings for me to attend. It will be fun. I hope you're not going to pull out of this, we haven't been to Paris for years. And we do have fond memories, remember?"

"How can I forget. I just don't want you pushing yourself too hard, that's all."

"Everything will be fine. I have plenty of time ahead of me to be bed-bound. I want us to enjoy ourselves. Have some fun!"

"I don't know if I can accompany you on your book tours. I am hoping to make a few business contacts, so I don't know how my time will be divided. I don't think I'll know until we fly out there how my schedule will pan out."

"Oh! Honey," I say, disappointed. "It will be so nice to have you beside me on my tour. Can't you arrange these meetings for another time? It's not as though we are talking about the other side of the world! I want you to be with me not with some business associate. I need you to be with me, honey. I need your support," I plead.

"I'll do my best, dear. You know I would rather be with you but I just can't make any promises. And, I don't want to make promises to my wife that I can't keep. I don't want you taking on any unnecessary stress by wondering when am I going to turn up. So, the best thing is to count me out but we will meet when we can."

"Well, that is not going to be much of a trip to remember, is it? Why don't you invite your friends along. That way, we can all get to meet one another. It might be a benefit to us all. Your wife is famous, you know. I could be a bigger asset than you think."

"That sounds like a good idea but you know what some of these people are like they are very straight. They live for business and nothing else."

"If I didn't know you better Jackson, I'd say that you were trying to hide something from me."

"Whatever gave you that wild idea?" asks Rupert looking embarrassed that his negative response could lead to me making such accusations. Well, I know it's nonsense, but one could be forgiven for thinking along those lines.

"I don't know. I just detect that you may not want me around. I hope that you are not doing a Dexter on me!"

"I hope that you're not accusing me of going to see some woman over there."

"Of course not! When would you have found time to meet a woman in France. And from my recollection we didn't spend a moment out of arms' length from each other when we were there. No, I don't mean that, silly! I mean, I hope that you are not ashamed of the way I feel: big belly and all that!"

"Now you're being paranoid. I would be pleased to introduce you to anyone, big belly or otherwise. I'm disappointed that you question my motives."

"Just checking. A woman needs her reassurances, you know."

"I gave you my reassurance the day we got married, you need look no further than that!"

Rupert

Sydney has summoned me to his office. It would be nice to say that we arranged a meeting, but that could not be further from the truth. He was calm but authoritative when he called me in Chambers and asked that I call round at his office on my way home. It was in a tone that was more of a command than a request. I could have said that I was too busy to attend but I, too, welcomed the opportunity to have a talk. Maybe even try and find out what he really knows about my affair with Linda. And, why he has stopped sending me work and not found a designer for Linda, despite such a promising start. I can guess, but I need to hear him say it. If it is a matter of clearing the air with him then I am prepared to do so. Not so much for me, we don't need the work, we are financially secure for life, but I love what I do and have no intention of retiring this side of fifty years old. As for Linda, an assignment with a top British designer would do her the world of good. And it wouldn't do any harm to her confidence either, which has been pretty low since Wilson's suicide.

The taxi driver dropped me off outside this opaque glass fronted office in Dean Street, just off Oxford Street in London's fashionable West End. The end of the journey could not have come soon enough. The taxi driver claimed to have dropped off many of the world's top models at my destined location. He kept telling me how he knew them all very well and then felt the need to bombard me with a string of what I believe to be the Christian names of some of these models; they meant nothing to me.

The double glass doors to Charles' Artists Agency open automatically as I approach them. The walls in the reception area are adorned with many pictures of models on the front covers of popular magazines. Presumably, these are pictures of models at the agency. Surprisingly, I recognise many of them, which shows how much models are involved in what I would call, "day-to-day advertising" as well as catwalk modelling. I think I even recognise one or two of them from that party Linda and I attended, where we met Sydney and Chantelle.

"Hello," comes this warm and inviting female voice from behind a large dark mahogany reception desk. I stop admiring the pictures and refocus on the task at hand. I am here to meet Sydney at his command.

"Hello, my name is Rupert Jackson and I'm here to see Mister Charles."

"Oh, yes, Sydney is expecting you," says the lady, who then gives me directions to Sydney's office without informing him that I have arrived. I sense an air of opulence about this place as I make my way through the wide corridors towards Sydney's office. I knock on the big timber door, which seems to be of the same type as that of the reception desk.

"Come in Rupert," I hear Sydney's voice emit from behind his office door.

Sydney greets me with a firm handshake the moment I enter his office. If Dexter and Sydney were to settle their differences in the boxing ring, I would say that Sydney would just have the edge. That is, if physique is anything to go by.

"Thank you for coming over at such short notice," says Sydney, cutting short the pleasantries.

"As you know, your friend Dexter is making all these ridiculous allegations about me. Now, I would crush the little worm but Donna thinks that that would only be succumbing to his little scheme. Trust me, Rupert, he doesn't want to pick a fight with me. I have people like him for breakfast and shit them out before lunch. I don't think I have to spell it out any more than I have. Do you understand what I am saying?"

"I understand clearly," I reply. I don't know what it is about this man but he does command respect. I wouldn't treat him with any less dignity than I would a judge. There is this air of authority about him that makes you reluctant to test whether the perception is real.

"I haven't spoken with Dexter for a long time. I've tried to contact him on numerous occasions but I understand from his secretary that he is very busy," I add.

"I have no doubt he is busy, but busy doing what? Busy giving Donna stress. Donna is not taking this very well. I don't like what all this is doing to her, so I am asking you to make contact with Dexter and put an end to this, right now! And I don't want Donna to hear a word of my involvement."

"I will do the best that I can, but, needless to say, if Dexter is hooked on doing something, then nothing short of a miracle will stop him doing it."

"Then I suggest that you learn how to perform miracles," says Sydney. He seems damn serious about what he was asking. Somehow, now didn't seem like a good time to mention my forthcoming meeting with Dexter. I have been pestering Dexter's secretary every day for the past week, trying to get hold of him, in order to try and talk some sense into him. After many attempts, I eventually got through. I think that either he was fed up with me calling and leaving messages every day or his secretary threatened to resign through having to constantly lie to me. It was clear, however, that Dexter did not want to talk, but he nonetheless agreed to meet me. Dexter is stubborn and I wouldn't expect him to change his mind after only a chat with me. There was a time when I could be confident that I could, but those days are no longer with us.

"I hear what you're saying Sydney, but I am not Dexter's keeper. He is a big man and does fairly much what he likes."

"Like I once said to you, you scratch my back and I'll scratch yours," he reminds me.

"And what exactly does that mean?"

"I think you know exactly what that means!"

"Well, from my recollection, I haven't received any work from you for some time, not that I would do what you ask in return for work, of course. I feel I should make that perfectly clear."

"Rupert, I'm a very wealthy man. Do you really think that I have made my money through caring which lawyer does my work? I couldn't care less! I couldn't tell one bad lawyer from the next. Get the message?"

"My misunderstanding, obviously."

"How is your friend, Linda?" he asks. It was only a matter of time before her name came up. At least I should now know what he knows. I already know what he thinks about me being with her. That has been obvious.

"I think that she is all right," I reply. "The last time I spoke to her she was still searching for a designer for Paris."

"Yes, she has called me a few times. Unfortunately, there are only a few people requiring the service of our official photographers."

"I thought that Linda was an official photographer."

"She is, but there are many other photographers searching for designers, so some will have to face disappointment."

"Linda was under the impression that a person of your influence could find her a place."

"She is right, but like I said there are other deserved photographers awaiting their chance."

"I don't know whether you have seen her work, she is very good."

"I have and she is very talented but so are many other photographers, so why would I want to do Linda a favour unless something was done for me?"

"I don't see what she could do for you when she hardly even knows you. Anyway, by the look of things it looks like you have everything you want."

"Materially, you could be right. Let me tell you something in confidence, that is, if you don't already know, I asked Donna to marry me and she is yet to give me an answer. I don't blame her. Her mind is otherwise engaged with this Dexter saga. The longer this goes on, the less I feel confident of getting a positive reply to my proposal. I would think kindly on anyone, or their girlfriend, if they were to help alleviate any unwanted distractions. Do I make myself clear?"

"I'm not admitting to anything but I know what you are implying. You do know that blackmail is illegal in this country."

"I'm not trying to blackmail you, Rupert. You want a favour done for your little girlfriend, then you will have to work for it. Nothing is free in this country, as I'm sure you're well aware."

"You know something, I always thought that you were a decent chap, but now I'm not so sure."

"It's called playing hard. I thought you would know all about that in your profession."

"There is only one thing you've overlooked," I reply. "You want Donna's hand in marriage more than I want Linda to go to Paris. Linda is talented. She might still have time to find a designer without your help. If she doesn't make it then it will be a big disappointment to her, but it wouldn't be the end of the world. So, after all that, I might choose not to cooperate. You see, in a roundabout way, you probably need me more than I need you. In fact, I don't need you nor your work at all!"

"Don't count on that, Rupert. If I don't get what I want then my tongue might just become a little loose and start revealing things that you would wish it didn't."

"Like I have already said, I'm not admitting to anything nor do I, come to think of it, know what you are talking about. I think I best leave. We have both made our positions perfectly clear and don't think that there is anything useful left to say." I say this and make my way to the door without so much as a parting hand-shake. My departure is clearly less amicable than my arrival.

"Don't push me Rupert, I might know a lot more about your bit on the side than you realise," says Sydney. With that comment I slammed the door and made my way out of the building.

That meeting with Sydney made me feel very uncomfortable. I felt that I had let myself down. I had let him get the better of me. I should have kept my cool. He knows that he's got me over a barrel, that was clear from my reaction. What exactly does he know? Does he know anything more than mere suspicion? Not knowing the answers to these questions could be worse than the answers themselves. And how did I get caught up in all this? Others have affairs and it's no big deal. I have an affair and suddenly it's the concern of every man and his dog. And above all, I don't think Sydney will tell Pat what he suspects. She is going through a difficult pregnancy at the moment and such news will not make her feel any better. Not even Donna would risk informing Pat of such news. More to the point, however, who will believe him? Although there is the question of why would he tell such a lie? I suppose when you put it that way, he is more likely to be believed than not. To put it crudely, I have been well and truly shafted. I feel worse now than when I have had a bad day in court, and believe me that in itself is bad! Dexter will simply have to play ball because Sydney might truly know more about Linda and me and is not bluffing. It's a risk I can't afford to take. Clearly, I now have an interest in the outcome of Dexter's action against Donna and need it to stop, otherwise this could be the beginning of a very unpleasant situation.

Dexter and I arranged to meet at Blue's wine bar in Chelsea. He was adamant that he did not want to meet at the club. This saddened me somewhat, as it indicated that the club was no longer our main meeting place, where we had so many good times over the years. I do sometimes ask myself how it ever came to this. How did Dexter and I allow ourselves to drift apart so easily? We were the best of friends, but no pretence could make us believe that that position has not changed now. I could see that Dexter's Porsche was parked opposite Blue's. He's early for a change. Maybe the prospect of responsible fatherhood has made him punctual and reliable. I could see him at the far side of the room. Our eyes meet and we acknowledge each other.

"Hi buddy," he says looking past me. I look over my shoulders to see whether he has mistaken somebody else for me, but there doesn't appear to be anyone else in particular to which such a welcome could have been addressed.

"Hi mate," I reply. Dexter seems happy to see me, but appears to be a little on edge. I suppose his apparent unease is a sign of how our friendship has degenerated in recent times. Especially, when one considers how close we once were. I relished in supporting Dexter, when many would try and put him down. I saw it as a debating exercise, because most of the time I knew that what my opponents were saying was in fact true. But, I was never one to shy away from backing the underdog, not that I would put Dexter quite in that category: he could fend for himself, and often would!

"How have you been?" I ask.

"I've been just fine, working hard. You know how it is," he replies. He appears to be nervous, which is most unlike him.

"Are you all right?" I ask. "You seem a little nervous."

"Yes, I'm fine. I'm just looking out for a friend of mine, who said that he would join us for a drink."

"Oh! Anyone I know?" I ask. He certainly did not mention that we were going to meet anyone else.

"No, I don't think so," he replies, still checking the door every time it opens. "He said that he would be here any minute now."

"I was hoping that we could spend some time alone, catching up on old times."

"I thought you said that you wanted to discuss Donna." I think tonight he would prefer to talk about anyone but Donna.

"Yes, I would like to discuss her as well, but first I would like to chat with my friend like the old days."

"Well, we can still do that. We don't have to be alone to chat about the past."

"What has come over you? Since when did I need to put forward an agenda before I meet up with you?"

"You don't need an agenda. In fact, we don't need to speak at all. Need I remind you who arranged for us to meet, and it wasn't me."

"Dexter, what's wrong with you, man?"

"Nothing's wrong with me. I feel just fine. Here comes Josh, now," he says. I turn round to see this tall man with a Groucho Marx-type face with the moustache. He looks stern-faced as he makes his way towards us.

"Hi Josh, glad you could make it," says Dexter. "I take it that you know Rupert."

"How do you do?" says Josh, extending his hand.

"Have we met somewhere before?" I ask Josh, who does not seem to have a friendly face, nor does he come across as the kind of person that smiles very often.

"Not exactly," Josh replies, remaining non-committal.

"I won't beat about the bush," says Dexter. "Josh is here to be a witness to everything we say."

"A witness?" I respond, sharply. "What on earth do we need a witness for? Can someone please tell me what the hell is going on? We arrange to have a drink and a chat and suddenly we have someone witnessing our conversation. Have you gone mad? I'm not staying here for this. I think this time pal you have really flipped your lid." I get up from my chair and grab my coat from the chair next to me, ready to leave.

"Maybe I have, but then again it's not every day that your best friend stabs you in the back, is it?" asks Dexter facing me.

"Who has stabbed you in the back?" I ask, confused.

"You know well what I'm talking about, so don't even try to deny it. I have proof. Josh here is a private investigator and he has unearthed some incriminating evidence against you. Evidence that even I refused to believe at first, until I pieced everything together, and then it all started making sense. You betrayed me badly. I knew I had my enemies, some justifiably so, but I thought that I could always count on you. I never thought that they had infiltrated my most inner circle!"

"Dexter," I plead, "I don't know what the hell you're talking about. Why have you hired a private investigator?" I watch Josh and immediately resent him being here. I need to talk to my friend who has clearly been brainwashed by this man.

"Dexter, let's talk about this in private. I'm sure that there has been a big mistake."

"I don't think that that would be a good idea. Anything that needs to be said can be said in front of Josh. I trust him, which is more than I can say I do for you." This is painful, it really is. Here is a man that I used to play squash with once a week. We would discuss things that were strictly private between us, things that weren't even discussed in front of the others. Now, all I can detect is animosity for something that I know nothing about, but more to the point, something that he did not see fit to speak to me about first! Our dirty linen is being washed in public, in front of a man who I don't even know and, worse, a private investigator. I thought that private investigators only existed in the movies! This must be a wind up.

"I know about you and Sydney," says Dexter, casually.

"Are you sure that you want to discuss this in front of him?" I ask. If some man has been following me around without my knowledge, then I certainly wasn't going to address "him" by his name, as if we were about to become friends.

"Continue," insists Dexter, coldly. I have a good mind to leave. I don't have to stay. I'm neither afraid of Dexter, nor his guard dog. But, I shall remain, say my piece, and leave. The rest will then be up to Dexter. To tell you the truth, I have had enough of all this and just want to leave them all to it.

"I met Sydney this week. He wanted me to try and persuade you to stop your action against Donna. I can't see the crime in that! I have been trying to stop you continuing with it as well, as we both know it to be a fruitless cause. And, the only reason you're doing this is to get back at Donna, although God alone knows why!"

"Don't try and play smart with me, Jackson," says Josh.

"Who the hell do you think you are calling me 'Jackson'? You'd better have some respect! It seems to me that you may have already caused enough trouble, but we shall get to the bottom of this, then I shall deal with you in my own way." Josh was giving me that smug look that made me want to punch him in the face; if I were a violent man then I would have no hesitation. With any luck, Dexter might give this smug face a knuckle sandwich in place of me!

"What Josh is saying, is that he has the evidence of you contacting Sydney whilst I was seeing Donna," says Dexter, who almost appears to be embarrassed at what is going on. I knew that not even Dexter could put on this tough exterior in front of me for very long. I wouldn't have minded if his allegations were so strong that he felt that he needed someone else present, to arbitrate, but not this idiot! I think that I could stomach Ashley better than this man or, better still, someone known for his fairness and honesty, Sam.

"Dexter, this has all been one big mistake. I hope that you haven't given this thing any money for his lousy work because he's got the wrong man, not that I can see where all this is heading to, but I was not in touch with Sydney whilst you were with Donna. In any case, so what if I had been? I don't get the picture!" Dexter looks even more puzzled than I am and indicates to Josh to explain.

"We have evidence to show that there was a conspiracy against Mister Livingstone, to oust him out of his relationship with his fiancée, Donna."

"This is absurd!" I interrupt. "No disrespect Dexter, but you and Donna didn't need any conspiracy to break up your relationship, you two were doing that perfectly well on your own. And, anyway, irrespective of how close you two were to me, do you not think that I had my own problems to be dealing with, than to try and split you two up? Why would I want to do that? There were allegations made against me tonight that just don't add up. And to tell you the truth, I am very disappointed that you did not come to me first and tell me these bizarre allegations yourself. I may have laughed at you, but at least we would have seen them for what they really were, instead of falling out over them. Where did you get this evidence from anyway?"

"I'm not at liberty to say," replies Josh. "But, what I can say is that for many years you were calling Mister Charles, the ex and present boyfriend of the lady known as Donna, at various telephone numbers. This was going on, despite you pretending to be a close friend of Mister Livingstone. It is clear that, upon you securing what Mister Charles wanted, namely Donna, you were briefed by Mister Charles' company as a reward for your efforts." I am beginning to wonder what this man knows about Linda. I could feel my grip on this whole situation slipping slowly away from my hands. If he knows about Linda then I am in trouble. This man clearly likes his job too much to think what such allegations of my affair could do to my wife.

"Were you the man who was calling my Chambers sometimes, but refusing to leave his name?" Josh seems not to know what I am talking about. I am not too sure why I asked the question myself, curiosity I suppose. I can see how some people can get caught up in situations without quite knowing how they got there. I've got Sydney on my back and I have Dexter on my back. There's only so much load I can carry.

"I have never called your office. I'm a professional. I could be the only other person in a room with you and you wouldn't even know that I was there. No, my tracks aren't that easily traced." Josh appears to be insulted that I even considered, let alone suggested, such a thing.

"I hear what you have said, but I can tell you that I have never ever made a call to Sydney's home or office, when you were with Donna. I couldn't even remember the man when I met him."

"And when was that?" asks Josh. I pause for a while to get this right. The silence that ensues shows that I was possibly on the ropes. This was the second time in a week that I had let my guard down. It was a habit I was not enjoying. Could Josh know about that party in Buckinghamshire all those moons ago? I don't think so. It was an invitations-only party. He couldn't possibly have got through all the tight security that night. I would have to gamble.

"I met him when my wife first invited him and Donna to our house for a meal."

"Is that so?" replies Josh. Dexter turned to Josh and nods his head. Josh takes out the celebrity magazine, *Breeze*, and shows me a photograph of Sydney, Chantelle and me chatting at the party. I gambled and I lost. I've lost the trust of my friend.

"There is a reason why I did not mention that," is all I can say. I offer nothing further. Dexter seems unable to look me in the eye, as if he had wanted me to disprove what was being alleged against me, if only to repair some of the damage done to our friendship.

"Would you like to shed some more light on that?" asks Josh. If he doesn't say, then I shan't volunteer.

"I can't, but whatever it may seem, you have got it all wrong. I would never have come between Dexter and Donna, if anything I would stand up for him when everyone was telling Donna to leave him. Dexter, you can vouch for that!"

"Don't say anything Mister Livingstone. This is a well known ploy by culprits to get the victim on their side. It's like high-pressure sales tactics, you get trapped and end up agreeing to anything." Dexter obeys this command and says nothing.

"Dexter, this guy knows nothing about us." As I say this Josh takes out an envelope and rests it on the table. I could feel the hairs raised on the back of my neck as I anticipate more damning evidence. All I need now is a set of photographs of Linda and me naked in her flat. Then both sides of the dispute could blackmail me, with me being the obvious loser, whatever the outcome. I open the envelope, cautiously. I can see records of what seems like every single telephone call that has been made from our house. I recognise numerous telephone numbers that appear to support the authenticity of the statement. In particular, I recognise Sydney's number. His number appears a few times. I feel like asking Josh how he managed to get this information which, I would have thought, was confidential, but I guess a private investigator has his sources.

"I don't know what to say, other than this must be some mistake. Either that or I have been framed. Dexter, tell him, I would stand up for you, even when my own wife was putting you down." As I say this, we all stare at each other. They can't possibly be thinking that Pat would be caught up in all this.

"I hope that you are not thinking that Pat is behind this?" I ask directly to Dexter.

"You've confirmed what I have been thinking all this time. I said to Josh that, if it were you, then you must be one damn good actor to have fooled me over all these years. But, we had to put you through this to make sure."

"Dexter, you and Pat may not have been the best of friends but Pat would not have meddled in your business to this extent. For God's sake, give her some credit!"

"You must admit Rupert, she never liked me from day one. And, besides that, the evidence is there. Do you doubt its authenticity? If you do then I challenge you to contact your telephone company and ask for a copy of all these statements. I will pay for any costs you incur. I promise you, you will get the same answer." I feel stupid. How could Pat be in touch with a man such as Sydney in all these years and not tell me? What was on the agenda? To dethrone Dexter? I feel sick!

"And by the way," continues Dexter, "your secret is safe with me. Linda seems a nice girl!"

I feel so humiliated. Maybe Dexter has got things wrong. There couldn't have been a conspiracy against him. Pat wouldn't have gone so far. There are far more important matters in her life than Dexter. Maybe Pat was having an affair with Sydney behind my back. I find that almost as hard to believe, as I am sure Pat would about me. What if she did have an affair with him? After all, he seemed extremely fond of her when we met at the party and he made no effort to hide it. If she was seeing him, then I would not be able to trust her again. And, if you have no trust in a relationship, then what is the point in carrying on? I know I'm being hypocritical, but Pat doesn't know about me with Linda and if she knew, she would put me out so fast my feet wouldn't touch the ground. I know that! We all know that! But, it was never a thought that Pat could have an extramarital affair. It was a case only of what would happen to me if I "played away", as if it was only conceivable that I was capable of "stooping so low". How I yearn to go back to my simple life. I wanted excitement. I've tasted it and now I want to go back to my uneventful corner. Actually, things weren't that bad. We had a great life. We have a great life. It's just that I wanted to experiment a little and that has led to all kinds of problems and consequences. Consequences that appear to far outweigh the crime. Let me get this clear in my head. If Pat was having an affair with Sydney, then she will say that, I know. I would have to kick up a stink because I would feel humiliated and cheated. Sydney might tell Pat about Linda. And, what would Donna make of all this? My head is swimming with questions. This can't go on, I must get some answers – tonight!

I can see that all the lights are off. I can't simply go to sleep without thrashing this matter out tonight. I make as much noise as I could reasonably have expected to make at this time of the morning, but she seems dead to the world. I wait a minute contemplating what I should do. I can't sleep. My mind is posing too many questions.

"Pat," I whisper, so as not to scare the wits out of her. I sense a little shuffle but nothing substantial. I take a bolder step by nudging and whispering her name again, only this time a few decibels higher. I sense life.

"What's up honey?" asks Pat, semi-conscious.

"Pat, we need to talk," I reply. I turn on her sidelight to force home the issue that we really do need to talk.

"Can't it wait until the morning?" she asks in a last gasp effort to salvage what sleep she still has left in her.

"Sorry, dear. It can't," I reply adamantly.

"What's so serious that it couldn't wait until the morning?" asks Pat not sounding at all pleased at having been awoken, in a "it better be good" tone. Trust me, this was worth waking up for.

"I would like to talk about Sydney," I reply, looking to detect any element of guilt, a guilt that could nullify any plea of innocence. There was nothing that I could read too much into. But, she was alert.

"As you know, I was due to meet Dexter tonight. He brought along a private investigator in order to quiz me about all sorts of crazy allegations. He claims that someone from our household had been in touch with Sydney during the times that Dexter and Donna were together. I told him that that was absurd." Pat does not join me in my assessment of the allegation. I could tell that this story was not entirely alien to her, and maybe "absurd" might not have been the word that she would have used in response.

"Is there something that you want to tell me Pat?" I know the question is a bit crass, bearing in mind that it was me who woke her up for a chat, but at these times logic flies out of the window and you rely on perception. Surprisingly, I feel no anger towards her, but I'm scared. I'm scared that what I am about to hear will tarnish the image I had of my wife for ever! I had always viewed Pat as being above anything so low. I was the lucky one. I had broken my wedding vows. Pat was the one that everyone came running to for advice on everything. She was the best-selling author whom everyone loved and she was mine, only she had been someone else's too. And how do I save face without my seeming weak, for both Dexter and his private investigator know. The truth of it all is that I couldn't leave Pat, as I know she would do to me if she had found out about Linda. And you know what? That pains me. It hurts because I feel like I have been reduced to being someone who can be disrespected and, yet, can do nothing about it but take it on the chin: a chin that can take whatever is dished out. Some people will sympathise with the cheated husband, others will laugh. No guesses for which will be the loudest.

"I shan't lie to you," says Pat. "I was in contact with Sydney, but I can explain."

"Please do, but spare me the gory details," I reply. I might be labelled a wimp, but I am not about to make it easy for her.

"What are you talking about, Rupert?"

"I thought that is what you were going to tell me."

"Well, it clearly isn't what you have in mind!" she replies in vexation. "I bumped into Sydney some years ago, shortly after he and Donna had separated. One day I was having lunch in The Crypt in St. Martins-in-the-Fields with Yolanda James, that's how long ago that was, because I haven't seen her for years, when Sydney walked in with a male friend of his. He and his friend joined us. He kept telling me how he really missed Donna, but thought that what had happened between them was for the best. We exchanged telephone numbers. I had no intention of calling him. Donna had a new love in her life and I was not about to get involved in her business. Out from the blue, one day, Sydney called. It was clear that he was enquiring about Donna. I was honest with him. I told him that her life was a shambles with Dexter. I never told Donna that he was in touch and I definitely wasn't about to tell Dexter's best friend that Donna's ex-boyfriend was enquiring about her! I had nothing to do with the breaking-up of Dexter's relationship with Donna. It amazes me that after all that he has done, he still thinks that he is blameless. Dexter caused him and Donna to part, nobody else." I listened intently as Pat told me what had gone on. I could feel both relief and yet let down that Pat was part of a secret that she felt she could not share with me. We are back on an unlevelled playing field; I'm the one that's cheating!

"I assume that you knew about Chantelle."

"If you're asking me whether I knew that Chantelle was Sydney's ex-wife, then the answer is yes."

"And does Donna know now about your communications with Sydney whilst he was in the wilderness?"

"No, she doesn't, although it hasn't always been easy. I almost came close to telling her once, when she was practically going out of her mind trying to figure out how Sydney could have known so much about her when they were apart. She put it down to a spy of some sort."

"So I guess Sydney has a lot to thank his spy for!"

"Sydney did not need any encouragement from me," confirms Pat. "And, I certainly wasn't his spy! At the first window of opportunity, he was in there. He went for what he wanted."

"You don't know what a relief it is to hear you tell me this, but

I can't believe that you kept this secret away from me for so long."

"I had to. I had no choice. Had I told you, then I might as well have told Dexter himself!" I couldn't deny what Pat was saying. I foolishly defended Dexter on too many occasions, knowing perfectly well that I disapproved of the way he was treating Donna. The irony about it is, when Dexter and I were together, alone, I would tell him how wrong he was. It was as if I felt the need to defend him to the outside world, in case I was ever caught doing the same. Hypocrisy is never viewed with high esteem.

"And what did you think had gone on between Sydney and me?"

"Nothing," I reply sounding like Bambi, the cartoon deer. I feel stupid. However, I would sooner be happy feeling stupid for having got it wrong, than not feeling stupid but depressed for having got it right! "I didn't know what to think," I continue. "All I know is that I want to be with my wife and my child and I don't want anything or anyone to come between us."

"Come here, you fool," says Pat. As she put her arms around me, I knew that the game was up. I can trust Dexter. He will not tell Pat anything. He knows that I did not betray him. I shall contact him tomorrow and tell him exactly what Pat has told me. Dexter can take it any way he likes. I will contact Sydney and tell him that I have tried to talk Dexter out of his action against Donna, but he didn't want to know. Sydney can do whatever he likes. I will no longer be held to ransom by him or anyone. I cannot please everyone all of the time. And, the big one, tomorrow I shall end my relationship with Linda. I cannot please two women. It was fun whilst it lasted, but I have a wife and child to look after. Maybe I can love two women, I don't know, but I can only have one, and that one has to be my wife: my wife who is carrying our first child. I had forgotten who was the most important person in my life and that will be no more. Before no time at all, I could see that Pat was fast asleep. I would now have to plan for the day ahead: the calm before the storm. But, every storm has a cloud and every cloud has a silver lining. Tomorrow night, I will be reflecting on a day that brought the ending of a chapter with Linda and the beginning of a new chapter with just my wife, my child and myself. Nobody else is invited nor welcomed. Goodnight!

I called Linda and told her that I had to see her tonight. In our short but compact time together I had never made such a short-notice request. With my place being a "no go" area, I insisted on me going over to her place. And, as privacy was the order of the day, we had to stay indoors, out of ears' reach of Sydney's or Dexter's informers. I recall the first time I went round to Linda's place. I remember telling myself that if she makes a move for me then I would tell her that I was a happily married man. Who was I kidding? I knew then, at the back of my mind, that I would be too weak to resist any advances. I wanted her as badly as she wanted me. That evening will remain with me for ever. Linda will remain with me for ever, but in spirit only. They say that "once an adulterer then always an adulterer". For me, I am content. I am free and I am strong. I had an affair with Linda Walters, not just any woman. I could only have had an affair with Linda. It was lust, but it was lust for her and her alone. I will not cheat on my wife again!

Since Wilson's death, Linda has paid little attention to her appearance. In short, she looks a mess. The paternalistic side of me wants to use all the resources at my disposal to help her get back on her feet, but Linda would be too proud to accept anything from me, post-separation. She is still very attractive even when not at her best. It is not hard to see why I fell for her in such a big way. I come out in goose pimples whenever I recall that dance at Yvonne's party. That was the beginning of us.

"You look tired," says Linda, as she rearranges the daffodils in the vase on the dining room table.

"I am," I reply. "I have been up most of the night tossing and turning, without a wink of sleep."

"What's troubling you?" asks Linda, with sincerity. I can't help thinking that under different circumstances, I could have been asking for Linda's hand in marriage, but reality is far from that ideal.

"It's us, dear. It's that time that we both knew would have to come at some time but wished that it would be postponed for ever." I turn and walk over to the window. I could not face her. I look out of the window at nothing in particular. My back is facing her, so it is safe to continue. "We always said that if anyone was likely to get hurt because of our relationship then we should call it a day. Well," I pause there, so as to check that what I am saying is what I really want. I check for the green lights all over my body. My brain is the first to return a green light. My whole body is tense as we await the signal from the heart. The seconds ticking away seem like minutes, if not hours. My heart is playing tricks on me again. It should not be taking this long. Last night the brain and heart were in agreement. Now is not the time to go their separate ways. There is a mad rush of excitement, as my heart sends signals to my brain; amber then green. It's approved! "I've been thinking about us a lot recently and I think that we should end our relationship. Before you say anything, I would like you to hear me out in full. You have given me some of the best times of my life. I will never forget the moments we spent together. All times were good times. But, the fact is I am married and I don't think that we could sustain our relationship much longer before someone else gets hurt. I am aware of at least three other people that know about us. God only knows who else is aware. It was one of the saddest days of my life when Wilson died. I told myself at the time that we were not to blame. I don't know whether that is true or not, but I can't help myself feeling so guilty. I am still very fond of you and I am probably in love with you, but that doesn't change the commitments that I have elsewhere. I would like us to continue being friends if we can." Linda remained stone-faced throughout and didn't appear to want to interrupt what was being said.

"How can we continue being friends when we were only ever lovers?" she asks.

"Well, I would like us to be friends," I assert.

"And do you think that that will stop suspicions? How will they know whether we are sleeping with each other?"

"I guess they won't."

"Exactly! What this really amounts to is you easing your conscience, isn't it? You've had what you wanted and now you can toss me aside, as if I were nothing."

"Linda, that is not true and you know that!"

"Don't try and patronise me, Rupert. I'm more than capable of expressing what I think. I don't have to be a lawyer to do that!"

"I don't understand. We knew from the outset that what we had was a temporary thing. We got close but we knew that, due to circumstances, it could not last for ever unless I left Pat. And, that has never been on the agenda."

"I'm not asking you to leave your wife but I do feel used. My career is in a mess, I'm in a mess, my ex-boyfriend committed suicide and you walk out on me. You've showed me what this was really all about. You never cared shit for me. All this, 'I will be there for you', was nothing but crap. You've showed your support at the first opportunity that I am no longer attractive to screw!"

"Linda, you are obviously upset. I understand that, but you are being grossly unfair. I care for you a lot, it's just that my life will be far too complicated if we were to continue. I will always be there for you. That offer will always remain open but we just can't continue. Pat is going through a difficult pregnancy at the moment," I confess, for the first time, "and it wouldn't be fair on her. You wouldn't wish someone to do the same to you would you?"

"Get out, Rupert!" shouts Linda. "Get the hell out of my life! I hope you rot in hell!"

Donna

Sydney has asked me, on two occasions, whether I have considered his proposal. I don't want to keep him hanging on for ever, but with all that is going on at the moment, marriage is the last thought on my mind. I have got Pat being very sickly with her pregnancy; she is worrying me. I have Jo who is all set for the biggest event of her life. And, I have Dexter; no more need be said about him, other than to say that matters have got really nasty. Rupert has been very supportive but I don't trust him. I don't mean to be cruel, but I have always thought that Rupert could have been a lot more influential over Dexter than he has been willing to exercise. I'm not saying that Rupert should try and rule Dexter; that would be impossible, in any case. But those guys are very close, so they must have some influence over the other. What, therefore, is Rupert saying to Dexter in order for Dexter to continue with this ludicrous claim? I say no more! Sydney doesn't quite share my view of Rupert. He is confident that Rupert wouldn't back against us. Why he has such faith in him, he alone knows.

Who would have envisaged that I would be going through what I am now? You expect people in my predicament to be parents who both share and enjoy bringing up their child, but that is clearly not the case here. Dexter was the silent parent. He reminds me of Joanna Kramer, the role played by Meryl Streep in the film version of Avery Corman's *Kramer versus Kramer*. I see Ted, the role played by Dustin Hoffman, in myself, of course. I hope my fight doesn't get as nasty as theirs did! We are playing two different games, but sharing the same rules. Only those rules might be more suitable to one game than the other. The system should not allow such actions to happen. And Dexter knows that I can't fight dirty. I don't want to hurt him. I will do only what is necessary for me to keep my child, but he would do whatever is necessary to hurt me.

If Sydney, or anyone else for that matter, were to know of my meeting Dexter here today, they would call me crazy. Sydney will simply go mad! I contacted Dexter. When Pastor Benjamin was preaching the message on Sunday he referred us to what Brother Paul said in First Corinthians, chapter six, where our brother dares any of us to bring a matter before the law and not before the saints. Brother Paul reminds us that the saints shall judge the world and are we therefore "unworthy to judge the smallest matters?" After that message, I knew that I had to see Dexter and try to resolve our differences between ourselves, although I don't think Dexter is the sort of saint Brother Paul would have had in mind! I don't want Dionne's future being presided over by a stranger, who is simply doing her job for the day. I don't want my child's welfare to be dealt with as though it was on a conveyer belt: the third case on in court number two in the matter of "D". The thought of such an experience makes me ask, what has my baby's short life been reduced to?

Dexter was clearly taken aback when I called him. This was the first time that I had got through to him. He was obviously in the mood to talk, but didn't want to talk whilst at work, so I agreed that I would meet him in Blue's. I have never been here before, but he seemed to know it very well. It could have been worse: he wanted to come to the flat. I would not feel comfortable with Dexter back in the flat. When I put him out, I had put him out for good and no peace pact could tempt me to go back on that! He was adamant at first, then he seemed to appreciate where I was coming from. Probably thought it better that he cooperate with me, than fight me. If he does have Dionne's interest at heart in any way, then he would know that it is better for us to talk. He didn't even ask to see her. In fact, he hasn't attempted to see her since he left. Is this someone who is serious about fatherhood? The problem for him is that we all know that this is not about Dionne but about me and him or, more to the point, Sydney and me. We spent so long trying to agree where to meet today, one wonders how on earth we are going to agree a suitable arrangement for Dionne. I couldn't believe it, when I turned down his request to meet at the flat he then suggested meeting at a wine bar that Sydney and I always go to whenever I meet him in town for lunch. Sylvester's Wine Bar is a stone's throw from Sydney's office. He always goes there. It is a popular venue but of all the wine bars in London and Dexter chooses the one that Sydney is most likely to call in on. Talk about coincidence!

"It's good to see that some things never change," I say as he approaches my table, twenty minutes late. A lot is hanging on today because if it goes wrong then the dirt will really fly!

"Sorry, I got held up," says Dexter. He seemed hell-bent on making small talk, as if to avoid the main issue. He almost seems pleasant. I have always viewed Dexter as a very immature man. He would behave badly when out with his friends, but the moment he is on his own he is almost as good as gold. He is a Doctor Jekyll and Mister Hyde personified.

"Dexter, what is it you really want from me?" I ask straight and to the point.

"I don't want anything from you, Donna, I just want to make sure that my daughter is well looked after."

"And what makes you think that you can do that? Apart from Dionne's date of birth, you know nothing about her. You are a stranger to her. The best thing for Dionne is for her to be with her mother. The funny thing about all this is that we both know how much having to look after her will cramp your style. It's almost as if you can't afford to win your claim."

"I only want what's best for my daughter," he repeats stubbornly.

"So you say," I respond in the most unbelieving way I could articulate.

"If you and Sydney were to part then I might have to reconsider my case."

"Dexter, don't try to insult my intelligence. You know what I think? I think that you are jealous of Sydney. You kept telling me that nobody would want me. You either want me to be on my own or with some worthless person like yourself!" He shuffles uncomfortably at my attack. He seems to have lost some of that thick skin he used to wear so well to his sole advantage.

"When people are fighting they say anything. I didn't mean any of those things, I'm sorry. Contrary to what you might believe, I still like you and don't want to see you make a big mistake."

"A big mistake!" I shout to the embarrassment of both of us, as the other customers turn and look in our direction. "Listen to yourself, you're like a spoilt child. If you don't get what you want then you sulk. You get nasty. Children are like that but they grow up and grow out of it. You clearly haven't!"

"There's a lot that you don't know, trust me Donna. It's because I still care for you that I am doing what I am. Sydney is not the guy you think he is. He's involved in all sorts of things. Have you never asked yourself why he came back to you?"

"Did it ever occur to you that he might actually like me or, better still, be in love with me. Or, is that still too hard for you to envisage. Only you could offer me such wonderful charity!"

"And has he told you that he has a criminal record for being in possession of drugs?" asks Dexter.

"What! You're lying. If that were the case then I would have found out about it by now." I seriously feel like throwing my drink over the beast and leaving matters to the court. I recall Brother Paul's message but Dexter is no saint, he is too evil. "If only you know how I am keeping you from being destroyed," I continue. "If it weren't for me, Sydney would have had your arse a long time ago. Sydney is a heavyweight, I warn you, don't mess with him."

"I don't blame you for showing loyalty to your boyfriend, I would do the same, if someone were to say the same about you."

"Don't patronise me, Dexter. If I were you, I'd stop these very serious allegations, before it is too late to save yourself and your career. Anyway, what proof do you have to support your allegations?"

"I'm keeping my cards close to my chest. I won't reveal anything until we get into court. If I ask you for nothing else, I ask that you question Sydney about his criminal record. I bet you he will be shocked that his little secret is out."

"Well, let's just say that I don't believe you."

"And I guess that he hasn't told you about his past with Chantelle?"

"How do you know about that?"

"I take it that's a 'yes'; then don't dismiss all that I say. I tell you, I know a lot more than I'm letting on."

"I am so glad that we are not together. I don't know what satisfaction you get from destroying other people's lives, but if you are expecting a 'thank you' from me then you can forget it, I despise you! It was a big mistake coming here to see you. I shouldn't have bothered!"

"Donna, if only you would realise it. You are as much a victim of what is going on, as I am."

"You're not a victim, Dexter," I respond and laugh out loud, dramatically, at the same time. "You are the assailant. You deserve all that you get, and all that is coming your way. I sometimes used to think that what Pat was saying about you was a bit strong, but I now realise that her views were tame."

"I wouldn't bark up that tree if I were you, as you might find your friend becoming a foe. Like I said, everything isn't always the way it seems."

"If you are now trying to tell me that Pat also has a criminal record for possessing drugs, then I would seriously wonder what you have been taking yourself! Your allegations seem to know no boundaries. They go from one extreme to the next. Just when you think that that is it, then you come out with another gem. Where does it stop?"

"You don't have to believe me, but don't say that I didn't warn you. Sydney and Pat were having an affair when we were together."

"That has to be the most ridiculous thing I have ever heard fall out of your mouth, and I have heard some masterful works of fiction from you over the years."

"Why would I lie?" asks Dexter, failing to see the funny side of my comment.

"Because you always do!" I confirm.

"What I mean is, it would be stupid of me to make these allegations, knowing perfectly well that you could easily check out my story."

"And you expect me to believe what you are telling me, based on that theory, do you? A theory from a known serial liar!" I had heard enough for one day. I was already gesturing to leave, before I finished my comment.

"You don't have to believe me, at your peril. But, don't say that I didn't warn you, then you will see who it was that really cared," says Dexter. If he said anything more I couldn't say, because by this time I had heard enough and just wanted to leave. I could feel a migraine coming on, fast!

Josephine

"Jo can I see you, now?" asks Don on her mobile phone.

"I'm sorry, baby, but I'm just about to commence a meeting."

"Okay, I'll speak to you another time," says Don, in resignation.

"Hey, Don, what's the matter?"

"It doesn't matter. We can talk another time," she replies.

"No, I can talk for a while. We're waiting for our photographer, who has not yet arrived. What's up girl?" I repeat. "You sound stressed out."

"I am!" replies Don, sharply. "I've found out that some of that drug stuff that Dexter has been saying about Sydney might be true."

"Oh no, honey! Where did you get that from?" I ask.

"Someone I know told me," replies Don, reluctant to reveal her source. Fair enough. Don and I are close but not as close as she is to Pat. "Problem chats" are something she would normally have with Pat, or with Pat and me, rarely with just me.

"Are you sure she's got this right?" I ask.

"I can't be sure, but if this comes out in the hearing then I might lose my child."

"You most certainly will!" I second. "Have you spoken to Sydney about this?"

"I haven't spoken to him today. I have only just found out for myself, but he has always denied Dexter's earlier allegations. I thought it would have been an insult to ask him whether what Dexter was saying was true. I just assumed that it was lies. Now, I'm not so sure."

"Well, you're going to have to talk to him, girl. I'm sorry that I can't see you now, but I must attend this meeting. As soon as the meeting is over I shall come over straight away. What has Pat got to say about this?"

"I haven't spoken her. It's not anything that I want to trouble her with." Don's comments were so uncharacteristic that she seemed unable to structure her sentence properly. "In any case," she continues, "I don't want to burden her with my problems. She is hardly in a fit state to take on somebody else's troubles."

"Maybe so," I say, "but you can't leave Pat out of this, you know that. What say we meet at her place later tonight and talk this through? Has Sydney left yet?"

"Yes, he should be in the air now and is due back tomorrow morning. He will be going straight to the office, so I shall speak to him about this tomorrow night. I really trusted him, Jo. I've been so unlucky, Dexter and Sydney. Some women get one bad apple in a lifetime; I get two!"

"We'll discuss this later, girl. We must get down to the bottom of this. Such rumours could be damaging to your case if people start believing in them."

"That's what I fear most. I'll try and see you about eight."

"See you later, girl."

"You've let me down again," I say to Leon, who has missed another meeting.

"But I was out with some friends last night, and things got a little out of hand. I'm sorry baby," he replies, still slurring his words. I swear I can smell the alcohol through the telephone. He doesn't turn up for the meetings and then gives me that sweet-talk nonsense. I know that the others are getting pissed off about it, but are keeping their comments to themselves. It's not an atmosphere that I want to create with my team, as their work is just as much on show as mine. I don't care what Leon does in his spare time, but when he is due to perform for me, professionally speaking that is, then I expect his full commitment. Business must come first.

"I think that you are taking advantage of our relationship," I say. "Leon, we all need this to go well."

"Hey, baby. What's happened to that talk about me being good. I can turn up in Paris on the day of the show, and turn the place inside out! When people see your designs they'll be queuing up in the streets of London, Paris, Milan and New York, just to see them." I can tell that the alcohol has numbed his brain. He probably couldn't even remember what planet he was on, let alone remember our meeting.

"When are we going to see you, in order to go through the plans for the show?"

"I can come round tonight, baby, and we can discuss the show then."

"I need to get the whole team down for their view. This is not a one-woman show, this is a team effort."

"That's fine, baby. I'll come round to the office, then we can have our own after-show entertainment. You know how you like that!" I don't think his comment was intended the way it came across: keep the woman satisfied and all will be all right. This makes me feel cheap! I like men, I make no bones about it and I certainly don't make any apologies for it, either. But, I am also a strong believer in respect and the moment a man starts to lose that, then I start to lose my interest. Leon couldn't think of anything as complicated as disrespect in his intoxicated state. And, in any case, give him his dues, he is a gentleman. He's just rarely a sober gentleman!

"Leon, darling! Don't let me down again, as I don't know how long I can keep defending you against the others."

"Baby, you're the boss. If they don't like it, then kick their ass into shape. My baby won't hear a bad word being said against me, right?"

"Right! You just make sure that you turn up later," I command.

Leon walked through the door apologising for being late. I was afraid to light my cigarette, in case I set the building alight. The fumes emitting from his breath were enough to get us drunk, by just being in the same room. I was ashamed and embarrassed. He seemed to be taking his talent for granted. He just did not seem to take anything too seriously, or so it appeared. How can he feel pressure, when he is forever stoned? Being stoned out of your brains, in order to avoid pressure, is not a way to deal with the adulation. Leon was beginning to piss people off. I knew, because I could tell by the sarcastic reactions to his comments. Any such sarcasm, however, would have gone completely over his head. If this was how he deals with pressure, it worries me senseless that Paris might be too much for him.

"Next week we get to show what we can do," I say, continuing with the meeting without so much as a welcome for Leon. "Our careers can go three ways: they can plummet into oblivion without trace; they can maintain the status quo, which is not too bad; or, they can rise to the point where we are all going to do very well indeed. I believe that we are all heading for the last. Our collection is great! I think it could possibly be our best to date. Let's bowl them over!" I raise my glass of champagne and the rest of the team follows suit. Leon had clearly had enough alcohol in his blood system but demanded more. When he finished his "down-in-one" act, he made a nuisance of himself, troubling everyone by asking whether they had a can of lager in their drawer. The disdainful looks were not enough for him to get the message that he was becoming more and more unpopular by the minute. I know that had I not been in charge, then I would have known of the views that were probably circulating amongst the team.

"Hey, baby, you ready for some of that loving?" says Leon at a volume that must have been heard by most in the room, if not all. I wonder how he manages to ride that motorbike of his in this state. He's likely to get himself arrested, if he attempts to ride that machine home.

"Sorry, Leon," I whisper, "but a friend of mine needs me tonight."

"Hey, baby, I need you tonight. What about me?" Leon shouts, to my embarrassment.

"Let's go into my office and discuss this further." I can see Virginia glancing over in our direction, her look of contempt says it all.

"No, if you're going to stand me up, then I want everyone to hear," he shouts.

"Leon," I warn, "you are making a scene." People were now pretending that it was business as usual, but I knew what they were thinking and probably saying. I don't blame them, Leon was also beginning to wear my patience thin.

"Baby, don't leave me tonight," Leon continues in his fake cry.

"Bring your friend round and I will give her a good time also. You must have told her how good I am."

"That's it! I've had enough of you," I say, raising my voice to match his. "You can get the hell out of this building, and if you're not in a better state by tomorrow, then you can kiss us all goodbye!"

"I'll give you all more than just a kiss! You all need me! I'm the one that everyone is talking about!" Adam came over to help Leon out of the building.

"Get off me, you freak!" shouts Leon as he tries to struggle his way out of Adam's hold. "Don't try and play the bitch-woman with me, you know it don't work. Everybody, I've made your boss scream with pleasure. She's a lousy screw!"

"You're fired!" I shout.

"I don't work for you," I hear him say, as Adam led him out of the door. I take some time to compose myself, after what has taken me by complete surprise. So much for Leon being a gentleman. Class-A lover, my foot!

"You all right, boss?" asks Adam.

"Yes, I'm fine," I reply, clearly shaken.

"Come on team, let's get back to work," commands Virginia. She always seems to know the right thing to say, at the right time.

"I don't believe it," says Pat. "I don't think that this is something that Sydney would have kept from Don, especially as Dexter had made these same allegations before. He would know that she would have found out eventually, so it would have been better to come clean now."

"I think that is the problem: if he were to confess to having drugs around, then Don would have to get rid of him. There are no two ways about it! She can't afford to expose Dionne to such risk."

"But surely we would have heard something about it in all this time. The world is not that big a place around here to hide such a secret."

"You could be right, Pat, but who knows what he has been up to, whilst he and Don were apart? For all we know, he could have been locked up in prison for years. How would we know? I can't say that I knew anyone that well, who would have been in touch with him during those years in the wilderness, do you?"

"There is something about this whole affair that stinks," replies Pat. "I don't like it one little bit. Where is Don, anyway? It's not like her to be so late."

"She said she would be here sometime after eight. I hope that she's all right."

"I can't get her on the telephone and her mobile seems to be permanently switched off," says Pat, looking extremely worried. "I hope that Don hasn't done anything silly. I can't believe that she didn't feel it right to call me. I could be on my death bed and I would still get up to help you girls, if I could."

"To tell you the truth, when she rang me this afternoon, I thought that she had either spoken to you earlier, or that she had tried to contact you and couldn't. It just goes to show that you can be with someone and not really know them. Look at Leon: apart from his drinking problem, he seemed a perfect gentleman. But the moment I told him that I couldn't be with him tonight, he turned into a beast! It's like as if some of these guys suppress what they're really like until one day the real them comes out and that's when their primitive manner comes to light. I've had my fair share of bad luck, so I know what I'm talking about. Why do we play this love game anyway?"

"I didn't know that you were playing that game. Your men never seem to be around for very long," says Pat, in jest.

"I can't afford to get myself messed up in this emotional game. And when I do fall for a guy, he turns out to be gay, so what chance have I got?"

"Oh Earl, now that was a hunk of a man. I can hear that voice now. Earl would make Barry White sound like he's singing in a falsetto! You definitely missed out there, girl."

"There was nothing I could do. But, for me, Pat, I don't get too close long enough to get that hurt. I am perfectly content living that way. I have my career to look after and I want to be a major success in my own right, before I start sharing my life with somebody else. When I'm as successful in my field, as you are in yours, then Mister Josephine might get a look in, until then he can wait."

"You were a successful business woman long before I even thought about *Four Seasons*. Success is very subjective and if one is going to use that as a measure, then it is very easy to move the target so that it can never be achieve."

"But you know what I'm like Pat, when I give more than I should, I lose my head. However, I've matured since my break up with Jeremy. Those days are long gone. You've done well. You found yourself a good man at the first time of calling."

"Wait a minute!" says Pat. "You should be the last person to say that. I had a crush on that Andrew what's his name, when we were at Crossfields."

"Having a crush is not the same as falling in love."

"The heartache and worry is probably the same."

"Maybe. All I know is, that feeling is like failing your exams, but twenty times worse. I don't think that Tennyson could have experienced such heartache when he wrote, "'tis better to have loved and lost, than never to have loved at all," because had he experienced such an emotion, then I don't believe that he would have graced us with those words."

"It doesn't seem like Don is going to turn up. Maybe she's gone by her parents."

"But why would she go there, when she knows that we are waiting for her here?" I ask. "Something is wrong, Pat." Pat is trying Don's telephone number again and asking whether she is in, and if she is, then to pick up the receiver: Pat is having no luck.

"I don't know what's going on Jo, because I know that she got my earlier messages because the beep on her answering machine came on almost as soon as she gave her welcoming message. That tells me that she got my message and wiped it off, but has not returned the call. That is so unlike her. I'm worried!"

"I think that we should give her until tomorrow morning, and if we don't hear from her by then, I suggest we raise the alarm."

"I hope that won't be too late," says Pat, showing genuine concern.

"Let's hope not. Talking about late, I must remember to give that friend of Rupert, Linda, a call, now that Leon is no more."

"Linda!" repeats Pat, "I don't recall Rupert mentioning this Linda. What does she do?"

"All I know is that she is a photographer."

"Oh yes," says Pat after seeming to consider her name for some time. "I know who she is. I didn't think he knew her that well. I remember meeting her once or twice when Rupert was at Bar school. She used to go out with one of Rupert's class friends."

"I just hope that she is good. What are your plans for next week?"

"Well, it now seems that Rupert is going to be free to travel around with me. At one time, he couldn't guarantee spending much time with me over there, but recently he has gone well out of his way to make sure that we have a great time. I have quite a lot of signing to do, and in between that, we are going to travel around the city. I love Paris, so I can't wait. Rupert's attitude to the whole trip has suddenly changed in favour of the idea, so he's no doubt looking forward to it. And, the highlight, of course, is my girl causing waves. I suspect that Don will be spending most of her time with Sydney, so I don't think that we will see her much before your show."

"You know Pat, in all the years we have known each other, we have never all been away together at the same time, so this could be a trip of a lifetime."

"You're right. Let's make sure that we arrange another trip when we come back. How about just us girls?"

"I like that!"

"Well, let's do it. I'm sure Don won't object," says Pat, confidently.

"Well, girl, it doesn't seem like Don is going to show her face around here tonight, and I've got to be making tracks."

"Okay Jo," says Pat. "I'll keep trying her. If I get through to her, I shall call you."

"That's fine, Pat. I might even try myself. One of us should hopefully get through to her," I reply, and make my way out of the flat and into my car. I'll try Don before I call Linda. It occurs to me that I haven't even got Don's telephone number stored into the memory of my car phone. Call it convention, I don't know, but the usual line of communication is normally through Pat, so I've had little cause to call her direct. I check her number in my electronic organiser.

"Don, are you there, it's Jo," I say, speaking into her answering machine.

"Hi Jo," says Don.

"Girl, where have you been?" I ask, relieved that she is okay. I was beginning to fear the worst, although I didn't mention this to Pat in order to save her any further anxiety. "Pat and I have been worried sick, thinking about you, wondering where you were. Where have you been?"

"Sorry, Jo, I didn't feel like coming round, again."

"Didn't you get the messages Pat left on your answering machine?"

"I haven't answered my phone to anyone tonight," Don snaps. Don is clearly in no mood to be pushed. Either way, it surprises me that Pat is in the class of "anyone" that she did not answer her phone to.

"Are you okay?" I ask.

"I don't know how I am at the moment, I wish that I could rewind today and play a different tape. Today did not go as I had planned it. I was full of optimism this morning, and now I couldn't be more pessimistic if I tried."

"Did you speak to Sydney tonight?"

"He rang me from Milan but I didn't answer his call, either. I didn't want to give him time to concoct some half-baked story by giving him any advanced warning. I need to see his reaction when I put the allegation to him."

"I think that could be the best move. Well, you must let us know how everything goes. Presumably, Pat hasn't got through to you as yet?"

"Not tonight."

"Well, she is probably trying to get through as we speak. We said whoever got through to you first should contact the other, and let them know. As you are going to speak to her when she calls, can I leave it in your hands to inform her that we have already spoken?"

"I'm still not answering my phone!" replies Don. She is angry but it's clearly not geared towards me.

"Okay, baby. I'll call her," I reply.

"I'll ring you tomorrow, Jo. Thanks for calling." I try to call

Pat but she is on the line. She's probably got through to Don right away. Hopefully, she can make more sense out of Don's behaviour than I. Now, to call Linda Walters.

Rupert

I feel like a weight has been lifted off my shoulders. I don't know how long I could have continued walking down that path with Linda, without collapsing under the burden of guilt. After that night with Pat I knew that I was playing with fire and it was only a matter of time before I got burnt. Linda took our split worse than I thought she would have. I was always of the opinion that we were together only because I wanted us to be. What I mean is that it would end only when I wanted it to. I knew that Linda had feelings for me, but she knew that I was married and I never once gave her the impression that I would leave Pat. And yet she still didn't make it easy for me or, should I say, for us. I don't think that we will be friends. She was probably right when she questioned whether that could happen when we were never friends in the first place. Our friendship coincided with our affair. Take the latter away and you have a void. That void might be too large for a pure friendship to fill, if we were to carry on seeing each other. I suppose there would always have been the danger that we might give in to temptation and continue where we left off. However, you never know, things might be different after a long cooling-off period. I wouldn't count on it, though. I knew that I was proposing solutions that wouldn't, in reality, work. But, there was some minor comfort in Linda having to say "no", rather than me having to be the bearer of the full bad news. I knew that we couldn't be lovers one day, and simply be friends the next. It is not so much that I couldn't trust Linda to keep her hands to herself, I don't think that I could trust myself! This way, history will show that it was a mutual separation, albeit not quite with equal enthusiasm. That night when I left Linda's place I felt like I had been cleansed. My soul felt free from burden. It's hard to explain that feeling, but I knew that within all that quagmire of mixed emotions, was something in there that told me that what we had done was for the best. I remember sitting in my car before

I went home that night, gathering my thoughts and, for the first time in a long while, I was looking forward to the period ahead. I was looking forward to being more of a support to my wife. I shall be there for my child. I shall be there to devote my time, fully, to both my wife and my child. I came close to missing out on one of the most important periods of my life and felt that I had to catch up. Catch up on what, I'm not entirely sure, but suddenly I wanted to spend as much time with Pat as possible. They say that you never know how much you love someone, until they have gone. I never knew how much I loved my wife until I woke up one day and realised that, if I were to carry on with my affair, I could lose her. I could lose her for good! As sure as we are born to die, is as sure I am that Linda and I would have been found out eventually with the inevitable consequence. I didn't want to be like the thief who is never satisfied with his loot. He carries on stealing until he is caught. That night I wanted to spoil Pat as much as I could. If I could have bought her roses and Swiss chocolates at that late hour then I would have done. I committed myself to being by her side throughout her forthcoming book tour. There was no more of this business trip nonsense. That was only a façade, in order to try and spend time with Linda when we were over there. It might also be a blessing in disguise that Linda will not be in Paris at the same time, because it will be very uncomfortable. Anyway, even if she does find a designer at this eleventh hour, Paris is a big place. The chances of bumping into each other are pretty slim.

Donna

I couldn't face Pat, yesterday. I have too much respect for her to confront her with a one-sided allegation. I have to have the story either denied or corroborated by Sydney. Anyone else and I wouldn't have had a problem. I would have told them what I heard and demanded to know their side of the story. Obviously I don't want this allegation to be proved right. I don't want to lose both Sydney and Pat as friends. I have always looked up to Pat. I think that a lot of people do. She's talented, thoughtful and incredibly bright. She has reached the highest in both academia and as a novelist. How can anyone fail to be impressed by someone with such glowing credentials? She is a star, there is no doubt about that! But, that star begins to dim the moment you hurt those that put their full trust in you. And, when you start to betray those who love you, then any admiration soon fades away. And believe me, it would have taken only something like being with Sydney without my knowledge that could cause me to lose that admiration. It's unfair that anyone should carry such burdens, but if you put yourself in those positions, then you are a target from those who respect you for what they thought you were. I wondered how it was that Sydney knew so much about me when we weren't together. They probably both discussed my business during their pillow talk. What I can't figure out is why she continually put Dexter down. Surely, it would have been in her interests for Dexter and I to have remained together. But then, I'm not a doctor of philosophy, so who am I to question how such minds work? Like Dexter said, it seems that we are both the victims of this scam. I haven't even got round to thinking about Rupert in this matter. At least I wasn't with Sydney when this affair was going ahead. And Pat could not ask for a more faithful husband than Rupert. Lord, I hope for both our sakes, Dexter has got this wrong. I do ask myself though why hadn't Pat told me that she was in contact with Sydney? What could possibly be so secretive that she could not tell me? Why hasn't Dexter told Rupert? Damn! I should have asked him. Dexter cares little for Pat, so he would have told Rupert the moment he knew. But Rupert clearly doesn't know, otherwise I would have known, or there would be some tell-tale signs. Pat and Rupert are probably closer now than at anytime I have known them, so he couldn't possibly know. It seems that I will have to deal with this alone.

I shall ask Sydney to move out tonight. This past twenty-four hours has made me realise that too many things in my life over the past few months have happened, too fast. I want to be me. I want to live for me, not for somebody else. Sydney often asked me to move into his house in Hampstead, but I wanted to stay in what was my own. Now I want to be alone in what is my own. As for marriage, I don't know. That obviously depends on how our discussion goes tonight. But either way, it would not be in the foreseeable future, if ever! It was wrong of me to have accepted Sydney back into my life so easily. There should have been a period when we got to know each other again, not simply continue where we left off. That was always heading for a disaster. I thought the person I was with was the person I fell in love with, all those years ago. But in truth, I don't really know him at all. Dexter was right, with those gorgeous supermodels at his disposal, why does he want to be with me? There must be something other than just love. How can he love me, when he doesn't really know me? I know I told myself that nobody knew me as well as he does, or did, but I would have told myself anything, just to convince myself that what I was doing was the right thing. And let's face it, saying that he knows me better than most is not saying very much, is it? I haven't had a serious relationship other than with Dexter and Dexter spent most of his time getting to know other women!

I recognise the sound of the engine in Sydney's jeep. He has not stopped calling me since he's been back. Well, this is the moment I have been waiting for. I shan't cause a scene. I am too tired for all this confrontation. I feel unbelievably calm. I guess, when you've had as many fights with Dexter as I've had, you become hardened to these occasions. When he left I put that life behind me. All I want now is to be left alone with my daughter.

And I've decided that I shall make arrangements with Dexter for him to see Dionne whenever he so wishes. She's our child and I would want him to play an important part in her upbringing. There is no reason whatsoever why Dionne should suffer, because her parents are no longer together.

"Baby, where have you been? I've been calling you since yesterday," says Sydney, looking genuinely worried. He attempts to cuddle me in some fashion but I make no move in reciprocation. He clearly hasn't noticed my cool response because he continues with his act nonetheless. "Donna, what's the matter?" he asks, as it must feel like he is cuddling a wet fish. Now is not the time to be expressing emotions. Well, not that kind of emotion, anyway!

"A lot of things are the matter," I reply coldly. "Where shall I start? How about I start with Pat, then we can move on to your drug conviction."

"Who told you about that!" says Sydney evidently surprised.

"Does it matter who told me? What matters is the truth of the allegations. I think your reaction is the biggest indictment, wouldn't you say?"

"It's not what you think, Donna. Stay with me on this one. It is definitely not what you are thinking."

"How do you know what I am thinking, Sydney?" I ask. "You don't even know me; how on earth can you tell what I am thinking? To think I was going to marry you."

"Donna, hear me out first before you make any hasty decisions. The most serious is the drugs matter."

"Really? And do you think that I take lightly you being with my best friend all this time behind my back, not to mention Rupert, who is also an innocent party caught up in this?"

"Okay! Okay! I shall deal with the Pat matter first," he says whilst pacing up and down the room trying to deal with the bombardment. This is exactly what I wanted, no preparation beforehand. No lies planned, just the truth, as painful as that might be.

"I can only presume that you haven't yet spoken to Pat, because if you had, she would have told you the truth."

"I'll leave Pat to her conscience and her husband. At this point, you're my concern," I reply sternly.

"I bumped into Pat with a friend of hers, some time shortly after we broke up. I was enquiring about you and we agreed to exchange telephone numbers. At first, Pat never called me, but I would make the odd call and ask about you. She would tell me how things were with you and, of course, with Dexter. That is all there is to it. There is nothing more. Forget me, we have been apart for some time, but I can't believe that you would have thought that Pat would have got involved in anything like that with me. Tell me that you didn't approach Pat with this."

"I didn't approach Pat with anything; I'm approaching you. Why the big secret? Why didn't you just simply contact me yourself?"

"Ask Pat; I pleaded with her not to say anything to you. I didn't want to be seen as meddling in your relationship, especially when you were pregnant with Dionne."

"So it was Pat who was your spy?"

"Are you asking me or are you telling me?"

"I'm serious Charles, this is not over yet."

"Yes, Pat was my informant. Believe me, she did nothing wrong! I can't believe I'm having to say this. Pat would not say a single word against you and you should know that better than I. I'm sure pleased that you didn't tackle Pat with this, because it would have been regrettable. If Pat didn't tell you about us being in touch then how did you find that out?"

"I don't think that is important at this time. I hope that you have as good an answer for this drug offence, as you did for Pat." This one I can see isn't as easy as the former.

"If Dexter is behind this then I'll kill him. I swear I'll kill him."

"It wasn't Dexter, I haven't seen or spoken to him for ages. Anyway, that is not the issue, you kill whomever you like, just as long as you give me a straight answer, and you are not residing under this roof. An addict and a murderer will be too much for me to bear."

"I did have a record for handling drugs, but it was a small amount and it was a long time ago. I was young and foolish. I was caught with two grammes of marijuana when I was once at a fashion show. It was for personal use. There was no evidence of me trying to supply to anyone. That's all it was. Nothing more."

"I can't believe what you are saying. You knew that Dexter had made these allegations before, so why didn't you tell me then? Why did you leave it for me to find out from somebody else?"

"It was such a long time ago. I only received a fine, it was that minor. And that offence would be spent by law, so I wouldn't have had to say anything to anyone about it."

"Forget the bloody law!" I shout. "I'm talking about us: me and you. You had nearly lost me my child. That was careless and selfish."

"Donna, I'm telling you, it was a long time ago. I don't know who is feeding you this information but they should not have had access to it. They should have known, surely, this information will not be admissible at the hearing?"

"There isn't going to be a hearing, because I am going to make arrangements with Dexter so that he can see his daughter whenever he so wishes. I don't want Dionne to be confused as to the identity of her father," I say coldly.

"Are you saying what I think you are saying?" asks Sydney.

"I think that we should have some time apart, and see how we really feel about each other."

"I already know how I feel about you," he pleads.

"Well, if you feel the same way later, and I feel the same way too, then there is no reason why we shouldn't get back together, but at this moment I need a break. I need to find myself and know what I am truly about." Sydney said nothing during my declaration. I knew that he wouldn't have taken this easily, but he knew that he was fighting a losing battle, and just stood there hanging his head. I think that I could have detected a tear in his eye but I wasn't too sure. As for me, I feel calm but slightly dazed. The sea of emotions has finally taken their toll on me.

"You don't need to take all your belongings unless you want to," I say. "I'll forward your mail to your office, as and when it comes in."

"Don't worry, there won't be any mail. All my mail goes either to my home or to the office."

"Well, an envelope arrived for you today by recorded

delivery."

"Are you sure that it's for me?" asks Sydney with a confused frown, probably wishing that he had got up on the other side of the bed this morning.

"It's got this address typed on it and it's got your name on it, so I guess it must be yours," I reply. Sydney takes the envelope off the table and examines it, as if checking to see whether there could be some mistake. Satisfied as to its legitimacy, he proceeds to open the envelope and inspect its enclosures.

"There are some photographs of you and Dexter and a letter."

"A photograph of Dexter and me!" I say and walk over to Sydney in order to view the photographs myself. I could see that these were photographs taken of my meeting with Dexter, yesterday. All the photographs have the time and date imprinted on them. That bastard Dexter has set me up!

"What is this all about, Donna?" asks Sydney as he passes me the letter. The letter was typewritten with no signature. It says 'Thought you would be interested in the latest pictures of the many secret meetings between your Donna and Dexter. They meet whenever you go away. Donna wants Dexter back but he is not interested." I could feel my blood boil as I read this letter. I have been well and truly stitched up.

"I thought you said that you hadn't seen Dexter for a long time," says Sydney, wasting no time in putting the direct question to me. It was only a minute ago that he was being interrogated, now it's my turn.

"I saw Dexter yesterday," I reply, in submission.

"Would you like to tell me more?" asks Sydney which despite the implied option, I don't think he would have accepted any answer but "yes".

"I met Dexter yesterday with the intention of trying to settle our differences. I can only think that he brought someone else along with the aim of causing further confusion between us."

"Well, he's succeeded hasn't he? Please tell me the truth, Donna. All this talk about you wanting me to leave, is it because you want Dexter back?"

"Of course, not! I just need some space."

"It was Dexter that told you about my conviction, wasn't it?"

he presses. Why should I lie anymore. Dexter says that we are both victims. Time may well prove that to be the case. That, however, does not mean that we need to be allies. There are too many people around me trying to do what's best for me. It is about time that I decided what was best for myself.

"Yes, it was him!"

"I knew that," replies Sydney with venom in his eyes. "Can't you see what he is trying to do? It's obvious. He's been jealous of me since we've been back together and he wants to split us up again. Why else would he tell you about a past of mine, that was so long ago it is almost irrelevant, and yet, at the same time, send these photographs to me. I know that these photographs are from him. He might as well have signed his name. Don't let him win Donna. Don't let that man continually ruin your life."

"He won't. I know how to deal with him."

"I think it is time I dealt with this man. I don't want this man interfering in my affairs when I come back from Paris. I take it that our trip is still on."

"No! I want a clean break now. I don't want to give the wrong impression. If we are meant to be, then we will be, but, for now, I just want to be left alone."

Sydney left most of his belongings behind. I could only think that this was in hope that we are not yet finished. I do wonder why he wants to be with me so much. I suppose years of self-doubt, built up during the Dexter era, makes one doubt their attractiveness to somebody else. Especially, when that somebody else's working day is in the proximity of so many beautiful women. Why me? I keep asking myself. What have I got to offer that nobody else has? Simple, I suppose. Me!

Patricia

"I spoke to Donna today and she told me that she will not be going to Paris," I say. "She and Sydney have agreed to cool things for a while. I think that the pressure of the custody case is really getting to her."

"Surely, now is the time she needs Sydney to be around," says Rupert, flicking through another of his books on parenthood "made simple".

"You would have thought so, wouldn't you? Having said that, she is beginning to show signs of strain. She seems to have undergone a complete personality change. She kept Jo and me waiting here for her the other night, without turning up. She didn't even call to say that she couldn't make it. I suppose I would be the same if you were to try and take our baby away from me, especially after going through so much pain for nine months carrying it and giving birth to it. It must be hard to take."

"I would never do such a thing. Anyway, I would have no cause to."

"Are you saying that Dexter does?"

"I'm not saying that at all!" replies Rupert defensively. Give him his dues, he has been overly supportive of me over the past few days. I'm not saying that he wasn't supportive before, but now it is more overt. He has reduced his workload, which might have something to do with the fact that he no longer has to work as hard as he used to. But then again, we were never quite paupers and he would still work all the hours God sends. Over the past few months, I don't think that a weekend went by without him having to work somewhere. He was obviously working on a big case because, for the first time since he has been practising, he has had to do so much research away from Chambers. I'm just thankful that he had chosen to spare me the details of what must be an incredibly boring case. Not that many of his cases are otherwise, but I like to try and show some form of interest, although it's not easy when, for example, the case involves lost cargoes and damaged ships. Try keeping awake during a discussion on the strengths and weaknesses of those cases. And, frustratingly, they always seem to settle at the eleventh hour, in any case, so why bother? I'm convinced that there is an unwritten code that you should threaten to go to court, then you agree a settlement just before the big show. And then everybody goes through the act of appearing surprised. It's like playing a poker game, without the tension. I remember my cousins on my mother's side would hold a surprise party for my aunt's birthday every year, and every year she would appear to be surprised. I see obvious patterns of similarity between my aunt's surprise birthday parties and Rupert's shipping cases: it's called inevitability. What is also inevitable, is that I am going to have another child. I definitely want another. This pregnancy has not been easy, Lord alone knows that! Well, that's probably not, strictly speaking, true because if I didn't tell people who asked how I was coping then they could tell. The mornings are the worst. Morning sickness really does mean that you feel sick in the mornings! When I awake from my daily siesta, I feel fine, but after a night's sleep, I feel nauseated. It's not very nice! No sickness is pleasant, but at least for most people, sickness comes around only once in a while. I also find that this sickness makes me feel lethargic to a point of almost being lazy. I no longer promote the book, although I shall be taking advantage of the opportunity of being in France. My normal sleeping pattern has gone completely out of the window. I read until very late, to avoid going to sleep, because of the inevitable sickness that will ensue. I have never yet managed to stay awake all night. More sleep and less activity leads to even more sleep and lesser activity! I have, however, started doing some research for my new book on my computer by surfing the World Wide Web. A trip to my university or central library seems too much like hard work at the moment. So my mind is relatively active when it is not dormant during my many hours of sleep. My book, which I intend to write after the birth of our first-born, will be a follow-up to *Four Seasons*. It will not be a sequel, in that the story will not continue. *Four Seasons* is fiction, my new book will be a scientific study into the lives of the many other Jessicas out there. Whether that book will be as big a success as *Four Seasons* remains to be seen. The interesting thing about my success as a writer is that I have never coveted the title of a best-seller. I wrote a book and that was the end of the matter as far as I was concerned. If it sold, it sold, and if it hadn't, so be it. I feel embarrassed when people give me the praise that I have been fortunate to receive. Now that I have witnessed the power of the pen, however, I do have many other projects in mind. Projects on subjects that interest me as a person, and as a woman. If I can achieve only half of what some of my heroines, such as Alice Walker, Toni Morrison or Zora Neale Hurston, have achieved, then I would have made some contribution to the enrichment of some people's lives. It means that I can put some of that education of mine to good use. I want to help in the continuation of people's education. I see the world as one big classroom. We are forever learning, but some do better than others. I would like to help bridge that gap between those who do well and those who don't. I know that a lot of what I want to achieve may sound like fantasy thoughts. Maybe some may say that I have too much time on my hands to think. But, if God has given me a talent, as others seem to think I possess, then it would be a sin not to put that talent to further good use. Enlightening people to the ways of others, apparently different to themselves, helps "put to silence the ignorance of foolish men". And we all know where ignorance can lead: to prejudice and hate. I don't want this for myself and I certainly don't want that for our child. I want our child to respect the cultures of others, as well as its own. I give this message whenever I go out on tour, and I am so pleased by the positive reception. I know it all sounds rather philosophical, but with expectation dies hope, and without hope we have nothing.

"I have a special surprise for you, my queen," says Rupert, hardly managing to contain his excitement.

"And what surprise is awaiting me?" I ask.

"I have managed to book us into the same room, in the same hotel we stayed in in Paris all those years ago."

"We can afford to stay in the Paris Ritz, you're such a cheap-skate," I say, while making a fake punch towards Rupert's arm.

"I want it to be like it was before."

"Oh you're such a romantic."

"I know! They don't make gentlemen like me anymore," says Rupert, clearly pleased with his accomplishment.

"I'm not too sure about that," I reply, dampening his ego. "Jo promised to pass by tonight, before she flies out tomorrow. She said that she would call on her way back from seeing your friend, Linda."

"Linda!" replies Rupert, with apparent shock.

"Yes, you have Jo to thank for that. I didn't know that you two were that close."

"We're not! I met her at Yvonne's party. She invited us to a private viewing of her photographs. Do you remember?"

"I do, but I don't recall you saying much about it. Is she still with that guy from Bar school?"

"Wilson," he informs me. "I'm sorry to say that he committed suicide a few months ago."

"Oh my God! When did you know this?" I ask, surprised that he hadn't mentioned it to me before.

"She told me only recently, but I didn't want to trouble you with any bad news whatsoever," he says. I become pregnant and suddenly people think that I should be shielded from all bad news, as if the news on the television and radio are any more comforting.

"I'm not that feeble. I barely knew him. Were they still together when this happened?"

"No!" replies Rupert hastily. "Their relationship had finished a long time before. She thinks that he was under extreme pressure at work and had one or two problems at home."

"What a waste of a life!" I say. "There have been times in my life when I have been so depressed I've felt that I can't go on, but, when push has come to shove, I could not do anything more than weather such depression. Nothing is ever as bad as it seems. How did she take it?"

"Understandably, she took it badly, even though they were no longer together. She let herself and her career slide. That is how she managed to contact me. I must have mentioned that I knew Jo and that she was part of The Best of British Fashion. She called me in desperation and asked that I ask Jo to put the word around that she was looking for a job."

"You should have asked Sydney, I'm sure that he would have helped."

"I didn't think of it," replies Rupert as the door bell rings.

"That must be Jo," I say.

"Hi baby!" says Jo in her usual dazzling style.

"Hi girl! Are you ready to bowl them over?" I ask.

"I sure am!" says Jo full of enthusiasm. "Everything has fallen into place, just at the right time. I saw your friend, Linda, tonight," she says turning to Rupert. "She is brilliant, I like her. I told her that I was coming over here tonight, she sends her regards."

"So are you going to employ her?" asks Rupert.

"I am indeed. I left her packing her bags and getting ready for tomorrow's flight."

"I look forward to meeting her again, after all these years," I add.

"You two would get on well, you have something in common," says Jo.

"Steady Rupert!" says Jo as Rupert, for some reason, nearly spills his wine on the Persian rug.

"You were saying Jo, that Linda and I have something in common."

"Oh yes. Linda, too, is pregnant!"

Part Four

Rupert

Jo may as well have said that I had a terminal illness. I don't believe that I could have felt any worse, either way. I thought that I had to be dreaming, and that I could escape the nightmare upon pinching myself, in order to wake up. I pinched and pinched but nothing happened, other than making me feel sore! Could Jo have been mistaken? My mind rummaged through its dictionary for words rhyming with "pregnant". Ironically, it is the one word that drew the least blanks, which is more than I can say for my sperm count, obviously! I nearly shat myself when Jo uttered those immortal words. I managed, just, to control my bowels from accomplishing that fate. I wasn't so lucky, however, with our Persian rug. I succeeded in my efforts the second time around what I had avoided at the first. That is, accidentally, spilled my wine on it. Both Jo and Pat looked onward with dismay that I could get so emotional over a friend being pregnant. If I could say, "you too would be in this state, if you were me", then I would have done, but I wasn't about to incriminate myself unnecessarily, no matter how shaken I was. I wanted to call Linda tonight, but thought better of it. I would have to see her and discuss what will happen next. She might tell me that the child is not mine. If it isn't mine, then it will have to be Wilson's. I want it to be Wilson's. I hope so, but I don't think so. When did Linda conceive? From my calculation... Oh my God! It could have happened any time, from "that" first time to the last. I'm so angry. Why didn't I ask her whether she was taking any contraceptives? She knew I wasn't! She wanted this to happen, she must have done. What did she expect to happen, other than what has occurred. I don't even want to think about Pat, that is another matter with its own consequence. And why didn't Linda tell me that she was pregnant and that it might be mine? Maybe there lies my glimmer of hope. She never told me, because it was none of my damn business. It was none of my business because it's not mine. No! I've already explored that. She knew Jo was coming over tonight so she must have known that Jo would have told me. 'She sends her regards', says Jo, and she sends me this poisoned message. How did she expect me to react? More than just spill my wine, I would suspect. What did Linda think this would do to Pat? Pat is supposed to be carrying my only child. Oh no! I haven't given a thought to Bertran and Veronica. They're due over here soon for the birth of their first grandchild. Bertran specifically asked me to look after his daughter when they left England. I have failed. I have failed us and I have failed them. I have let everybody down. I played a dangerous game and lost. I am ashamed. What did I think I was doing, anyway? I was a home-loving man, trying to play the field of a gigolo. I didn't know what I was doing. Others get by. Dexter has been doing it for years. I am not like Dexter or any of the others he symbolises. I have had to learn my lesson the hard way. I haven't even got Dexter to turn to. I could do with his advice now. Damn you Dexter! He might already know. That Josh guy seems to be very much on the ball. The bloody man seems to know my business inside out. This will ruin me, if I am not already ruined. If I had known that this would have happened then I would not have ventured into a territory where I belong not. If I knew how I would feel I would not have trodden where I had not trodden before. But I remember that day. The very first time Linda and I made love. I can still visualise it, as if it were only yesterday. And the judgement, "I sentence you to a life of shame and guilt". That has haunted me ever since. But the sentence didn't fit the crime. I was weak and many men have fallen at the feet of more than one woman at any single time. Why should I then be punished so harshly? I love my wife, I have never pretended otherwise. Lord, please help me in my hour of need. I need you. I beg upon your mercy. I ask for help but know not yet what I want. I haven't even thought through my options properly. What are they? I can have another child or not; the latter desirable, the former disastrous. I can't have another child, other than with my wife. I tell myself that there is more than one solution to that which is desired. I don't believe in abortion, or I don't think I do. I remember that debate at Oxford, "Life or Murder". I was for Life but I did have some reservations. I was open to persuasion on some issues. Conceiving a child through the lovemaking of two consenting adults, however, was not one of them. Views do, however, change. I want to pray that Linda loses the baby but that is immoral, if not downright sinful in itself. I must see Linda before she flies out tomorrow. Maybe Linda doesn't want a child, my child. Maybe she doesn't even like children. If not, then she can take any fatal decisions she desires. I can then wash the blood off my hands. She would never have to know where I stood on the matter. And then again, there is Pat. I can't keep putting her to the back of my mind. I feel for her more than I feel for myself. If Pat finds out about my other child; another child that does not carry her blood; another child that is mine and not hers; another child that is part of my life and not part of hers; my child that was carried in the womb of another woman. I could go on and on. It doesn't get any easier. And what happens when that other child is sick, do I leave my wife and child at home, to attend to my other child with another woman? Oh Lord! What have I done?

Donna

Sydney still calls me every day. He doesn't have to say he's sorry, for me to know that he is. He has, nonetheless, apologised numerous times. I too am sorry. I am sorry for how our relationship, brief as it was, panned out. I thought that the second time around really would be better than the first. I think that all I did was remember how we were before and yearn for it to be the same again, only this time it was not. And, I'm not too sure that it can or ever will be. I am different from the Donna of all those years ago. I have changed. Sydney, too, is different and has changed. It wasn't difficult to rekindle what we had before, because we simply played the role of the past. When we know each other as well as we do, then that was never going to be too much of a challenge. Mind you, I ask myself, do we really know each other, anyway? Can we ever recover the lost ground of the past few years? Can anyone? Also, Chantelle will always be a part of his life. She obviously wasn't part of his life when we were first together, so it could never truly be as before. I don't mind Chantelle. In that respect, I trust him. He wouldn't do anything to hurt me or jeopardise any kind of relationship we might have. I know him well enough for me to say that! I think he feels the same about me, and he would be right. I haven't abandoned all thoughts of being with Sydney. In fact, I could think of no one else I would rather be with, only not now. I do need my space. I do think however that Sydney put down my wanting a moratorium from the intimate side of our relationship, to feelings I might have for Dexter. I had to put him right, before he could convince himself that such absurdity was true. I can't say anything about Dexter that hasn't already been said, and meant. Who is to say that Dexter wants me back, anyway? Not wanting me to be happy with anyone else and wanting me back are two entirely separate matters. And that ignores the question of whether I want him for myself, which I clearly don't. It is regrettable that anyone could even consider that I might be considering having him back. I can only believe that my forgiving nature of the past has clouded people's opinion of me. That easily forgiving person, I'm glad to say, no longer exists. That person left, along with Dexter. Like I said, the night I kicked Dexter out, a man will have to see me on my terms or not see me at all. Call it selfish, I don't mind, for when I get hurt, it is that same forgiving heart of mine that feels the pain most. Selfish? No. Self-preservation? Yes. They can take it or leave it.

It was easy. All I had to do was to tell Dexter that Sydney and I were no longer a couple and he was a different man: "different" being the operative word, of course. Surprisingly, he didn't ask too many questions. A Dexter-of-old would surely have gloated at his mini success. He messed up my life when we were together, and he could mess up my life when we weren't. I had submitted to him and he was pleased. He was everything to me short of being my pimp. And I wouldn't put it past him to try and attain such control, only he would be my sole client! When I told him that he could come round to the flat for the first time since his rapid departure, I thought that he would have dropped his trousers there and then, he was that excited! He seemed very happy when we spoke, reminiscing about the old times. I listened and added nothing, as he was doing well for the two of us all by himself. Not all was bad, of course. I wouldn't have stayed with him all that time, if it were all bad. I hear that familiar sound of his Porsche's engine. It occurs to me that I had never been invited for a drive in his prized machine. I wonder if this apparent prohibition was extended to his other women? I don't think so. But, anyway, that is all behind us, now. We have a bright new future ahead of us. It wouldn't take much for us to be like we were before, because there wasn't much there.

"You've lost more weight," says Dexter, whilst handing me a bunch of mixed flowers. He makes his way into the front room, his eyes roaming like a surveyor, looking for any disapproving signs of Sydney.

"You always knew how to charm a lady," I reply. Dexter looks well, although he has gained a little bit of weight. I put this down to good living and not so much clubbing.

"I meant only well, no maliciousness intended," he apologises. He appears to be a little nervous, unsure whether he should treat the flat as solely mine or ours. He is treading carefully. He has been given an opportunity and he was not about to blow it by coming across as too self-assured about his position.

"Where is my baby?" he asks.

"She is fast asleep."

"If memory serves me well, she used to be a late sleeper, playing until the late hours of the night and then falling asleep due to exhaustion. I miss her."

"She hasn't been sleeping too well recently, so I think that such lack of sleep has finally caught up on her."

"Can I see her?"

"That wouldn't be a good idea," I reply hastily. "As you remember, she is a light sleeper."

"Oh yes, I do," he says. In fact this is not true. Once Dionne was asleep, an earthquake couldn't waken her, but as Dexter was not the one to attend to her in the night, he is not in a position to question its correctness. Despite his limited involvement in the upbringing of Dionne, Dexter does like to think that he knows a lot more about his daughter than he really does. His pride forbids him from admitting to himself that he knows as much about the behaviour and idiosyncrasies of his daughter as does our milkman!

"You don't know how pleased I was to get your call, inviting me over. I never thought that I would ever step inside this flat again."

"It's ironic that you feel that way, because it was me who had to convince you that the flat had potential and was worth buying, remember? You wanted to buy that old shack that looked as though it was ready to collapse any day."

"Yes I do," he admits. "But then again it wouldn't have been the first time that I got something wrong, would it?" he asks, working the charm.

"You were right about Sydney though, weren't you?" I say, giving his big head exactly what it loves most: praises!

"Like I said before, Donna, my only care was for you and my

daughter. You are still officially my fiancée, remember? Neither of us broke that off. Why do you think that is?"

"You tell me!"

"Because we need each other. What are we, without each other?"

"Is that why you made sure that Sydney and I would break up?"

"I couldn't make you break up with Sydney. If you didn't want to finish with him then it wouldn't have happened. I really believe that there is a force out there that neither of us has any control over. It compels us to be together."

"If that is true, Dexter, how come I only feel the force of your envy and nothing else."

"I admit that I played dirty, but you still invited me round tonight. Am I beginning to make sense? You need me without fully appreciating it," says Dexter. Modesty was never his strongest point!

"I don't think that I can ever trust you, unless you came clean. Tell me, how did you get that criminal information on Sydney?"

"It's better that you don't know," he replies.

"How can I trust you, if you can't even tell me something which wouldn't make a blind bit of difference to me? As you said, I wouldn't have separated from Sydney unless I wanted to."

"Okay, all will be revealed. I hired a private investigator to find as much information on Sydney as he could. I also contacted an old friend of mine to tap into the police records to see if there was anything on Sydney. I couldn't believe it when his name came up trumps. I knew with that ammunition Sydney couldn't touch me, even if he wanted to. I had him exactly where I wanted him. I could make matters very uncomfortable for him, the longer he hung around you."

"I can't believe that you got someone to get into the police records."

"That is nothing. We managed to get our hands on all Rupert's telephone records as well. That is how we managed to find out about Sydney and Patricia."

"You went all out to achieve this end, didn't you?"

"You know me Donna, I play dirty and I play to win," he says, boastfully. "Where am I now? I am sitting in the front room of my flat with my fiancée. Where is Sydney? He is probably licking his wounds and regretting that he ever crossed paths with the mighty Dexter."

"You're obviously proud of yourself!" I say. Self-congratulations is Dexter's biggest pride.

"You could say that. The longer I sit here chatting away, the prouder I become. It's good to be back. I can't wait to hold Dionne in my hands. You're right she is a heavy sleeper, I haven't heard a sound from the baby monitor since I've been here. You expect to hear at least a little shuffle or something. Are you sure that she is all right?"

"Watch what you say, I know my daughter!"

"Sorry! Sorry!" says Dexter raising his hands in the air as a symbol of surrender. "Only showing concern."

"And what was it with the photographs?" I ask. Dexter chuckles.

"That was a last minute thought. My investigator took the pictures. He is good. Do you know that I didn't even know when he took them? I knew that he was going to take them, but I didn't see him. He was in total disguise. Isn't that daunting? If I couldn't find him and I hired him then how could anyone else see him? He's good. I thought that in case you went soft on Sydney, then the photographs would cause enough confusion in order to raise mistrust. As I know, once one has mistrust, it is hard to regain that trust again. Look at what I had to do just to get you back, but it was worth it. I guess now you could call the photographs the icing on the cake." He is in a good mood. Tonight has gone well so far. If he continues at this rate he could be having his breakfast here in the morning. He had his two hands behind his head and smiling to himself, probably reflecting on how easy it was to walk back into my life after all that had gone by.

"Hello Dexter," says Sydney. Dexter nearly jumps out of his skin at the sight of Sydney standing in the doorway.

"What is he doing here?" asks Dexter clearly shocked.

"Oh, sorry," I reply. "Did I not mention that Sydney was next door. It must have slipped my mind while you were congratulating yourself."

"But I thought you said that you two were finished."

"We are, but we're still good friends."

"I don't want him in my home," says Dexter without even so much as a glance in Sydney's direction. As far as Dexter was concerned Sydney was not worthy of his acknowledgement.

"You forget that I still have all that incriminating evidence against him. I can't see a court taking too kindly to having such a criminal around a baby. I have a good mind to take my child away with me tonight."

"Over my dead body," I reply.

"If that's what it takes!"

"You have a funny way of showing how much you care for Donna and Dionne, if you are now prepared to step over Donna's dead body just to get what you want," says Sydney to Dexter.

"Keep out of this, fool!" replies Dexter, "I am talking to my fiancée." I had already alerted Sydney to Dexter's potential verbal lashing. Sydney has so far stuck to his promise to me, and not retaliated. If two grown men want to try and prove their manhood by reverting to physical violence, then they can do so anywhere but in my home.

"It will take more than a threat of a spent conviction to get rid of me," says Sydney.

"Don't push me. I wouldn't think twice to prove what a criminal you really are."

"You might think twice after all that you've revealed tonight," Sydney replies.

"Didn't your mother tell you that you should never listen in on big people's conversations?" asks Dexter, sarcastically. Sydney stares right at Dexter but he still appears to be keeping his cool in the face of such abuse. I'm impressed!

"Who is going to believe that shit that I came out with tonight? The courts tend not to believe in the lies of convicts. I think that even someone as stupid as you, should know what I am getting at. Who are the courts likely to believe? Are they likely to believe a convict trying to protect his girlfriend, like you, or a respectable lawyer, such as myself? I know who I would believe, but then again I do have a vested interest."

"Forgive me for being, as you put it, stupid, but I would have thought that it would believe both me and you." Dexter looks confused by Sydney's reply. "I say that," he continues, "because, in truth, we are saying exactly the same things. I shall only repeat to the court what you have confessed to on this tape." Brilliant! Sydney held up a cassette in his hand to show Dexter where all his bragging was well and truly recorded. "I don't think that the courts or your professional organisation will look too kindly on a lawyer using such underhanded methods of resolving his own domestic disputes. Now, let me see, which is the most damaging, the illegal access to police records or the telephone records. I would say, in my stupid self, that one could soon be securing a criminal record for one's self. And then, there is the other matter. Your professional organisation can't have one of its members bringing the profession into disrepute. So, in my, to remind myself, stupid mind, I think that such a person would be struck off so fast they wouldn't know what hit them." Dexter was clearly in a daze at what had hit him so unexpectedly. It all happened so fast. Sydney can hardly contain his excitement. Everything has gone exactly as we planned it. I knew that Dexter wouldn't be able to keep his big mouth shut. All one has to do is tell him that he is smart and he would then have to tell you how smart he is. He looks at the tape machine in the corner of the room. It was empty. Dexter has been outfoxed.

"How did you manage to get that tape?" whispers Dexter, barely audible.

"Well, let me put it this way. Dionne may be a heavy sleeper but you wouldn't have heard her if she were the heaviest-snoring baby in the world, because she's not here. But, as for my tape recorder and me, we were very quiet. In fact so quiet, I could have taped your conversation via the baby monitor. And further still, in case you are thinking that you need only take hold of this cassette, forget it. There is another copy of your conversation on a tape many miles away from here. Everything you said was sent simultaneously via my mobile phone to a tape recorder elsewhere. And you'll be pleased to know that the operator paged me to confirm that all went well. He said that you came across loud and clear. I think his words were that your "voice travels well". Sydney was relishing in watching Dexter silenced. Dexter had met his match. The usually arrogant and conceited Dexter cannot even look me directly in the eye. "Now, if you were me, what do you think that you would have done with this hot cassette? Let me see, you were prepared to ruin my relationship with Donna in order to satisfy your needs. I think that you even branded me a pimp. So I think that we could safely say that you wanted to ruin me with little chance of recovery. Now, I'm a man who never believes in getting even; an eye for an eye and a tooth for a tooth, are not for me. I believe one should dish out worse than one has received. In that way people learn a lesson they are unlikely to forget." The atmosphere has got an eerie feel about it at the prospect of Dexter losing everything he has worked for. The career that gave him a special status in society and made him a catch for the ladies was now on the verge of being snatched away from his grasp.

"Now," continues Sydney, revelling in this moment, "whereas I agree with you, I regret the day that our paths ever crossed. I say that, because it saddens me that I know someone like you. You are one very unhappy creature. However, you will be happy that you crossed my path and not somebody else's. I had a good sleep last night. The future looks bright. And I am going to promote the biggest event in Europe over the next few days. I feel generous. I'm in a compassionate mood. I tell you what, to keep it within the spirit of your profession, I shall deal with you justly. I could spare a wretched soul from the lion's den but as this was not solely my fight I should ask what my fellow judge thinks we should do." Dexter had still refused to look me in the eye. For all that shit Dexter threw at me, it is me who now has his fate in my hands. The tormented is now the tormentor.

"Well," I reply, "it has been a long hard few days fighting this claim for Dionne. I am tired and I am in no mood for a fight. This action will have to be dropped. However, if it were to continue, I am sure that I can find enough strength to fight on and make a formal complaint about the illegal activities of a particular legal representative of the country. Also, I'm sure that those who helped you in acquiring such illegal information will not be too pleased at being implicated."

"Okay, I think that is clear," says Sydney. "You are to inform your representatives to discontinue the action for custody of Dionne, tonight."

"Tonight!" replies Dexter.

"Yes, tonight," confirms Sydney. "You will call your representative at home while you are here, in order to start the ball rolling. Donna and I have already drafted a letter for you to sign right now, and send to your representative, confirming what you are going to instruct him on tonight." Sydney hands Dexter the letter. He reads the prepared text. He has been caught, hook line, and sinker. Knowing Dexter as well as I do, he would be burning inside. To be shamed is one thing. To be shamed before me is unthinkable! Dexter signs the letter. Sydney and I look at each other and can hardly contain our joy. This nightmare is finally over. I have my baby and I am happy. Dexter is finally out of my life.

"Will I be able to see Dionne again?" asks Dexter, without the boastful tone of voice that graced me only a few minutes ago.

"Dexter," I reply, calmly, "I have never wanted to deprive you of seeing your child. You are welcome to see her, whenever you wish."

"Thank you." It was embarrassing. Dexter sat there a defeated man and Sydney and I were unsure what to say. We hadn't thought this far ahead. To be honest, I expected more of a fight from Dexter but I guess that I just underestimated the strength of our case. And knowing Dexter, Mister Houdini himself, I was not entirely confident that our plan would have succeeded until I had witnessed the implementation, myself. Dexter rose from the couch and walked out a dejected man without uttering a further word. No goodbye! Nothing! I suppose that can be viewed as an improvement from the last time he departed from this flat when he called me a bitch!

"I think that is what one calls a good job well done," says Sydney with a grin a Cheshire cat would be proud of.

"Yes, thank you," I say and put my arms around him for a comforting cuddle.

"It was my pleasure," he replies.

"I'll have an answer for you when you come back from Paris," I say. He raises his head and looks at me. I can feel the sudden increase in heartbeat pounding from his body and against mine.

"Okay. You don't have to rush, you know that, don't you?"

"If I were you, Charles, I wouldn't say another word on the matter. I might just change the way I feel at this moment."

"My lips are sealed," he replies, as he closes his mouth and mimics the act of zipping his lips together.

"How did you manage to get that cassette player to work?" I ask out of curiosity.

"I didn't!"

"Lucky you had a friend who could record the conversation via your mobile phone then, isn't it?"

"What friend? There is no friend and there is no cassette, but Dexter doesn't know that and what he doesn't know won't hurt him," says Sydney with that mischievous look I had grown to love in him but despise in Dexter.

"You're not a criminal," I reply, "you're a crook!"

Rupert

Last night must have been the longest night of my life. The morning couldn't have come around soon enough. I didn't sleep a wink. That isn't surprising. I wanted to sleep, but I couldn't. I wanted to sleep, if only to give myself a chance of waking up from a dream. I was not afforded that luxury. I had to keep awake throughout the whole night with the knowledge that what was happening to me was no dream, but real. I left Pat in bed fast asleep totally oblivious of the day that lay ahead. I thought long and hard about calling Linda. I got up many times throughout the night to call her, but knew that whatever had to be said had to be said in person. We had to talk face to face. I can't remember what time Jo said that they were due to fly out, so I had to get to Linda's place early. There isn't much I can do now, I know. The damage has already been done. But I have to talk to her. I'm not even too sure what it is I want to say. But, in situations like this it has got to be better to talk than not. Linda might even spare me the indignity of seeing both my wife and my ex-girlfriend together, both carrying my child! I curse the day I first came to this flat. I swear, if only I could have looked into a crystal ball and seen into the future, I wouldn't have got involved with Linda.

Usually when I come here I park my car in another street and walk the rest of the way. Today, as if to save on every minute of valuable time, I have parked my car right outside her home. There is more at stake here than being seen by someone that I shouldn't be. That would be an ice cube in comparison to the iceberg of my predicament. I look into Linda's front room for any signs of her. She is nowhere to be seen. It would not have been too difficult for her to have seen me as I approached the flat and decamp into another room. I never did like ground-floor flats. I ring the intercom and hear no reply. Linda knew that I would have come round. She knows that I would be worried out of my skin. I ring the intercom again in case she is at home and didn't hear the ring the first time or, if she is, to let her know that I know that she's in there. She must be in because she was supposed to be packing for today's flight. She couldn't have left already. Maybe I should ring Jo to find out the details. No, that would be silly. I never ever ring Jo. Stay cool. Linda knows that I would be in this state. I am not a Mister Cool Lover Boy. She knows that, so she tells Jo that she's pregnant knowing damn well that Jo is going to tell me. I did well to drop only my wine! Believe me there was strong pressure to discharge a bodily matter on the carpet that wouldn't have been a pretty sight! I peer into the breaks between the drawn curtains to the front room. I must look pathetic. All I need now is to be stopped by the police for attempted burglary or, worse, being a perverted Peeping Tom. I hear life!

"Hello!" says Linda's voice blurring out of the intercom.

"Hi Linda, it's me, Rupert," I reply. Linda let me in without any apparent hesitation.

"Sorry that I didn't answer the door earlier, but I was in the bath. I have a busy day today," she says, wearing a white bathrobe.

"I know, but you knew that didn't you?" I ask. Seeing Linda in her bathrobe makes me think of what I am giving up. What I shall never have again. My head is telling me that I was wise to end this affair, below is telling me that I am a fool to have given up what was readily available. People have affairs for years but I could only manage a few months before it all goes wrong. Had it not been for the predicament we find ourselves in I know that I would have made advances towards her. The forces of sex are stronger than control but this time I have to be resilient. That's not to say that Linda would be obliging in any case!

"Jo told me that you are pregnant," I say breathing heavily, more from anxiety than from breathlessness.

"Yes, I am," comes the frank reply, as if to say, "so what?"

"And you had no intentions of telling me?"

"Why should I? It's not your problem and it's definitely none of your business."

"Are you saying that the child is not mine?"

"If that's what you want to believe."

"Please Linda," I say impatiently, "answer the question. Is the child mine?"

"Well, I haven't been sleeping with anyone else in the past few months but you, so I guess it is."

"When did you know this?" I ask, raising my voice for the first time.

"Look Rupert, I have a busy day today and I'm in no mood for an argument."

"No mood for an argument? You are carrying my child and you didn't even have the decency to tell me, but you tell a friend of mine. What kind of woman are you?"

"Don't you dare come here, raising your voice like you own me. I am the same kind of woman that you wanted to screw at your pleasure whenever your damn wife failed to sexually fulfil you, which seemed to be most times, by accounts. That's the kind of woman I am! So don't you come round here acting like you are some kind of saint."

"What do you intend to do with this child?" I ask, ignoring her outburst and the sexual competence or incompetence of Pat.

"What do you think I intend to do? I am going to have it. You couldn't possibly be thinking that I would have an abortion! I'd sooner kill you than kill my own child!"

"I wish I had never set eyes on you," I say angrily and spitefully. "I can't believe that I let my guard down so easily. I guess when someone puts it in your face it's hard to resist."

"Get out, before I call the police to drag you out," shouts Linda. I obey and walk into the passage to make my way out. No! Why should I make this easy for her? She is ruining me and seems to care less. "You're a bitch!" I say stopping short of opening the front door, "I never use such words on a woman, but you're a worthy exception. You know what this will do to me and you don't care. You couldn't give a damn!" I am now shouting so loud that my voice begins to tremble both from strain and emotion. The neighbours must be able to hear what is going on. I don't care, I am already in the shit, trying to get out. There must be married men out there in my predicament who would be only too pleased to have been "let off the hook". My ex-girlfriend wants nothing from me. She wants no acknowledgement. She doesn't even want me to leave my wife. She wants nothing! So what the hell am I complaining about? I wasn't brought up that way. I have seen how my father abused my mother, and I vowed never to be like him. Never! God forbid that I could be treading down that same disgusting road as he did. God, my mother and my conscience are looking down on me in distaste. Look what I have become. I am now what I have always despised in another man. I could see that someone is standing on the other side of the front door. The person was either just listening to what was going on or afraid to enter the war zone. I couldn't care less anymore. No one knows me around here. And once I walk out of that door, I shall not be showing my face around here again.

"If you don't get out of here, I am going to complain to the police that you are harassing me," shouts Linda at a volume not much lower than my own.

"If you think that you can have my baby and start causing me trouble then you really don't know me. I'm warning you, don't you dare come anywhere near my wife or this harassment will seem like nursery play in comparison." Linda is shouting and acting hysterical. Tears are building up in her eyes, I think more out of rage than anything else. The scene is becoming more and more unpleasant by the second. I hear her intercom buzz and can now hear a door open upstairs.

"Get out! Get out! You bastard and don't you ever show your face around hear again or your wife will know what kind of cheat you really are!"

"Hey what's going on down there?" asks a male voice coming from upstairs. I can hear the footsteps making their way across the upper landing. I hate myself for saying those hurtful things. I loved this woman and I can't say that I am not in love with her now. I didn't mean the hurtful things I said, but time does not afford me the opportunity to take them back now. I have the threat of police over me, a neighbour coming down to see what all the noise is about, and someone at the door. I wish I could start this morning all over again. This is definitely not how this morning was supposed to work out. We were supposed to have a nice talk and agree on the best way forward. I have to leave. I shall try and talk to Linda again in Paris. I shall have to escape from Pat for a short while. I can't risk seeing her the next time with Pat being in the same room. After all that I've said I don't know what

Linda is likely to say with Pat being around. And let's face it, Linda will be in a stronger position with Pat in the vicinity, than not. I can see the bottom half of what looks like pyjamas of a man walking down the stairs. I am in no mood for a further full-blown confrontation with a neighbour, as well. I hear the intercom buzz again. A next-door neighbour is also probably trying to find out what all the commotion is about. The state Linda is in anyone who sees me will think that I have laid a hand on her, which I didn't and wouldn't but they wouldn't know that. I can't afford to be associated with such falsehood. I must leave. I shall just rush by the neighbour on the other side of the door and make a quick exit. With any luck, my departure will be so swift that the neighbour wouldn't even recognise me if we sat next to each other on a train. Linda can explain what all the noise was about, albeit from a one-sided point of view. That is the least of my worries. I can see more of the neighbour coming down the stairs and I open the door to leave.

"Rupert!" calls out Jo in total shock.

"Jo! What are you doing here?" are the only words that I can find. My heart is now pounding so hard I take deep breaths to get my heartbeat back to normality. Jo looks at Linda and sees the state that she is in. Please God, please don't make Jo be the one that was behind the door all this time. If so, I'm dead!

"No," says Jo, "No! No! No! Tell me I'm wrong! Tell me that you are not pregnant for Rupert." Such confirmation is not forthcoming. Jo shakes her head and backs away from the door. She is now shaking her head uncontrollably in disbelief. Linda is crying with her head in her hands. The neighbour just seems puzzled by the whole event. Jo walks out of the gate. I have to stop her. I know exactly where she is heading. This can't happen.

"Jo!" I call out. I can see heads peering through curtains at various houses as I follow her down the road.

"Jo! Come back, please." I catch her by the arm and pull her around.

"Get your filthy hands off me," commands Jo. "I am not your piece on the side. How on earth you can do this to Pat, I will never know."

"Jo, I'm begging you, please don't tell Pat. I will do anything for you. Anything, just name your price," I plead in desperation.

"You disgust me," replies Jo. "I don't want anything from you. I am going straight to Pat now and tell her all that I have heard, then you are on your own. I have known Pat since my childhood. Whatever gives you the idea that I owe you any allegiance over her? You better have a good excuse that's all I can say. You even tried to use me to get your girlfriend to come to Paris so that you could have both your women in the same place. Rupert, I hate you!" I let go of Jo. I must do something, fast. I have to get to Pat before Jo does. Where is my phone? Damn! I left it in Linda's flat. I've got to get it, but she would never answer the door to me again. I'm more likely to get the police up my arse. I need a phone box. Why can't you ever find these bloody things when you need one? I'm running like a mad man trying to find a phone box. Sod's law, there is not a single phone box in sight. I will have to try my luck and drive home. Jo must have at least five minutes on me. I run back to the car and see that people are still peering out of their windows. I glance at Linda's flat. The curtains are still drawn. Shall I ask her for my phone? No. That is not a good idea. She will either send it to me or it is already smashed and disposed of. Fortunately, I didn't leave my car keys, otherwise I would have had no chance of getting back home in a reasonable time. I start the car and speed down the road as fast as I can. My marriage is on the rocks and I have to save it. There is only one option. Survival!

Jo has beaten me to it. From my calculation she can't have had more than about three minutes unless she herself drove like a mad woman. I would have got here quicker had it not been for those damn sleeping policemen in the road. One road I drove down slowed the car down to an unreasonable ten miles per hour. I still have time in order to get in my plea. I slam the door and run towards the flat. There are children playing football near the car. One day those kids are going to break my windscreen with that football of theirs. That reminds me did I lock the car door? These kids will steal anything that's not bolted down. I run back and check the door lock. I hadn't locked it. This has lost me some vital seconds. Jo likes to talk. Hopefully, she is giving an elaborate account of what she heard. With any luck she's yet to get to the crunch. I run up the stairs and make my way into the flat. There is talking but it isn't very loud. I then hear coughing like when someone has been crying and they start to choke. I walk into the room and search for the words but the words fail me. Pat is holding her stomach. Jo has her arms around Pat. Pat knows. Pat looks up and sees me. Jo doesn't bother. The assassination is successful!

"Pat we need to talk," I say.

"I have nothing to say to you, Rupert," she replies.

"Pat I need to talk to you in private," I plead.

"Jo you stay right where you are," she commands. "If you have something to say then you can say it in front of Jo." This is awkward because I don't know what exactly Jo heard, so I don't know exactly what she told Pat. Whatever Jo heard, it is clear that she got the main gist of it.

"Pat, I have made a big mistake."

"I don't want to hear any excuses of how sorry you are," she interrupts. "I am going by Donna for the day and when I come back I want you out of here with all your belongings, and I do not want to see your sorry face again!"

"Pat, we have been through too much together. I'm begging you please give me a chance. I need you Pat. I can't live without you. Please don't do this to me." I am pleading for my life. Jo is present and I feel no shame. I cannot lose Pat over this.

"'Do this to you?' Did I hear you correctly? You have been having an affair and you make another woman pregnant. And you ask me not to do this to you. Are you sure?" I can see that what is happening is eventually beginning to sink in. I can see the white in Pat's eyes turn red as if she has burst a blood vessel. I sense the rage building up. A sight I have never had the displeasure of witnessing until now. I look down to where the stain on the Persian rug is still showing. Suddenly I hear a loud shout and then feel a thud to the side of my head. It feels like my head is about to explode. Pat's fist had connected to the side of my head. It must have just missed my temple, otherwise I'm sure that that punch would have killed me. Pat was lunging at me, screaming and shouting. Jo tries to hold her back, but the strength of Pat is too much for her who can't be much over only half Pat's size and weight. Punches and kicks are landing all over my body. I try to defend myself by holding on to her hands, but this only makes her worse. Jo has given up. My baby kept flashing through my mind. If Pat doesn't calm down she could lose our baby. I must leave. I can come back later. She would have calmed down by then. Maybe not. This will never be over. I must leave. I shout out that I will leave but Pat is still in hysterics. I now have a massive headache both from that punch from Pat and a morning full of hysterical women. I run out of the flat.

"That's it, run back to your woman," shouts Pat. "She deserves you." Pat is following me down the stairs. Jo ensues but can do little else. She is calling on Pat to calm down and to go back inside. Pat is following me out onto the forecourt and is shouting more abuse at me. I can see people looking to see what is going on. I don't think that I have ever been the centre of attraction for so many people in my life, as I have been this morning. The kids are still playing football, unaware of the commotion that is going on. I run towards my car. No, I shall leave it. It would look like cowardice to jump in the car and speed away.

"If I set eyes on you again I will kill you!" shouts Pat. Some of the children stop their game and turn to see what is going on. They seem amused. I am walking fast but not running. I can hear Pat crying and Jo trying to console her. I can see that we are both now the centre of attraction for everyone. There seems to be a million eyes everywhere. I can see that one of the children playing football has decided to start the game without the others paying attention. His moment of glory has arrived where he can score a goal. Probably his only chance for the entire game. He takes a shot and scores. He is jubilant and raises his arm to the imaginary roar of the crowd. The ball goes into the road and he runs after it. I would have got the ball for him, but I have my own problems. I turn back to see where Pat is and feel a punch straight on my left eye. I see a flash of light and then it goes dark. I'm temporarily blinded in my left eye. I run and can see the boy run towards the road for the ball. Pat is now chasing me. I can hear her shouting but I can't make out the words. The punches both to my eye and the side of my head seem to have dulled my hearing.

"Pat I'm going! I'm going!" I shout. I can see a lorry coming down the road. The ball is heading towards the road and the boy seems determined to get the ball. The lorry driver does not appear to see either the ball or the boy. I can sense what is going to happen in the way you have that instinctive feeling that an accident is about to occur, and you keep watching. I can see everything.

"Stop!" I shout to the boy. "Don't run over, a lorry is coming." He is so pleased with having scored a goal he seems not to hear what I am saying. He runs out in front of the lorry. I can hear the screeching of breaks. I ran out to try and divert the boy. I can hear Jo and others shout out something, but the amalgamation of voices and the pains in my head mean that I cannot hear what is being said.

"No!" shouts Jo above the sound of everyone else. I then hear a second screeching of tyres and then a massive bang from behind me from a car travelling in the opposite direction to the lorry. There are screams from everywhere. There is pandemonium. I turn my head all the way round to my left as my left eye is by now fully closed from Pat's punch. I can just about see that there is a body lying in the road. Pat is laid out cold on the tarmac. Jo is going berserk and is being held back by someone in the crowd. I run towards Pat who seems to be totally unconscious. The drivers of the lorry and the car both run out to see what is happening. I can hear a woman making her way through the crowd saying that she is a doctor. I recognise the woman as one of our neighbours. We had exchanged nothing more than courtesies prior to today. Now she is called upon to tend to my wife.

"Doctor, she is pregnant!" I shout. Already I can hear an ambulance in the distance.

"Stand back!" shouts the doctor to the crowd surrounding her and looking down at Pat lying in the road in a pool of blood that is flowing from some part of her body, I'm not sure where. "She needs air," says the doctor. Thank you Jesus, that means that she's alive. The doctor checks the pulse of Pat's left hand. She looks concerned.

"What's the matter, doctor?" I ask. My right eye catches a glimpse of Jo. I can see nothing but shock and horror written all over her face. The doctor does not answer my question. The doctor then puts her left ear onto Pat's chest. Her face looks even more concerned than it did a few seconds ago.

"Doctor," I shout, "my wife and our baby are going to be all right, aren't they?"

"I'm sorry," she says, "your wife is dead!"

The Church of God has never held so many people at any one time since its construction in 1789. Family, friends, admirers, supporters, fans and the adulterer is present. It was Rupert who had the unenviable task of having to call his parents-in-law to inform them of the tragic news of their daughter's death. The news came late. Bertran and Veronica were already in mourning by the time of his call. The news had already been broadcast on local radio and television stations around the world. "The talented academic and author had been killed in a tragic accident this morning following a row with her adulterous husband" is the headline that fairly summarises the common theme used by the world's media. Rupert heard the bawling of Veronica when he spoke to Bertran. Bertran was in no mood to talk. Veronica's wail was heard all over the Bahamas, if not further beyond. This only led to Rupert feeling worse for the part he played in the death of their daughter. The Thompsons had left their only prize in his hands and he had betrayed them.

Bertran and Veronica had wasted no time in making their way to London. They were due to come to England a few months later, under different circumstances. That was supposed to be a happy reunion with their daughter. They had planned to fly to England, in order to witness the birth of their first grandchild: the child their daughter wanted so much. Veronica had to be supported rather than be accompanied by Bertran as they made their way into the church. Donna and Jo sat together on the front pew reserved for members of Pat's family. Pat would not have wanted it any other way. No one had blamed Jo for her involvement in Pat's death, other than Jo herself. Jo was so upset that she had to cancel her part in The Best of British Fashion show. She and her team agreed not to go to Paris. Jo had replayed that fatal moment over and over again in her mind. She blamed herself for being too good a friend. She should have taken stock of herself and thought of how Pat would react to such news about her cheating husband. She knew Pat would not have taken such news lightly. Jo was telling herself that she, Jo, was too hasty. She should have spoken to Rupert first. He wanted to talk but she wanted to remain loyal to her best friend. The best friend she had known since eleven years old. She and Rupert could have reached a deal. Donna disagreed. She assured Jo that she did the right thing. Jo would have felt worse had she not told Pat and Pat had subsequently found out from somebody else. Jo was surprised and grateful to get a call from Earl who had heard of the tragedy whilst in Los Angeles on business. He caught the earliest flight back to London in order to lend his support to Jo and to pay his last respects to Pat. Jo had spared a glance for Leon but he could not be seen. In fact Leon's drunken behaviour had become rapidly worse since his sacking by Jo. It was the first time that the talented photographer had had the indignity of experiencing such treatment. It was unclear whether he had even heard or was capable of hearing the news of Pat's death.

The service was delayed for nearly an hour as the large multitude of people standing outside, who could not find room inside the church, waited for loudspeakers to be installed so that they could hear the sermon. One would have difficulty in finding a dry eye either inside or outside the church. It seemed like Pat had touched many lives in one way or another. Shortly before four o'clock a black hearse made its way through the jostling crowd towards the entrance to the church. Those standing outside started to shuffle uncomfortably, as the reality of what had happened and who had been lost to the world began to sink in. The organist was playing the music to Lyte's, "Abide with me". The eerie sound of the sombre music touched a nerve. The sound of unrestrained crying and grieving filled the air. The pressure was clearly too much to bear. The mass outbursts outside seemed to trigger off more bawling and wailing inside. The Brazilian Mahogany coffin was slowly taken out from the back of the hearse. Rupert, Sydney, Samuel and Ashley held the coffin and lofted it onto their shoulders. Dexter had offered his help as a mark of respect to Pat but Rupert declined his offer. Led by Pastor Benjamin, they marched slowly into the church. People watched in disbelief. "What a waste," many were heard to have said. Dexter was sitting at the back of the church. He had, in fact, got to the church early but wanted to remain anonymous by keeping well out of the way. Earl was a few pews in front of Dexter. He hadn't known Pat that well, but had admired her work and what she stood for, as, it seemed, had many other people. There was a loud bawl from Veronica as the coffin holding her daughter's body passed by her side. Bertran tried to grab his wife as she headed for the marchers but slipped and fell to the floor. There was chaos as Veronica reached the marchers and tried to get to the coffin. She was weeping for the life of her daughter. She then shouted at Rupert and accused him of murder. She lunged towards Rupert, which nearly caused him to drop his end of the coffin. He stumbled, but managed to keep the coffin aloft upon his shoulders. The other carriers stopped in their tracks in shock. This outburst caused a ripple of murmurs within the church. Pastor Benjamin moved to his left to halt Veronica before such passion was relayed to the others and cause a near riot in the Lord's House. The atmosphere was tense. Rupert was not welcomed at his wife's funeral. "He should have stayed at home with his girlfriend," said many. Linda was rumoured to be in hiding. With the help of Jo and Bertran, Pastor Benjamin managed to get Veronica back into her seat. Pastor Benjamin regained his position in front of the coffin and indicated to the marchers to continue.

"Jesus Christ said I am the resurrection and the life. He that believes in me, though he were dead, yet shall he live," repeated Pastor Benjamin as he led the marchers down the aisle towards the altar. Pastor Benjamin, and the marchers finally reached the front of the altar. His once well-pressed gown was dishevelled and creased from the tangle with Veronica. Rupert was visibly shaken by Veronica's attack. There was a seat vacant next to his parents-in-law but he declined to fill the position. Rupert found a seat on the other side of the aisle safely away from Pat's parents and in particular, Veronica. There seemed to be space forming both sides of Rupert as he sat down. No one wanted to be associated with him. He was public enemy number one. A leper wouldn't have suffered such repellence. He had caused the death of the one whom they had all grown to love: the one whose death they were now mourning. The congregation was still recovering from what they had just witnessed. Pastor Benjamin watched over the mass of people and thought to himself that in all his years in the Ministry he had never undertaken such an important funeral in his life and was unlikely ever to again. He composed himself. He took a deep breath and raised his arms to indicate a request for calm amongst those in attendance. After only a few seconds calm befell upon the church. Composure was restored and Pastor Benjamin was ready. He placed the microphone in a position that would benefit the listeners outside and spoke, "Let the service begin."

Rupert

"We are all gathered here today," commences Pastor Benjamin, "on this very sad occasion, for the funeral of Patricia Veronica Jackson. A young life cut short in its prime..."

The attack on me by Veronica really shook me up. I once had the love of that woman. She loved me as her own son. She treated me as her own son. She has lost a daughter and I have lost a wife. And like Veronica and Bertran, I too have little to live for.

"I first met Patricia when she was only eight years old..." explains Pastor Benjamin.

I have received bags filled with mail every day since the news of Pat's death was known. I have received a few letters in sympathy, but most have been in disgust. I have taken and accepted the blame. It is nobody else's fault but my own. Not Linda's, not Jo's, but mine.

"And as the songwriter says, 'in life, in death, O Lord, abide with me...'" preaches Pastor Benjamin.

Linda and I played a dangerous game and have both paid a heavy price. I feel sorry for Linda because her only crime was that she happened to have an affair with the wrong man at the wrong time. But our affair ultimately ended the lives of two people. Two lives lost for an affair that we both knew was never going to last. It couldn't!

"I shall now ask those who wish to say a few words to come forward and say their piece," requests Pastor Benjamin.

Bertran walks forward to the rostrum. Veronica is in no emotional state to address the congregation. Bertran stands still and in silence. He makes several attempts to utter some words but the pain appears to stifle any output. Bertran and I got on very well. Since my telephone call to him informing of Pat's death, he has neither spoken to nor set eyes on me.

"I can't believe that I will never see my daughter again," starts Bertran. "I can't believe that my wife and I will never hear that sweet little voice again. To the world she was a woman but to us she was our little girl. She had so much to live for. She gave so much to others and had much more to give. I remember her ringing us the night before she died. She was telling me about the plans she had when she came back from a trip abroad. She had so many great ideas in order to help enrich the lives of other people. She wanted to do so much." Bertran's voice begins to break. He stands still for a while in a gallant attempt to continue, but his emotions get the better of him. Samuel leads him to his seat. Samuel then gives a few words. Pat had plenty of time for Samuel. He is a genuine and honest man. A few more people speak. Some of whom I know but most of whom I don't.

"Pat was like a big sister to me," says Donna. "She was always there for me and looking out for me," she continues. She pauses and looks towards Sydney. "I only wished that I could have thanked her before she left," ends Donna. Sydney then gave a few words of nothing but high praises for Pat. The message was mainly coded and would have made little sense to the congregation other than to Donna, Sydney and myself. Some people who had not known Pat personally but had read her book, or had attended one of her talks gave their words.

"Pat and I met when we were just eleven years old and we had been the best of friends ever since," says Jo. "She was unarguably the nicest person anyone could ever have wished to have met and have as his or her best friend. She was kind and would go out of her way to help others. She would speak out against all kinds of prejudices. She was a caring person. I have not had a moment's sleep since that tragic day. I have nothing but questions swimming around in my mind. 'If only I had done this' and 'if only I had done that', I keep saying to myself."

"You did the right thing, girl!" shouts someone from the congregation.

"I take some responsibility towards what happened to Pat that day," Jo continues. Choruses of "no" follows her confession. Jo seems overwhelmed by such response, as if her heart had been freed from such guilt there and then. She is crying with what seems like a mixture of happiness for the verdict and sadness for Pat. She makes her way back to her seat where she is met with a hug from Donna. Nobody else has come forward to speak. I watch and wait. Pastor Benjamin looks in my direction. I have spoken at many functions in the past and have addressed the most difficult judges in the land. And yet, I have never felt as nervous as I do now. I was long presumed guilty until proven innocent; to most people I am guilty, myself included! I know that I am in for a hard time if I speak. Pastor Benjamin looks in my direction again, as if to say that the stage is set. It was at the sole discretion of the other speakers whether they wished to speak or not, but I have an obligation. I have spoken to Pat in private but I have an obligation to report how I feel to the public. Pastor Benjamin is not going to let me pass on my duties. He has been my sole comfort ever since Pat's death. He would want me to say my piece and then leave the rest to God, for He is the ultimate judge. Pastor Benjamin gives what looks like a final indication to me to take the stand. I decide against it. I have already spoken to Pat in my heart and cannot go through it all over again. Pastor Benjamin concedes. He understands.

"Brethren," says Pastor Benjamin, "I would like to thank everyone for their kind words given on behalf of Patricia. I would now like to ask..." I stand up. I hear murmurings. Pastor Benjamin stops what he is saying and looks me straight in the eyes. Our exchange says it all. I cannot go home with this burden. It is too heavy. I will have to address the people.

"I think that our brother Rupert would like to have a few words," says Pastor Benjamin. I walk forward and face the congregation for the first time for the afternoon. I hadn't realised how large the church was and the multitude of people. There are people packed from wall to wall. I can see that people are trying to squeeze in at the entrance, as I take my place at the front of the church. There is no doubt in my mind that every ounce of what I am about to say will be scrutinised by my prosecutors in waiting. The murmurings have stopped and are replaced with a hush, waiting for me to speak. I take my time.

"I loved my wife, contrary to what many of you may have read or believe. I did wrong and I have paid the heaviest price imaginable. I know that everyone of you today blames me for Pat's death. I have received so many 'hate letters' I lie awake waiting for my assassin. And yes, I do read all my mail. I read them in search of that one letter that might just give me a little support. That letter that would sympathise with what I am going through. No one here today knew what a wonderful life Pat and I had. She was special. Our life together was special. We had our disagreements, couples sometimes do. But, to think that I would in any way wish on Pat what has happened, is beyond all belief. You all blame me for what happened the other day. The truth is I also blame myself. But I don't deserve to be told that I never loved my wife. I made a big mistake. No one here today is perfect. He without sin cast the first stone. There are probably even some of you who are cheating on your partner sitting or standing next to you, but I would never judge you. Who am I to judge? Who are any of us to judge? How can we be more concerned with the mote that is in another person's eye and not the beam that is in our own?" I look around at the congregation trying to look into the eyes of each and every person. "I don't ask for your pity, you are all entitled to your opinions. But when you attack me and get it wrong, you hurt not only me but others, also. You hurt people who are not only grieving for a friend but are grieving for a loved one or a daughter." I stare at Bertran and Veronica. Both heads are lowered. "Finally," I say and turn to look at the coffin. "Pat, I will miss you. I will miss your smile, your laughter, your support and the good times we had together. You may not be with me in person but I know that you are in spirit. Goodbye!" I walk back to my seat.

"I would like to thank Brother Rupert and, in fact, everyone else who gave a few words today. I would now like to invite anyone who wishes to pay their last respects, to make their way forward towards the coffin and then please make your way out of the church. While those of you are paying your last respects, the song 'I Will Always Love You' will be played."

People make their way to the front to see Pat's body lying motionless in her coffin. I sit there bowing my head and listening to the sounds of cries that passes me by. A few people are kind enough to pat me on my shoulder as they walk by. I hear Whitney Houston's voice unaccompanied, emit from the speakers which sends shivers down my spine. The a cappella at the beginning of the song is so pure and angelic I cry in memory of my Pat.

"Everything will be all right, son," I hear a voice say. I recognise it to be that of Bertran and look up but see no one immediately in front of me. I turn to my right and see the back of him and Veronica, walking away. If only they could find it in their hearts to forgive me for what I have done, the healing process will never be complete, but it may at least begin.

Sydney, Ashley, Samuel and myself carry the coffin to the graveside in the grounds of the church. Everyone's head is bowed as Pastor Benjamin gives a final prayer. He finishes his prayer and indicates to us to lower the coffin into the void.

"Today," continues Pastor Benjamin, "you go to sleep to wake again with your Father."

He sprinkles earth on to the coffin as it is lowered.

"Ashes to ashes, dust to dust." It is all over. Patricia Veronica Jackson, Rest in Peace. Amen!

There is an eerie silence among those of us who are still in the grounds of the churchyard. I can see Dexter standing by himself at the exit gates. He had spent much of his time fighting my wife and yet paid his last respects to her. The crowd has now dispersed. The event of the day is well and truly over. Now is a time for mourning and preparing to face the rest of my life without Pat. I see that Dexter was waiting around. I walk over to him.

"Hi mate!" I say to Dexter.

"Hi Buddy!" he replies. We embrace each other as men do these days.

"Well, it's just us two, it seems," I say.

"Excuse me," says this man who seems to have come from nowhere, "may I have a word with you please."

"Sorry," I reply, "I shall not be giving any interviews."

"I'm not from the media," replies the young man, "I would just like to have a private word with you." I look at Dexter. I have had enough for one day and I am not about to be taken away to be later misquoted or worse.

"Whatever you have to say," I respond, "you can say it in front of my friend." The young man is clearly nervous and starts to stutter as he speaks.

"I have come to tell you about your father."

"My father!" I repeat, "I haven't seen him for years."

"I know. I tried to call you a few times, but you were unavailable and I refused to leave my name because I was not sure that you would have returned my calls."

"Oh, so it was you who kept calling me. What did you want?"

"I was calling to tell you that your father was unwell and he wanted to see you."

"And?" I reply. After the day that I've had I was not about to care for someone I cared nothing for.

"Your father passed away a few weeks ago," says the young man. I show no reaction to what was said. I feel nothing and I am not about to pretend.

"Well, like I said, I haven't seen him for years and we all have to go some time." I see that the young man was offended by what I had said. It has been a long hard emotional day and I could not give a damn what a stranger thought about my reply, callous or otherwise.

"Who are you, anyway?" I ask. The young man seems hesitant, as if still taken aback by my cold response to the news about my father.

"I'm your brother on your father's side."

"My brother?" I repeat. I become light-headed and feel that I am about to faint, as my legs give way. Dexter steadies me, otherwise I was sure to fall. "Oh my God!" I whisper to myself. I have failed in every sense of the word. "I sentence you to a life of shame and guilt", comes into my head again, not for the first time since Pat's death. I vowed never to be like my father. And what have I done? I have done to my wife exactly what he did to my mother even down to having a child with another woman. I hate myself. I am exactly what he was; like father, like son.